TIKKUN OLAM

RESTORING WHAT WAS LOST

ANA WATERS

For new releases, special promotions, announcements, and
ordering information:

Instagram @ anawatersbooks
Facebook @ anawatersauthor
linktr.ee/anawaters

For the Davis family. May the Lord bless you back one-hundred fold because I could never repay all you've done.

"Restore us to yourself, Lord, that we may return; renew our days as of old."

— LAMENTATIONS 5:1 NIV

CHAPTER 1

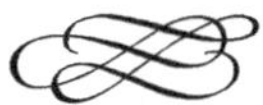

"After eighteen years together, my husband told me he never really loved me. I thought he'd lost his mind," I said, unburdening myself to my coffee shop buddy of two weeks. Ruefully, I added, "I still can't believe I'm sharing my life story with someone I met because I couldn't decide between vanilla or cinnamon shots in my latte."

My nameless friend shrugged. "Sometimes you meet people but feel like you've known them forever. My rabbi growing up called that *beshert*. Two people destined to meet."

"So, you're religious?" I asked, though hardly much of a practicing Jew myself.

She barked out a self-deprecating laugh. "Pretty sure they would have taken me out and stoned me by now."

I grinned back at her. "I can relate. Once upon a time, I had a shotgun wedding."

"And then two *decades* into the relationship, your ex suddenly doesn't love you anymore. Yeah, right," she said, blowing a raspberry.

"That's how he tried to sell it anyway. Like he had some magical epiphany."

My friend rolled her eyes.

Gaining a full head of steam, I continued, "He tried blaming our failing marriage on me, of course. Eventually, he confessed to cheating on me with my best friend from high school. He wanted a sugar mama, not a wife, and he found that with her. They broke up last March, and then he says he found Jesus. Now, he wants me back and acts like I'm just supposed to forget everything that happened."

Myriad emotions crossed my friend's face while a steaming cup of *Vincenzo's* coffee sat motionless in her hand.

"Am I oversharing?" I asked. Her honey brown eyes that ordinarily expressed warmth and humor showed wariness instead. "Maybe they put truth serum in the flavor shots."

"Not oversharing," she replied after a lengthy pause. "It, um, just hits close to home."

I raised an eyebrow. "Did you have someone cheat on you too?"

She took a sip before answering. "Let's just say I've been on both sides of the cheating situation."

"Have you ever been married?" I asked with my usual candor.

My coffee buddy surprised me when tears filled her pretty eyes. "Almost."

"Ah," I said in slow understanding. "Didn't work out?"

"Yeah, you could say that."

Another customer entered behind us and placed his order. My nameless friend startled and turned deathly pale. Excusing herself, she barreled out the front door.

"What was that about?" I murmured above the rim of my cup. Taking another fortifying sip, I checked the wall clock. Ten more minutes before another work day commenced at Culver, Incorporated.

"Poppy?"

Surprised that I missed the telltale sound of jangling keys and squeaky loafers, I glanced up at Culver's top, east coast producer, Ted Margolin.

"I didn't realize you'd started coming to Vincenzo's too," he said.

"You can thank your wife for turning me into a regular here. The last time we met up for brunch, Rebecca told me I had no idea what I was missing." I lifted up my cup in salute. "She wasn't kidding. The grounds at home are great, but I love the old world Italy feel of this place."

Ted's expression seemed as pained as my coffee buddy's when a silver car sped away in the parking lot. "I thought that was her."

"Who?" I asked.

Ignoring my question, Ted said, "I saw you guys talking through the window, but her back was to me. That's definitely her, though."

"Who?" I repeated.

"Jessica Goldstein."

Realization dawned as I pieced together Rebecca Margolin's description along with that of my former coworker, Taylor Horner. Knowing both Rebecca's and Taylor's stories firsthand, I marveled at not recognizing Jessica sooner. Everything Jessica had shared with me over coffee only fleshed out the narrative I'd already heard.

"How do you know her?" Ted asked, pulling me from my thoughts.

"I don't," I said. "We struck up a conversation a few weeks ago in line, but we never exchanged names. She's just a familiar face when I scrape together some extra nickels for Vincenzo's."

"Extra nickels, huh? Do I need to talk to Phil about properly compensating our marketing department again?"

I shook my head. "Your wife has already threatened to get me a Vincenzo's gift card because she knows anything else I would just spend on my kids. I have three little mouths to feed and clothe. They take priority over Mommy's fancy bean water."

I expected a grin from the father of two toddler girls himself, but Ted frowned. "My wife isn't a gossip, Poppy, but she did share some details about your situation. Have you and your children settled in okay?"

I grimaced, not liking the idea of anyone at work knowing about my personal life. Strangers seemed safer somehow. Then again, Jessica Goldstein was only a stranger because we'd never been formally introduced.

"Sorry, Poppy," Ted said. "I didn't mean to violate any confidence shared between you and Rebecca."

I exhaled a slow sigh. "She's your wife. I get it. I do appreciate the concern, and yes, we've adjusted to living in my parents' basement. We've been there for over two years."

As the entry bell jangled against the glass door of Vincenzo's, I saw another coworker of mine enter the small coffee shop. Joe Trautweig stopped short and smiled at both of us.

"Private party, or can I join too?" he asked, winking at me.

I found myself involuntarily blushing at an attractive, single man showing me a shred of attention. And I felt ashamed, knowing I had a broken marriage and three, devastated children at home. Clearing my throat, I said, "That's okay, Joe. I need to get to my desk anyway. Ted has bestowed the marketing department with yet another Request for Proposal."

"I think the letters 'RFP' might be the most hated letters in all of commercial insurance," he said, giving me a conspiratorial grin.

I swallowed down a lump of panic and turned my full attention to Ted. "Gentlemen, I'll see you back at the office."

Snatching my worn coat and shoulder bag, I attempted a quick exit. Instead, I heard a laughing Joe call my name. I turned and saw him extending a cup toward me along with a warm smile. "You forgot your coffee."

Our fingers brushed, and awareness sparked along every nerve ending. Meeting Joe's pale green eyes, I knew immediately I was playing with fire. As old as I felt with a tweenager and two other children in elementary school, I had not forgotten the sensation of physical attraction.

"Thanks," I mouthed, feeling my accelerated heartbeat down to my toes.

"See you in the office, Poppy." Joe made my name sound like something beautiful rather than the result of former hippies naming their only daughter after an opioid producing plant.

Against my better judgment, I ventured a closer look into pale eyes studying me as if truly seeing me for the first time. The mutual startle as our gazes collided sent me reeling. I circumvented any further conversation with a curt nod and flew through the glass doors of Vincenzo's.

I tried to exorcise any demons with each stride toward the Culver Incorporated highrise and shook my head at the confusing turn of events. Once I arrived at my desk, I took a final swig of coffee and plopped into my chair. Hopefully, Joe Trautweig had offsite meetings the rest of the day. Life was complicated enough without the effect those pale eyes had on my insides.

Phil Robbins, my CEO and the youngest seventy year-old I'd

ever met, rapped on my office door frame. "Poppy!" he exclaimed. "Just the gal I was looking for!"

I grinned. "What is it this time, Phil?"

"Oh, go easy on an old man in his dotage. I've got an RFP ready to land on your desk by early afternoon."

"The mighty Margolin beat you to it," I said, holding up a voluminous packet of paperwork ready to be copied, pasted, and manipulated to fit another potential client.

Phil tsked. "Poppy, you know we're working on hiring some help for you, right? I respect your time constraints because of after school care, and I want you to know I would never tell you business takes priority above family."

I glanced over to the framed photo of three much younger and more innocent cherubs who had no idea Daddy slept with Aunt Leah on the side. Following my gaze, Phil took in their adorable faces.

"Cute kids," he said. "Does this mean I won't have to worry about shotgun weddings, baby announcements, and then losing yet another graphic designer in our office?"

"Been there, done that," I said, matching Phil's wit with some of my own.

"How old are they?" Phil asked.

"Natalie, my oldest is now almost twelve. Ryan is nine, and Madison is five."

Phil nodded. "They all look like you."

I grinned, proud of that. The less I saw of my ex, the better.

Noting my bare left hand, Phil showed uncharacteristic restraint and left his question unasked.

"Margolin should be stopping by in a few minutes with updates for the Guildcorp renewal document."

"On top of the RFP?" I asked with a raised eyebrow. "Never a dull moment around here."

Phil chuckled. "He said he's bringing you a bag of Vincenzo's coffee as a preemptive apology for how much work he's got for you."

"I ran into Ted this morning," I said, ignoring the other two people I'd also encountered. Before Phil could question my awkward pause, I added, "I can't believe the mighty Margolin thinks he can bribe me with expensive coffee."

"Oh, and biscotti. I forgot to mention that."

From all accounts, I knew Ted Margolin wasn't a perfect man, but I certainly envied Rebecca at times. Compared to the louse my poor kids had to call a father, he may as well have been the messiah.

"Right on time," Phil smirked as the trademark sounds of the mighty Margolin announced his arrival.

With a wide grin, Ted entered the office. "I come bearing gifts. My wife suggested I pick up a second bag of biscotti for your children." He held up the bags of goodies for me to ogle.

Thankful for the mention of "my wife," it kept my thoughts in line. I would never do to Rebecca Margolin what had been done to me. More than that, I considered Rebecca a real friend even if I disagreed with all of her Jesus preaching.

"What time is Bible study this weekend?" Phil said, turning to Ted in private conversation. "We might try to join you this time."

"Same time as always, old man."

"If I could remember, I wouldn't need to ask," Phil retorted. "Show some mercy on me in my golden years, you whipper snapper."

Laughing, Ted turned to me and said, "I heard Taylor's coming up next month for her brother's wedding."

"Is she bringing Ian and the baby? I can't believe her little boy is almost one."

Ted grinned. "The whole gang will be reunited. Should be interesting with Kyle and Abigail there too."

I startled at the mention of Jessica Goldstein's brother, reminded of the incredibly small and interconnected world of Parkview.

"So Abigail is the new, uh…?" Phil prodded.

"Fiancée," Ted answered. "Goldstein finally found his unicorn."

Phil's smile was genuine. "Well, then I'm glad for him. I still don't understand how you kids are best friends all of a sudden, but then, I never thought I'd be attending a Bible study at the mighty Margolin's house."

Content to let them talk around me and absorb the information, I kept my mouth shut. Their conversation grew more superficial once they remembered my existence.

Ted cleared his throat and said, "Poppy, I'll have Lexie stop by later with the Guildcorp info. I didn't realize how long I was shooting the breeze with the old man."

Phil found an opportunity for one of his usual jokes. "Just pretend I've got dark, curly hair and two of the most adorable girls ever made, and I'm a dead ringer for your better half, Margolin."

I stifled a laugh that came out sounding more like a suffocated sneeze.

"*Gesundheit*," Phil said with panache.

The golden sparkle in the mighty Margolin's eye meant he saw through my sneezing facade. "Phil, why don't we let Poppy get back to work? Also, get someone in here to help before my wife starts tackling my RFPs at home."

Raising my eyebrows at that last statement, I was filled with immediate dread. I wondered if I would fall by the wayside like so many others who had tried and failed in my job position.

And I needed this job.

No matter how many years it took to get out of my parents' basement, I was determined to accomplish something for my children that had absolutely nothing to do with Jared Michael Levine.

CHAPTER 2

I worked an hour of overtime, texting my mother and asking her to pick up the younger two kids from after school care. My oldest daughter and mini-me, Natalie, took the bus home from middle school.

"I have dinner!" I announced, carrying paper bags full of drive-thru sandwiches and fries.

My mother tsked in disgust at the grease stained bags I deposited on our kitchenette counter. "Why don't you let me cook for the kids when you work late, Poppy?"

"Because they're my kids, not yours," I replied, kicking off my low heels.

"Fries and greasy sandwiches? I didn't raise you to eat such unnatural food. I think the bag is more biodegradable than what's inside."

"Roast beef! Yes!" my boy with the bottomless stomach cheered. "Mom, did you get curly fries too?"

"Of course, Ry-Ry." I smiled at my only son, at the overgrown curls I didn't want to cut, and the splash of freckles across his nose.

Ryan rolled his eyes, but he still hugged me around the middle. I held him too long, and he pulled away, embarrassed.

"Mom! Where's my salad?" Natalie demanded as she sauntered into the kitchen. Her tone was so grating, I considered force feeding her the french fries instead.

"Over there." I gestured toward a wider paper bag next to my purse.

With a haughty sniff, my firstborn retrieved her special order dinner and took it into the family room.

"Some gratitude wouldn't kill you," I called from the kitchen.

"I think she's on her period," my son said, wise beyond his years. "She's even crankier than usual."

My mother and I exchanged a knowing glance and stifled a laugh. Jared would have appreciated a moment like this before he had emotionally checked out of our lives.

"Mommy!" my five year-old squealed, running into the room. She launched herself into my arms.

I happily caught my baby girl, giving her a hearty squeeze and savoring the perfect little necklace her arms made around my neck. It helped ease the pain of her sister's tweenager angst.

After I sat down to eat dinner with my children, my mother resumed her usual passive aggressive mutterings about calories, my frumpy clothes, and her non-obese grandchildren needing to worry about their cholesterol.

"This isn't all we eat, Mom," I said around a mouth of curly fries. "It was a long day at work."

"Dear, don't talk with your mouth full," she said primly.

With my back to her, I rolled my eyes, forgetting the two

children watching me. Madison didn't hide her giggles. Ryan's gaze darted back and forth between Mom and Grandma.

"She just wants you to eat healthy," Ryan said, his face serious. "What happens to us if you die of a heart attack?"

Eyes wide, I said, "Who told you that?"

"Grandpa says you need to lose the extra weight because you're a triple bypass waiting to happen," Madison parroted perfectly.

I turned in my chair to face my mother. "Seriously? Like my kids need anything else to worry about right now? What were you thinking?"

"It was your father, not me. Go take it up with him," she said, wiping off an already clean kitchen counter with a sponge.

"I plan to. When is he due back from his bowling league?"

"He's usually home by ten."

Convenient, since I'd already be in bed, passed out from another grueling day of being both mother and father.

"I don't know why you're making that face, Poppy. At least your father is getting some exercise."

"I didn't realize two beers and a German pretzel were also part of his new diet regimen. Is this some new, Oktoberfest weight loss plan?"

Madison laughed even though she didn't get the joke. To my kindergartener, Mommy was the funniest person in the whole world. To my fourth grader, I was confusing. To my middle schooler and soon-to-be *bat mitzvah* candidate, I was all embarrassment save those rare moments she remembered we were supposed to love one another.

It wasn't a perfect setup, but it was ours, and we were much happier without Jared Levine in it. Not that it stopped him from knocking on my parents' front door at nine o'clock at night anyway.

My mother fetched me from the sofa as I devoured my favorite author's newest novel. I was ill prepared to face my ex with no makeup, no bra, and a mismatched shirt with pajama pants.

"You could have warned me," I hissed as my mother shoved me outside.

"Think of the children," she whispered back. "It would be nice to see the two of you getting along at Natalie's bat mitzvah. Just try, Poppy."

The sound of the closed door behind me felt like a fight bell commencing our sparring match. Jared wasted no time in perusing my appearance.

"Don't bother telling me I look good." I crossed my arms over my chest in both defiance and modesty.

Ready with the hard-sell, Jared said, "I've been doing a lot of praying."

I held up a hand to cut him off. "It's been a long day, and I don't have time for your Jews for Jesus spiel."

"It's called *Messianic Judaism*," he said with an indignant sniff. "Real Jews don't worship in a church."

"Whatever you say, Jared. Just tell me what you want so I can get back to my book."

"Still reading those R.D. Hampton novels?" he asked.

"And here I thought you were too busy coming up with ways to lie and cheat on me to even notice what kind of books I like."

Regrettably, Jared didn't take the bait. "Those books took up most of your nightstand, Poppy. They would be hard to forget."

Thinking about my old nightstand made me think about the bed we once shared. It reminded me of all the times I thought my husband and I were making love, yet he was simply making do until he could run off with Leah Halpern. Resentment burned the back of my throat.

"I know I've already said this a hundred times, Poppy, but I made a huge mistake. The Bible says—"

"Save it," I snapped. "I don't want you, and I don't want your Jesus. The kids have school in the morning, and I need to get to bed."

"I miss you, Poppy. I miss us. I miss our family."

"You should have thought of that before you started sleeping with my best friend. And what about 'finally finding real love' after faking it with me for eighteen years? Either work on a legitimate divorce settlement with me or stop stalling on a mediation date. You know we can't go to court without it, and you're not going to win by holding me hostage in a marriage I don't want anymore."

His dark eyes implored mine. "Don't you think we owe it to our kids to try?"

"Don't you think you owed it to our kids to actually love their mother? To find our children more interesting than whatever game you downloaded to your phone or computer? Where is all of this coming from, Jared? Is it because Leah kicked you out when she realized you're just looking for another mother to spoil you? My days of catering to your whims and mood swings are over."

"Leah didn't kick me out, Poppy. I left. I found *Yeshua*, and I couldn't live in sin with her anymore."

"We both know His name is Jesus, so quit trying to turn it into something it's not. You sound insane. This is even more crazy than the performance you gave about secretly carrying a torch for Leah all these years."

"I made a mistake," he said, searching my eyes. "Let me make it up to you."

I compressed my lips into a thin line. "Jared, you talk a lot about your 'mistakes,' but I'm still waiting to hear you be sorry for what you actually did."

"I *am* sorry, Poppy. I've told you that already."

"No," I fired back. "You're sorry for what your choices cost *you*. I have yet to see an ounce of remorse or grief for what your choices cost *us*. You abandoned your children, Jared, not just me. You left me to explain why Daddy didn't live with us anymore, why we had to sell our house to pay for divorce attorneys. For Pete's sake, I had to go crawling back to my parents to have a roof over our heads! I endure their constant nitpicking and meddling because I could never afford Natalie's bat mitzvah without their help. *You* are responsible for that!"

His head lowered. "I didn't realize that."

"Of course you didn't, you selfish jerk! The only person you ever think about is yourself. How dare you show up at my parents' home and expect some vague, non apology to fix everything you've broken!"

"Tell me what to do!" he begged. "I'll say whatever you want me to say. Just tell me there's hope for us!"

I shook my head in disgust. "You shouldn't need me to spoon feed you the words, Jared. I'll start believing any of this *mishigas* is real when you stop giving me blanket apologies and you start owning your actual behavior. You know what you did. You know how you treated me our entire marriage. Why don't you start with some of that?"

"I know you've been lonely for a long time, Poppy. You told me you started reading romance novels because you couldn't get those things from me. I'm offering it now. I've changed, I promise. I want to have a real marriage with you."

Tears burned my eyes. For all of Jared's self absorption, he still knew my deepest weakness. He interpreted my prolonged silence as a crumbling of my defenses and leaned in to kiss me.

He pressed his lips to mine, and I succumbed for a brief

moment, temporarily swept away in emotions and sensations long forgotten. I melted easily into his arms as if no time had passed.

"Poppy," he breathed against my mouth. "I knew you'd come around."

Slapped back into reality, I pushed Jared away with comic book strength. "Don't ever touch me again," I snarled. I wiped his kiss from my mouth and the stain of Leah Halpern along with it. "Sex won't fix the mess you made, and I'm tired of you manipulating me with it."

Jared raked a hand through salt and pepper hair that had added more silver since the last time I'd seen him. "How do I make this right, Poppy? You complained I stopped showing you affection, but apparently that's not what you want anymore. What am I supposed to do?"

Holding back the barb I wanted to unleash, I studied my soon-to-be ex-husband, not quite sure what to believe.

"There's nothing you can do," I finally said, "other than grant me my divorce so we can move on with our lives. Congratulations on stealing a kiss. It won't happen again."

"You used to love my kisses."

"You used to pretend you loved *me*. Or maybe you were just pretending that it was Leah who followed you like a puppy in high school. Leah who gave you her virginity. Leah who gave you eighteen years of her life and three children."

He winced. "I know, Poppy. I completely understand why you hate me. I know Yeshua has already forgiven me, and I hope you can too one day."

"You are unbelievable!" I fumed. "Why can't you just apologize like a normal person? You destroyed our family, yet somehow you still manage to feel sorry for yourself."

"I see," he said coldly.

Hoping to catch him off guard with something other than anger, I said, "Look, we are past the point of no return here. I don't love you anymore, and I want you out of my life. We have three, amazing children who don't need to be exposed to any more of your dysfunction."

His gaze hardened. "My faith is not a dysfunction."

"I'm talking about *you*, Jared. You don't know how to be alone. You've always had some woman taking care of you, taking responsibility so you wouldn't have to grow up. I just had no idea I'd been sold a bill of goods when I married you."

"There's somebody else, isn't there?" he demanded. "That's why you don't want me kissing you. It's the guilt."

Before I could bite back a chuckle at the absurd turn of our conversation, I found myself saying, "Yes, it's somebody from work. We just started dating a few weeks ago. I'm not ready to introduce him to the kids, but he treats me well."

Jared crossed his arms over his chest. "Does he know you have children?"

With my mind immediately conjuring up the image of my mystery man, I replied, "He sees their pictures all the time. And unlike you, he thinks I'm amazing. He told me so just the other day."

"How do you know he's not some creep pedophile? Don't you remember the scandal with that pastor in Winthrope last year?"

"He's not a pedophile."

"Does he know you're still married?"

"If by 'married,' you mean because my husband is too cheap to pay his divorce attorney and keeps stalling on our proceedings, then yes, he's well aware of the situation. We had quite an interesting conversation at the Culver awards banquet last month."

I amazed myself at being able to fabricate an entire relationship based on a smattering of conversations and the brushing of fingers on a coffee cup. Joe Trautweig would certainly be surprised.

"Is he coming to meet your folks for Thanksgiving?" Jared asked.

"You're not invited, so what difference does it make to you?"

"Call me curious to see how quickly this relationship is progressing."

Ignoring him, I took a step backward and reached for the front door knob. "Jared, I'm going to bed. Don't stop by unannounced anymore. If you want to see the kids, just ask. You know they love you and are always happy to see you, but you can't expect me to share their enthusiasm. Not after what you've done."

"Office flings don't usually end well. I might just call this guy myself." Jared raised an eyebrow and watched me for a reaction.

I glared back. "Joe has never made me cry. Unlike you, I might add."

"So, is this you living out one of your romance novels, Poppy? This Joe guy swoops in on the white horse and woos you with his *courtly love?*"

Of course, the one thing Jared would remember from my steamy, historical book collection was the medieval practice of forbidden love between a married woman and her unmarried male admirer. In the Hampton novels, the wife usually chose forbidden fruit and ran off with her lover. It certainly explained the scowl on Jared's face.

I sighed wearily. "Just go home, Jared. My love life is none of your business anymore. You made that choice when you abandoned me for my best friend. We both need to move on."

Not giving him a chance to respond, I slipped back into the house and ignored my mother's questioning glance from the living room. Undoubtedly, she'd been eavesdropping anyway. I trudged downstairs back to the basement apartment, wiping the tears that fell freely down my face.

The idea that Jared Levine wanted his wife after nearly two decades of taking me for granted just felt tragically ironic.

CHAPTER 3

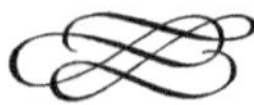

After a sleepless night conjuring up any manner of drama Jared Levine might stir up, I braved another morning at Vincenzo's. The complimentary coffee pods at Culver didn't offer double shot espresso needed to deal with a jerk ex-husband looking to cause trouble.

"Fancy seeing you here," Joe Trautweig said just behind my ear. His baritone voice tickled the fine hairs on my neck and sent goosebumps down my arms.

I managed to gracefully choke, trip, and stumble right into the condiment counter.

"Poppy, are you okay?"

I stared up into jade eyes, mortified at the lie I'd told Jared, but even more embarrassed that part of me wished it was true. Joe blinked once then glanced down at the R.D. Hampton bodice ripper bulging from my purse.

"I see you're a fan of the classics."

Blushing like my tweenager with her latest crush, I fumbled to put a lid on my coffee.

"Maybe you should ease off of the double shot," Joe said playfully, seeing my order handwritten on the side of my cup.

Willing myself to be the Poppy Levine of old, I squared my shoulders and faced Joe head on. "Rough couple of days. No worries, Joe. I'll see you back at the office."

Grabbing my cup, I sat down in a leather chair. He sat down opposite me.

"Did I do something to offend you, Poppy?"

My head jerked up in surprise. "What?"

Joe held my gaze, and I forced myself to maintain eye contact despite a rumble of butterflies. "I was beginning to wonder if I had done something wrong," he said. "I've been getting the impression you can't stand to have me around."

I shook my head. "Sorry, Joe. I just have a lot on my mind. I promise, it has very little to do with you."

He didn't look mollified. "Are you sure that's it?"

"It's nothing I can really talk about," I said through a tight smile, "but rest assured, we're totally cool. I've got no bone to pick with you."

He nodded as if he believed my lame story, but a muscle flexed in his jaw.

"Oh, wow! Two days in a row?" Jessica Goldstein exclaimed, catching my eye as she picked up her order. Noting Joe's presence beside me, she asked, "Who's your friend? He can't possibly be the ex-husband."

I sucked a deep breath and inwardly cringed. Seeing her misstep, she said, "Sorry. That just went from awkward to embarrassing."

Taking it all in stride, Joe stood up and extended his hand to Jessica. She smiled prettily for him, and I noticed Joe respond in kind. Though I felt a pang of jealousy at her beauty and lack of baggage, I wouldn't begrudge Jessica the opportunity to meet a wonderful man.

They chatted for a few minutes, and I stared glumly down at my coffee. They'd probably have china patterns picked out by the time I finished my espresso.

"Poppy?" Joe asked.

I glanced up, surprised he wasn't still engaged in conversation.

"Where'd she go?"

"Your friend said she didn't want to interrupt and just stopped over to say hi."

"There was nothing to interrupt," I blurted out. At Joe's confused look, I added, "That is, I mean, we're coworkers. We happened to be in the same coffee shop at the same time. It's not like she walked in on a date or something. Besides, you two looked like you had plenty to chat about."

Joe raised an eyebrow. "Well, can I at least walk you back to the office?"

"I don't need an escort, and I'm sure you'd rather talk to my friend anyway. She's probably much better company this morning than I am."

Fighting back claws of envy I had no right to feel, I grabbed my purse and made sure to take my coffee with me. I berated myself for wanting Joe to ignore my boundary and chase after me. I berated myself for being so good at pushing him away that it worked.

I stepped off the elevator outside of our office suite and ran directly into Culver's mother hen, Miss Belle.

"Oooh, child, who kicked your dog?" she said, looking me over. "You've got the weight of the world on your shoulders today, Poppy Levine."

"I'm fine, Miss Belle. I'm just waiting for my coffee to kick in. Do you need the elevator?"

"No, baby. I came by the front to give some copying to Brooklyn." She inclined her head toward our receptionist seated just beyond double glass doors.

A second elevator dinged, and Joe stepped out. His posture immediately stiffened, but he offered a small jerk of the chin to acknowledge the two of us. He walked briskly into the office, probably feeling Miss Belle's gaze the entire way.

Once he disappeared around the corner, she lasered in on me. "Spill it."

"Spill what?"

Her narrowed eyes and pursed lips kept my feet stuck like glue in their place. "Don't act like you couldn't cut that tension with a knife, baby girl. I've seen all this before."

"There's nothing going on, Miss Belle. Believe me."

Understanding lit her eyes. "There's nothing going on right *now*, but maybe one of you was hoping for more, right?"

"That's ridiculous!"

"Mmhmm," she said, looking me up and down. "That's what I thought."

I sighed. "It's not what you—"

"Poppy," Brooklyn called, poking her head between the glass doors, "you've got flowers at the desk."

"Thanks, Brooklyn. I'll be there in a second."

Miss Belle shook her head. "Lord! I'm getting too old for all this soap opera drama."

I exhaled an exasperated sigh. "Miss Belle, there is no drama. Just a misunderstanding."

She glanced over at the enormous bouquet of mixed roses now placed prominently on Brooklyn's desk. "That don't look like *nothing*."

I rolled my eyes.

"Don't you want to know who sent them? Somebody spent a lot of money on flowers to get your attention."

"Fine, I'll go look. Happy now?"

"No need to be nasty!" she gasped, appropriately clutching her pearl necklace.

"I didn't ask for your advice or interference, Miss Belle. I'm sure you mean well, but it's just making a difficult situation even worse. Can you just trust me that you don't have the entire story? Jumping to conclusions isn't helping anybody here."

She relaxed her pursed lips. Somewhat. "Well, go see who sent you the flowers. At least then you'll know if there's a reason to be so snippy with everybody."

Determined to put the matter to rest, I opened the glass door for Miss Belle and followed her inside. Dread and anger filled me with each step toward the front desk. I didn't have to wonder who sent the obnoxious bouquet. Jared Levine would waste no time in marking his territory and issuing a challenge to my imaginary boyfriend.

"Beautiful!" Miss Belle said, coming up behind me. "That's got to be three dozen roses in there. I love when they make the bouquets with all the different colors."

"Except I hate roses," I muttered. "Eighteen years together, and he still can't remember that."

"Aren't you going to open the card?" Brooklyn asked. "Oh, this is so romantic! Flowers at work has got to be one of the sweetest things ever. It looks like your secret admirer doesn't want it to be a secret anymore."

Trembling with adrenaline, caffeine, and growing rage, I opened the envelope and read, *To many more kisses in the future. Your loving husband, Jared.*

My inner voice escaped to the outside in a seething hiss. "I'm going to kill him."

Brooklyn and Miss Belle exchanged nervous glances. I crumbled up Jared's disgusting manipulation ploy and threw it into the garbage.

"Brooklyn, feel free to take those home and enjoy them," I said.

"But they're so beautiful! Are you sure you don't want them?"

"I hate them," I said through gritted teeth. "I absolutely *hate* roses. I've always hated roses. He knows I hate roses, but he's too selfish to remember or even care."

Brooklyn's jaw fell open at my outburst at the same time Joe approached with a document needing to be scanned and emailed. He looked from Brooklyn, to Miss Belle, to me, and then to the flowers. His eyes came back to rest on me, question and concern in his eyes.

With forced gaiety, I announced, "Brooklyn, I'm so glad you like the roses. I think they'll look really nice on the coffee table for any visitors coming by today. They're all yours after that."

Still in shock, she nodded and then sat back down at her desk. Joe approached her with his email request, and I made my escape to my office. Not sure where else to turn, I sent Rebecca Margolin an emergency text message as soon as I sat down.

Jared has gone completely unhinged.

Rebecca's response was swift. *Both babies up all night with stomach bugs. Totally exhausted and tired of cleaning up vomit. What's going on?*

Too much for text. Sounds like your hands are full.

The joys and oys of motherhood. If I can get the girls to nap, I'll text you back later.

I took a shaky breath, wishing I could give into the pity party I felt rightfully entitled to partake.

When Joe called my name at my doorway, I startled and screamed out loud.

Then, I promptly burst into tears.

Indulging myself for a few minutes, I gave way to silent sobs, not wanting to humiliate myself any further by causing a scene. Joe remained for the duration of my hysterics, standing above me with a box of tissues. I glanced up, surprised he didn't flee in abject terror.

"Thanks," I whispered, taking the box. Figuring I couldn't make myself any less attractive than I already felt, I relieved the pressure in my nose and went through two more tissues before I could breathe again.

"Better?" he asked.

I looked up, suddenly realizing Joe had shut my office door.

He pulled a conference chair around my desk to sit down next to me. "Poppy, what's going on? I've never seen you like this. Brooklyn said the roses at the front desk were for you, but you..." his voice trailed off.

"Had a complete meltdown," I finished for him. "That about sums it up."

"Is this what made you so jumpy at Vincenzo's?"

I nodded. "My ex dropped by my parents' house last night trying to woo me back. He sent those hideous flowers as a follow up. I just don't want any trace of him here at work."

Joe's pale gaze searched my face. "That makes sense."

"Eighteen years I was with that man, and he still thinks a bouquet of roses is all the effort he needs to make."

"So, you're trying to reconcile?"

"No!" I said a little too loudly. "I'm trying to get out! The imbecile thinks sending me flowers I absolutely despise will somehow change my mind.”

“Despise?”

“Despise,” I repeated emphatically. “Roses are clichéd and not my style at all. Give me a bouquet of daisies or mums any day of the week. Jared and I have had this fight so many times. He completely ignores what I want, then gets offended when I’m not falling down in gratitude for what *he* thinks is best. Typical for Jared, his grand display has nothing to do with *me* and everything to do with looking good to others.”

“Anything I can do to help?”

I laughed bitterly. “I don’t think so, Joe, but I appreciate the offer.”

He placed a hand on my shoulder. “If you ever want to talk, I’m happy to listen. I have plenty of my own horror stories to share. My ex-wife might even make your ex-husband seem normal by comparison.”

I chuckled softly. “I may just take you up on that.”

The sparkle returned to Joe’s eyes. “I hope you do.”

We stared into each other’s eyes, and the rest of the room grew hazy. Joe opened his mouth to say something just as Miss Belle came barging into the room.

He bolted awkwardly from his chair and excused himself. Miss Belle, meanwhile, leaned against my office door frame while he hurried past her. She folded her arms over her ample chest with a smug look on her face.

“Mmhmm,” she purred. “That’s what I thought.”

CHAPTER 4

"LEAH! LEAH! HE SIGNED MY YEARBOOK!" I SQUEALED. I pulled my best friend closer to the lockers so no one else at Hillcrest High discovered my undying love for Jared Michael Levine.

"Are you serious?" Leah gasped, clutching her heart over her cropped cardigan.

"Look! Right here!" I opened my yearbook to prove it was no hallucination.

"Poppy. Cool Name. H.A.G.S. Jared," she read aloud.

"Can you believe it? He wants me to have a great summer," I said, translating his yearbook acronym.

"That's it? I thought he wrote something a little more personal."

I flipped a mass of curly tendrils out of my eyes to reread his message. "Don't you see? We're totally meant to be. We're like Russ and Raquel from *Buddies*!"

Leah's frosted lips thinned. "I guess."

"What's wrong?" I asked.

"I don't know, Poppy. I mean, he's a senior. You're a sopho-more. Guys usually like older women. You know, with *experience*," she whispered.

"Well, I'm not going to give my flower away to just any guy. It's supposed to be with someone you love."

Leah rolled her eyes. "Nobody believes in that anymore."

"Oh yeah? Well, how many guys have you done it with?"

My best friend cleared her throat. "I'm not saying I've gone all the way, but I totally could if I wanted to. My friend Stephanie from cheer camp says her boyfriend knows someone who would do it with me. And he's in college too."

"My dad says guys will go out with just about anybody as long as they think they can get some. He says I'll know when it's the right one."

"Which means daddy helps keep your chastity belt on, but it doesn't exactly improve your love life," Leah said, pulling at her knee-high tights. "Poppy, I think your parents would be happy if you died a virgin."

"What's wrong with them being protective? You know they have a good reason to be."

"Over protective," she corrected. "Guys like Jared aren't interested in a goody two-shoes who doesn't know what she's doing."

I frowned. "Leah, I know you've kissed a lot of guys, but what's wrong with waiting and wanting things to be special? I mean, you only get one first kiss, right?"

"You've never been kissed before?" she gasped.

"Announce it to the whole school, why don't you? Oh my gosh! What if someone heard you?"

"But you've never even kissed a guy! Are you trying to become the first Jewish nun?"

"Billy Halston tried to mack on me after homecoming last

year, remember? It was gross and wet, and it doesn't count because I didn't want him to kiss me."

Leah shook her head and rolled her eyes. "How are you going to know what you're doing with a guy like Jared if you don't get any practice first? What about your neighbor? The big guy?"

"Ew!" I gasped. "Moose Grunwald? As if!"

"But he's friends with Jared."

"Leah, that makes no sense. Why would Jared want to go out with me if he knew I made out with his friend?"

"Some guys like a challenge. You know, like forbidden fruit."

"I guess," I said with a shrug. "I know people already think I'm some dateless loser because I'm not showing off my midriff or wearing micro minis all the time. No offense," I said, gesturing toward her fitted top, tartan skirt, and platform loafers.

"Poppy, you're my best friend," Leah said. "You might be dateless, but I'm not friends with losers. You were the only girl in our P.E. class last year who let me borrow a pair of shorts when I forgot mine."

I smiled. "Friends are supposed to be there for you."

Leah matched my grin. "When the rain falls and more."

Looking at each other, we both did the *Buddies* theme song clap and burst into giggles.

After exhaling a contented sigh, I pressed my yearbook to my chest. "I still can't believe he actually signed it for me. Did you see what he put as his senior quote?"

"Looking for love in all the wrong places," she recited immediately. Without warning, Leah's blue eyes doubled in size as something caught her attention behind me.

"Hey ladies," Jared said. His perfectly gelled pompadour and mischievous smile made my knees feel like jelly. With a jerk of the chin, he added, "How's it going?"

Surprising even my sixteen-year-old self, I maintained an air of nonchalance. "It's all good."

Jared leaned his elbow against a nearby locker and leisurely looked me up and down. "Nice overalls," he said, which to my teenage brain somehow translated to, "Will you marry me and have my babies?"

"Thanks," I replied easily. Turning to my best friend, I said, "Hey, Leah, I think your stepmom is going to pick us up soon. We better get going. Nice to see you, Jared."

As I pulled Leah with me, she looked at me in shock.

"Poppy!" she hissed. "What are you doing? Jared came over to talk to you!"

"Playing hard-to-get. Is it working? Look over your shoulder, but try to be subtle."

"He's gone."

I whipped around, only to see Jared following both of us with his eyes. He grinned, flashing two, melt-your-heart-into-butter dimples.

"Leah, you ruined my dramatic exit!"

"Poppy, I'm helping you get a date. You could try thanking me."

Jared sauntered over. If not for my cork wedges, he would have towered over me by a good six inches. Had any pair of eyes ever been so dark and dreamy?

"Moose Grunwald is throwing a graduation party on Saturday night. You should come. Both of you," he said, winking at Leah. "Do you know where he lives?"

Leah frowned. "Two doors down from Poppy. Her parents will probably call the cops because of all the noise."

I kept my composure for Jared's benefit. "Leah can be a little dramatic sometimes. My folks are totally cool. I mean, they named me 'Poppy,' right?"

Leah now wore the look of hurt, ice blue eyes flashing anger.

"Two doors down, huh?" Jared said, oblivious to the silent war between me and my best friend. "How come I never knew the prettiest girl in school lived so close?" He gave me a sideways smile that obliterated my feigned indifference. My cheeks pinked, and Jared's eyes took on a knowing glint.

He touched the fabric flower clip nestled amongst my eons of curls. "See you Saturday?"

I nodded wordlessly and assumed Leah would eventually pick her jaw off the floor.

"Cool. See you there," he said. "Oh, and you too, Lila."

Twenty-two years later, I chuckled to myself, remembering how Leah fumed for days about Jared not remembering her name. My expression sobered, wondering if that's when our rivalry began.

"Was it ever about Jared or just getting back at me?" I wondered aloud.

"Mommy, can you sign my permission slip?" Madison asked, putting an end to my trip down nostalgia lane. I returned my attention to the chicken and frozen vegetables cooking in the skillet.

"What am I giving you permission to do?"

"Field trip," she said with a toothy grin. "We're going to a farm."

"Sounds gross," Natalie said from the breakfast table. "Who wants to be around a bunch of smelly animals anyway?"

Seeing Madison's crestfallen expression, I glared at my twelve year-old. "Do you have to do that to her, Natalie? Shoot down every little thing your sister gets excited about?"

"What?" she said in faux innocence. "Suddenly horses and cows don't smell like poop anymore?"

When my five year-old's shoulders trembled in silent tears, Mama Bear came roaring. The words escaped my mouth before I thought better of it. "Those barn animals smell about as delicious as those middle school boys you're always crushing on."

Madison laughed, but Natalie looked like she'd been slapped. She burst into tears and fled the room. I sighed.

"Thanks, Mommy," Madison said, looking up at me with admiration. "Nati says she doesn't always mean what she says, but it still hurts."

Tears stung my eyes, hating this entire mess, and hating Jared Levine more than I ever fancied myself in love with him. I flipped the knob off on the electric stove and located my first-born crying in the bedroom she shared with her sister.

"Natalie?" I called, knocking softly on the door.

"Just go away! I know I was being mean to Maddie, but it's not fair!"

I opened the door and stepped into the room. "What's not fair?"

Natalie looked into my eyes, tortured pain reflected in them. "How come she gets to be happy, Mom? It's like the divorce isn't even happening to her."

Inching closer to my daughter, I asked, "Are you saying our whole family should be depressed all the time? That we can't be happy even though we might be sad about some other things?"

"Well, you're always depressed," she said, gesturing at me.

I nearly choked on her words. "Is that what you think?"

"Daddy said he started dating Aunt Leah because you were never happy and always complaining. He said he could never do anything right. He said Aunt Leah made him feel good about himself."

Refusing to stick my daughter in the middle and argue against her father's fabrications, I tried a different tack. "Natalie, do you think it was a good idea for your dad to tell you all those things about me?"

"Well, they're true, aren't they? I mean, you always wear the same clothes, and you cut off all your hair when Daddy left. It's like you stopped caring."

"I was *grieving*, Natalie. I still am." I eased onto the twin bed with her. "I fell in love with your father the second I met him, but he broke my heart. How would you feel if Caden Jones treated you that way? You've been in love with him since school started."

"Why is it wrong for me to want my parents to be married and not hate each other?"

I pushed a wayward curl behind her ear. "It's not wrong. And by the way, I don't hate your father. I do hate what he did to us, though."

"Can't you try to make it work?" she pleaded. "For us?"

"I did try, sweetie. For a long time. I would still be trying if Daddy hadn't left us. I didn't ask him to leave, Natalie."

"Oh," she said quietly.

"If your father and I could be married in a way that's healthy and good for all of us, I would do it. I just don't think that's possible anymore."

"Daddy says that all things are possible with God."

"He's not wrong," I admitted, "but I don't think God wants us to make ourselves miserable so other people can be happy."

"Were you miserable, Mom?"

I nodded. "Yes, honey. So was Daddy. He thought Aunt Leah would make him happy."

"But she didn't," Natalie said, highlighting the recent chain of events.

"There are things your father needs to sort out in his own heart that have nothing to do with me or Aunt Leah."

"Could you guys get back together if he did?"

I couldn't douse the hope in my daughter's eyes, not after she'd just bared her soul. "We'll see," I hedged, kicking the can down the road. "In the meantime, can you please make an effort to be nicer to all of us, especially your baby sister?"

Natalie's curly head bobbed. "Yeah, and I hope you and Daddy can be nicer to each other too."

Bounding off her bed like a completely different kid, Natalie took a direct path to Madison. Accompanying giggles followed shortly thereafter.

I touched my shoulder length curls. My first act of rebellion against Jared and his lies had involved taking a pair of scissors to my own hair.

Desperate times.

CHAPTER 5

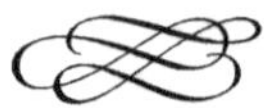

"How'd you manage to get out of the house?" I asked Rebecca Margolin three days later over brunch.

My friend sighed dramatically. "I begged my mother-in-law to babysit. She'd brave worse than a potential stomach bug just to hug and kiss her grandbabies."

I smiled. "When Jared left us for Leah two and a half years ago, my mother-in-law grew more distant. Jared has the version he spreads about what happened with our marriage, and I think it hits too close to home for Barbara."

"How so?" Rebecca asked.

"She was divorced when Jared and I started dating, and then things got tense between the two of them when she married his stepfather."

"But you actually like the stepdad, right?"

I nodded. "Gary and I always got along. He tried talking to Jared about how he treated me, which Jared resented like h...oh, um, like heck," I amended.

Rebecca grinned, lighting up the room. "Thanks for that."

I winked at her. "I do my best. I save my salty language for my morning coffee buddy."

Mrs. Margolin cleared her throat and took a sip of water. "Ted mentioned a little something about that. How is Jessica doing?"

"Are you looking for dirt or just general information?" I asked. "I know you two have a lot of history, but I want to respect Jessica's privacy. She has no idea who I am or that I know you."

"Just general info," Rebecca said. "Jessica's life fell apart around the same time mine came together."

"You've mentioned that. Jared actually knows her ex-fiancé."

"Seriously?" Rebecca asked as our server placed our entrees in front of us. I watched her offer up a quick prayer before she picked up a piece of turkey bacon. "How does Jared know Nathan Fein?"

"Let's just say your book made quite an impact at *Beth Shalom*."

Rebecca gave a sideways grin. "You mean my less than flattering portrayal of what they do at the messianic synagogue?"

"Well, there's that, and then there's outing Nathan's porn addiction to the world. Jared likes to use that as a strike against you. He calls you bitter and unforgiving."

"I've been called worse," she said with a laugh. "Nathan's addiction and gaslighting are what caused Jessica to implode. I'm glad he finally got help, but it doesn't change what happened to my friend."

"Which is exactly what I told Jared. Nathan is some *macher* in that synagogue now and married with a baby, so putting a tarnish on their pristine image didn't go over very well. Jared seems to be climbing up the ladder there too. He's bought into all of that *mishigas* hook, line, and sinker. He's constantly shoving all of this Bible stuff in my face, acting like he's a better Jew than I am."

"What does he think about all the Scriptures regarding adultery?" Rebecca asked pointedly.

I rolled my eyes. "He prefers to quote the ones about forgiveness. Somehow Jared's cheating was my fault, as is my unwillingness to overlook it now that he's lost his meal ticket."

"Meal ticket?"

I took a bite of home fries before answering. "Leah's loaded. She works at her father's company, and by 'works,' I mean that she gets a salary and travels the world. She'd probably run the place into the ground if she actually cared enough to take an interest."

"How did the two of you remain friends all these years?" Rebecca asked. "You seem like complete opposites."

"Leah has put on airs for as long as I've known her. Beneath all the designer clothes, though, she's lonely and insecure. I was one of the few people who saw behind the persona and let her be herself."

"And then she stole your husband. So much for gratitude."

"He wasn't much of a husband, Rebecca. I always felt so unworthy, and Jared used that to his advantage. I wore myself ragged trying to be good enough for him."

"When it should have been the other way around," she said, offended on my behalf.

"You've mentioned how narcissistic abusers deliberately target someone with qualities they envy. I'm living proof."

My friend nodded around a mouthful of scrambled eggs. Swallowing, she said, "Then, they tear you down and make you feel like all of those wonderful qualities are worthless. They have to destroy any bit of you that makes them feel inferior by comparison. My father loved to demean anything I said about the Bible, acting like I didn't know what I was talking about."

"How's that prison sentence working out for him?" I shot back. "Quite a rap sheet for Mr. Holier-than-thou."

Rebecca responded with a sunny smile. "That's the beauty of no contact—I don't have to know. According to my aunt, my mother will be getting out of jail soon for her part in his crimes."

"Any plans to see her?" I asked.

"She's done more than enough damage to last me a lifetime. I won't let her anywhere near my children."

"I'm not sure I believe in marriage anymore after what Jared did to me."

My friend looked sad. "The world does not begin and end with Jared Levine."

"No, but he refuses to admit defeat now that he realizes he can't just waltz back into our lives. He came over about a week ago and said he loves me and wants to have a *real* marriage now. I don't think he has a clue what that even means. Frankly, I'm not sure I do either."

"What did you tell him?"

"Take a wild guess." I stabbed into my omelette with unusual vigor.

Rebecca grinned. "And what did he say?"

"He wanted to know if I was seeing someone else. Typical for Jared, he assumes I must be guilty of cheating too."

"Did you tell him to stop projecting his behavior onto you?"

I blushed.

Rebecca raised an eyebrow.

"I'm already catching flack about this from Miss Belle," I began.

"Someone at work?" she asked in surprise. "The only person

who's single over the age of thirty is..." her voice cut out as her eyes went wide. "Are you and Joe...?" her hand gesticulated wildly as she pieced it all together.

"Nothing's going on," I said.

"If nothing's going on, why is Culver's resident granny giving you grief about it? Miss Belle is pretty perceptive."

"And nosey."

Rebecca smiled. "Yeah, that too. She means well, but sometimes she gets carried away."

"The whole thing has turned into a Shakespearean comedy."

"I've been dealing with baby throw up and diarrhea all week. I could use a chuckle or two."

I laid out the situation as succinctly as possible while Rebecca fought back laughter.

"So, let me see if I have this straight," she said. "You lied to your ex to get him off your back."

"Right."

"Except you think you caught feelings for Joe, and all signs seem to point to him returning them."

"Right."

"But Joe doesn't know you lied to Jared and told him that you're already dating."

"Correct."

"So, your fictional love interest has no idea that you made up a relationship with him, only to wind up having actual feelings for him anyway."

The situation felt even more ridiculous hearing it out loud. "Like I said, Rebecca, Shakespearean comedy...or tragedy, depending on how all of this works out."

"Poppy, is there any chance of you reconciling with Jared? Before you complicate things for you, for Joe, and especially for your kids, you have to know the answer to that question. Anything else is just a recipe for disaster."

I sighed heavily. "Jared says he's found Jesus, that he left Leah because he couldn't 'live in sin' with her anymore. Now, he eats, lives, and breathes all of this Messianic Judaism stuff. Sometimes he sounds like he's turned over a new leaf, and other times, it's the same old Jared with a super spiritual coating. I still don't feel like he's taking responsibility for everything leading up to the affair or for how he treated me during our marriage. He just wants to shove it all under the rug and expects me to do the same."

I didn't miss the wince on Rebecca's face.

Continuing on, I said, "My parents told me Rabbi Cohn gave another sermon on the dangers of Messianic Judaism. I don't mean to offend you, but he raised a lot of valid reasons why it just can't work. Jared's hypocrisy just proves his point."

"About Messianic Judaism as a denomination or about Jesus being the Jewish Messiah?" Rebecca asked. "Because they're two, totally different things."

I shrugged. "I didn't realize there was a difference."

"Let me ask you this," she said. "Would you want people to base their opinion of traditional Judaism on how you personally practice it? Do you think that your behavior speaks for the entire Jewish community? That every person who calls themselves a Jew observes the holidays and traditions exactly like you do?"

I conceded the point with a wry smile. *"Touché,"*

"You know the story with me and Ted," she said. "We've tried visiting every kind of church, synagogue, and even messianic synagogue looking for something that fits who we are. We've found good. We've found misguided. We've even found a few cults masquerading as houses of God. We just haven't found the place that works for us and our situation."

"Doesn't that prove Rabbi Cohn's point?" I asked. "You can't find a decent house of worship because what you're worshiping is all wrong."

"Or," Rebecca countered, "the issue isn't about Jesus, but about people worshiping things other than God. Instead of a congregation like we read about in the Bible, we've got spiritual country clubs offering social activities and motivational speeches. This isn't just a Messianic Jewish issue, but one that's affecting the entire Body of Christ."

"The what?" I asked, thoroughly confused.

Rebecca smiled encouragingly at me. "I forget you didn't grow up hearing all of the Bible-ese."

I exhaled a short laugh. "That's for sure."

"Have you talked to Ted about any of this?" she asked. "I'm sure he'd be happy to answer any questions you have."

"I'm not looking to get converted here," I said, shifting uncomfortably. "Jared has already tried pitching me all of the Messianic talking points. He keeps going on about *Jewish identity*, this and that. It's like he wears it as some kind of merit badge. Look, I'm Jewish, my kids are Jewish, but we don't go around advertising it like Jared does. Sometimes, I think he's having an identity crisis. You know, on top of the midlife one."

"We can change the subject," Rebecca said, watching me. "Poppy, I don't want to upset you, and you know I love you for who you are. I'm not just your friend to force you to believe anything. I hope you know that."

"I do," I said, "but I appreciate you saying it anyway. You and Taylor have this special bond that sometimes makes me a little jealous."

"Shared suffering will do that," she said, "and you're a card carrying member too. Do you have any idea what you're going to do with this Jared/Joe situation? Too many 'J' names anyway. Can you forget both of them and fall in love with a Simon or something?"

I laughed. "Back in high school, Leah told me I should go make out with my neighbor to get some practice. Maybe I should look up Moose Grunwald and see if he's still available."

Rebecca choked violently on her water, so much so, I wound up across the table patting her on the back.

She looked up at me, eyes red from the exertion. "Warn me next time, okay?"

"Warn you about what?"

"The next time you want to drop a bombshell on me."

I reached over and handed Rebecca the offending glass of water. "Care to explain?"

"You're talking about Patrick 'Moose' Grunwald, right?"

"Yeah," I drawled.

"He was Jessica's married boyfriend. The one she used to get back at Nathan for cheating on her. He's definitely not single, Poppy, and you wouldn't want him if he was."

CHAPTER 6

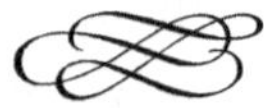

I STUMBLED BACK INTO THE OFFICE AFTER MY LUNCH with Rebecca. The web of connections between my past and my present sent me directly into the break room in search of caffeine.

I brewed the strongest roast coffee pod I could find. "Come to Mama," I purred, taking a deep drink.

A male voice cleared his throat, stifling a chuckle.

Fumbling with my cup, I wondered how and why Joe Trautweig managed to be at the wrong place at the most obscenely wrong time. Mortified, I said, "That was for the coffee!"

His eyes sparkled with humor. "How was lunch with Mrs. Margolin?"

"How did you know? Are you stalking me or something?"

"I saw you and Rebecca through the restaurant window."

"Ah."

"So, are you two pretty close?" he ventured.

"I'd say so. Why?"

"Just curious. Margolin has a Bible study group at his house. Is that the same stuff your ex got into?"

"Not at all," I said. "I disagree with the Margolins and their Jesus *shtick*, but I know they're sincere about it. Jared just parrots whatever he hears from the pulpit."

"Well, what do you think about it?" Joe asked, inching closer to me.

"What do you mean?"

"Do you think they're right about Jesus being God's son, that it's possible to be Jewish and Christian at the same time? I had lunch with Margolin the other day, and what he said made a lot of sense."

I met Joe's green gaze, wondering at his line of questioning. My pulse quickened as curiosity quickly shifted into the hum of attraction again. Turning my attention to my coffee cup, I finally said, "I don't think this is an appropriate conversation for work hours."

"Because I want to talk about religion, or because you're feeling the same thing I am and you're not sure what to do about it?"

"I don't know what you're talking about," I lied.

So, you're telling me I'm imagining the attraction between us? I'm not blind, Poppy, and neither are you."

His boldness and outright declaration gave me the courage to meet his eyes again. "Joe, you know I'm still married—even though it's not by choice. No matter how much I hate what Jared did to me and my kids, I will never retaliate like that. I'm not selfish enough to do that to my children."

"I understand."

"Why are you pursuing this anyway? It's a dead end."

"Is it?" His jade green gaze seared into mine.

I closed my eyes and reopened them, feeling like I stood on

the edge of a cliff. "What are you hoping is going to happen here?"

"The heck if I know, Poppy, but I haven't felt this way around a woman in a long time. I'm willing to figure it out together if you are."

I frowned. "While that sounds very romantic, it's not realistic. I don't have the luxury of casual dating or casual anything else. My kids come first."

"I'm not asking you to sacrifice your children for me. I would never even suggest that," he said, closing the distance between us and grabbing my hand. "Maybe this is nothing more than two lonely people finding some life experiences in common, but isn't it nice to know we're not dead anymore? That we get our souls back after what they did to us?"

"She really messed you up, didn't she?"

Joe's sad smile reached his eyes. "My wife wasn't well, mentally."

"What do you mean?"

"The doctors diagnosed Catherine with severe, borderline personality disorder. Her mother is one of those Bible thumpers, and she was convinced Catherine needed an exorcism from a Jezebel spirit."

My blood ran cold.

"You look the same way I did when she suggested it."

I shivered, still put off by the idea of demons and evil spirits. "It's just not something you hear about other than horror movies."

"Catherine eventually became violent, flushing away the meds her psychiatrist prescribed. She said she hated feeling numb all the time."

"Wow," I breathed, "and you had no idea when you got married?"

Joe shook his head. "Catherine was vivacious, charming, and made you feel like the most special person in the room. The first four years of our marriage felt like bliss, like the fairytale ending to a perfect love story."

"So, what changed?"

"We had a miscarriage. Catherine never got over the loss of the baby. It was like something snapped. First, she blamed the doctors, then she blamed the FDA for all of the chemicals and pesticides in our food and water. Eventually, she blamed me."

Hearing the approach of voices outside the door, I released my hand from Joe's and backed away toward my lukewarm coffee. I grabbed the styrofoam cup and placed it in the microwave just as Lexie Arterton and another new hire walked in.

"Hey guys," Lexie said, glancing from Joe and then back to me. "What's up?"

Recovering quickly, I said, "Finishing up Ted's RFP and working on Phil's. How are things going with all of your January 1 renewals?"

Lexie gave a long suffering sigh. "I'll be glad when they're over."

Joe's lips pressed into a tight smile, clearly wanting the other ladies to vacate the room.

"So um, what brings you to the breakroom?" Lexie asked, turning to Joe. "Do you have some projects to dump on the marketing department too?"

"I've got a few things for Poppy. Just wanted to get her up to speed first."

Lexie nodded, satisfied with his answer. She turned the conversation to our newest coworker, a recent college grad with very little interest in what the rest of us old folks had to say.

"Meet me in the hallway," Joe mouthed and then walked out of the room.

My hands shook as I pulled my coffee out of the microwave. Lexie migrated from the kitchenette to the lounge area of the break room, and I took a moment to compose myself.

"God, if you're listening," I whispered, "I need help here. I feel like I'm drowning. I don't know exactly who you are, only that this whole praying thing seems to work really well for my friends." After an awkward pause, I added, "Amen."

Keeping my coffee in hand in case I needed to use it as a weapon, I walked slowly to the back door. I took a deep breath, half hoping Joe gave up waiting for me. Instead, I found him leaning casually against the wall scrolling on his phone.

"Hi," I said.

"Brought your coffee with you, eh?"

A corner of my mouth lifted. "Just in case you get any funny ideas."

"Like what? Kissing you in the middle of the office?"

"Exactly like that, actually." I took a sip to steel my nerves.

"I've been wanting to ask you out for a while, Poppy, but I didn't know how to do it. When I found out you were in the middle of a divorce, I backed off and tried to give you space."

"So, what changed?" I asked, eyeing him over the rim of my cup.

"The award banquet last month," he said, a twinkle in his eye. "You were so relaxed and at ease. I think it was the first time you and I talked about anything that wasn't work related. It was also the first time I saw you without your usual ponytail. You're stunning, Poppy, and your ex-husband is a moron."

I blushed and took another sip of coffee. "Thank you on both accounts. I may disagree with you about the word 'stunning,' but I won't argue about Jared. He's also plenty of other words I can't repeat in front of my children."

"Is there a chance the two of you will reconcile? I don't want to waste my time or yours."

"Rebecca asked me the same thing over lunch, and I still don't know the answer to that question."

"Are you saying there's a chance for us?" he teased, his face boyishly hopeful.

I knew the answer deep in my gut. I wanted to shake a fist up at heaven, but God had answered my clunky prayer.

"Joe, I think it's best if we stick to a professional, working relationship."

"Women like you don't come around often. I'm willing to wait for the divorce to become official."

"What if I wind up getting back together with Jared? Will you pine for me the rest of your days?" I said half-kiddingly.

Joe's expression soured, sucking the air out of my sails. "It's an attraction, Poppy, not a romance novel. Don't flatter yourself."

Offended, I said, "When your spouse cheats on you, *Joe*, the last thing you do is flatter yourself. A part of your soul dies, the part that believes 'this could never happen to me.'"

His mouth opened, apparently ready to insert the other foot.

Cutting him to the quick, I said, "Please, don't waste another second on me, because I certainly don't intend to return the favor."

Shoving past him, I marched back to my office, holding my tears at bay. Still angry, I fired off a text to Jared that said, *I've told you for eighteen years that I hate roses. What did you hope to accomplish other than proving how little you know me and how glad I am to finally be rid of you for good?*

Jared's response came back quickly. *What are you talking about?*

Don't play dumb. You had three dozen roses sent to my office. The only thing worse than the flowers was the disgusting note that went with it.

I watched ellipses show Jared typing as he fired off another speedy reply. *I promise I have no idea what you're talking about. I didn't send any flowers.*

Who else would send me a $100 worth of roses, tell me, "looking forward to more kisses," and then sign it "your loving husband?" You're the only one who fits the bill.

Did you check with your mother?

Irritated, I shot back, *What does she have to do with this?*

She called me and asked how our meeting went.

My heart sank to the floor. Harriet Berman would absolutely pull a stunt like that. Harriet Berman never understood why I hated roses, insisting there must be something wrong with me because of it. Harriet Berman would absolutely work on Jared's behalf whether he asked her to or not. And in typical, Harriet Berman fashion, her meddling would inevitably cause more harm than good.

Poppy? You still there? Jared asked. *Are you mad that I told your mom we kissed?*

Yes and yes.

Do you at least believe me about the flowers now?

Jared, are you serious about winning me back?

Taking longer this time, he finally wrote back, *Yes.*

Then, we need to establish some ground rules. Number one, you leave my mother out of it. Living under her roof is hard enough.

What about this guy you've been seeing?

I glanced through my open doorway to see Joe in conversation with Phil. My heart constricted, wanting something I shouldn't and simultaneously wanting to reject the thing that made the most sense.

I'm not sure about anything right now. One date. You don't shove your Jesus junk at me, you keep your hands to yourself, and we don't talk about Joe or Leah. Deal?

Done. Where are we meeting?

Los Bravos by my office. This is my work late day anyway. You get sixty minutes of my time, and no more. If you're late, all bets are off.

You won't regret this, Poppy.

"But I already do," I said, feeling like I'd hoisted up the white flag entirely too soon.

CHAPTER 7

I DIDN'T BOTHER UNDOING MY PONYTAIL OR attempting a more flattering hairstyle. I also didn't bother freshening my lipstick or rubbing out the small, oil stain on my shirt either. Anything to repel Jared Levine seemed like a win.

He surprised me by entering the restaurant right on time, his wedding band gleaming on his ring finger. He followed my gaze and said, "I thought it was time to put it back on."

"A bit presumptuous, don't you think?"

Jared offered the lopsided grin that used to turn my knees into mush. Twenty years of heartache now rendered that smile into nothing more than a car engine refusing to start. The sparkle died in Jared's eyes.

"I should have known this wouldn't be easy," he said.

"What did you expect?" I snapped. "That I'd come running back the second you dropped a few breadcrumbs? We're not in high school anymore."

"Can we continue this conversation over dinner?" He jerked

his chin toward the hostess who had returned to her stand. "Party of two," Jared said to her.

She nodded and led us to a secluded booth. I sighed, less than enthused with the dimmed lighting and intimate ambience.

He didn't hide his irritation as he gestured for me to sit down. "You're the one who asked for a date."

I plopped down resentfully. "I'm going to need a drink."

Neither of us said much as we read over the menu and placed our orders. Jared unloosened his tie and enjoyed a few sips of his beer. I hoped a half a glass of cabernet might calm my anxiety.

"So...how was work?" he asked, studying me over the basket of chips.

"Fine," I said. "How are things at the bank?"

"Fine," he replied, a smile hovering on his lips.

After another lengthy pause, I grabbed a chip and a heaping pile of salsa. Half of the salsa made it into my mouth, and the other half landed next to my existing stain. I dabbed my napkin into my water glass and began to wipe furiously.

"I'd offer to help," Jared said, "but I think you might chop off my arm."

"Very likely," I said, rubbing out my anxiety into my shirt. Little white pellets appeared, making the stain more obvious. Even worse, the excess moisture revealed far too much of what lay underneath.

I looked up, seeing Jared's eyes were drawn to my dampened chest. "Get your mind out of the gutter," I snapped. "This isn't Moose Grunwald's graduation party, and I have nothing to prove to you anymore."

Jared's expression sobered, remembering that night also.

"What I did was wrong, Poppy. I shouldn't have pressured you to—"

I cut him off. "You're right, you shouldn't have. I also shouldn't have listened to Leah's horrendous love advice either. I was just as worried about disappointing her as I was with you."

"I thought you said Leah was off limits."

"She is. I just wanted you to know that I also hold myself responsible for what happened." At his raised eyebrows, I sneered, "Oh, don't look so shocked, Jared. I was young and stupid, just like you."

"I never loved her. I was miserable, and Leah was an easy way out of our marriage."

I pursed my lips, struggling to maintain control of my emotions. "I can't do this with you right now, Jared. I shouldn't have brought her up. Please, just drop it."

He surprised me by honoring my request. "So, your mom sent you flowers, huh?"

"It appears that way."

"And she forgot you hate roses too?"

"Oh, she didn't forget," I said, drinking deeply from my wine glass. "My mother just thinks she knows better than me. I'm not allowed to have an opinion she doesn't approve of."

"Can I ask you something, Poppy?"

"You can ask. I may or may not answer."

He grinned. "It's nice to have you back. I've missed your spunk."

"You hated my spunk."

"No, I didn't!"

I scoffed. "What version of reality are you living in? You spent twenty years trying to shut me up. You shamed me for it. Called me ungrateful, controlling, and mean after I stopped enabling you. It took me way too long to realize just how truly selfish you are."

Jared held up his hands to halt my tirade. "Hey, now! This isn't meant to be couples counseling."

"Not that you ever went."

"Look, I understand why you might have some anger toward me," he began.

"Might?" I choked. "You stole my youth, Jared! You selfishly stole my innocence and then betrayed me in the lowest form possible. All of a sudden, you get Jesus, and then you expect me to magically trust you again. Sorry pal, but life doesn't work that way."

"You're getting a little loud." Jared's gaze darted around the restaurant. "People are staring."

"Then they'll really enjoy seeing me walk out on you," I said louder than necessary. I felt emboldened by a full glass of wine on an empty stomach. "I knew this was a mistake, but at least now, I have proof. Give me my divorce, Jared."

"You need to calm down and consider what you're saying," he said with infuriating condescension. "Why don't you just..."

I didn't hear the rest of his statement because I stormed out of the restaurant and ran as fast as I could toward the office parking deck. I continued on autopilot, not sure if Jared would follow me, but knowing I just needed to escape.

"Poppy!"

I whirled around to see Joe Trautweig walking toward me, his car situated four parking spaces from mine.

"Are you okay? What's going on?" His eyes swept over my tear stained cheeks and landed on my wet blouse.

I gripped the sides of my cardigan over the stain in embarrassment. Joe flushed appropriately.

"I need your help," I said.

"Poppy, you're starting to scare me. What's going on?"

"Can we save the professional relationship thing until tomorrow? Right now, I just need a friend."

"Sure," he said immediately. "How can I help?"

"I need you to take me home."

"Excuse me?"

"I don't feel safe driving, my ex-husband may or may not be on his way over here, and I need you to drive me. I'll pay for you to get a ride back and pick up your car, but I need your help. Please!"

With a curt nod, Joe took the car keys from my hand and opened the passenger door of my minivan. I cringed at the fast food bags and other debris littered within the vehicle, but Joe either didn't notice or thought better of commenting.

He adjusted the driver seat and mirrors just as Jared came into view at the bottom of the parking deck level.

"Go! Please!" I yelled.

With a screech of tires, Joe took off, leaving Jared Levine shouting my name. He stared in shock at the male driver behind the steering wheel of our family car.

"Where am I heading?" Joe asked once he turned out of the parking deck.

"Danbury," I replied. "We're off exit 17."

Joe nodded, easily guiding the van toward the interstate.

"Well, that was certainly dramatic," he said.

"In my novels, the evil villain usually wears chainmail and rides a destrier. Thankfully, Jared arrived on foot."

"Destrier," Joe said, testing out the word. "I assume this is some kind of horse."

"I looked it up, so yes," I said with a laugh. "It's a fancy, medieval war horse ridden by noblemen and warriors. They used a palfrey for everyday riding."

"Fascinating," he said with a grin. "It seems you get both entertainment and a little history lesson with your novels."

"And uncomplicated, vicarious romance without all of the mess of real life. The book has a happy ending no matter what trials your hero and heroine face."

"I see why you like them."

"R.D. Hampton just has a way with words. I got into her books twelve years ago after Natalie was born."

"Needed to keep yourself occupied?" Joe asked.

"Natalie nursed constantly, and I read the books to help stay awake. By the time Madison surprised us with her arrival, I had repurchased them all as e-books so I could read in the dark. I have a few other authors I like, but I always go back to the Hampton novels when I need a pick me up."

I watched Joe smile in profile as he turned off the exit to Danbury. "Left or right?" he asked.

"Left. You'll make another left in about two miles on Sycamore Lane."

"My parents live off Pinecrest," he said.

"Two streets away? Well, that's convenient. Do they go to *Beth Tefillah* like everyone else in this part of town?"

"*Beth Emunah*," he replied. "They decided to try out the Conservative synagogue after all of the scandals came out with Rabbi Epstein. They didn't bother finding out if Rabbi Cohn was any better."

"So, what does that make you?" I asked.

"Undecided."

I felt the sides of my mouth curve into a smile. "Fair enough."

Joe made his turn, and I guided him through the subdivision. Never more thankful for the secondary basement entry into my parents' home, Joe surprised me by offering to walk me to the door.

"Do you want to come in?" I asked.

"Won't that be weird with your kids?"

"My mother took them out to dinner. They should be back around eight."

Joe glanced at his watch. "Sixty minutes."

"Exactly," I said, fumbling for the keys in my purse. "Just enough time to say, 'thank you,' call you a ride, and scare you off once you see the state of our home."

Joe grinned. "Glad you're not trying to impress me."

I chuckled as I opened the door and flipped on the light. Overhead, fluorescent lighting revealed breakfast bowls still on the kitchen table, three backpacks strewn on the floor, and at least five pairs of children's shoes piled by the door.

"Cozy," he said, following me inside.

"Well, it's definitely *lived in*," I said, dumping my purse on the kitchen counter. "Did you eat dinner yet?"

"No, but I can pick up something later."

Joe's grumbling stomach begged to differ.

Reaching into a cabinet, I pulled down a loaf of wheat bread, peanut butter, and apricot preserves. "Can I interest you in a PB&J with some pretzels on the side? If you're a good boy, I may even throw in some applesauce."

Joe returned my quip with a wink and a grin. "Yes, please! I promise to be on my best behavior."

I chuckled as I began assembling our sandwiches. "I hope your palate is prepared for my ridiculous, culinary abilities. I challenge even the mighty Margolin to outdo this feast. I bet he and Rebecca have never tried making *this* before."

Joe laughed, the corners of his eyes crinkling. I blushed as I handed him a meal worthy of any kindergartener's discriminating taste buds.

"Cheers!" he said, raising his sandwich in salute.

"*L'chaim*," I responded in Hebrew.

Joe and I ate in companionable silence, and as promised, I bestowed him with a complementary container of applesauce.

"Does everyone in the marketing department share a deep and abiding love for all things Joey's Real Food?" he asked, glancing at the label.

"That's my mother's doing. She buys the groceries, and I don't argue with her. For now, I'm playing nice until we can get out of here."

"Speaking of," Joe said, as high beam lights poured through my thin, kitchen curtains, "it looks like we've got company."

CHAPTER 8

I PEEKED THROUGH THE WINDOW TO ENSURE IT WAS my mother arriving home early rather than Jared making another surprise visit. For all of her flaws, my mother handled the children with ease, doubly impressive since my father had scheduled poker with the boys on the same night. I exhaled a sigh of relief when I saw my children exit her SUV, laughing and talking loudly as they approached the door.

"Should I go hide?" Joe asked.

"Just play it cool and follow my lead. Madison and Ryan should be fine. Natalie is the one who will probably give you the cold shoulder. If you're lucky."

"What about Mother Dearest?"

I grinned, picturing my mother rage over wire hangers. "Turn on the producer charm, mention that you're Jewish and single, and then say complimentary things about me. My mother sucks all that up like you're complimenting *her*."

"Ah, she's one of those."

"You have no idea," I said as my children burst through the front door with Grandma.

"Oh, Poppy, you're..." my mother stopped dead in her tracks once she saw Joe stand up from our small table.

"Not alone," I finished for her. Taking perverse delight in seeing her squirm, I walked over to her and said, "Mom, this is Joe Trautweig from work. I was having some car trouble earlier, and he very kindly offered to take me home."

"Was that *all* he offered?"

Ignoring her, I pasted on a sunny smile for my children. "Hey guys, I want you to meet my friend."

Madison and Ryan eyed Joe cautiously, probably noting the similarities to their father in work clothes. Joe wore gray slacks, a pale blue shirt, and a royal blue tie. Whereas Jared preferred to stay clean shaven to accentuate his dimples and chin cleft, Joe sported a well-trimmed beard dotted with patches of silver.

Joe held up a hand and waved to the kids. Ryan's expression remained dubious, but Madison seemed to approve. "My Mommy needs friends," she said. "Sometimes I hear her crying in her room at night."

I moved quickly to put my hand over her mouth. "Maddie, I don't think Mr. Joe needs to know all of that. Why don't you kids go put on a movie?"

"On a school night?" Ryan asked.

I nodded vigorously, eager to end my public humiliation.

"Awesome!" he yelled and ran into the next room.

I glanced through the window at my oblivious tweenager still on the patio outside. According to her cell phone screen, Natalie seemed torn between which filter to use on her photos of dinner. Thankful for her temporary distraction, I refocused on the battle inside my home rather than the inevitable one to come.

Ryan had eagerly vacated the kitchen, but Madison remained unmoved, continuing to stare at Joe.

"Aren't you going to go watch your movie?" he asked her gently.

"My Mommy deserves to be happy. Can you help her be happy?"

I pressed my lips together, blinking back tears. Joe glanced down at Maddie and then back up at me. "I'll do my best."

Madison broke into an ear splitting grin, suddenly looking at Joe like the free toy in the bottom of a cereal box. "Thanks, Mr. Joe!"

He inclined his head with a wink, and Maddie hugged his leg in gratitude. Joe reached out to pat her hair, but he caught my eye first to make sure it was okay. I fought back the lump in my throat, nodding that he had my permission. Still anchored around his leg, Maddie beamed up at him and said, "You're the best, Mr. Joe!"

I took a steadying breath while my mother practically swooned.

Joe's smile seemed sincere. "Well, I appreciate that very much, Maddie."

She released his leg, running to join her brother in the family room.

"He's definitely charming, I'll give you that," my mother said close to my ear.

I took a few steps toward the table, needing to put some distance between me and the warden. My plastic smile faded as Natalie entered, finally pulling her eyes away from her cell phone to realize we had an unexpected visitor.

"Hi, I'm Joe," he said, extending his hand toward my twelve-year-old doppelgänger.

Natalie eyed his hand like he might have the plague

slathered on his palm. Looking over at me, she said, "Mom, who is this guy, and why is he here?"

I took a protective stance to shield Joe from my angsty tweenager. "Joe is a friend from work. You missed the explanation while you were reading through the comments on your instantpics of dinner."

Natalie shot me the evil eye. "So, this is just your friend, right? Not like some new boyfriend or anything? You promised you would try to work things out with Daddy, remember?"

Joe glanced over to me, his eyes questioning.

"Natalie, I said if it was possible for your father and I to have a healthy relationship that I would try to make it work. Anyway, it really doesn't matter, because Joe is just a friend."

"A very handsome friend," my mother said under her breath.

"Are you going to marry my mom?" Natalie asked. "Because she's still married to my dad, and I don't need some dirtbag trying to take his place. My parents are getting back together." Defiance burned in her dark eyes.

"Your mom and I are just friends," Joe answered smoothly. "She needed some help tonight, and I offered. That's what friends do for each other, right?"

Her eyes narrowed. "I don't like how close you're standing to my mom."

"Enough with the third degree, Nati." I hoped the use of her childhood nickname might placate her. "Joe is just waiting for a taxi to come pick him up."

"Where's his car?" my mother asked.

"Back at the parking deck at work," I answered for him.

"Poppy needed some help with the van, and I offered. No fuss, no muss," Joe added. "Everything's fine. False alarm car trouble."

A strange look came over my mother's face as she watched

the two of us. With a satisfied smirk, she practically purred, "Since *everything's fine* with the van, you should drive Joe back and let him save a few shekels. Unless you already called for a ride. Did you?"

"Not yet," I drawled.

"I can handle bedtime with the kids. Go make a night of it with your friend here and enjoy some time out of the house. You never do anything for yourself anyway."

My mouth opened and shut. How was this the same woman who sent flowers on behalf of her odious, former son-in-law?

"But be sure to freshen up first," she added, glancing disdainfully over my frizzy ponytail and stained shirt.

I looked at Joe, not sure how he'd respond to my mother's machinations. His pale green eyes held humor and a spark of something else.

"I would love to see what Poppy looks like freshened up." He winked at my mother as if they shared an inside joke.

Shocking me even further, my mother blushed.

"Mom?" Natalie asked, her confused gaze darting between me, Joe, and Grandma. "What's going on?"

My mother spoke up first. "She's just giving her friend a ride back to his car." Wrapping an arm around Natalie, she turned her toward the family room. "Since your mother usually looks so *schlumpy* at work, I thought it might be nice for her to dress up before she goes out. She deserves a bit of a break every now and then, doesn't she? After all, she works so hard for that company, and they don't even appreciate her." Her voice trailed off as she walked away with Natalie.

"Poppy, you don't have to do any of this," Joe said quickly. "I said what I did to get the heat off of you. I'm not looking to go back on our agreement from earlier."

I took a step toward him, admiration swelling within me.

"You asked me for a real date. After what you did for me tonight, you've more than earned it. Give me about ten minutes, and I'll be ready to go."

"That's all you need?" he asked, surprised.

"My clothes are staying on, so there's a lot less work involved." I gave him a saucy wink and a grin.

I left Joe laughing in my kitchen as I raced into the lone, basement bathroom. After yanking out my low ponytail, I pulled handfuls of water through my curls to liven the stretched out strands. I freshened up my makeup with powder and blush, then applied a ruby red lipstick I hadn't worn in at least five years. My reflection displayed a woman I'd nearly forgotten.

"Welcome back," I said reverently.

I changed into a pair of fitted jeans, v-neck sweater, and black boots, satisfied with my transformation.

Joe's eyes widened when I emerged back in the kitchen. "Wow," he said, drinking in every inch of me.

"Don't wait up," I called to my mother in the other room.

"Wouldn't dream of it," she trilled back.

I grabbed Joe's hand and led him outside, giddy and reeling from the turn of events.

"That was almost too easy," he chuckled. "I didn't think I'd have your mother in my corner so fast." We arrived at my van, but he did not release my hand. Instead, he tightened his grip and brushed his thumb across my knuckles.

I glanced to our joined hands and back to Joe. "I feel like a teenager sneaking out, but with my mother's permission. I know she's up to something, and I don't trust this nicey-nice routine one bit."

His pale eyes twinkled under the street lamps. "Either way, it's free babysitting on a school night, right?"

I chuckled softly. "That it is."

"Poppy, you're beautiful," Joe said, looking me over once again.

I blushed, unused to such open admiration. Hoping to deflect, I said, "Your 'wow' in the kitchen communicated that already."

Joe's grin took ten years off his face. "Did you put on red lipstick just to discourage me from wearing it? Because you're much more charming than I think you realize."

"Boys and girls who are *just friends* don't share lipstick." I stuck my tongue out at him for good measure. "And the red was for my own benefit. I haven't worn this color since before Madison was born."

"I'm honored."

I shrugged. "It's just girly warpaint, Joe. Don't get too excited."

He laughed again, and I realized I enjoyed the sound of it immensely. Deep, joyous, and from the soul.

"Poppy Levine, you certainly have a way with words."

"It helps keep me employed," I quipped, savoring our flirtation more than I wanted to admit. "Obviously, we have to head back to Parkview, but was there anything in particular you wanted to do?"

"Other than getting your lipstick on me?"

"Other than that. Just friends, Joe." I pulled my hand from his.

"How about we drive down to Parkview and enjoy a nice stroll? I'm still full from the sensational dinner you prepared, but maybe we can grab some tapas or dessert later."

I grinned. "Just the word 'tapas' makes me hungry. I'm totally game."

"You know, after our conversation in the office today, I never imagined the day would end up like this."

"No kidding."

Joe's expression sobered. "I want to apologize for my comment about the romance novels, Poppy. I regretted it the second it came out of my mouth. It was insensitive and demeaning, and I'm sorry."

"You're forgiven," I said with a smile. "Thank you for that."

He smiled back. "You're welcome."

"Do you want to hear something crazy?"

"Crazier than being chased out of a restaurant by your ex-husband and then asking me to give you a ride home? I'm intrigued."

My smile widened. "Crazier than that."

"Go for it."

"I actually prayed today in the break room. I asked God to help me figure out what to do with you and Jared."

"Is that why you told me you think we should keep our relationship professional? Because you'd be breaking a commandment if you went out with me?"

I shook my head. "I just needed to figure out if I could work things out with Jared first. You were too much of a distraction. Quite frankly, I never thought I would be interested in any man outside of my extensive reading library."

"So, are you saying I'm the answer to your prayers?" he asked, eyes twinkling.

"Not in the way I expected."

"What do you mean?"

"I needed closure, one way or the other. I needed to know beyond a shadow of a doubt if I could work things out with Jared before I even considered anything with you. When I found out my mother sent the roses, I thought maybe I'd misjudged him."

"And?" Joe asked.

"I think Jared *wants* to believe that he's changed and become a new person, but the only change I see is in how he attacks me. When we were married, Jared hid behind Leah as his excuse for mistreating me. Now, he's using Jesus to do it. Any hope I had of saving my marriage died tonight in that restaurant."

CHAPTER 9

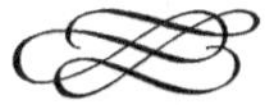

"That doesn't mean I'm ready to jump into anything right now," I added quickly. "I like you, but there's still a lot of healing I need to do. So do my kids."

"Was Madison right about you crying yourself to sleep at night?"

I cringed, hating feeling so exposed.

"Nevermind," he said. "We can save that conversation for another time. Meanwhile, I promised you a walk around Parkview and some food."

"You really are a good guy," I said, meeting his eyes.

"But my timing sucks."

"It is what it is," I said. "If you wanted to get Jessica Goldstein's number and ask her out, I'd be more than happy to help."

The corner of Joe's mouth lifted. "I think you want that to be true, Poppy, but we have chemistry, whether you admit it or not. You deserve to be happy." As he held my gaze, the air between us grew thick. He took a step toward me.

"Not like this." I held up a hand to halt his forward progress. "If I fall into the same trap Jared did, then it makes me no better. I would be an even worse hypocrite for doing to Jared exactly what he did to me. I can't let my kids go through that again. If this is too much for you, then I'm begging you to stop. I waited twenty years to have Jared look at me the way you are right now. "

"Look at you like what?"

"Like the most beautiful woman you've ever seen. Like you see someone special, worthwhile, and worth loving."

"You had to throw in the 'L' word, didn't you?" he asked.

"It's what we're both looking for, isn't it?"

His smile faded. "Isn't everybody?"

I sighed. "Joe, you said you don't want to waste your time or mine. If all you're looking for is sex, then you've got the wrong gal. I'm not willing to put myself through a new kind of heartache just to fill the void that Jared left."

"I didn't drive you home hoping for a booty call," he said with equal frankness. "I do want more than just sex, Poppy, but I can't tell you that I'm searching for happily ever after either. I don't know if I believe it exists anymore."

"I'm right there with you."

Raking his hand through his hair in agitation, he said, "This is impossible! I can't play at 'just friends' with you, Poppy, but I also can't offer what I know you're looking for either. We don't know each other well enough, and a real relationship with you also means a relationship with the three children inside of that house."

"Now, do you understand my dilemma?"

"Completely."

I leaned back against the side of my van. "The situation is already complicated enough. Adding sex, romance, or whatever you want to call this thing between us even more so."

Joe looked down at me, his eyes searching mine. "I guess we have to decide if the risk is worth the reward."

"You have to stop looking at me like that," I whispered.

He took a step to my right, then turned and leaned back against the van beside me. Glancing over, he said, "Poppy, if we try this 'just friends' thing, we'll basically wind up dating without any of the physical stuff. Eventually, we're both going to cave."

I sighed. "I know."

"How much longer until your divorce is finalized?"

"That's really up to Jared. He was gung-ho ready to end our marriage and move on with Leah, but then he woke up one day with this epiphany about Jesus. One second, he's telling me that he should have picked Leah instead of me back in high school. The next, he says that God can restore our marriage if I'll just forgive him and take him back."

"So, it's really just all about Jared," Joe said. "He makes everything your fault while taking responsibility for nothing."

"Bingo. He wanted a no-fault divorce at the beginning, and I refused. After he left, I realized how much happier we were without him, even though we lost our house because of all the attorneys' fees."

"I'm so sorry, Poppy."

"The only thing worse than losing the house was having to come crawling to my parents to tell them we had no place to live. I couldn't afford to keep my kids in the same school district. I had to threaten Jared with incarceration before I saw a dime of temporary child support."

Joe shook his head. "That's disgusting."

"Somewhere along the way, Jared claims he found Jesus. Conveniently, this was about the same time I heard through the grapevine that Leah kicked him out of her downtown loft. I absolutely hate gossip, but my mother holds no such scruples. She gets the dirt at her Jewish Federation meetings. I know she wants me and Jared to get back together."

"After what he did to you? That's insane!"

"Natalie's bat mitzvah is next summer. My mother wants it to look picture perfect for all of the synagogue friends she needs to impress. Rebecca calls it *pseudomutuality,* where everyone agrees to go along with a public perception even though it's a total sham."

"Nice," Joe smirked. "It sounds like you're getting the passive from your mother and the aggressive from your ex."

From beyond the open basement door, I heard my mother call, "You can talk over drinks or dinner. Stop putting on a show for the neighbors, and go enjoy your evening!"

"Speak of the devil," I said for only Joe to hear.

He winked at me.

"Eager to get rid of me?" I called back to her.

She rolled her eyes. "Poppy Esther Berman, I'm eager for you to go on a date and have a life. Get to it!"

As if that was the final word on the matter, she slammed the door shut.

"Poppy Esther?" Joe asked, testing out the sound of my name.

"What do you expect with Jewish hippies for parents? If we were Catholic, they might have named me Mary Jane."

Joe laughed, bringing a full smile to my lips. He reached a hand toward my face, then withdrew it. In a choked voice, he said, "I think we should get going."

We sat in silence on the twenty minute drive back to

Parkview, the absence of traffic eliminating thirty minutes off of my usual commute time. I pulled the minivan next to Joe's luxury sedan and turned the engine off.

"Here we are," he said.

I glanced over at him. "You know Miss Belle is going to be all over us like white on rice tomorrow, right?"

Joe chuckled. "I think she missed her calling as a *yenta*. She still likes to take credit for Ted and Rebecca getting together."

I shook my head. "I've actually read Rebecca's autobiography. Wishful thinking, I'm afraid."

"I'll have to check it out," he said absently. "In the meantime, I think we should take a raincheck on our tapas and stroll."

"Why's that?" I asked. "You tired?"

"No, not tired," he drawled.

I looked at Joe, and his eyes held mine captive. My palms began to sweat against the steering wheel.

"You should probably go," I whispered.

His eyes never left mine. "Yeah, I probably should."

The piercing shriek of my cellphone cut through the tension like a gunshot. We both startled, me clutching my chest as if my heart would escape from my rib cage.

He handed me the clamoring device. "It's your mother."

"Mom?" I asked, trying to regain my breath. "What's going on?"

I listened to her panicked ramblings about Madison, an upset stomach, and never being able to resell her house if I didn't come home and clean the carpet immediately. I wondered if my mother concocted the story, but I heard Maddie moaning in the background along with Natalie's dramatic shrieks of horror.

"I'll be home in thirty minutes," I said. "Hose Maddie off in the shower, and I'll deal with the throw-up when I get back. I just bought some apple cider vinegar for the laundry, and that will take care of the smell."

Satisfied with my answer, my mother spent a few more minutes making herself the victim of a mess she wouldn't have to clean.

"Okay, Mom, if you want me to come home, I need to get off the phone."

I rolled my eyes at my mother's petulant response and looked at Joe in apology. I ended the call, then turned to him and said, "Puking child to the rescue."

"Blessing in disguise, hmm?"

"I think we both need some time and distance. I can't afford to have my emotions overcome my logic right now. This whole day has been a rollercoaster, and we were about to do something incredibly stupid."

"I'll wait," he finally said.

"Wait for what?"

"I'll wait for this mess to be over with Jared. I'm not ready to let you go."

My heart thudded loudly. "Are you sure about this?"

"Yeah. Yeah, I am."

"Even though I'm a package deal with puking kids?"

"It would take a lot more than some throw up to stop me."

I nodded slowly. "Okay, but we can't do this alone in the car stuff anymore. Not unless I see Jared chasing me down in the rearview mirror anyway."

"I don't want you to feel guilty when you kiss me, Poppy. And I don't want the weight of Jared Levine on my back when I kiss you either."

"Where does Catherine fit into all this? Is she out of the picture? Remarried?"

"Deceased," Joe said quietly. "She wrote a note saying she wanted to see our baby and couldn't live with the pain anymore. She overdosed on her psychiatric medication."

"Oh my goodness! Joe, that's awful! No wonder you don't believe in fairytale endings."

"I was content never being married again, let alone even date."

"And that's why this is such a big deal for you," I said, piecing together the details from our earlier conversation.

"I didn't know if I would feel anything other than numbness for the rest of my life. My picture perfect story became a horror movie."

"You know I understand." I placed my hand on top of his.

My cell phone trilled, my mother sending out several frantic texts asking if I'd left.

"No rest for the weary," I said, rolling my eyes.

As I pulled my hand off of Joe's, he recaptured it. "I will be here waiting on the other side. I'm not Jared Levine, and I'm not going anywhere."

Taking a risk, I leaned my forehead against his. Joe's hands immediately found their way into my hair, tangling themselves in my curls.

"Do you promise you'll be there?" I asked, my voice tight with emotion. "When all of this mess is over with Jared?"

"Twelve years ago, I never thought I would feel this way again. I'm not going anywhere until I get to kiss you, Poppy Levine."

"Berman," I whispered. "Poppy Berman."

I lifted my head to stare into those jade eyes, tumbling into feelings that made even my steamiest romance novel feel like a cheap, carbon copy. There was no substitute for mutual desire, and it made my heart skip a beat before returning with a heavy pound in my chest.

My phone rang again. Joe and I both turned our faces toward the offending little monster shoved into my drink holder.

"Remind me to thank your mother," he said, releasing my hair. "I don't think either of us would have survived the night without her."

"I'll see you tomorrow in the office." Despite my casual tone, my whole body felt alive in ways I thought had died along with my love for Jared. My mind replayed the sensation of Joe's hands in my hair and how much I wished for more.

"Good night, Poppy." His eyes lingered on my face before opening the door and exiting the van.

"Good night," I whispered once he was gone.

CHAPTER 10

I KNEW THE RETALIATION FROM JARED LEVINE WOULD be swift and ugly. He didn't disappoint on either front. I woke up to a monsoon of text messages from my soon-to-be ex-husband, livid, accusatory, and convinced I'd led him into the parking deck only to humiliate him.

I waded through the notifications to turn off my morning alarm on my phone. "Fifty-six messages, Jared? How did you find the time to write a novel in one night?" Scanning through a few of them, I began to laugh. "Well, it looks like Mr. Holy Man forgot he wasn't supposed to have a potty mouth anymore."

"Mommy?" my five year-old said from the doorway. "What's so funny?"

I slid my phone under my pillow before my baby girl learned four-letter words not found on her kindergarten, sight-reading list. "Morning baby," I said, extending my arms out to her.

Madison wasted no time snuggling under the covers with me. She tucked her head in the crook of my arm, her back to me. Smiling, I stroked the curls at her temple.

"Did you have a good time with Mr. Joe?" she asked.

"We had a nice talk."

"I like him."

"I do too, baby."

"Do you think Mr. Joe would want to come over and play dolls with me?"

I chuckled. "I'll have to ask him, sweetheart. Sometimes boys don't like playing with girl toys, but I'm sure he'll be very glad that you wanted to invite him over."

"Mommy?" she asked, her voice sounding smaller.

"Yes?"

"Natalie says you're kissing Mr. Joe the way Daddy kissed Aunt Leah. Was she telling the truth or a lie?"

With a clean conscience, I said, "It wasn't a lie Maddie, just a misunderstanding. Mr. Joe is my friend, remember? We don't kiss our friends like husbands and wives do."

"Oh," she said quietly, processing the new information. "Do you think you will ever kiss Daddy again?"

Amused by both her curiosity and precociousness, I smiled. "I don't think so, baby. It's probably best that Daddy doesn't kiss anybody for a while. He needs to work on some ouchies in his heart."

Turning her head back to meet my eyes, she said, "Do you still have ouchies on your heart, Mommy?"

I nodded, then stroked the velvety skin of her cheek. "Yes, but they hurt a little bit less every day."

Madison rolled over and placed her hand on my heart. "God," she prayed, "please heal my Mommy's heart and take away all of the ouchies. In Yeshua's Name. Amen."

Before I could *kvell* at my daughter's heartwarming prayer, I realized she used the Hebrew name for Jesus. I frowned.

"Mommy, what's wrong?"

"Where, um, did you learn to pray like that, sweetheart?"

"From Daddy," she said happily. "He said Yeshua is God's Son, and if we don't want to go to hell, then we have to believe in Him."

"Jews don't believe in hell," I said, trying to maintain a calm I didn't feel. Jared's abusive text messages didn't faze me one iota. The nonsense he poured into an innocent, five year-old's head, however, left me positively irate. "I understand Daddy wants to be a Christian now, but—"

"Oh no! Daddy's not a *Christian*," she said, making the word sound like an insult. "He's a Messianic Jew. He says Christians made up a bunch of new rules and aren't following God the right way. They have pagan holidays they pretend are really for God, but they're not."

I flattened my lips into a line, not trusting myself to say anything else.

"Mommy?"

"Yes?" I choked out.

"What's a pagan?"

I sighed deeply, longing for a cup of freshly brewed Vincenzo's before I had to answer questions like these from my kindergartener.

"Mommy?" she asked again.

I glanced down into a miniature pair of my own dark eyes highlighted by sunlight peeking through my window blinds. "You're very smart, you know that?"

"Mommy," she pouted, her lower lip overtaking the upper, "you're not answering my question."

I sighed. "So you asked about a pagan?"

She nodded.

"Well, Jews believe in one God. Christians believe in three

gods. Pagans worship statues and idols, nature, and things like that."

I expected the look of confusion I saw on Madison's face. "Three gods, Mommy? Daddy says he believes in one God, and Jesus is God's son."

Not sure how to explain to a five year-old what I could no more explain to myself, I shrugged my shoulders. "Sweetie, I can only tell you what I learned from my rabbi. He said that Christians believe in three gods, but they pretend that it's one."

"Is that what the Bible says?" she asked, sitting up on her elbow to study me.

"The Bible?" I repeated with a nervous laugh.

"Yeah," she said, face brightening. "Daddy reads the Bible every day. He says Jews don't ever read the Bible, but they just do whatever the rabbi tells them. Is that what you do, Mommy?"

Jared's hypocrisy felt stifling. "Your father must read the drunken sailor Bible," I said bitterly, unable to control myself.

"The what?"

Trying to rein in my emotions, I smiled overly bright. "Maddie, it's time to get ready for school, okay? I need to talk to your father about the things he's telling you. It sounds like you're a little confused."

"Oh, I'm not confused," she said, bouncing off my bed. Her tangled curls bounced a few seconds after her. "I prayed for Yeshua to come live in my heart, Mommy, and He does! Daddy said he was so happy, and all the angels are having a party in Heaven."

The image of Jared Levine's windpipe being crushed beneath my hands felt tantalizingly real.

"Mommy?" Madison said. "Are you okay? Did I do something wrong."

"No, baby," I said, shaking off my murderous thoughts. "I just need to talk to Daddy about a few things. Why don't you go get dressed before your sister spends forever grooming herself?"

While Madison skipped her way to the bathroom, I snatched my phone to re-read Jared's stream of abuse and hypocritical accusations.

Still not home, Poppy? How did you convince anyone to get in bed with you anyway? Must have had the lights off. Did you tell your boyfriend how much you like it when—?

"Pig!" I yelled, throwing my phone across the room. I let loose a string of my own foul words, giving my ex a run for his money.

"Mom?" Ryan said from the doorway, his voice timid.

I whirled around. "How much did you hear?"

Eyes wide, he said, "All of it. Is that what you really think of Dad?"

I fought back tears of frustration, longing desperately to tell my children the sick, psychological games their father played with all of us. At the same time, I knew I'd scar them for life if I gave in. Inhaling a shuddering breath, I blinked back emotions cresting too close to the surface.

"What did he do?" Ryan said, taking a step toward me. "Did Dad hurt you again?"

Jaw set, eyes narrowed, my son made one fearsome warrior. I smiled gently at him, silently beseeching a God I wasn't sure even existed for the right words to say.

"Well, did he?" Ryan demanded.

I nodded. "Yeah, Ry-Ry. He got mad about my friend, Mr. Joe, and said some things he shouldn't have."

My son raised a dubious brow, looking far older than his nine years. "Must have been pretty bad if you were using all of those swear words, Mom."

My lips thinned, trying to figure out a truthful answer without oversharing. "It was, Ryan, but I shouldn't have been using bad words either. I'm sorry you heard all of that."

His chin jerked, acknowledging my apology. "I'm sorry, Mom."

"What are you sorry for, Son?"

"I'm sorry for everything Dad did to you."

Tears blinded my vision. I flopped down on the bed, desperate to keep my misery from spilling over onto my children. Ryan sat down next to me, rubbing his hand on my back. The tears came harder, and I felt the shame of my child offering comfort rather than the other way around.

"It's going to be okay, Mom," Ryan said soothingly. He mimicked the same tone I used for countless cuts and scrapes over the years.

I studied my fourth-grader who seemed more like a man than his forty-year-old father. I reached over and patted his knee. "Thanks, baby."

He nodded. "You don't deserve the way Dad treated you, Mom."

"You mean Aunt Leah?"

He shook his head. "No, Mom. Before that. Dad was always mean to you and yelled at us. I asked him to play catch with me one time, and he told me to ask you since he was busy on the computer. I told him he's always busy, and then he screamed and told me you'll just do it better than him anyway. He never had time for me."

When my son's eyes grew moist, the comforter quickly became the comforted. I cupped the sides of his face in my hands and said, "You are one incredible, young man, Ryan Andrew Levine. Your father has no idea what he missed, and

I'm so sorry he hurt you the way he did. You're right that he hurt me too."

My son buried his face against my heart and wept, and I cried along with him.

From the doorway with a toothbrush hanging out of her mouth, my oldest said, "What's with him?"

I waved her off, and Natalie responded with a near audible roll of the eyes. She harrumphed back into the bathroom and slammed the door.

"It's okay for boys to cry, isn't it?" Ryan asked, his eyes imploring mine.

"Sometimes crying is the only way we can get rid of all the feelings we have inside. It's a *good* thing," I said, immediately reminded of all the times Jared berated our son for showing any human emotion. "Not everything your father says is true, even if he believes it is."

"Is Jesus a liar because Dad is a liar?"

I paused before answering. "I don't know the answer to that, Ry-Ry. I have some wonderful friends who say they believe in Jesus, and then we have your father. What I do know is that Dad acted exactly the same way before he said he believed in anything at all. I don't think that has to do with Jesus being a liar but with the choices people make."

"Makes sense," he said. "Thanks, Mom."

"You're welcome, Ry-Ry. Thank you for helping me feel better."

"I helped? Are you sure?"

I beamed at him. "More than you know, baby."

He grinned back, the sparkle returning to his dark eyes. I patted him on the shoulder, his cue to get up and get ready for school. Once the bathroom cleared of children, I raked water through my curls and pulled up the crown with a hair clip. What functioned as a standard hairdo back in the nineties now served as the perfect way to get some lift in the curls around my face.

"It's a new day," I whispered to myself in the mirror.

Glancing down, I took note of the soggy bathroom that survived three children and my revitalized, hair care regimen. With an amused sigh, I wiped up the mess and headed toward our kitchenette. All three of my children sat at the table inhaling their cereal.

Ryan and Madison seemed like their normal selves, but Natalie remained mute during our standard, rushed breakfast. I watched as she kept her gaze lasered down at the chocolatey goodness in her cereal bowl.

Catching the eye of the younger children, I inclined my head toward Natalie. Both of my babies shrugged and returned their attention to their breakfast.

"Aren't you going to eat, Mommy?" Madison asked.

"No, baby. My friend, Miss Rebecca, gave me a gift, and I'm going to pick up a bagel and coffee after I drop you and your brother off at school. Natalie, you need to finish up, or you're going to miss the bus."

Nodding wordlessly, she stood up, her chair scraping against the tile floor.

"Are you okay?" I asked as she walked past me to retrieve her backpack.

She handed me my cell phone. "I needed to use your phone to find mine, and I saw—"

I gasped in horror.

"I thought he'd changed," she said, finally meeting my eyes.

The sadness and despair reflected back tore my heart out. "I know, baby."

"Did he always treat you like that, Mom? Even before Aunt Leah?"

"Yes, sweetie, but I never wanted you to see this," I said, holding up my phone.

"I know," she whispered. "Why did you let me think you guys could get back together if this is what Dad is really like?"

"I was trying to protect you, honey. I never wanted you to see this side of your father."

"But I've said so many mean things to you, Mom. I thought you were just being hard on him. That's what Dad always told me."

"Your father says a lot of things, Nati. I just didn't want to be the one to tell you it's not true. I wasn't sure you'd believe me even if I did."

Her downturned mouth showed the grief and disillusionment of a conman coming off of his pedestal.

From outside, the bus honked, shaking both of us from our painful musings. Natalie kissed me on my cheek for the first time since she was Madison's age and ran out the door.

Her siblings sat with eyes wide as saucers, wondering who had replaced their surly sister with the sweet child I remembered. Putting on the brave face I had mastered over the past three years, I announced, "Bowls in the sink and grab your backpacks. Time to go!"

CHAPTER 11

Settling into my favorite nook at Vincenzo's with a fully schmeared bagel and coffee, I pulled out my R.D. Hampton novel to escape for a few minutes before work.

Tingles raced down my fingers as the hero and heroine finally declared their feelings for one another. My breath caught as they prepared for their first kiss after one hundred pages of flirting, fighting, and longing glances. Their forbidden love was finally coming to fruition, and I could almost imagine myself standing there in medieval garb, breathlessly anticipating those words of love spoken to my own, aching heart.

"Morning, stranger!"

"Oh my gosh!" I shrieked, nearly upending my bagel and coffee in one fell swoop. I placed a hand over my heart and blushed at the stares of the other java junkies.

Jessica Goldstein laughed and helped mop up the bit of coffee that splattered onto the end table. She eased into the seat opposite me. "I like your hair," she said, gesturing toward my curly mop. "Why don't you wear your hair down more often?"

I shrugged. "Ponytails are easier, and sharing a bathroom with two children and a tweenager also makes it a challenge. Meanwhile, you've got hair for miles." I paused to admire the perfectly formed waves cascading down her back.

"Well, I don't have to share a bathroom with anyone, so it's a little easier I guess."

After an awkward pause, I took another bite of my bagel, hoping a mouthful of food would help slow down everything I wanted to say but probably shouldn't.

"So, tell me about this Joe guy," she said, eyes alight with mischief. "He's cute! Are you guys dating? Does your ex know?"

I swallowed audibly.

"That bad, huh?"

"Short story is that Joe and I are just friends, but Jared isn't happy about it regardless."

"Scared of some competition?" she asked, sipping her latte.

"Not exactly, Jessica."

Her face drained of all color. "How...how do you know my name?"

So much for the wonder bagel.

"Do you remember last week when you flew out of here in a panic?" I asked.

"Yeah," she drawled.

"Well, I work with Ted Margolin."

Her jaw dropped. "You work at *Culver*?"

"In the marketing department," I said, going for broke. "I had absolutely no idea who you were until Ted told me."

Her expression tightened as did her tone. "So, that means you've heard all about me, right? Are you going to condemn me to the lowest parts of hell like the rest of the holy rollers?"

Thankful for a twelve year-old who also possessed a strong

flair for the dramatic, I calmly raised an eyebrow. "Seriously? After everything I've told you about my ex? And my name is Poppy, by the way."

"So, Rebecca and Taylor actually *allow* you to be friends with me?" she asked with a sneer.

"Allow?" I laughed. "Rebecca just wants you and your brother to be happy. That's all she's ever wanted."

Jessica's expression turned a normally lovely countenance into something nearing grotesque. "You don't get to talk to me about my brother," she growled.

"Excuse me?"

"That little rat, Taylor, turned Kyle into some crazy, Jesus freak, and then she goes and writes a book about him anyway. She had no problem sharing everybody's secrets, including mine!"

I grimaced, seeing the situation from her perspective. Tentatively, I asked, "Are you still seeing Moose?"

"Moose?" she repeated, her anger momentarily forgotten. "Nobody calls Patrick that except for his old fraternity brothers. How do you know him?"

"His parents live two doors down from mine, and we went to high school together. I had lunch with Rebecca recently, and when I mentioned his name in passing, she literally choked."

"Wow," Jessica murmured, her face returning to a more pleasant expression. "So, you don't hate me then? For what I did to Taylor or for helping a married man cheat on his wife?"

I shook my head. "Jessica, I just know you as this cool chick I met in the coffee shop. I've enjoyed all of our morning chats, and I'm in no place to judge anyone."

She inhaled and exhaled slowly, still unsure.

"And for what it's worth, I think all of these Jews for Jesus people have completely lost their minds. The Margolins, even though I know you have a history with them, at least seem sincere in what they believe. Jared sent me fifty text messages dripping in profanity that my twelve year-old accidentally discovered this morning."

Her eyes went wide. "Oh, no! That must have been so hard for her."

"The look on her face just ripped my heart out. It's bad enough he's already poisoned my youngest baby with all of this Yeshua-Jesus garbage. Now, I've got the older ones growing up too soon because they have to accept their father is a complete..." I struggled for a PG-rated word while Jessica went ahead and supplied the one I had in mind.

I hid my face in my palms, taking a cleansing breath before removing them. "I just can't believe I married someone like that. I was so blind, and now my kids are the ones paying for my stupidity."

"Look, you may have married a jerk, but at least you didn't cheat with a married jerk already knowing what he was," she said, condemning herself.

"Why did you do it? What was so great about Moose Grunwald that you sacrificed your best friend for it?"

She took a sip before responding. "To be honest, I don't even know anymore. I must have flashed my engagement ring around the office a million times before that awful Thanksgiving four years ago. Patrick didn't seem to notice me until the ring suddenly disappeared."

"What happened with your ex?"

Jessica's expression became closed and resentful. "Rebecca didn't fill you in already? I thought the whole world knew by now thanks to her little memoir."

"Humor me," I retorted dryly. "You know what they say happens when you assume, right?"

Jessica looked sheepish, but contrite. Heaving a sigh, she said, "I caught my former fiancé looking at teenage porn. This was after he sold me on all of his Messianic Judaism *chazarai* and a million lectures on sexual purity before marriage. He made me feel dirty about my past, like I should have been living according to standards I didn't even believe in."

"I'm familiar with the predicament. Jared is about as big a hypocrite as they come."

She shook her head. "Maybe it's that crazy synagogue they attend. For all of my brother's mishigas with the Jesus stuff, it's the one thing he and I both agree on."

"What happened after you broke things off with your fiancé?"

"Well, I was devastated, of course. My parents were furious at Nathan...and at me. This was supposed to be my dream wedding, and instead, we were just flushing money down the toilet. If I ever get married again, I'm going to skip all the hoopla and just go to the courthouse."

"That's what we did," I said, polishing off my bagel, "but I was also pregnant with Natalie. My mother didn't want to live down the disgrace of her daughter standing under the wedding *chuppah* already carrying her future grandchild."

Jessica offered a sympathetic smile. "Well, Patrick has two kids, but half the time, he can't remember their names. I knew what I was doing getting involved with him, but I didn't care. I wanted to get back at Nathan for all of his lies and hypocrisy. Looking back, I see how stupid it was."

"Anybody nicknamed *Moose* sounds like the idiot best friend in an '80s teen movie. Don't be too hard on yourself."

Jessica gave a throaty chuckle. "I would love to see the look on his face if he ever heard you say that."

"By all means," I said, sweeping my hand in grand gesture.

She grinned back at me. "Patrick quit the firm once word got out about our affair. He didn't have a prenup with his wife, and he was going to lose a ton of money. None of the women in the office will talk to me anymore, and the men either act skittish or think they can help themselves to Patrick's leftovers."

"They're lawyers! It's not like they don't know about sexual harassment laws."

"It's because they're lawyers, they think they can get away with it," she said. "I'd lose a fortune trying to prove anything, and the partners look the other way because everyone's making money for the firm. I'm just the peon paralegal and easily replaced."

"Can you work somewhere else?" I asked. "You shouldn't have to put up with that kind of abuse."

She waved a hand dismissively. "I'm used to it. It's fine."

"No, it's not fine," I said, my voice rising along with me out of my chair. "Why don't you submit your resume to Culver?"

Jessica laughed bitterly. "You're joking, right? Why would I go from one awful work environment to another? I'd have to see Ted Margolin plus all of the gossips who still talk dirt about my brother. I'm not much of a graphic designer anyway."

"But you know how to handle deadlines, pay attention to detail, and roll with documents in a constant state of flux, right? I can show you the ropes of graphic design. Plus, most of our documents already have templates in place, or you can copy an existing file."

"I don't know, Poppy. I think it's just going from one fire into another."

"Look," I said, tossing my cup and empty plate into the trash, "my only qualifications when I got hired was a digital photo album I put together for Natalie's ninth birthday and some old secretarial work. I don't think either of the Margolins have it in for you, and it might be a good way for everyone involved to gain some closure. I know I could use some."

"I'll think about it," she hedged, taking a deep drink of coffee.

"That's all I ask." I reached over and patted her shoulder. "In the meantime, I have to go deal with my own hot mess at work. Thank God, it's Friday."

CHAPTER 12

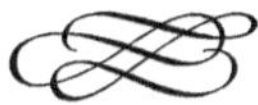

I BRACED MYSELF AS I STEPPED OFF THE ELEVATORS, not sure if I would find another bouquet of gaudy flowers on the front desk or my ex in the flesh ready to stake his claim.

"So far so good," I murmured, waving hello to Brooklyn as I took the long way to my back corner office.

Pausing to scan for any telltale signs of unwanted intruders, I found myself pleasantly surprised and relieved to be all alone. I hung up my coat on an empty chair and tucked my purse into a storage drawer.

"Hi there," I heard from the doorway.

The warmth in that baritone voice put a blush on my cheeks. I glanced up, knowing my smile met my eyes.

"Hi," I replied.

"You look beautiful," Joe said, eyeing my new hairdo, "and this style suits you much better than the ponytail. All you're missing is a flower in your hair."

My blush deepened. "This is how office rumors get started,

Mr. Trautweig. What brings you to the marketing department first thing in the morning? Business or pleasure?"

"Well, it's always a pleasure doing business with you," he said with a wink.

I rolled my eyes and smiled wider. "Keep it up, funny man, and you'll have Miss Belle giving you the what-for."

"I do actually have some work for you." He stepped further into the office and handed me a packet of papers. "I marked up the Harding presentation so we can use it as a template for Geneva Group. All of the information you need is on the work request form." His eyes shifted to the blue sheet of paper clipped on top of his red-inked mess.

I flipped through thirty pages of barely legible revisions. "Looks like fun," I deadpanned. "Definitely business today."

"Trautweig!" Ted exclaimed from the doorway. "Trying to sneak in your documents ahead of mine?"

"The mighty Margolin needs a little competition," he parried easily. "Poppy's work day goes by more quickly, and she's not stuck staring at your RFP's all day. You really should be thanking me for giving our amazing marketing department a break from all of your projects."

"I'll be happier once I get some help," I said.

"Hear, hear!" Ted joked.

"Speaking of," I said, turning my gaze to Culver's top, east coast producer, "Ted, I need to talk to you about something. It's kind of important."

"Do I need to leave the room?" Joe asked, the humor slipping from his mouth.

I smiled at him in apology. "Yeah. It's kind of personal."

"Personal?" Ted asked, confused. "And you need to talk to *me* alone?"

"It has to do with our mutual friend at Vincenzo's," I said. "The one who sped off in the parking lot."

The mighty Margolin nodded. Turning to Joe, he said, "She's right that it's personal, Trautweig."

"Anything I should be concerned about?" Joe asked, though he immediately saw how inappropriate his question sounded. "I mean, you're not quitting or anything, are you Poppy?"

"No, nothing like that. It has to do with Ted and Rebecca. Sorry to make it sound so cryptic."

Joe's expression remained dubious. My own smile grew strained as Ted looked back and forth between the two of us, an eyebrow raised in question.

Joe coughed and said, "Right. Well, Poppy, you've got the document, and please let me know if you have questions or can't read my writing."

"You should have been a doctor," I teased, hoping to let him save face, "but I think I'm used to your penmanship by now. I'll let you know."

Joe smiled tightly and exited, leaving a very perplexed Ted Margolin still standing in my office.

"That was more than just a little weird," he said. "Everything okay?"

I shrugged with the same nonchalance I used when Jared Levine first showed interest back in high school. "Totally fine. However, I do need to talk to you about something, and it's important."

"Shoot," Ted said, sitting down in a conference chair across from my desk.

"Well, I talked to Jessica again this morning."

"Okay," he drawled. "What do you need to tell me that you think I won't want to hear?"

"I told her she should come work with me in the marketing department."

Ted's mouth opened and closed, and he blinked rapidly.

"I just wanted to know what you thought about that. Would you have a problem interacting with Jessica on a daily basis and having her work on your documents?"

Ted cleared his throat. "I was not expecting you to say that, Poppy."

"I know it's a bit of a shock. She has just as many reservations as you do, by the way."

"I'm sure," he said, his tone hardening.

"Look, I know things didn't end very well with Jessica and Rebecca, but we're all adults, aren't we?"

"But why here? Doesn't Jessica have a cushy job with that married boyfriend of hers?"

My tone was pure ice. "Judgmental much?"

Ted looked incredulous. "You have to be kidding me, Poppy. Your husband cheated on you, and now, you want to share an office with a woman who's exactly like his mistress."

"She is nothing like Leah!" I snapped, banging my hand on my desk. "I'm sorry Jessica's not as perfect as you or Rebecca, but I do believe she is a good person who made some mistakes."

"So, does that make *Jared* a good person who made some mistakes?" Ted asked, throwing my words in my face.

"Those are two, completely different situations."

"Try me," he fired back. The steel in his eyes reminded me why so many in the insurance world considered the mighty Margolin a formidable opponent.

I refused to be intimidated. "Jared is a hypocrite who hides behind his Jesus shtick to launch guilt trips on me. He doesn't show remorse for anything that he's done, only that he's had to suffer the consequences for it. Jessica genuinely regrets her choices and deals with the repercussions daily at work."

"Cry me a river. If Jessica thinks office gossip is bad at Schwartz, Zendler & Hoffer, she has no idea what she's in for at Culver. I'm sure Kyle could tell her a thing or two about what he experienced here."

"You know, for someone who calls himself a Christian, you sure don't sound like one," I said, growing increasingly irritated with the mighty Margolin.

"Sin is sin."

"Do you think being sexually harassed daily is enough of a punishment?"

His mask of anger slipped. "What are you talking about?"

"Jessica's boyfriend left the firm trying to avoid an expensive divorce. She still works there, but the other lawyers think she's fair game since she already slept with one of their colleagues."

Ted's mouth thinned into a straight line. "I wasn't aware of that."

"Of course not. You were too busy judging her."

"It's not that easy, Poppy. She also hurt my wife. Badly. And in case you've forgotten, Taylor Horner is your friend too."

"I haven't forgotten anything, Ted. I'm just amazed that someone who can forgive Kyle Goldstein for everything he did to hurt our friend, Taylor, is so quick to condemn his sister. Seems a little hypocritical, don't you think?"

Ted glared at me for a long minute before breaking eye contact and sighing heavily. "You're right," he said, "but I can't tell you that things wouldn't be incredibly awkward around here. Did Jessica say she wants the job?"

I shook my head. "She has the same reservations you do. This was all my idea."

"What if she comes here and pulls the same stunt that she

did at her current job? What if she hooks up with Trautweig, for example?"

Hoping to keep my jealousy at bay, I replied coolly, "Since neither one of them are married and their love lives are none of my business, what they do on their own time is not my concern. I just know that I am in desperate need of help in this office, and Jessica is in need of a change of scenery. Maybe, if you can pull your head out of your self-righteous backside for one second, you would see that even people like Jessica Goldstein deserve a second chance too."

"Brava!" Phil called from the doorway, clapping his hands.

"Phil," Ted warned. "Stay out of it."

"Who is this Jessica Goldstein person? Any relation to the other Goldstein who used to work here?"

"His sister," I answered before Ted could. "She's looking for a new job. She happens to be a friend of mine, and I think she would be a great fit for the marketing department."

"I've heard enough," Ted said, rising from his chair and storming out of the office.

"What bee flew in his bonnet?" Phil chuckled. "I haven't seen the mighty Margolin that hopping mad in a long time."

"Disagreement of opinion," I said.

"So, what's the big deal about hiring the sister? He's all buddy-buddy with her brother now, so I don't understand the hostility."

"Old grudges, I guess. Jessica hurt Rebecca, and Ted wants to protect his wife. I can't say I blame him in that regard." I frowned, wondering if I had overreacted to the situation despite wanting to accuse Ted of the same behavior.

Phil raised both eyebrows. "What does protecting Rebecca have to do with Goldstein's sister working here? Rebecca is at home with the girls anyway."

"Ted would have to work with Jessica, and from all accounts, they can't stand each other. I guess that could make things pretty awkward."

My CEO exhaled a bemused laugh. "So, tell me again why you think this is a good idea, Poppy? Sounds like you're just borrowing trouble."

"Jessica's in a tough situation with her current job, and I thought I came up with a solution that helps everyone. Maybe I was wrong."

Phil nodded. "Give the mighty Margolin some time to cool off. His temper has gotten a lot better since he married Rebecca, but he's just as human as the rest of us. Meanwhile, Goldstein's sister still has to apply for the position and qualify for it. Whether she's your friend or not, we can't afford to train another person for this department and have to let them go. Too much turnover around here as is."

"So, what brought you to my office anyway?" I asked, ready to change the subject.

Phil's expression immediately brightened. "You've been nominated for Culver Super Star along with a few others. We'll be announcing the winner at our Friday birthday celebration, but I thought you'd want to know how highly we all think of you here."

"Thank you," I murmured, his kind words a balm from my heated conversation with Ted.

"The kicker is that the guy who nominated you is the same one who was in here arguing with you."

I smirked. "Maybe he'll withdraw his nomination."

"Margolin is a pragmatist and stickler, Poppy, but he's always been a man of his word. One little fight doesn't change all the hard work you've put in. We all notice how you rarely take a lunch break. You don't get paid for that hour, but you work through anyway. That counts for something around here, and we appreciate how well you support the associates in this office."

I exhaled a deep breath, ready to move on from the entire disaster. "Thanks, Phil." Gesturing to my pile of work requests, I said, "Time for me to earn that reward."

He smiled, his blue eyes twinkling as they often did. "I'll think you'll be just fine, Poppy Levine. Also, have you noticed Trautweig pacing around your office pretending that he's not waiting for me to leave?"

My eyes widened in genuine surprise, but I recovered quickly. Pulling Joe's document request from my copious stack, I said, "Must be a pretty important presentation, Phil. I wouldn't overly concern yourself about it."

My CEO nodded as if we shared an inside joke. "If you say so, my dear."

I rolled my eyes dramatically, stealing a move from my tweenager's playbook. "You and Miss Belle really need to knock it off with the matchmaking. Sometimes a man and a woman can just be friends. It happens every day."

Phil took another glance outside the door, apparently catching Joe's eye and grinning broadly. "Whatever helps you sleep at night. See you around."

I snickered softly, both amused and annoyed at the perceptiveness of my CEO.

When I heard footsteps approach my office, I didn't bother to lift my eyes from the computer screen. "You know, you probably should stop dropping by my office and get to work."

"Probably should," Joe said with a smile in his voice. "You okay?"

"Yeah. Just busy. I have to get to work, or I'm never getting out of here." I glanced up, meeting his pale eyes. "I'm not blowing you off, but I'm absolutely swamped. Work comes first right now."

"Duly noted. Lunch?"

"Too soon. Too suspicious."

"So, what now?"

I stared into his eyes, having to content myself with the same longing glances found in the pages of my novels. "We work, we wait, and we hope for a better ending than the last chapter of our lives."

Courtly love was certainly not designed for the faint of heart.

CHAPTER 13

FORTUNATELY FOR ME, AND PROBABLY FOR JOE TOO, business called him out of town over the next two weeks. Joe's absence also kept Phil and Miss Belle off the scent of romantic tension lingering just below the surface. After Jared's tirade failed to produce the eruption he anticipated, he retreated into petulant silence. He made no inquiries into visiting the children, and the older two didn't ask. Madison asked if Daddy was sick, and I simply said Daddy had put himself in time out.

"So, your mother tells me you've been seeing someone," my father said, coming alongside me as the kids played catch in the backyard.

"I was beginning to wonder if you were a ghost, Dad. We've barely seen you lately."

He ran a hand over thinning, gray hair still shaped in a bowl cut. The former hippie kept some traces of his youth well into his early seventies.

"I've been busy," he said unconvincingly.

"Well, you've missed the last three dinners with the kids,

and had you been around, you would have met my friend too," I said, emphasizing the idea of *not my boyfriend.*

"Friend *schmend*," he retorted. "You don't bring home a handsome, Jewish man and introduce him to your children unless something's going on."

I turned to face my father head on. "Dad, we really are just friends."

"Just like you were really going to the library with Leah rather than sneaking over to the Grunwald boy's house back in high school, right?"

"Seriously, Dad? That was over twenty years ago."

"What about all the sneaking out with Jared Levine when you were still underage?"

"What about it? I was young and stupid, and I'm paying for that now." I gestured toward my children. "Three, innocent lives got sucked into that dysfunctional vortex."

My father folded his arms over his chest, resting them against his sizable belly. "I just don't understand how Jared Levine can be the love of your life for two decades, and now you won't even try to make it work."

I studied my father, irritated by his obvious parroting of whatever my mother asked him to say. "I mean this with all due respect, but Mom is going to have to accept the fact she won't get a picture perfect bat mitzvah next June. Up until Jared had his Jews for Jesus epiphany last year, he was even more eager than I was to end our marriage. I assume you haven't forgotten."

His mouth turned grim. Apparently not.

I pressed on. "We didn't have a real wedding because Mom didn't want to be shamed in the synagogue that her only daughter had been shacked up with her high school boyfriend for eight years and forgot to take her birth control pill. We both know Jared never would have married me otherwise."

"Poppy, how can you say that? After everything you did for him. Sacrificed for him. You could have been a journalist and worked in news broadcasting."

"I remember," I said, easily recounting every communications class from college. "But Jared wanted to get his MBA, and one of us had to work to help pay the bills. I loved him, Dad, and our relationship was fine so long as everything was all about Jared. He didn't care about me, my job, or my dreams, only that I continued to center my entire existence around him."

"You never told me this," he said quietly.

"I never realized I sold my soul for Jared's nonexistent love. It wasn't until he told me about the affair with Leah that I finally saw him for the pathetic, narcissistic pig he's always been."

"I saw it," my father said, "but you swore up and down that you loved him, so I kept my mouth shut."

"I did love him, Dad, but he never loved me back. Frankly, I don't know if Jared even understands what love is. I think he associates *love* with being in control, and God somehow designed the world to be under his thumb."

My father scoffed. "You make him sound like one of those sociopaths on the crime shows your mother watches."

I raised an eyebrow. "They all have to start somewhere."

"Not in front of the kids," he chided. "I know you have strong feelings, especially because of what happened with Leah, but he's still their father."

I matched my father's determined stance with arms crossed over my own chest. "One second you tell me you knew all along, the next, I'm not allowed to believe the same thing. Which is it, Dad?"

"Why do you have to make everything so dramatic, Poppy? I agree that Jared is a selfish brat. I never said he was ready for his own segment on *60 Seconds*."

"Mommy! Watch!" Madison called, twirling in her tutu top and matching leggings.

Glad for a respite from the growing animosity, I walked over to my daughter and clapped my hands. "Beautiful spins, Maddie. Can you show me some more?"

She happily obliged, spinning until she toppled onto her bottom.

"Nice going, Maddie," Natalie teased, though I heard no malice in her tone.

Dusting herself off like a champ, Maddie began her twirling again in earnest.

Her determination reminded me a lot of myself in younger years, of that unwillingness to accept defeat even against my better judgment. Trying to make Jared Levine love me, to truly see me as a person rather than a means to an end, became my mission for nearly two decades. I thought back to those early years of our marriage when Natalie was just a baby and Jared began his first job as a mortgage loan officer.

"Did a bomb go off in here?" he scoffed, walking through the front door of our two-bedroom apartment.

I juggled Natalie on my hip while I dabbed at the baby puke running over both sides of my shoulder. Along with a plethora of baby toys adorning our carpet, our lone couch sat covered in a mountain of laundry. Dishes I'd meant to wash remained unmoved as our colicky, firstborn child refused to nap at all.

"Jared, can you take her for just a second? I've needed to pee for the last hour and a half."

My husband looked down his nose at me, affronted I would even ask.

Rolling my eyes, I placed Natalie in her swing. I cringed at the sound of her immediate wails when I finally had thirty seconds to relieve my bladder.

"What's for dinner?" Jared asked, loosening his tie.

He did not mistake the "I will murder you in your sleep" look on my face.

"What?" He held up his hands in innocence. "You're the one who gets to be home all day. Is it so hard to stick a frozen pizza in the oven?"

"Jared, I haven't slept in five months," I said, trying to get my husband to understand. "The only place I can get Nati to sleep is on my chest, and it's a little hard to get much of anything done that way."

"Clearly," he sneered, once again eyeing our messy apartment.

"If it bothers you so much, *dear,* you could always try pitching in once in a while. It's not like we have some magical laundry fairy who comes and washes your clothes and puts them away for you."

"It never bothered you before," he said, dumping his briefcase on top of my pile of newly laundered baby clothes.

I knocked it to the floor. "Are you kidding? I just washed these, Jared!"

"I can't breathe in this place. How hard is it to clean a tiny apartment and take care of a kid, Poppy? It's not like you have a real job."

"Because keeping a child alive is just a piece of cake," I clapped back.

"Is this more pregnancy hormones, or can you try acting like my loving wife again?"

I muttered under my breath about the whopping *two* diapers Jared had ever changed, and at that, he treated a simple diaper like a chemical waste spill. I turned to see Natalie asleep in her baby swing, and my shoulders slumped in relief. Jared flipped the television on, content to complain about being hungry rather than offer to make food or clean anything.

"Could you keep it down?" he called into our tiny kitchen. "I can't hear the TV."

If only for the sake of our sleeping daughter, I didn't bang the dishes even louder out of spite. Instead, I finally put my kitchen to rights, grabbed an empty laundry basket, and brought the clothes into our bedroom to fold.

Picking up our cordless phone, I tucked it into my shoulder as I called my best friend for support.

"Why can't he just grab some food on the way home?" Leah said in my defense.

I folded a onesie then frowned at the spit-stained collar. "Jared is a total mama's boy. The only way he survived two years of college without me was bringing laundry home for his mother to wash."

I could envision Leah's wince on the other end of the phone.

"Anyways, enough about me," I said. "How are things going with Roger?"

"Meh," she replied. "He wants me to move in with him, but I told him I'm not looking for anything serious."

"Leah, you've been dating off and on for four years. Don't you think that's long enough to know if you want to spend the rest of your life with the guy?"

"Not all of us have the good fortune to get knocked up and have a shotgun wedding." The venom in her tone stopped me cold.

"Are you jealous?" I gaped. "I know you enjoy teasing me,

but I can almost feel the resentment seeping through the phone line."

"Excuse me?"

"You heard me. My bed is buried under laundry, I'm wearing the same, spit-up covered shirt from yesterday, and my husband can't be bothered to help. You act like I'm living some fantasy."

"You're right," she said dismissively, "I have no reason to be jealous of any of that."

I felt Jared's presence in the room before I saw him. "I'll have to call you back." I hung up before Leah could reply. I suddenly didn't feel like talking to my best friend anyway.

"So, uh, the baby's asleep," Jared said, eyeing me in that familiar way. His gaze roamed freely over my figure.

"You're joking, right?" I held out my stained shirt better suited as a rag. "I haven't taken a shower in almost a week, and you still expect me to make dinner."

"I made a sandwich." He loosened his tie and tossed it haphazardly into the basket of newly folded clothes. I sighed internally, somewhat moved by the idea he tried to make an effort for himself.

"Did you make one for me too?" I asked.

His eyes shifted before returning back to mine with intensity. He walked over to me and rubbed his hands up and down my arms. "Why don't you go take that shower you deserve, and I'll make the best tuna melt you've ever had in your life."

"What about the laundry?" I glanced over to my half-done pile.

"How hard is it to fold some clothes? I can do it."

I bit back a retort, enjoying the feel of his hands and the scent of my favorite cologne. I sighed into Jared's touch, and his eyes took on that same, knowing glint that turned my insides to goo ten years earlier in high school. His caress slowed, shifting from comforting to intimate.

"Are you sure?" I asked.

"I'll show you how it's done. Maybe it will even inspire you to work a little harder during the day."

I pursed my lips but said nothing. Instead, I savored my fifteen minute oasis into the Hawaiian tropics provided by my plumeria body wash.

By the time I emerged from our bedroom, wet curls falling down my back, Natalie was awake and fussing.

"She's hungry," I said, noting the telltale cries and my body's reaction to them. I carried Natalie to our garage sale recliner and nursed her. True to his word, Jared brought over the aforementioned sandwich along with some chips.

"*Bon Appetit*," he said, affecting an accent.

"Thank you," I said sincerely. "It was a rough day."

He smiled. "Happy to help. Maybe I could interest you in a back rub later."

"Sounds like heaven."

He rested a hand on my shoulder, his warmth immediately seeping through my thin bathrobe. "I have a few other ways to take you to paradise, Poppy."

I nearly choked on my sandwich, unused to such a ridiculous pick up line since the early days of our relationship. My eyes teared with silent laughter, and I tried to keep from spitting food onto my precious nursling.

"She's beautiful," Jared said, finally noticing our daughter.

I relished a few, quiet minutes of motherhood. "Yes, she is."

"So are you," Jared added huskily, his eyes burning into mine. "I probably should have started with that when I came home, huh?" He smoothed away a damp tendril that had fallen onto my forehead.

I smiled back at him. "It would have helped."

"Think she'll go to sleep in her crib?"

"Probably not, but we can try again."

I attributed Natalie's decision to suddenly sleep through the night as what saved our marriage until Madison came along.

CHAPTER 14

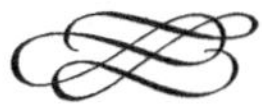

"I can't believe you left me home with all three kids!" Jared yelled not two seconds after I walked in the door with groceries.

I ignored him and deposited several bags on the kitchen counter to alleviate the strain on my back. Feeling his glare from across the room, I turned around and suppressed the urge to roll my eyes. "So, what exactly is the problem?"

"Natalie won't listen, Ryan poured cereal all over the carpet, and the baby threw up on me." He gestured toward the massive stain on his chest.

"Sounds like a pretty typical day." I pulled out boxes of cereal to toss them on top of our refrigerator.

"You think this is funny, Poppy? You dropped all of your responsibilities on me so you could go gallivanting across town!"

Whirling back around, I hissed, "Excuse me?"

"You heard me."

My eyebrows shot up. "Do you really want to talk about

gallivanting, Jared? What's with all of these business conferences lately? You just up and go without a thought to me or the kids. When you actually manage to be physically present with us, you're checked out emotionally. I'd have better luck talking to a wall."

"You're the one laying around at home in your pajamas while I'm out making money. You have no room to complain," he growled.

"You can't handle all three kids for one hour so I can go food shopping, yet when *I'm* home with them for hours on end, it's apparently no big deal. Pick one, Jared, because you can't have it both ways."

I slammed a few cans into the pantry while I caught my older children scurrying out of the room in my periphery. I sighed heavily, tired of the constant fighting with my husband.

"Help me understand," I finally said, "why you've been running off for all of these work conferences, especially since we've had such a hard time juggling a third baby. I talked to your boss because Larry has always been so supportive of you having a good, work-life balance."

"You did what?" he roared, his face mottled in rage.

Startled by the unholy expression, I backed away and into my refrigerator. "Jared?" I said weakly.

"Why would you do that?" he screamed. "What's the matter with you!"

Madison startled from her play kitchen and began to wail. I rushed over to soothe my toddler, even more dismayed to realize she'd been left in the filthy diaper I'd asked Jared to change on my way out the door.

My initial fear gave way to Mama Bear fury. "Are you such a selfish cretin you'd give our daughter diaper rash just because you can't be bothered to change her? Just *one* diaper, Jared? Are you truly that helpless, that completely useless?"

"You're the one who's useless," he snapped. "You got fat and ugly and stopped taking care of yourself. And you're bitter, Poppy. Do you really have to wonder why I don't want to be around you?"

Temporarily distracted by changing my squalling baby and her reddened skin, Jared's words finally sunk in. My hands shook as I slathered on the baby ointment and folded her into a clean diaper. I desperately wished the truth in front of me was nothing more than a horrible dream.

"Who is she?" I asked quietly.

The red seeped from Jared's face into white. Recovering quickly, he puffed out his chest. "I don't know what you're talking about."

I found the tube of ointment and threw it at Jared with my free arm. My husband's eyes widened in shock.

"Did you just...?" he spluttered.

"Answer the question," I demanded. "Can't stand to be around your ugly wife and your awful kids? Always have an excuse to bail on family time? Suddenly not interested in sex when you used to hound me for it constantly? I'm not stupid, Jared, and you're not as good a liar as you think you are."

He folded his arms over his chest, then grimaced at the whiff of baby vomit on his shirt. I rolled my eyes.

"I'm not in love with you," he said with cold condescension.

I uttered an unladylike expression.

"More of your usual venom?" he sneered.

"More of your usual blame shifting?" I retorted, switching Madison to my other hip. "We both know you're the world's lousiest husband, Jared. You're selfish, lazy, inconsiderate, and you expect me and the kids to cater to your deluded versions of perfection. You won't allow any of us to have an independent thought without your royal permission."

I set Madison down amidst some wooden blocks left abandoned by her older brother. As expected, she picked up one to gum on it. I walked back into the kitchen to face Jared head-on.

He looked me up and down derisively. "It was a mistake marrying you, Poppy. But you just looked at me with those big, puppy eyes, and it was too easy to settle."

I inhaled a sharp breath at his cruel words, disgusted and disillusioned by what my life had become.

"I gave up everything to be with you," I said, outraged. "And my thanks is having you cheat on me? By having you tell me you *settled* for marrying me?"

"I liked being adored," he said, lifting up my chin with his finger, "and nobody was better at it than you."

I slapped his hand away. "How dare you!"

"We haven't been happy for a long time, Poppy, and you know it."

I glared at him. "And you're going to blame me for that too, aren't you? Who is she, Jared?"

"Nobody you know."

"Who?" I demanded.

His eyes shifted away.

"Don't you dare lie to me, Jared Michael Levine! Clearly, you've been doing that for eighteen years already. Who is she?" I yelled.

I regretted my outburst immediately because I heard footsteps at the top of the stairs. All three children heard my world come crashing down with the utterance of one name.

The betrayal of my best friend and my husband left me winded as if physically punched in the gut. Jared hastily packed a suitcase after leveling me with more accusations and lies to excuse his behavior. I fought back each verbal knife wound as best I could, later sobbing myself to sleep when I could mourn privately.

Blinking back tears, wondering when the ongoing misery would finally end, I refocused my eyes on my office computer two and a half years removed from that awful day. The document I had been editing resembled word salad more than a commercial insurance summary.

"I need a drink," I muttered, rubbing my eyes then wincing at the eyeliner I inadvertently rubbed off as well.

I sighed.

"Bad day?" Miss Belle asked from my doorway.

"Bad memories," I said, wiping my fingers on a tissue. "What can I do for you, Miss Belle?"

"The mighty Margolin asked me to check on the Triple J renewal."

"He still mad at me?" I asked. I knew either Ted or Rebecca had filled her in on my request to hire Jessica Goldstein.

"Busy," she said, "and you still got your Culver super star award, remember?"

Half of my mouth lifted. "It was a nice surprise."

"Looks like you got some new makeup and a haircut too," she said, eyeing my layered and highlighted curls. "Poppy, you're a new woman."

"Wish I felt like it," I said morosely.

Miss Belle's lips thinned. "Is that no good, philandering ex-husband of yours giving you trouble again?"

I shook my head. "I just want the pain to go away. I don't know if I can move on from what happened without some kind of closure. I know my kids need it too."

"Some folks like to preach about 'forgive and forget,' but I don't think they understand what forgiveness really means."

I scoffed. "I'm not even at the point of forgiveness yet, Miss Belle."

"Well, I ain't talking about the kind where people pretend like nothing happened and then just never mention it again. That stuff festers and will eat a body up."

I tilted my head as I considered her words. "Go on."

She walked closer toward my desk. "My mama always talks about forgiveness as making peace with the past and releasing the debt."

"How do you make peace with something you don't understand? How do you make peace with someone who wants to destroy you?"

"It ain't about making peace with a person who deliberately hurts you, baby. It's about making peace with the situation. You accept what happened, you deal with all your demons, and then you let go."

"But you just said you don't believe in forgive and forget," I said, confused.

"You'll always have the scars, Poppy. I'm not telling you to ignore them. Letting go means you stop trying to relive what happened and change the past. You accept that it is what it is, and then you work on moving forward with your life."

"How do I get to that place?" I said desperately. "I'm so tired of feeling this way."

"It takes time, baby. You have a lot of hurt to work through and a lot of regret. Time and distance always help."

"Hard to do when he's the father of my children."

She nodded. "Nothing is impossible with God, child."

"So I've heard," I said, rolling my eyes. "The no-good cheat likes to quote that Bible verse when he's trying to manipulate me into getting back together."

Miss Belle chuckled. "Didn't anybody ever tell you the devil likes to quote Scripture too?"

"Really?"

Miss Belle's eyes took on a knowing glint. "Oh yes, baby. The devil likes to take the Word, twist it, play with it, and get folks believing all kinds of mess to justify what they're doing."

"I've never heard of that."

"Honey, not everybody who says, 'Lord, Lord,' belongs to Jesus. Christ talks about it himself. Lots of folks claiming they did all kinds of good deeds and spiritual things, but Jesus rebukes them all, telling them that how they treat the little people is how they treat Him. Makes a body think, hmm?"

I nodded, letting the new information sink down. "Very interesting."

"Don't take my word for it, baby. You can read it yourself in the Bible."

"I'm not interested in reading any books right now." Turning away from her potent gaze, I ignored the pang of guilt knowing I had a newly finished R.D. Hampton novel in my purse.

"You wanna fight fire with fire, Poppy Levine? Go read these verses your ex-husband likes to quote. Read them in context with the rest of the Bible. Shock his cheating socks off when you tell him exactly what Jesus has to say about his scheming ways. If you know the truth, you won't fall for any of the devil's lies. You might even surprise yourself with what Jesus says instead of what your ex-husband *pretends* He says."

"I'll think about it."

"I always liked the book of *John*," she said. "The gospel book, not the little ones later on."

I shrugged, having no idea what she meant.

Miss Belle grinned. "Some folks like to turn Jesus into Santa Claus ready to give them whatever they want on their wish list.

They act like their church has all the answers, and they know better than everybody else how to worship God and live right."

"Sounds familiar," I said, conjuring up several conversations with Jared regarding his congregation.

"Jesus had a lot to say to those religious folks back then, always busy condemning others but never dealing with their own sin."

I met her eyes again. "Jesus was anti-Semitic. I've heard the rabbi at my synagogue talk about it."

Miss Belle smiled tolerantly. "Baby, He was preaching to his own kin, calling out sin in the family. Am I racist for telling my niece she ain't living right shacked up with her baby's daddy?"

I grinned in response. "Can't argue with that."

"Good," she said, her dark eyes glowing. "Read it for yourself, and see what you think. The sooner you can see and accept the lies for what they are, the sooner you can get free."

"I just want peace, Miss Belle."

"You'll find that too, baby. My Jesus has never let me down."

CHAPTER 15

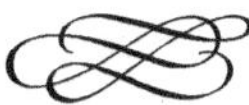

"This doesn't look like the latest R.D. Hampton," Joe said, standing over me a few days later. I sat outside enjoying the sun and fresh air on a bench near the Culver highrise.

The sun in my eyes partially blocked my view of him, and I shielded my face. "Welcome back. How was all the client wining and dining? Did you miss me?"

"Terribly," he said with a grin. "I stopped by to see you earlier, but you looked swamped."

"Wanna sit?" I asked, gesturing next to me.

Joe obliged, picking up the leatherbound Bible between us. "Anything interesting in here?"

I shrugged. "I don't understand a lot of it, but Miss Belle made a good suggestion the other day, and I thought I'd take her up on it." Taking back my borrowed book, I laid it gently in my lap. "She told me to fight fire with fire."

"Meaning what?"

"She said Satan quotes the Bible."

"Satan being Jared?" Joe asked, his eyebrows raised in semi-humor.

I laughed. "Satan being Satan, I guess. She was making the point that people like to misuse the Bible, and maybe I should read what it says for myself. Miss Belle said the next time Jared tries to hit me over the head with Bible verses, I can set him straight."

"Ah," Joe said, "context is king."

"Exactly."

He studied me, his eyes flickering over my hair and outfit. "You look great, Poppy."

"It's amazing what a haircut and some shellack will do."

Joe pulled a face. "Not what I meant. Makeup is nice, but it doesn't put a sparkle in your eye. That's something new, by the way."

"Maybe it's all the Bible reading," I teased.

"I was hoping you were just glad to see me," he said, his mouth curving into a grin.

We maintained eye contact, and my heart began to pound in my chest. "It's good to see you," I finally said, drowning in pale green eyes.

Joe looked away first, glancing down at the open Bible in my lap. Reading aloud, he said, "For God so loved the world that he gave his one and only Son, that whoever believes in him shall not perish but have eternal life."

"*John 3:16*," I said. "I never knew what that meant when people wrote it on banners at football games. Makes a little more sense now."

"Do you wonder if you'll get struck by lightning for reading the New Testament?" he asked. "I remember my parents saying something about that growing up."

"If Jared Levine can get away with everything he's done and

still survive a thunderstorm, I think I'll be okay reading the New Testament."

Joe grinned. "I've missed you, Poppy."

I smiled. "Likewise, Mr. Trautweig."

We gazed into each other's eyes for another moment before Joe cleared his throat. Blushing, I looked away.

"This *just friends* thing absolutely sucks," I said.

"Really sucks."

I dared another glance back up. "But it's necessary."

Joe sighed and leaned back against the bench. "It definitely increased my desire to clobber Jared Levine with a two by four."

I laughed. "You'll have to take a number for that."

"How are the kids doing?" he asked.

"Okay, I guess. Natalie hasn't spoken to Jared since she found his text messages and confronted him about it. Jared blames me for that, of course."

"Of course," Joe said. "It's your fault he got caught rather than his own fault for saying those horrible things in the first place, right?"

"Nailed it," I said, closing the Bible with a flourish. Holding it up in my hand, I said, "This is a very interesting book, by the way."

Joe offered me a sidelong glance. "How so?"

"Just not what I expected."

"What did you expect?"

I shrugged. "Fire and brimstone, maybe? A list of rules? This book of *John* reads more like a story than a list of dos and don'ts."

"Interesting," Joe murmured.

"Jesus didn't mince words with these Pharisees, I'll tell you that much. Called them 'sons of Satan.' No wonder Rabbi Cohn thinks Jesus is anti-Semitic. He said Jesus came to make a new religion. History would suggest he's right."

Joe considered my point. "I've heard that argument before. I asked Margolin about it, actually."

I turned to face Joe more fully. "What did Ted have to say?"

"He said the Bible presents Jesus very clearly as the Jewish Messiah promised in the Old Testament. He also said that the Judaism we practice today is based on a lot of manmade rules, and Jesus was right to rebuke the Pharisees for teaching their own laws as if God said them."

"I didn't know that."

"He asked me about different things Jewish people do, like lighting candles on *Shabbat* and beating our chests on *Yom Kippur*. He asked if I knew where the traditions came from, or if I just accepted everything as something Jewish people do."

"So, what's the answer?"

"I told him I didn't know."

I smiled. "At least you're honest."

Joe returned my grin. "He gave me a lot to think about. He also told me to read it for myself."

"Just like Miss Belle," I said, finishing his thought.

"By deductive reasoning alone," Joe began, stroking his beard, "if these Christians had something to hide, they wouldn't tell us to read for ourselves, would they?"

"Probably not."

"Yet, both of our rabbis are almost superstitious about us reading the New Testament. Like we'll be contaminated or brainwashed somehow," Joe said.

"Rabbi Epstein used to say the Torah was so complicated that not even the rabbis understood it. My bat mitzvah Torah portion felt like some cool story but nothing to do with *The*

Bible," I said, using air quotes. "To me, the Bible was a Christian thing."

"Do you think it's weird that Christians just go right to the source, but Jews are told we need the *Talmud* to interpret the Bible for us?" Joe asked, referring to the Jewish rabbinical commentary spanning more than two millennia.

I considered his point. "Well, according to Rabbi Cohn, Christians are ignorant and misguided by interpreting the Bible the way they do, but Jews are okay because we have a bunch of rabbis telling us what we should think. That doesn't sound like projection at all, does it?"

Joe exhaled a slight snicker. "Not at all, Poppy."

"What if Jared is right?" I said in sudden amazement.

Joe's expression grew wary. "What are you saying?"

"We're not getting back together," I said quickly. "Even if Jared's right about Jesus, he's wrong about everything else. Based on the little that I've read in the Bible, Jesus doesn't seem to be a big fan of religious hypocrites."

"And I've known plenty of religious Jews who were crooks and liars too," Joe said, contemplating my words. "To call someone out for being a hypocrite doesn't automatically make them anti-Semitic, does it?"

I recalled Miss Belle's near replica statement, puzzle pieces beginning to come together. "The Orthodox Jews don't consider the Reform to be real Jews, let alone what they think of people like the Margolins or Kyle Goldstein. Does that make them anti-Semitic for discriminating against other Jews?"

Joe smiled broadly at me. "Well, don't we sound like a couple of heretics?"

I laughed. "I've never been one to just meekly go along with things. My mother will attest to that. She'd flip her lid if I told her any of this."

"Might be worth it just to see her face," Joe teased, his eyes twinkling mischievously.

I rolled mine in response. "You forget I still have to abide under her roof. A moment of pleasure is not worth the nagging to follow."

"I wish there was something I could do to help," Joe said, his expression turning serious. "I hate that you're stuck in this situation."

"Not your job," I said firmly. "I'm touched that you'd offer, but you know I can't accept anything."

"Have you made any headway in that regard? Maybe a check to Jared's attorney to help get the ball rolling?"

"I wish. Until Jared gives up this idea of winning me back being synonymous with 'winning' period, I'm stuck. Since he's paying child support, I can't cite 'desertion' as an eventual way out of this marriage. I'm not even sure we could get an emergency hearing right now." Turning to face Joe I said, "Look, I'm not asking you to wait around for me. I hope you know that. You're allowed to get on with your life, and I won't begrudge you if you want to date. You could do a lot worse than Jessica Goldstein."

"Why do you keep pushing her at me, Poppy?"

"Why not? She's younger than I am, has a lot less baggage, and you guys seemed to hit it off at Vincenzo's."

"I appreciate the self-sacrifice, but I'm not so desperate for a relationship that I'd settle for something less than what I really want."

The intensity of Joe's gaze and the emphatic pronouncement of his words made my mouth go dry.

"Don't give up on us yet," he said, taking my hand in his.

"Where were you twenty years ago?" I murmured, tears wetting my eyes. "Why couldn't we meet back then?"

Joe's eyes warmed in compassion. "Head over heels in love with Catherine. Already planning our wedding. The timing would have been all wrong. You wouldn't have those three, amazing kids if not for Jared Levine. You can at least be thankful for that."

I grudgingly took my hand back from Joe's, enjoying the contact too much to maintain the wall I knew we needed between us. "Jared likes to quote this Bible verse about all things being possible with God. Do you think that's true for you and me?"

"I can't imagine God looking down on what Jared has done to you and your kids and being happy with it."

"Would you consider praying with me?"

"Now?" he asked, visibly startled.

"Why not?"

"In public?"

"Are you chicken, Joe Trautweig? Afraid of what people will think if you pray in the middle of our office park?" I clucked a few times to remove the look of terror from his face.

Joe's expression grew sardonic. "You're going to regret issuing a challenge, Poppy."

"Why's that?"

"I rarely back down from one."

"Good to know."

He grinned. "You wanna pray or should I?"

"Doesn't matter to me. I don't know what I'm doing any more than you do."

Joe lifted his chin, indicating I should go first.

I closed my eyes and bowed my head, mimicking what I had seen Rebecca, Taylor, and Ted do countless times before.

"So, um, God, if you're listening," I said, "we don't really know who you are, who Jesus is, or if you're real, but we could use some help." I cracked open an eyelid to see Joe looking at me with an adoring smile. Gulping and hastily reclosing my eyes, I continued, "I just want out of this nightmare with Jared, some stability for my kids, and a chance to be happy. So, if, um, that's not too much to ask, I would really appreciate the help. Amen."

I glanced over at Joe, nodding for him to say something.

He closed his eyes, pink with embarrassment, but clearly determined not to falter. "I don't know how this works, God, but this woman and I have both been through hell and back. We could use a break. I don't understand this Jesus stuff, but if you can somehow work it out for Poppy and me to have a shot at happiness, I'll know you're really listening. Amen."

I opened my eyes in surprise. "Did you just issue a challenge to God?"

Joe shrugged. "Guess so."

"I don't know if it works like that," I said. "I'd be a little scared of talking to God like that."

Joe stood up and held out his hand for me to rise along with him. "If there's one thing I've learned watching Margolin the last three years, it's that most people don't get the things they want because they're too afraid to ask. The worst someone can say is, 'no,' and then you're no worse off than when you started."

I placed my hand in his, standing next to Joe and enjoying one last look into pale eyes that sent a shiver through me. "Thanks for asking," I whispered.

"You're worth asking for." I felt the tension and internal struggle in Joe's grip. He didn't want to let go of me any more than I wanted to be released. Inhaling and exhaling slowly, Joe relinquished my hand and turned back toward our office highrise.

I followed just behind him, allowing myself a deep breath to regain control of my heartbeat and my equilibrium. I felt peace wash over me as we trekked back inside the building. I wasn't sure of what God had in store for either one of us, but somehow I felt certain both of our awkward prayers had made it up to heaven.

CHAPTER 16

WHILE ECSTATIC TO BE REUNITED WITH TAYLOR AND Rebecca the following weekend, I still felt guilty leaving my kids home with Grandma and Grandpa. I sat parked in the driveway, debating whether or not I should bail at the last minute. Instead, I re-read a few text messages from Joe.

Weird as it sounds, I enjoyed praying with you yesterday. Kind of feels like we're both on the same journey, doesn't it? My grandmother is probably rolling over in her grave, but she's already been in there for fifteen years, so maybe she enjoyed the exercise.

I laughed at his droll sense of humor.

Have fun with the girls, and please pass along a hello to Taylor and her family.

"Yeah, like she won't figure out what's going on in two seconds," I muttered.

A rapping on the driver side window startled me, and I dropped my phone on the floorboard.

"Get out of the driveway already," my father said.

"Do you need to back out, Dad?"

His hazel eyes scanned over my made up face. "No, but you need to get out and enjoy yourself. You'll never do that sitting in the car feeling guilty for having a life outside of your kids. I think they can survive one breakfast without you."

"When did you get to be so smart?" I teased.

"Probably about the same time you realized you weren't as smart as you thought."

I smirked. "Thanks, Dad."

"You look nice, Poppy. And it's good to see you taking better care of yourself. Those kids need you."

"I know. I'm working on it."

Tapping on the hood of the van, he said, "Get going already. The kids will be fine. Your mother said she's taking them for pancakes. If we leave soon, we can beat the weekend mall crowd."

I smiled, knowing that even my tweenager would enjoy a short stack and scrambled eggs.

Putting aside thoughts of Joe Trautweig, I drove from my parents' home west to Hillcrest, meeting Rebecca and Taylor at one of those tree hugger, locally sourced, all organic, blah blah blah restaurants that Taylor loved. With all of her food allergies, I knew it was one of the few places Taylor could eat safely.

Taking in my former coworker, I saw how Taylor glowed with both happiness and a Florida tan. She relayed the details of her brother's wedding from the night before with a dramatic flair. Her narcissistic mother had shown up to crash the party and wreak havoc.

"She waited until the 'does anybody object' part before she announced her arrival," Taylor groaned, digging into her vegetable and egg scramble.

"The books just write themselves, don't they?" Rebecca

quipped. Turning to me, she asked, "So, when's yours coming out, Poppy?"

"Probably when I can get my divorce finalized and then change the names of everyone involved to protect the guilty. Jared's dragging this out."

"Can't you prove the adultery?" Rebecca asked.

"Sure, I can. The problem is Jared's attorney withdrew from the case because he hasn't been paid in nine months. The only reason why he couldn't file a lien against our house is because it's already been sold."

"Does that mean you're stuck?" Rebecca asked. "Indefinitely?"

"No, it means I either pay for an emergency hearing, or we somehow convince Jared to go to mediation without a lawyer. He's currently ignoring all of my attorney's emails. At this point, I may have to wait on the state's statute of limitations and eventually go to trial anyway. He won't agree to a settlement because he doesn't want the divorce anymore. Jared keeps pretending he wants to negotiate then ghosts me when I press him to give me a date. I think he's waiting for God to strike me with a bolt of lightning and then I'll just 'come back to my senses.'"

Rebecca exhaled the same frustrated sigh I felt. "I'm so sorry, Poppy."

"Is he fighting for custody?" Taylor asked after a sip of orange juice.

I shook my head. "Jared deserted us and was forced by the court to support his own kids. We agreed to a general visitation schedule every other weekend, but that hit a snag when my oldest accidentally found abusive text messages from him on my cell phone."

Taylor and Rebecca gasped.

Noting their wide-eyed faces, I said, "Yeah, it was *that* bad. Natalie is not one to shy away from conflict, and Jared has never accepted responsibility for anything in his life. You can imagine how well that went over."

Taylor frowned. "So, you're basically stuck in divorce limbo. Would you consider going *no-fault* to get it over with?"

"Start all over?" I choked. "I can't waste another two years on Jared, and my Culver salary won't cover all the expenses without support. I was hoping to be free of him before my fortieth birthday. He's been jerking my chain for the past year and a half since he had this supposed Jesus epiphany. Jared says he wants to reconcile, but mostly that means I pretend he never hurt any of us, and then I go back to worshiping him and walking on eggshells."

"Can you get in front of a judge any sooner?" Taylor asked. "You mentioned an emergency hearing. Since Jared's deliberately stalling things, get all of your financial stuff together, write up a proposal, and see if your lawyer can push for a court date."

"That takes money, Taylor, and I have none to spare. My parents refuse to help because they're still hoping we'll get back together. Even if a very generous friend wrote me a check, it would look suspicious."

Taylor raised an eyebrow, but Rebecca seamed her lips together, knowing exactly to whom I referred.

"What about that helpfundme website?" Taylor suggested, never one to give up easily. "People could give anonymously, and Jared couldn't try to claim half of it. Or even if he did, at least the attorney gets paid, and you're free."

"Still too suspicious," I said, shaking my head. "Judges don't look kindly when you blast your dirty laundry all over the internet, especially since my kids or their friends could find it. I have a call to my attorney on Monday to see what we can do to expedite the process. I'm not looking to fleece Jared for money, just to be done with the marriage, make sure my kids are covered, and move on with our lives."

"Ted has a good friend who's a family law attorney," Rebecca said. Do you want me to pick his brain?"

"Eh, things are still kind of tense because of the whole Jessica Goldstein thing."

Taylor blinked rapidly then looked back and forth between me and Rebecca. "What Jessica Goldstein thing? What does she have to do with any of this?"

I cringed at Taylor's emphasis on the word "she."

Rebecca glanced over at me with an expression that said, "Do you want to tell her, or should I?" I nodded quickly, letting her know I was up to the challenge.

"I befriended Jessica at Vincenzo's without realizing who she was," I said.

"So, what's the problem?" Taylor demanded. "You know what she did to me and Kyle, and then there's sleeping with that married guy from her office. How are you okay with any of that after what Jared did to you?"

Rebecca laid a restraining hand on Taylor's arm.

"How can you be okay with this?" Taylor fired at our mutual friend. "Jessica didn't leave you unscathed either."

"Calm down," Rebecca said firmly.

Instead, Taylor's voice became shrill. "Did I enter the twilight zone or something?"

"Taylor, you know I love you like a sister," Rebecca said, "but you need to listen before you overreact."

"Overreact?" she repeated in disbelief.

Frustrated, I said, "I know Jessica hurt you, but she also opened the door for everything you've always wanted. You act like she ruined your life."

"Poppy's not wrong," Rebecca said, her tone more soothing than mine. "Kyle's choices aren't Jessica's fault, no matter how much you want to blame her for ruining that relationship. Besides, didn't you wind up with the better end of the deal? You have a husband who adores you and a beautiful boy. Jessica has none of those things."

"She doesn't deserve them," Taylor spat. "I'm not going to feel sorry for some skank who helped a married man cheat on his wife. And neither should you, Poppy."

Pulling a twenty dollar bill from my wallet, I slammed it down on the table. "I've suddenly lost my appetite. Taylor, have fun trashing someone who is still paying for her sins while you have your perfect, little life now. Not all of us can be as *blessed* as you."

My former coworker looked shocked and affronted, but I pressed on. "If becoming a Jew for Jesus—or whatever you freaks call yourselves—makes me as much of a self-righteous jerk as you are, then you can tell your Jesus I said, 'shove it!' You're more like Jared than Jessica is!"

"Poppy, wait!" Rebecca said.

"Sorry, but I've had enough of this." I snatched my coat and purse off the high backed chair. "Taylor, I can't say it was good to see you again, but at least I've seen the real you."

I stormed out of the restaurant without a backward glance. I saw Rebecca and Taylor through the window in rapid fire conversation, but I rolled my eyes in disgust. I knew I could reason with Rebecca and maybe talk to her later. As far as Taylor Horner was concerned, that relationship was done. Just another jerk hypocrite like Jared.

I ignored my ringing phone, certain it was Rebecca trying to play peacemaker. Instead, I began the drive down to Parkview, feeling like I was about to cross a bridge and never return.

Using my van's Bluetooth system, I commanded my phone to call Joe on speaker.

"You busy?" I asked, semi panting.

"Poppy? Are you okay? Aren't you with Taylor and Rebecca?"

"Change of plans," I clipped. "Can you meet me somewhere in Parkview? I'm about fifteen minutes away."

"Yeah. Did you have some place in mind?"

"How about your condo?"

Joe's prolonged silence had me wondering if my cell carrier dropped the call.

"You still there?" I asked, simultaneously dreading and anticipating the other shoe to drop.

"I'm here," he said. "Are you sure about this?"

"I'm not sure about anything right now, but I'm done with all of these religious *machers* and their Jesus."

"What happened, Poppy?"

"Judgey McJudgerton decided she's the only person allowed to live a happy life, and anyone who's ever wronged her should suffer indefinitely."

"Say again?"

"Nevermind," I said, as I began my descent off the Parkview exit. "I'll explain when I get there. Can you give me directions to your place?"

"Poppy, I really don't think this is a good idea. You sound angry."

"That's because I *am* angry."

Joe sighed before answering. "Look, I don't know what happened today, but I know both of these women love you. They're your friends."

"Yeah, they love me as long as I don't make a mistake or pick the wrong people to talk to at Vincenzo's," I said bitterly. "Man, I can't believe Jessica was right about them."

"Jessica?" Joe asked. "What does your friend from the coffee shop have to do with your fight with Taylor and Rebecca?"

"Everything," I said, pulling off the main road and moving my car toward the Culver highrise. "I'm at the deck. You can meet me here, and then we can walk somewhere, I guess."

"Do your parents have the kids?" he asked.

"Yeah. They expected I'd be out with my so-called friends for a big chunk of the day, so I've got at least four hours available."

"I'm sorry, Poppy."

"Sorry for what?" I pulled into a parking space and jerked the car to a stop.

"Sorry that things went so horribly this morning. You really don't sound like yourself. Are you sure you're okay?"

"I'll be a lot better once I see you."

I could hear the smile in Joe's voice. "Hard to say 'no' to that. I can be there in ten minutes. Will you be okay, or should I stay on the phone?"

"If I'm talking to you, I can pretend that Taylor isn't blowing up my phone right now with text messages."

"That would explain all the dinging bells," Joe said with a chuckle. "Are you sure you don't want to see what she's saying? Maybe she's apologizing."

"Christians don't apologize, Joe. They just gaslight you with Bible verses about how you need to forgive them for something they simultaneously claim they never did."

"Not every Christian is Jared."

"Maybe not," I conceded, "but way too many of them are exactly like him."

CHAPTER 17

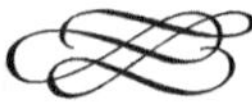

The second Joe arrived and pulled next to my minivan, I sprang from the driver's seat and flung my arms around him. He eagerly embraced me, but he kept his hands in a respectably platonic position.

"Poppy, what the heck happened?" he said against my hair.

I pulled back but left my arms around his neck. I craved his warmth and the sound of his voice. As I looked into beautiful, pale eyes, Joe's hand found itself along the side of my face. I leaned toward it and sighed contentedly.

"I'm just glad you're real," I breathed.

"Real stupid," he said, his eyes delving mine. "I'm beginning to think this was a bad idea."

"Do you remember what I said about not wanting to be a hypocrite like Jared?"

"How could I forget?"

"Well, Jared is always going to be a hypocrite, regardless of what I do. It's stupid to deny ourselves what we both want, isn't it?"

Joe removed my arms from around his neck. "Poppy, what are you talking about?"

"You know what I'm talking about, Joe. I'm taking the 'just friends' stipulation off of this thing we have between us." I searched his eyes, hoping to see the same desire I felt.

"You're upset right now, Poppy. As much as we both want something more than friends, we will absolutely regret it later. I didn't come down here to comfort you like that."

"But if you're looking at the future," I said with a note of teasing, "what difference would it make when we start our relationship?"

Joe's expression turned pained. "Poppy, listen to yourself. Who do you think you sound like right now?"

Shocked and horrified, I felt the color drain from my face.

"I'm sorry, I didn't know how else to say it."

My arms hung limp at my sides. "I'm an idiot."

"No, you're not."

"Yes, I am," I said more forcefully. "I stormed out of brunch with two of my closest friends, and all because of a stupid fight over somebody I barely know. Joe, what's the matter with me?"

He pulled me into another hug, his hands making comforting circles on my back. "Why don't you start from the beginning, Poppy?"

Leaning my head close to his neck, I caught a whiff of whatever cologne or aftershave I had only smelled faintly before. "You smell nice," I murmured.

"Focus," he said tersely, though I heard the smile in his voice.

I grinned against his chest. "This is nice."

"Poppy," he warned.

I chuckled. "I forgot how wonderful this could be."

Joe gave a resigned sigh, gently prying me off of him. I missed the feel of his arms immediately.

"Start from the beginning," he said, stepping further away to maintain a safe distance.

"You have more self control than I do right now."

"One of us has to stay strong, Poppy."

I sighed, feeling the weight of the world with me. "Why did we bother praying, Joe? What was the point? Less than twenty-four hours later, I lost a dear friend, and now I'm throwing myself at you like I'm Leah Halpern."

"You're not, Leah," Joe said, "but, it's obvious you're hurting and vulnerable. A lesser man would take advantage of you."

"A lesser man already did."

Joe raised an eyebrow. "What do you mean?"

Realizing what I'd implied, I shook my head emphatically. "Ancient history with Jared. Nothing recent, I promise. I can't stand the thought of that man touching me now."

His shoulders visibly relaxed.

Continuing on, I said, "I was thinking of my first time with Jared. It was my first time with anyone. I was only sixteen."

"Poppy, we don't have to talk about this. You've got enough going on today."

"I'm not upset about what happened anymore, only sad about how stupid and naïve I was. The truth was that I wanted Jared to take advantage of me. I had a best friend to impress too. I always felt stuck in Leah's shadow, never good enough or as pretty as her. Jared was the one thing in my life that she wanted but couldn't have."

"Until she did," he said flatly.

"Until she did."

A lengthy pause passed between us. I met Joe's eyes, and he

offered an encouraging smile. "So, what happened with Taylor and Rebecca?"

I sighed wearily. "There's just a lot of bad blood between Taylor and Kyle Goldstein's sister. I actually read Taylor's memoirs, but there's no love lost on Jessica's side either. She blames Taylor for Kyle's conversion to Christianity."

"So, Taylor doesn't like that you and Jessica hang out at Vincenzo's, is that it?"

"Taylor views it like I've betrayed her somehow. Fraternizing with the enemy and all that. Since her ex-husband also cheated on her, Taylor's even less inclined to like Jessica Goldstein."

Joe held up his hands for me to stop. "Poppy, I know Taylor wrote some kind of fictionalized autobiography, but I don't need all of the details. I don't fully understand Jessica Goldstein's connection to everything, and quite frankly, I'm not sure I want to. She seemed nice enough when I met her. Can we chalk it all up to a difference of opinion?"

I smiled sadly. "I wish it was that simple. I'm not looking to share any of Jessica's personal business, but it's hard to explain the situation without doing exactly that."

"Then don't worry about it. It's none of my business other than how it affects you. Whatever Jessica Goldstein's past transgressions, it sounds like you don't have a problem with them, but Taylor obviously does."

"Pretty much."

"It does seem silly to fight over it, though."

"I don't know what happened, Joe. It's like I just snapped. I got so sick of Taylor ragging on someone she barely knows. More than that, if it wasn't for Jessica interfering in her relationship with Kyle, Taylor would have never married Ian."

"Too much drama," Joe said with a shake of his head.

"And I've got plenty of my own to deal with," I deadpanned.

"I don't know why, but I just have a soft spot for Jessica Goldstein. I even talked to Phil about hiring her in the marketing department."

"You did what?" Joe's eyes snapped up to meet mine. "Is this the personal matter you needed to discuss with Margolin?"

I nodded.

"And he's got his own history with her, right?"

I nodded again. "Stupid idea, I know."

"What made you think of it in the first place?"

I searched Joe's pale eyes, wondering if he would understand. "Jessica's being sexually harassed at her job. I thought I could help by seeing if she could work at Culver instead. I need help in the marketing department regardless."

"Why would Margolin or Taylor object to that?" Joe asked, incredulous. "They're all Christians, aren't they? That doesn't make any sense."

"Jessica made some poor choices with another coworker. After he left, other men in her office thought she would do the same with them."

Understanding lit his eyes. "Oh, I see."

I smiled tightly. "Jessica was dealing with her own disastrous relationship when Rebecca and Ted got together. Taylor briefly dated Jessica's brother, but Jessica interfered in the relationship. They broke up because of it. Rebecca has moved on, but Taylor and Ted are still angry about things."

"And now they're mad that you've gone and stuck yourself in the middle—or more accurately—that you're not on their side and completely shunning Jessica."

"You've got it."

I could see the wheels turning in Joe's head. "When and how did you decide to champion Jessica Goldstein's cause? Why are all of her excuses for her behavior okay, but Jared's aren't?"

"What?" I choked. "I can't believe you're even asking me that!"

Joe placed his hands on arms to keep me from bolting. "Let me finish. I'm just trying to understand your reasoning, Poppy. I'm not accusing."

Trying to calm my racing heart and the surge of adrenaline coursing through me, I inhaled and exhaled.

Joe took that as a sign to continue. "What is it about Jessica's story that makes her different than Jared and Leah? I don't think you're condoning what she did, but I can understand the confusion Taylor and Margolin would have. Just help me understand, Poppy."

His soothing tone and imploring eyes helped cool my anger. "So, you're not judging me? Thinking that I'm a hypocrite?"

"Of course not!" he exclaimed. "If anything, it shows a lot of compassion and understanding on your part. I'm more concerned that Jessica manipulated you with some sob story and wants to cause trouble between you and your friends."

"I see," I said quietly. "I never even considered the possibility."

"Before you cut off Taylor and the Margolins for being a bunch of Bible thumping ogres, you have to remember that they've all been hurt by this woman. Maybe it doesn't seem like that big of a deal to you, but it's not your place to decide if their pain is legitimate. You're completely discounting your friends and trusting the word of a total stranger instead. I hope you can see why they'd be upset—and not because of old grudges."

Immediately seeing my own hypocrisy, shame washed over me. "Wow."

Joe tilted up my chin with his forefinger. "Look, I'm not saying you're wrong about Jessica. I'm just asking you to consider another perspective."

My lips trembled as I replayed the entire brunch scene in my mind with a new set of eyes.

"Oh, Joe!" I moaned. "I'm so stupid!"

This time, it was Joe who pulled me into his arms as I grieved over another mistake. I mumbled incoherently about my own foolishness while Joe spoke words of reassurance. Unlike Jared, he didn't take delight in a condescending lecture or act like consoling me entitled him to sex afterward.

I finally pulled away, unable to handle any more comfort. I knew I didn't deserve any.

"Poppy," he said gently.

I shook my head.

"Poppy," he insisted. "Look at me."

"I'm too ashamed."

He took a step toward me and cupped my face in his palms. I kept my gaze downcast, but he nudged me gently to look in his eyes. "It's going to be okay, I promise. And if it's not, I'll deal with Margolin myself."

"You can't do that, Joe. It's not your place."

"It was an honest mistake, Poppy. You're *allowed* to make mistakes, by the way. If these people are really your friends, they'll forgive you. They'll also try to understand where you're coming from."

"But Jessica," I argued. "Why would they forgive me and not her?"

"Poppy, there's a difference between forgiving someone and trusting them. If somebody runs you over with their car, you're not going to get back out in front of them again. Forgiveness doesn't mean you're required to trust someone who hurt or wronged you. That would be stupid. Trust takes time to build, and even longer to rebuild once it's been broken."

"Has anyone ever told you that you're a really smart guy? Smart and very, very handsome?"

He smiled down at me, green eyes twinkling like stars. "Not lately, but I don't mind hearing it."

I matched Joe's grin with one of my own. Caught up in the moment, I dreamily blurted out, "I think it would be very easy to fall in love with you, Joe Trautweig."

His arms fell away from me, and he stepped backward. He inhaled a ragged breath, his eyes burning a hole straight to my soul. "Did you mean what you just said?"

Feigning nonchalance, I said, "I didn't say I *am* in love with you."

My quivering insides called me a liar.

"We need to take a break from this...well, whatever this is," Joe said, gesturing between us. "Wanting you and not being able to do anything about it is torture. Giving in would destroy both of us, and I can't walk this tightrope anymore."

"What?" I breathed. "Joe, I don't understand."

"Poppy, I just...I can't do this anymore. I'm sorry."

CHAPTER 18

"So that's it?" I cried. "We can't be friends? We can't be anything?"

"Cooper & Jaye offered me an executive position, and I think I'm going to take it. Seeing each other every day at Culver just makes the situation harder. Turns out, I'm not as strong as I thought."

"Well, what happens when I'm free from Jared? Do you think I'm going to let you suddenly swoop back into my life because it's convenient for you?"

"You need to be completely free of him first, Poppy. You said so yourself."

"So 'waiting for me' lasted a whopping three weeks?" I fumed, angry at Joe, Jared, Taylor, and the entire world at that moment. "Is every man on this planet just a selfish liar?"

"I'm so sorry, Poppy. I shouldn't have pushed for a relationship. It was too soon. I'm going to wreck your life if I don't walk away now."

"Can't we just...why...why does Jared Levine have to ruin

everything?" I finally yelled in frustration. "Don't I deserve to be happy too?"

"Yes!" Joe said emphatically. "But I won't be the guy who takes advantage of you. Your kids would resent both of us, and that may never go away. It would also screw up your divorce proceedings. We'd make a bigger mess of things for everyone. I care about you too much to do that to you. I'm sorry."

"Well, I'm sick of 'sorry.' Go take your stupid job and leave me alone!" I fled into my van, slamming the door, and nearly rear ending an oncoming car in my haste to escape.

I pulled into a nearby gas station, shut off the engine, and sobbed hysterically. The thought of my three children out on their brunch date with their grandparents helped me keep darker thoughts at bay. Ending my own life would allow Jared to rewrite history and paint me as whatever villain suited his narrative. He would ruin our children trying to raise them in his own, narcissistic image.

"I hate you!" I finally screamed up at heaven. "I hate you! You ruin everything! I try to do things right, and you just laugh in my face. Do you get some kind of sick thrill watching me suffer? Well, do you!" I succumbed to another wave of tears and eventual dry heaves. I opened the driver side door and flopped my head between my knees. I needed to calm my stomach before I retched up an already bitter breakfast.

The sound of footsteps and crunching gravel punctured the fog of misery surrounding me. "What?!" I snapped. I wanted whoever it was to go scurrying off in the opposite direction. Jerking my head up, my eyes narrowed into slits as I beheld the last person on the planet I ever wanted to see again.

"You!" I hissed. "Did Jesus send you here to torment me? To make my life even more of a living hell than when we were married, Jared?"

"I'm on a lunch break from a business conference. I saw the van at the gas station, and you didn't look well."

"Ah, you mean those *business conferences* you attended with Leah," I seethed, instantly feeling the betrayal all over again. "Why can't you just leave me alone? I hate you, I hate your Jesus, and I want nothing to do with either one of you!"

"Poppy?" he asked weakly. "What's going on?"

In that moment, the floodgates broke. I jumped to my feet and unleashed every foul word I had only uttered in the privacy of my own bedroom. I bludgeoned Jared with one broken promise after another, the devastation he caused, and his utter contempt for anything other than himself. I beat my fists against his chest, letting him see the full scope of destruction he'd caused to my life and three, innocent children who deserved so much more from their father.

Jared surprised me by not fighting back. I expected him to yell over me, shut me up, and try to spare his public image. Instead, he let me expend the breadth of my grief until I crumpled to the ground in a heap.

"Just go away," I croaked, wiping my nose with the back of my hand. Realizing the futility of that effort, I clambered toward my van to find a tissue, but Jared beat me to it. He handed me a batch of white, paper napkins almost as a truce flag.

Snatching them from his hand, I cleaned my face and relieved the pressure in my sinuses. He hunkered down next to me, silent, and watchful.

"Why are you still here?" I asked low. "Came to gloat?"

"You needed me."

"I need you like I need a brain tumor."

"I probably deserve that," he said.

I glared at him.

"Did you mean what you said?" he asked.

"When?"

"When you told me that I ruined your life and that you're never going to be happy until you're free of me. When you told me that I've permanently damaged the kids."

I studied Jared's concerned expression before answering. It was a side of him I had yet to see since our marriage imploded: actual regret.

"Why aren't you attacking me with your usual accusations of bitterness and unforgiveness? What about all of the disgusting things you texted me? Where's the *real* Jared?"

He winced. "I'm sorry about all of that, Poppy. It was wrong, and I'm ashamed of myself. I'm even sorrier that Natalie saw any of it."

"She said you blamed me, Jared. She said you tried to force her into saying I let her see the messages on purpose."

"I did," he shocked me again by admitting.

I inched my body away from him. "Who are you, and what did you do with my ex-husband? What kind of game are you playing?"

"You probably won't believe me, but I had a come-to-Jesus."

"Another one?" I mocked. "I think the first one was bad enough."

"Your friend, Rebecca, was right about Nathan Fein."

My eyes snapped back to meet his. "What did you say?"

"He was downloading pornography onto the synagogue computers."

My jaw dropped. "How? How did he have access? How did anybody find out?"

"Nathan paid part of his tithes doing free IT work for the congregation. He designed the website, built their servers, and handled any technical problems. The police raided the congregation because he downloaded underage porn, and they tracked it to the synagogue."

Pushing aside thoughts of what Jessica Goldstein would do with the information, I turned my attention back to Jared. "What does this have to do with the new leaf you've apparently turned over?"

"Can we stand up, Poppy? This is killing my knees. I'm not eighteen anymore."

Rolling my eyes but obliging, I stood up on my own. I pushed away his outstretched hand of assistance. "So, finish your story, Jared."

"The synagogue covered up the scandal and called it a *terrible misunderstanding*. Rabbi Lebow told the congregation Nathan was taking a sabbatical for personal reasons and then praised him for working so hard at the temple and taking time to spend with his family. The real reason is because his wife took their baby and is staying with her parents during the police investigation. After that pile of lies, he preached a sermon about gossip and complaining, saying that God doesn't want us 'interfering' in other people's lives. He told everyone to be about *God's* business rather than anybody else's."

Disgusted, I said, "That must be why they welcomed you into that church too. What's a little adultery, right?"

"Poppy, I felt sick to my stomach. I couldn't believe what I was listening to. It was like watching a conman pull the fleece over everyone's eyes. Only a few of us knew what really happened, and Rabbi Lebow called a leadership meeting to discuss what we would tell anybody who didn't believe the company line."

"How could your rabbi guarantee all of you would keep quiet about it?" I asked, now genuinely curious.

Jared cleared his throat, then rubbed the back of his neck.

"All of us in that room have a past. Rabbi Lebow would happily share our dirty little secrets if we exposed any of his."

"Is that what following Jesus is all about, Jared? Preach one lifestyle, but live another? Gaslight and condemn victims as living in some kind of sin because they don't turn a blind eye to *yours*? Manipulate bystanders from using their brain so they believe whatever lies you force feed them instead?"

"No!" Jared's eyes went wide in desperation. "That's just it, Poppy. I saw myself, really saw myself. Everything Rabbi Lebow said from that pulpit was something I know I've said to you over the last eighteen months. It was like coming face to face with my own, personal demon. Rabbi Lebow caught my eye during the sermon and smirked at me. I ran into the bathroom to throw up."

"Is there any way for me to verify this crazy story, or am I supposed to actually take your word for it? You have to know how ridiculous this sounds."

"They sell CDs of every sermon. Rabbi Lebow is super weird about having any of his messages on the internet, but he makes them available for purchase."

I rolled my eyes. "Yes, God forbid he give anything away for free."

"Poppy, I'll buy a CD, and you can hear it for yourself."

"How do I know this isn't some trick to brainwash me into believing about Jesus? How do I know that any of this isn't some elaborate lie to avoid going to divorce court?"

"You don't," he said simply. "I'll mail the CD to the house. You can listen for yourself. Rabbi Lebow dances around the whole topic, referring to 'certain situations' and 'this is how rumors get spread.' He's indirectly referring to Nathan. His wife took down her marital status on FaceSpace and any pictures of her with Nathan. With his sudden disappearance from the syna-gogue, people are asking questions."

"Good ole social media," I deadpanned.

"Poppy, I've been selfish, and I know I hurt you and the kids. You were right when you called me a lousy husband and father."

I nearly laughed. "Has hell frozen over?"

When Jared didn't retaliate, I frowned.

It was then my prayer with Joe came rushing back to me, that feeling of God answering our awkward prayers about both of us being happy. Sadly, Joe and I assumed it meant being happy with one another. The sinking feeling in the pit of my stomach warned that I would be forever tied to Jared Michael Levine.

Frantic, I said, "I need to go. I've had all the drama I can handle for one day."

"Are the kids with your parents?"

"Yes, and you should go see them—Natalie especially. If you've really had some kind of come-to-Jesus," I nearly choked on the words, "then you owe it to the kids to take responsibility for what you did to me and to our family. I don't mean empty promises about the two of us getting back together either. You tell those kids you're sorry, and you mean it. You apologize to my parents for what you did to their daughter and their grand-children."

"What about you?" he asked. "What do you need to hear?"

"There's nothing you could say to me that I would believe right now. You've done nothing but manipulate and use me since the moment we met. I need actions, not empty words."

"And then what?"

"And then nothing," I said. "Apologizing to the kids and to my parents is what you should have done already. It has nothing to do with me. I'm not the only person you lied to and hurt, Jared."

He surprised me by nodding in agreement.

"No argument from you? No bargaining and blame shifting?"

He shook his head. "Poppy, I saw the devil smile at me from the bima a week ago. I will never be able to unsee that. I wrestled with some kind of demon in my sleep the next day."

A cold shiver ran through me.

"One second I'm sleeping, the next I feel like I'm being suffocated. I called out to Jesus, and the pressure stopped. I looked up and saw a black shadow slither across the ceiling of my apartment. I got down on my knees and repented of everything I could think of. I repented for getting you drunk at Moose Grunwald's graduation party and pressuring you into bed. I repented for all the lies I told you while we were married, for all the lies I told Leah to make her feel sorry for me."

"What?" I breathed.

Jared's expression looked pained. "Poppy, I played both of you from the beginning. Every time your back was turned, I was complaining to Leah about you. She didn't set out to ruin our marriage. I'm the one who kept stringing her along."

Feeling another punch in the gut, I took a deep breath, searching for a resolve I didn't feel. "How...how could you do that, Jared? To me? To Leah? What kind of a monster *are* you?"

"A snake," he answered immediately.

My jaw fell open at his easy admission of guilt.

"Poppy, have you ever heard of Leviathan?"

Immediately recalling Rebecca's own book, the passage that went right over my head yet left me with a queasy feeling in my stomach, I fell down hard on the floorboard of my open van door.

CHAPTER 19

"Poppy?" Jared asked, his eyes searching mine. "Talk to me. You look like you've seen a ghost."

"Who...who are you?" I gaped. "What happened to you?"

"Jesus," he said matter-of-factly.

"No, no, no." I stood up and pushed him away from me. "Don't you start with that *chazarai* again. You told me you found Jesus already and then became a bigger jerk than you already were."

"Poppy, do you know anything about spiritual warfare?"

"About what?" I said, dumbfounded. "Jared, you sound like a lunatic. Even worse than the crazies I left at brunch this morning."

"Poppy, I'm telling you that I woke up with a demon attacking me. It felt like a boa constrictor wrapped around me."

"You don't actually expect me to believe this, do you?"

"Honestly? No. I'm still not even sure if I believe any of it."

"So, now this snake thing is responsible for everything you

did wrong since I won't let you get away with blaming *me* anymore?"

Jared exhaled in frustration. "Ask Rebecca about Leviathan, okay?"

"Assuming she wants anything to do with me," I muttered.

"What happened? I thought you guys were friends."

I caught myself before I answered. My world felt off axis. It should have been Joe Trautweig offering comfort, not Jared "my god is me" Levine. It should have been Joe looking at me with concern in his eyes, not the worst mistake I ever made back in high school.

"Just go, Jared. I can't...I can't handle any more of this. If you're trying to make me lose my mind so you can get custody of the kids or not pay child support, it's not going to work."

"Poppy, I—"

"No," I said, strength returning to my voice, "we're done. And while you're at it, you owe Leah Halpern an apology too. She could have been happy with Roger or half a dozen other guys. My life isn't the only one that you've ruined."

"I know," he said quietly. "She won't return my phone calls or texts. I've been trying to apologize to her."

"Maybe I'll call Leah myself and find out if any of this is true."

"I hope you do," he said, shocking me yet again with his sincerity. "I don't know how to make this up to either one of you, but I won't stop until I do. I couldn't shake that I was supposed to be in Parkview today. It was to see you, Poppy."

I exhaled a mocking laugh. "Why is your god so hellbent on making my life as miserable as possible? What did I ever do to him? I'm a good person. I didn't deserve what you put me through. I deserve to be happy, and now that's gone too."

I realized my blunder as soon as the words spilled out of my mouth.

"Did you sleep with him, Poppy?" Jared asked. "You and this Joe guy from work?"

I glared at him. "That is none of your business."

"You're right, it's not. I just want to know how badly I need to hurt him for breaking your heart."

I shook my head in disbelief, the words on my tongue unable to pass through my lips.

"You're my wife, Poppy. I don't want anybody hurting you."

I laughed maniacally, sure I had finally lost my last shred of sanity. "*You* don't want anyone to hurt me, Jared?" I whooped some more, tears of laughter rather than sorrow trickling down my cheeks. As quickly as the macabre humor began, it ended. A surge of hatred started in my gut, rolled up my back, then blazed into a fireball exploding from my lips.

"Nobody has ever hurt me as much as you have, Jared Michael Levine!" My right fist connected squarely with his nose.

The whole thing happened in slow motion, Jared's head jerking backward, blood flying in the air and splattering all over his clothes and mine. Before I knew it, Jared and I found ourselves surrounded by police, an ambulance, and a fire truck. The gas station attendant had already reported us as a public disturbance.

Jared emphatically told the police he refused to press charges, even while the paramedics reset his nose. "I always wanted a nose job," he mumbled from the back of the ambulance.

"So the two of you are estranged?" Detective Vila asked, scribbling down my words on his notepad.

"We were in the process of a divorce. I don't know what we are now."

The detective hid a smirk as he glanced back at Jared. "I think you got your message across, ma'am."

I sighed wearily. "I think this must be the worst day of my life...you know, other than when Jared told me he never loved me and was leaving me for my best friend."

I expected a wince or some shred of sympathy from Detective Vila. Instead, he nodded robotically and continued writing.

"Not your first time hearing that one, huh?"

"My wife would probably do a lot worse than bust my nose."

I smiled. "I won't lie and say he didn't have it coming. A friend of mine burned her ex-husband's clothes."

"You're very lucky your husband isn't pressing charges. It doesn't help in a divorce or custody case." He tipped his head to hold my gaze from beyond his sunglasses. "If there's a chance the two of you can try to work this out for the sake of your kids, do it."

"But you just said..." I spluttered, unable to compute his contradictory statements.

"The fact your husband isn't pressing charges says a lot, ma'am. Just my two cents. Take it for what it's worth."

I wrapped my arms around myself, feeling the late October air bite into my bones. Noting several missed calls and frantic text messages from my mother, I finally wrote her back. I told her there had been an accident, but I was perfectly fine and on my way home soon.

"Poppy?" Jared said groggily, hobbling over to me.

He looked so pathetic with his bandaged nose, bruised eyes, and overgrown hair. My mind flashed from the greasy haired high schooler to the forty year-old in front of me with dried blood on his shirt.

"Can you take me home?" he asked. "Otherwise, I'll call a cab."

"Why? So you can tell the kids how horrible I am for punching you and then abandoning you? Gotta blame Poppy's anger instead of Jared's behavior, right?"

Ignoring my barb, he replied, "I need to ice my nose, and you're covered in my blood. Your mother is going to freak if she sees you like this."

"I already told my mom I was on my way."

"Then take me with you."

"How are you going to get back home, Jared?"

"Your parents have two guest bedrooms. I'll stay overnight."

I fired off some profanity laced thoughts about Jared sleeping anywhere near me.

Jared winced and held up his hands in innocence. "Look, I'm not running a con here. You want me to apologize to your parents and our kids, and I'm planning to do it."

"How convenient," I sneered. "You can get them to feel sorry for you with your bloody nose, and then they can gang up on me for punching you."

Before I could say anything else, Jared swayed on his feet. He collapsed against me, his full weight dragging both of us against the side of my van. I glared up at him before realizing his face was just inches away. He searched my eyes questioningly, and his head angled toward mine. Disgusted, I turned away and allowed the car to bear the burden of Jared Michael Levine instead of me.

"I don't blame you for hating me, Poppy. I don't blame you for wanting to leave me here. I'm not asking for help because I think I deserve it, or because you owe it to me. I'm asking for help because you're a good person, and I need you."

Of all the times I ever imagined Jared Levine laying down his pride and uttering words I'd waited twenty years to hear, I could never have conceived of a more insane set of circumstances. I pursed my lips and blinked back bitter tears.

"Fine," I said low. "Because I *am* a good person, and not because you deserve it. Can you get yourself into the van?"

"If you can get the door, I should be okay for a few seconds. My balance is off."

"I could tell," I muttered. I shook off the feel of the weight and warmth of Jared. It was too easy to slip back to the familiar and pretend the last four years had just been some horrible nightmare. The pain of unending grief made it a tantalizing offer. Instead, I reminded myself of all I had endured and the new strength that came with it.

"Just to be clear, I'm giving you a ride for breaking your nose. Don't read into it as anything else."

"Understood."

He shifted against the van to make room, and I gingerly opened the passenger door. Jared slid into the seat and leaned his head back. His eyes were already closed, and I hoped he'd remain unconscious during the trip back to my parents' house.

Instead, his eyes opened, and he stared at me. "You're beautiful," he whispered, "and I was so blind."

Despite myself, I laughed. "Your vision is probably blurry. Try to rest." I closed the door and pulled my cell phone out of my pocket to text my mother.

Finally leaving. Have a guest with me. Long story. Not what you think.

Are you on a date with your friend, Joe? No need to lie about an "accident" Poppy.

Pushing away thoughts of bitterness or wanting to take them out on my mother, I simply said, *Not lying about anything. Jared's with me. He's the one who had the accident. He'll be fine. Just needs a place to spend the night. NOT with me.*

As expected, my mother's petulance transformed into immediate helpfulness. She prattled on about bed linens and which guest bedroom Jared would prefer. I turned off my phone, irked at how quickly she'd betray me at the thought of golden boy coming home.

I glanced at my unwanted passenger dozing next to me in the van, saddened and sickened that I still found him attractive. After Jared's cold desertion, I expected to see horns poking through his full head of hair. Instead, he just grew more distinguished with silver overtaking his formerly dark waves. The lanky, high school dreamboat had matured and filled out into a silver fox. Too bad the silver hadn't made him any wiser.

I pulled my gaze away from him and refocused on the road. "He's just less threatening in his sleep. Get it together, Poppy." Shaking my head, I replayed all of Jared's revelations from that afternoon. "Leviathan," I said under my breath. "Yeah right! Just someone else you can blame."

I felt unease as I uttered the words, frowning as I recalled Jared's admission of guilt. I thought about the angry curses I had yelled up at God and the bitterness I felt over a wasted life beyond my three children. The taste in my mouth turned acrid at the thought of Joe and empty promises. Part of me wished I hadn't let my self-imposed morals get in the way. I wondered what would have happened if Maddie hadn't gotten sick and I'd gotten that first kiss in the parking garage. I wondered what would have happened if I hadn't opened my big mouth that morning and ruined everything.

I pulled into my parents' driveway and shifted the van to park. Defeated, I rested my head against the steering wheel.

"This is my life," I said, depression gripping me. "I'm going to be stuck for the rest of my life with a man I despise." Resignation to my fate left me feeling hollow as tears slid down my cheeks.

"Poppy?" Jared asked, stirring in the passenger seat beside me.

I hastily wiped my face. "What, Jared?"

"I love you."

I shoved my fist in my mouth and bit down hard, determined to keep the scream inside. My shoulders shook, wanting so desperately to release the anguished sob lodged in my throat.

"Poppy?" he asked again. "You okay?"

I inhaled sharply, determined I would never let the monster see me cry again. Silver hair or black hair, he was still dangerous. I steeled myself for the battle to come and for Jared's inevitable tale of woe at my expense.

"I'm fine," I clipped.

His eyes searched my face. "Can you help me out of the car? I think I'll be okay to walk, but my head is spinning. I might need to lean on you."

I released an exasperated sigh, getting out of the van and slamming the door with extra gusto. I wanted to punch a hole in the wall, but I settled for already bloodying Jared's face. Yanking open the passenger side, Jared stared up at me with purple rimmed eyes.

"What's wrong, Poppy?"

"You have to ask?" I hissed.

"Things are going to be different. I promise. I'm not here to make trouble."

"I'll believe it when I see it. So help me, if you try to pull one of your usual stunts, I will tell the children everything you shared with me. Especially about what you did to me and their Aunt Leah."

"I know," he said.

Bending over so I could help ease him from the van, I didn't expect my mother to come flying out of the basement entrance, apparently ready to welcome back his royal highness with the red carpet treatment.

"Oh Jared, it's so good to...oh!" she exclaimed, taking in his battered face. "What happened? Poppy, did you do this?"

I looked up at Jared, ready for him to start laying on the standard, tag-team attack.

"Little accident," Jared said casually. "Poppy was there to help me, and that's what matters. Harriet, I really appreciate you and Ron opening your home to me. I know I don't deserve it."

"What kind of people would we be if we neglected someone in their hour of need, Jared Levine? We've already been taking care of your wife and children while you've been...sorting things out."

I had no doubt Jared felt me stiffen at my mother's white-washed version of events. Not taking the easy escape offered by my turncoat mother, he simply said, "We can talk about that later. I just need to lie down. My head is killing me."

CHAPTER 20

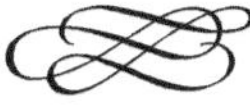

"Daddy!" Madison squealed, running toward me and Jared. She stopped short as she saw her father with his bruised and bandaged face.

Natalie and Ryan entered close on her heels, both of their brown eyes widening in shock.

"Dad?" Natalie said. "What happened to you?"

I looked again to Jared, expecting him to start the theatrics now that he had a larger audience. I assumed he'd have us in our usual spots on stage, me under the bus and himself on the sacrificial altar.

"It was a silly accident, kids. My own fault. Your mom did a great job taking care of me."

Natalie glared icy daggers at her father. "Shouldn't you be at the hospital? Or with Aunt Leah?"

Never one to let an opportunity go to waste, my mother quickly shushed her up. She talked up Jared as if he had saved a litter of kittens from a burning building. The fact she had no idea what *actually* happened was just an irrelevant detail.

Ryan glanced at his father's nose and then back at me. I saw the silent question in his eyes along with a gleam of mischievous delight.

With a nod, I answered his unspoken inquiry, and the teensiest of grins appeared on his face. He looked me over as if I wore a superhero cape taking out the big, bad villain.

"Does it hurt?" Ryan gestured toward Jared's bandaged nose. "A lot?"

Not missing the near hopeful sound in his tone, Jared looked at me with a pained expression beyond his two black eyes. Despite the fortress I'd tried to erect around my heart, a sliver of me felt compassion. I knew how I'd want to be treated.

"That's enough kids. Your father has had a pretty rough day. Grandma made him a place to sleep upstairs with her and Grandpa, and I'm sure he's ready to lay down."

I expected my mother to wrap her arms around poor little Jared, coddling him and reveling in her role as nursemaid. Instead, she shocked me by saying, "Oh, Poppy, didn't you get my voicemail?"

The bottom dropped out of my stomach. I knew exactly what Harriet Berman had planned before her ridiculous excuse spilled forth. The only surprise was utilizing my father as the catalyst. She reached out a hand to placate me, but the death glare she received kept her anchored in place.

"You need to stop," I said through gritted teeth. "It's not cute, and you're screwing with your grandchildren too."

"I'm trying to *help* my grandchildren," she hissed in response.

I glanced over to the deadweight still hanging on my shoulders, wondering if Jared was simply content to watch wife and mother-in-law fight over his sleeping arrangements. He certainly had no problems allowing my mother to bully me in the past. The Jared of old was long overdue for his arrival.

"Harriet," he said imploringly, but then swooned. He dragged me down with him, and my well-padded backside bore the brunt of the impact.

"Mom!" Natalie exclaimed, rushing toward me. "Are you okay?"

I grimaced as I could already feel a bruise forming on my hip. "I'm fine. Jared, are you all right?"

"Just dizzy. Poppy, I don't know if I'm going to make it upstairs. Can I crash on the couch for now? I'm not here to cause trouble, I promise. I'll call a cab first thing in the morning."

I sighed, uncaring of my mother's approval, but more concerned about the three pairs of Levine eyes watching my reaction. "Can you make it to the couch by yourself? I'm going to need a minute before I can get off this floor."

"Are you hurt?" The wide-eyed look on his face gave a rather convincing portrayal of a concerned husband. "You took most of the fall for me."

I held his gaze and dared him to lie to me again. "Yeah, what else is new?"

"Here, Daddy, I'll help," Maddie said, offering Jared a hand. She led her father into the adjoining family room.

Natalie helped me to my feet while Ryan grabbed a bag of frozen peas. He held up the makeshift ice pack and said, "Will this work?"

"It'll have to." I placed it against my side and limped over to the kitchen table.

Meanwhile, my mother's face held a far off glow. "The two of you are quite a pair, Poppy. You could have let Jared just hit the floor, but you didn't."

"Don't get excited, Mom. Jared fell on top of me. It wasn't my choice to break his fall."

"If you say so, dear. I'll go see if your father will relent on Jared staying upstairs with us." Her eyes darted over to the family room. "He does seem pretty cozy on the couch, though. Maddie covered him with a blanket, and she's tucking him in."

I grunted in response, not trusting myself to say anything that didn't involve profanity.

My mother exited for the stairs, pep in her step, and humming. I shook my head disgustedly and sat down at the breakfast table.

"Why does Grandma seem so happy he's here?" Natalie asked.

I rolled my eyes. "Take a wild guess."

"Perfect bat mitzvah," Ryan said, quoting one of his grandmother's oft-used phrases. "I think she's trying to get you and Dad back together like in that *Parent Plan* movie she made us watch a hundred times."

"Haley Bliss or the Lindsay Lowman version?" I asked, referring to the classic and the later remake.

"The really old one," Natalie said with a long suffering eye roll.

"I think it's from the nineties," Ryan added, instantly making me feel ready for an assisted living facility.

"Ah, the Lowman one," I said, chuckling at the subjectiveness of "old." I vividly remembered dragging Jared to see the movie back in high school only to have him coerce me into a marathon make out session instead.

"Daddy's asleep, but he's snoring," Maddie announced, joining the three of us in the kitchen. "Hi, Mommy." She walked over and rested her head against my arm. "You were gone for a long time today."

I smiled and rumpled her hair. "One of the longest days of life, baby."

"So, Dad is just sleeping here?" Natalie asked.

"Yes," I replied. A herculean display of self control kept from adding the word *unfortunately* to the end of that statement.

"I'm glad you took care of him, Mommy," Maddie said. "Daddy told me you helped him even though he didn't deserve it."

"Dad said that?" Natalie choked. "Are you sure you're not just making things up, Maddie? Dad isn't as awesome as he pretends to be."

Madison's full lips turned into an adorable pout. "I don't tell lies! Daddy said he needed Mommy, and even though he hasn't been nice to her, she helped him. He said Mommy is a wonderful person, and he's sorry we had to come live with Grandma and Grandpa."

The older two absorbed the new information, both looking unsure of what to do with it. I glanced over at the clock and realized the kids would be starving if they hadn't eaten dinner already. Hoping to curtail more uncomfortable questions, I asked if they were hungry. With a rousing chorus, all three declared empty bellies, and I whipped up grilled cheese sandwiches while Natalie and Madison peeled oranges for dessert.

I half expected Jared to make a surprise appearance and force himself into our "one big happy" around the breakfast table. Instead, the four of us ate in companionable silence while Jared slept off his pain meds and facial trauma.

The kids seemed generally unfazed by the presence of their father, perhaps because he remained unconscious on the sofa. They didn't fight me about bedtime or streaming one more episode on the TV. With the last kid in bed, I located an old,

R.D. Hampton favorite, pulled on a matching pajama set, and curled up on my leather recliner.

Though never one to bend the spines on my paperback books, my most well-read novel still showed signs of wear. The plastic film had been slowly separating from the cover beneath.

"Might need to replace you soon," I murmured, flipping on the side lamp next to the chair.

Jared stirred on the couch, and my heart stopped. Though I'd thought about simply reading in bed, I always enjoyed laying out in the family room to devour my novels. It felt more luxurious somehow, like I was doing something just for myself rather than holing up in my bedroom cave to sneak in some "me" time.

I read for about an hour, totally captivated by the story of my brooding, rugged knight and his forbidden lady. I'd practically committed the story to memory, but my breath still caught at the longing glances, stolen kisses, and dramatic kidnapping. The knight's anguish over his love most fair and her abusive husband finally caused him to take action and steal her away. No matter the cost, the hero of my novel was determined to make this woman his own. My eyes glazed over just as my hero and heroine reunited by a waterfall. Their dramatic kiss caused my heart to flutter as it had so many times before.

"Good book?" Jared asked from just beyond me.

My fluttering heart became a banging drum. My head remained fuzzy from my novel and the forgotten presence of my ne'er-do-well husband. I set the book down beside me on the end table.

"It's fine." I glanced into dark eyes no longer clouded with pain or fatigue. "You feeling any better?"

Jared stretched across our well-worn sofa. "Stiff, but otherwise okay. What time is it?"

"Just after ten," I said, looking at the wall clock. "Are you hungry?"

"Starving," he said with a grin, "but you don't have to make me anything."

"I wasn't offering."

Jared nodded, slowly sitting up. He picked up my novel and touched the same, worn edge I'd noticed earlier. "How many times have you read this thing?"

"A few times. Why do you care anyway?"

Jared steadied himself, his eyes never leaving mine. "Why are you so defensive?"

"You shouldn't be here," I blurted out. "This is *my* new home. We made this place without you in it, Jared."

His lips thinned. "How do I fix what I've done?"

"Fix what?"

"This," he said, gesturing at me. "How do I fix 'us'?"

"There is no *us*," I said, "not anymore. From your own mouth, that was all a lie. You just enjoyed being adored, and nobody did that better than me. Remember?"

Jared winced, clearly remembering that horrible day just as much as I did. "I never should have said that to you."

I shrugged. "It was the first time you ever told me the truth. I wasn't a person to you. I was a means to an end."

"I did love you, Poppy, and I do love you."

I shook my head. "You loved having me center my world around you and jump through hoops to keep you happy. You would actually have to know the real me in order to love me."

"I know that you hate roses. Your favorite color is yellow even though you never wear it. I know you own twenty different shades of red lipstick, and a back rub is all it takes—"

I held up a hand to cut him off. "We're not going there."

"So, this is it?" He picked up my prized novel again. "No love, no affection, just kids, work, and fantasy romance?"

I snatched the book from his hand. "Sounds just like our marriage, doesn't it?"

"And that's really enough for you?" Jared asked, his eyes searching mine. "What stopped you from making a go of it with this Joe guy?"

"You," I said, spitting the word like a curse. "Joe has more integrity in his little finger than you'd have in a thousand lifetimes. He didn't want to be selfish and ruin my life or my relationship with my children by doing what you and Leah have already done. It's bad enough that you've poisoned our kids with your lies about me. Joe refused to give you any more ammunition to hurt me or them."

Jared remained silent.

Hoping to bait him into the expected response, I said, "Cat got your tongue, or are you just trying to come up with another ridiculous reason to make everything my fault?"

"You're right," he said. "I did all of those things. I was selfish, and I thought I could keep blaming you for what went wrong. I used the kids as a weapon against you. I'm ashamed of myself."

I pursed my lips at yet another admission of guilt.

"Poppy, I—" his voice wavered, and for maybe the third time in twenty years, I saw tears fill the eyes of Jared Michael Levine.

"Are you actually crying?"

"Yes, and it hurts like...ow!" His hand flew to his bandaged nose.

"I don't regret hitting you," I said, hoping to stop the traitorous thawing of my heart. "You deserved it. And more."

"I won't argue with you."

Not liking the unpredictability of this new Jared nor its effect on me, I offered a curt nod, left the room, and locked my bedroom door.

CHAPTER 21

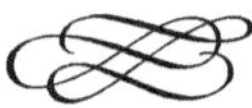

By the time I woke up Sunday morning, Jared was gone. Much to my relief, I found the children watching television as I entered our family room.

"When did Dad leave?" I asked, pushing a flop of curls from my face.

Ryan shrugged. "He wasn't here when we woke up."

"Did he leave a note?"

Natalie inclined her head toward our small kitchen. "It's on the table."

Nodding, I padded my way over, curious to see what Jared said.

Called a cab early this morning. Didn't want to impose on the rest of your day. Thanks again for taking such good care of me. I love you all. -Dad

I heard Jared's note crumpling in my hand before I realized what I'd done. "Oh," I breathed, staring down at it. Hearing my mother greet the children in the next room, I shoved the paper in my pocket.

"Where's Jared?" she asked with extra cheer.

I brushed past her toward the coffee maker. "Gone."

"Didn't he want to stay for breakfast? I baked cinnamon rolls upstairs."

"I'm sure you did."

I sensed the frown on my mother's face without even turning around. "Why do you have to make things so difficult, Poppy? Your husband suffers a terrible accident, and you can't even show an ounce of compassion."

Inhaling a deep breath to keep the irritation out of my tone, I said, "I believe compassion was bringing him home in the first place, Mom."

As expected, my mother stuttered and stammered for a response, always a hair below Jared in finding ways to scapegoat me because she couldn't control the universe. Bracing myself for the next wave of accusations and passive-aggressive manipulation, I poured grounds into the coffee maker and worked toward caffeinated sustenance.

"Well, is he coming back again to visit?"

"No idea." I poked in the fridge and located a carton of eggs.

"Poppy, I said I have cinnamon rolls upstairs," she chided.

"I'm surprised you'd make such *unnatural food* since you're so concerned about our health." I gestured toward the cage free, brown eggs she'd purchased. "Are you sure those cinnamon rolls were for all of us, Mom, or just because they've always been Jared's favorite?"

"I, uh…" she fumbled.

"Too bad you made that early run to the food store to get them because you probably missed the golden son-in-law on his way out."

My mother's eyes narrowed, her charade fully exposed. "What if I were to say you and the children need to move out so you and Jared can work on your marriage?"

Calling her bluff, I said, "Then, I'd also make sure to explain to your grandchildren how you kicked us out of your house when we had no place else to go. That they wouldn't be seeing their mean, old granny anymore. I'd also explain to Natalie that even though she's worked so hard on her bat mitzvah, we wouldn't be able to afford it. Thanks, once again, to Grandma."

"Poppy!" she gasped.

"What did you expect? You asked what I would do, and I'm telling you. Stop meddling in my marriage. How could you expect me to be anything other than resentful when you treat Jared like the beloved son and me like the horrible shrew he married?"

She placed a hand over her heart. "How can you possibly say that?"

"Cinnamon rolls," I said matter-of-factly. "Ignoring how your son-in-law lied and cheated on your daughter. Ignoring how he refused to financially support his own children until a judge made him do it. Ignoring how he suddenly became some Jews for Jesus freak and is teaching that garbage to your grandchildren. The *coup de gras* was finding out you sent roses to my office pretending they were from Jared."

Guilt flashed in her eyes before she hid it again. "Is that what he told you?"

"I hate roses, Mom. I've always hated roses. Not that it matters to the omniscient Harriet Berman who thinks she knows how other people ought to live their lives."

"So, I'm suddenly not supposed to be your mother anymore, Poppy? I shouldn't try to stop you from making horrible decisions that could not only ruin your life, but my grandchildren's lives also?"

I slammed my coffee mug down on the counter. "Do you understand that you're not God, and I'm not eight years-old anymore? Stop trying to control my life because you couldn't control what happened to River."

"How dare you speak to me about your brother!" she fumed. "You didn't have to watch him destroy his life with drugs."

"Of course, I did! Just because I was eight doesn't mean I couldn't figure things out. Even though you want to pretend I've been an only child my entire life, we both know I had an older brother. You used to brag about getting knocked up at Woodstock!"

"I never did that!"

I raised an eyebrow. "More things you're going to pretend I imagined, Mom? You couldn't stop River from taking his own life, so you try to micromanage every aspect of mine. You and Dad deliberately sheltered me so I would present well in the synagogue."

"Poppy, I..." she faltered.

Narrowing my lids, I finally went for broke. "Were you really ashamed of me being pregnant before marriage, or were you just trying to protect yourself from all the *yentas* gossiping at synagogue how you and Dad failed as parents again?"

I saw the truth in my mother's eyes, though I doubted her lips would part to utter it. It was one thing for my mother to think she kept her insecurities well hidden, shaming and nitpicking me instead. To acknowledge I fully understood her own shortcomings put us on a level playing field.

"Why are we dredging up all of this ancient history?" she asked with a dismissive wave of the hand. "It's obvious where your children receive their dramatic tendencies."

"From their grandmother. Clearly."

My mother and I locked in a stare down. This was my moment to seize control of an unbalanced relationship, and I intended to take it. If I could stand up to Jared, the monster, and force him to apologize to his children, I could take on his most ardent enabler.

"I love you, Mom. I loved River too. Trying to control my life is never going to bring him back. Meddling in my relationship with Jared and manipulating my kids has to stop. If you force my hand, I will move us out of here. I'm done with the games."

"Oh, Poppy," she moaned and slumped into the chair next to me. Her shoulders shook in silent tears, and I gaped at the genuine show of emotion.

"Why did you have to be so smart?" she asked, her watery gaze finally meeting mine. "Always too smart for your own good."

I responded with a tight, sad smile. "It's okay to miss River. It's okay to have regrets, but you can't change the past. You also can't change the decisions River made for himself. Those aren't your fault, Mom. They were his own choices. Keeping me under your thumb and controlling me won't bring River back. All it does is push me away."

"So, you don't hate me?" she asked through trembling lips.

"No!" I exclaimed. "You definitely have your moments, but I don't hate you at all. I do resent your interference and acting like you know how to live my life better than I do, but I also know where you're coming from. Why do you think I put up with it for so long?"

We stared at each other for a long moment, mother and daughter finally seeing each other free of masks, preconceived ideas, and resentment.

"So, what's going to happen with you and Jared?" she said, subdued.

I sighed. "I don't know."

"Is there any possibility of you two trying to make it work for the kids?"

I exhaled a bitter laugh. "Unless I become one of those Messianic Jews, I doubt it."

My mother's face pinched. "Is he really serious about all of that chazarai?"

"Apparently. Jared said he's had yet another come-to-Jesus and mentioned something about a demon in his apartment. Suddenly, he seems genuinely sorry for what he did to me and the kids. Not just butter me up and tell me what I want to hear, but actual remorse."

My mother shivered. "I don't like hearing talk about devils and demons, Poppy. You know Jews don't believe in all that."

"Jared said he's not sure he does either, only that he felt like he was being choked in his sleep. He said he woke up and saw some shadow slither across the ceiling of his apartment."

My mother shuddered more violently. "Enough, Poppy! I don't need nightmares."

"I'm not sure if I believe him or not, but Jared does seem different. More than the first time he showed up preaching all of that Jesus nonsense."

"Well, that's something, *Poppeleh*. Are you willing to give Jared a second chance?"

I rubbed at my forehead and the beginnings of a tension headache. "I don't know, Mom. I can't afford to get conned by him again. Our entire relationship was based on manipulation and control. I have no way to prove Jared hasn't just improved his tactics."

"I didn't realize that. You've been head over heels for that boy since you were sixteen years-old. He's also quite a charmer."

I smiled ruefully. "Don't I know it."

"Are you still seeing your Joe friend?"

"No. That's over and done with."

She stood up to fix her own cup of coffee. "Probably for the best."

"Why?" I snapped. "Because it means the path is free and clear for Jared to waltz back into my life?"

"Slow down," my mother said with steel in her tone. "Don't put words in my mouth, Poppy Esther."

"Fine."

She poured coffee into her cup, then joined me back at the breakfast table. "I saw the way Joe looked at you. You were a sitting duck."

"A sitting duck for what?"

She raised an eyebrow.

"So, what if I was? So, what if Joe and I had a relationship before the divorce was finalized with Jared? Am I supposed to live like a monk for the rest of my life?"

My mother patted my arm, though with comfort rather than condescension. "Two wrongs don't make a right."

My lips thinned. "Does that mean you're going to acknowledge that Jared cheating on me with Leah was actually *wrong*? Please, excuse my shock since you've all but welcomed your philandering son-in-law back into the fold as if this was some simple misunderstanding."

"Do you think you'd be so angry if you weren't still in love with Jared? Despite everything he's done?"

"No!" I shouted, jumping from the table. "I'm not in love with Jared at all! I'm disgusted with him. I'm disgusted with his behavior and with everyone else trying to pass it off as no big deal. All of you act like what he did to me and the kids was nothing!"

I expected my mother to counter my anger with her standard guilt trip. She often used my reactions as an excuse to avoid examining her own behavior. I braced myself for a histrionic display, even welcomed the opportunity to unleash some of my frustration with Jared on my mother. Instead, she remained silent and pensive.

"Mom?" I asked.

"You're right," she said quietly. "You're right, Poppy."

I sat back down, too stunned to speak.

Continuing, she said, "For almost your entire marriage, you made excuses for Jared. When he changed jobs so many times or didn't help with the kids, you always had reasons."

"I was covering for him. I was so ashamed of what our marriage really was. I thought if I pretended he was a model husband, he might actually start acting like one."

My mother nodded in understanding. "So, you were also covering for yourself?"

Tears pricked my eyes. "Do you have any idea how much shame I carried? I felt like such a failure. To the entire world, Jared was this devoted husband and father who never shied away from affection—as long as he had an audience to see it. I let him blame all of his faults on me, but I could never make him happy. Our marriage was a total sham, but who would believe the truth? Jared had his public persona, and I was prob-ably even more at fault than anyone for helping people believe it was true."

"I just want you to be happy, Poppy," my mother said. "I thought finding ways for the two of you to reconcile was what you wanted. I assumed once the anger passed, you'd fall right back into Jared's arms after he left Leah. That changed when I saw you with Joe."

"How so?"

"He looked at you like the kid who won the biggest prize at the carnival. At first, I thought you were just enjoying the attention, but I watched you defend Joe in front of Natalie. I hoped that maybe this was something you needed to get out of your system or would even help Jared come to his senses. Instead, I saw the two of you talking outside, and it looked like a made-for-TV movie."

I blushed. "Nothing happened, Mom. Not even a kiss."

"So, why did it end, Poppy?"

"Joe didn't want Jared's shadow on our relationship. He said he couldn't walk the tightrope of wanting to be more than my friend but not being able to act on it."

My mother looked impressed. "You don't find a lot of men with that kind of integrity."

"No," I said, thinking of Jared, "no, you don't."

CHAPTER 22

Following my heart-to-heart with my mother, I found myself on a ninety minute phone call with Taylor Horner as we hashed through our disagreement from Saturday morning. With tears and apologies on both sides, we waded through our differences, agreed to disagree on others, and ultimately left the conversation at peace with one another. She returned back to Florida on Monday, and I returned to Vincenzo's with her reassurances that she had no right to dictate whom I was allowed to consider a friend.

My favorite R.D. Hampton novel sat perched in one hand while I sipped my cinnamon latte in the other. I had swooned over the hero's heart stopping declarations of love at least twenty times before, but that day, his words felt empty and flat. No longer comforted by my bodice ripping version of *Chicken Soup for the Heart*, I frowned.

"Poppy?"

Glancing up, I found dark eyes peering into mine rather than the pale jade color I secretly longed to see.

"Wh-What are you doing here, Jared?" I slowly set my book down.

"I stopped by your office, talked to some guy named Ted, and he mentioned I might find you here."

I looked over at the wall clock and then back at Jared. "Don't you have to be at work?"

"Took a personal day. I needed to see you."

"Well, here I am," I said, "and, unlike you, I do have to work today. What do you want?"

"Are you free for lunch?"

"I...uh," I stumbled. My brain worked furiously to recall if there were any frozen meals left in the office refrigerator. Eager to change the subject, I noticed something very different about Jared's left hand. "Where did your ring go? You've been acting like getting back together is a sure thing."

He eased into the stuffed velvet chair across from me. "I'm learning not to take anything for granted these days."

I took a sip of coffee and wondered if I needed more caffeine to wake up from this ongoing dream of Jared Levine suddenly behaving like an adult.

"Just lunch, Poppy. No strings or expectations."

Before I could answer, Jessica Goldstein entered the front door. Her eyes lasered in on me and Jared, and they widened in surprise and recognition.

Jared's face registered similar shock.

With panicked, honey brown eyes Jessica said, "Poppy, I—"

I held up a hand to cut her off. "I wondered if your paths had ever crossed since you both have a certain someone in common. Guess I don't have to wonder if Moose ever introduced the two of you."

"You know each other?" Jared asked, his eyes darting between me and Jessica.

She crossed her arms over her chest. "I had no idea Poppy was the horrible ex-wife you painted for me and Patrick."

"Does Poppy know about *your* history?" Jared snapped, sounding much more like the Jared Levine of old. "Pot, meet kettle."

Making my lunch decision far less complicated, I offered a tight smile to both of them, stood up, and left the coffee shop. I ignored the sounds of both Jared and Jessica calling my name before they dissolved into an arguing match over who was responsible for my hasty exit. I marched to the Culver highrise, eager to disappear into my office and under a mountain of work requests.

Not long after, the sound of squeaking loafers and jangling car keys made their way inside of my office. "Poppy, how bad was my blunder?" the mighty Margolin asked with palpable dread. "Are you okay?"

"I take it you figured out the identity of my mystery guest."

"I texted my wife afterward, and she went ballistic. Are you all right? Did I send you into the lion's den?"

I shook my head. "No, the lion's den was Jessica Goldstein waltzing in and she and Jared recognizing one another."

Before thinking better of it, Ted asked, "Did they...?"

"No!" I exclaimed. "Not like that. Jared was friends with Jessica's ex-boyfriend. Apparently, the two cheating husbands went on double dates with their mistresses."

"Wow."

"I may need to find a new place for my morning jolt of caffeine."

Ted nodded. "Since it's nearly your birthday, how about Rebecca and I splurge on a few bags of coffee for you?"

"My birthday?" I repeated with a furrowed brow. "You guys

already bought me a mug and coffee back in March." I held up the well-worn container from my desk.

"Since it's your *birthday*," Ted said with a wink, "Rebecca and I would love to treat you to some coffee you can make at home or in the office."

I smiled. "You guys are awesome. Thank you."

"Does this mean Jessica won't be joining the Culver marketing team?" He didn't hide the hope in his tone.

I shook my head. "It was a dumb idea, and I wish I'd never brought it up."

"Good morning!" Phil sing-songed, poking his head in my office. "Did I hear it was someone's birthday around here?"

I rolled my eyes. "What can I do for you, Phil?"

Blue eyes twinkling, he replied, "I thought I overheard something about getting you some Vincenzo's on the go. Can I contribute to the keep-Poppy-caffeinated-and-happy fund?"

"By all means," I said, having learned long ago to accept a gift when it was offered. "Throw in some biscotti again if you're feeling generous."

Phil and Ted exchanged a glance and laughed.

"I'll do anything to keep you from following Trautweig over to Cooper & Jaye," Phil said. "The pay might be better, but their office faces the freeway. We've got a much better view of Parkview here."

Able to save face during Phil's sales pitch, I put on an impassive smile and said, "Well, I'm sure Joe is looking forward to the opportunity. Anyways, I have lots of work to do, and you both have 'birthday' coffee to buy."

Phil studied me, hardly fooled, but he kept his thoughts behind his lips.

"*Proverbs 10:19*," Ted said, glancing at Phil with humor in his eyes.

"Am I that transparent?" he asked.

Ted chuckled. "It's the lack of words that makes it the most obvious, old man. You used to love watching people squirm."

Relieved to discover this was some inside joke rather than a revelation of my potential relationship with Joe Trautweig, I let the two men banter in front of my desk.

I submerged myself in work, heedless to when Phil and Ted finally removed themselves from my office. I didn't expect Jared to show up at my door for lunch, and thankfully, he failed to appear. Instead, I located my lone, remaining frozen meal, ate at my desk, then took a stroll around Parkview.

I smiled at the latest bridal dresses on display at a swanky boutique.

"Fancy schmancy," I murmured to myself.

"See something you like?" Miss Belle asked, coming up beside me, "or are you tickled by the idea of some girl going down the aisle in that half-a-dress they got in the window there?"

I grinned. "Care to take a walk with me?"

"Bless you, child! I'd love to."

Eager to unburden myself and gain an outsider perspective, I unloaded the weekend's shenanigans to Miss Belle.

"Mm, mm, mm," she clicked, "you can't even write that kind of drama for soap operas."

I exhaled a short laugh. "If only."

"And I don't want to hear you making excuses for Mr. Trautweig either, Poppy Levine. That man had no business playing with your heart."

"He didn't play with my heart, Miss Belle. I respect him for not pushing forward with a physical relationship."

Pursed lips and raised eyebrows said otherwise.

"He was a perfect gentleman."

The eyebrow raised higher.

"What?" I finally asked.

"Just because the man didn't lay hands on you doesn't mean he didn't trifle with your feelings. I'm not saying you're completely innocent either, mind you."

"I would never claim to be. I pushed him pretty hard too."

"Yes, but Joe started it and got you playing with fire thinking about another man while you're still married to the one you've got. You said you wished it was Joe who walked into that coffee shop this morning instead of Jared, right?"

"Yeah," I drawled, not liking the ugly picture before me.

Miss Belle looped her arm through mine. "For everyone's sake, I hope your husband's latest come-to-Jesus is a real one and not more of his usual chicanery. You can't take God's Name on your lips and then not expect some kind of retribution for lying in His Name."

"What do you mean by retribution?"

She met my eyes for a long minute. "Poppy, what would happen if somebody did all kinds of people wrong, but they claimed they were acting on behalf of the President?"

"They'd go to jail."

"So, what do you think happens when they do it in the Name of my Almighty God?"

My eyes grew large. "I guess I never thought of it that way."

"Meaning, you never thought any of this God stuff was real," she astutely noted. "When you really believe in an Almighty God, the idea of using and abusing people in His Name should make you shudder down to your toes."

A chill washed over me along with the weight of her words.

"Whether it's this life or the next, every charlatan and no-good user will get what's coming to them. God isn't mocked, Poppy. People reap what they sow."

"That's scary," I said, wondering when I would receive my own bolt of lightning for my part in the Jared-Joe fiasco.

Miss Belle's stern expression softened as her eyes sparkled like jewels. "Baby, this is why we love and thank God for our beautiful Savior, Jesus Christ."

"Because of abusers?" I asked incredulously. "Are you saying I should be *grateful* there are people like Jared and his disgusting rabbi who abuse people in the name of Jesus?"

Miss Belle shook her head. "No, Poppy Levine. It wasn't just our sin that Jesus took on His back. It was our pain, our grief, and our shame. The cross has the final word. Jesus conquered sin. He conquered death. He conquered every disease, every sickness, every heartache when he hung on that cross for us."

"If that's true, Miss Belle, then why do we still have disease, sickness, and heartache? What good did dying on the cross do when people still choose to be so ugly? What about Jared claiming he follows Jesus and then treating me and the kids so horribly? How am I supposed to love Jesus for making Jared into a crazy man?"

"Jesus dying on the cross was a free gift to us, Poppy. We can accept the gift, or we can choose to reject it. We still have sin in this world because folks reject the light so they can keep living in darkness. The hope we have in Jesus isn't for all our pain and problems to disappear, but knowing He walks with us through our suffering."

"How does the cross conquer anything then?" My old wounds suddenly felt reopened and exposed. "Is Jesus going to make my husband's lying and cheating disappear? Does the cross fix me or my kids? Does the cross fix everything that's been broken?"

"The cross has the final word," Miss Belle repeated. "The hope we have in God makes us stronger than our trials or even the people running amok in our lives. We have joy in the middle of suffering. We feel loved even if we've been abandoned. Knowing that the Son of God laid down his life for us, that He loved us so much He died for us, gives us a joy and a peace this world will never understand. We can be a prisoner in chains but more free in our hearts than the richest man alive. Jesus took every burden on His precious back so we could know the sweet love of God. He lifts the pain of this life and comforts us with hope for the next. That is the true gospel of my Lord, Jesus Christ. We have been saved from our sins, saved from our pain, and set free from thinking we have to fight every battle on our own. Jesus has already won!"

Tears trickled down my cheeks as Miss Belle finished her powerful speech. I felt a deep yearning for something more than tradition or religion, for an elusive peace I saw reflected in this woman's eyes.

"What do I have to do?" I finally said. "How do I get what you have? I can't carry the burden of all of this anymore. I feel like I'm going to fall apart."

The tears on my cheeks now matched the ones coursing down Miss Belle's. With a firm and loving grip, she held my hands and led me in a prayer to confess my own weakness, helplessness, and sin. I repeated her words to declare Jesus Christ of Nazareth as my Lord and Savior. Although I feared the Jewish God of the Torah would strike me down for abandoning my people and my faith, I instead found peace and joy comforting me like a blanket. The weight of anxiety that normally slumped my shoulders lifted free, and I began to laugh and cry with joy.

"Oh, baby!" Miss Belle cooed, pulling me toward her expansive bosom like a mother hen. "Oh, baby!" she murmured into my hair. "Oh, thank you, Jesus!"

"Am I going to hell?" I wondered aloud. "Will I be punished for becoming a Christian and turning my back on Judaism?"

Miss Belle held me back at shoulder length. "Now, what kind of nonsense is that?" she thundered. "Going to hell for accepting God's salvation *from* eternal damnation? No, baby! This has nothing to do with being Jewish or any other race, color, or creed. Jesus died for *all* mankind. This gift is for everybody. You go ask Rebecca or the mighty Margolin if they have any problems loving our Savior and being Jewish at the same time. Jesus came to fulfill those Jewish Scriptures in your Bible. He came as the Messiah for the Jews along with everybody else."

I nodded, too stunned, shocked, and overwhelmed to process anymore.

"You still have my Bible?" she asked, maintaining eye contact with me.

I nodded.

"Then consider it my gift to you, Poppy. You read those words of Jesus, see how much He loves you, loves your kids, even loves that no-good Jared Levine. What God has given you today, nobody can take away. That joy you feel is the joy of your salvation. Hold onto it, and never let it go. When you feel overwhelmed with life and don't know what you're going to do, you remember that the cross has the final word. We all have to answer to Jesus, and He isn't sitting idly by doing nothing while we suffer."

"Thank you," I whispered. "Thank you for everything."

Miss Belle pulled me into another hug, and I wept.

CHAPTER 23

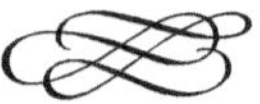

"AM I GOING TO GET STRUCK BY LIGHTNING?" I ASKED as I stepped inside the Margolins' home. Scooting past a hall tree overflowing with dolls and stuffed animals, I smiled as the two littlest Margolins chased each other around the room. Following just behind their high pitched shrieks was a silver haired woman I assumed was Ted's mother.

"Tabby! You give that bear back to your sister right now!" she called, her tone carrying enough gravitas to stop the older girl in her tracks.

The mighty Margolin approached with a boyish grin on his face. "Sixty-eight years-old, and she's still got it. Hey, Mom," he called to her, "I want you to meet somebody."

"Poppy! You made it!" Rebecca squealed from the kitchen. She nearly toppled over her mother-in-law as she raced to wrap me in a bear hug.

"I can tell she's just a little excited," Ted's mother grinned. "I'm Rose Margolin," she said, extending her hand to me.

"Poppy Levine." Meeting her eyes, I saw warmth and took an immediate liking to her.

Ted glanced over to a mantle clock. "You're early, Poppy. Not that we usually start Bible study on time, but we prefer to have the house a little more presentable."

"He means that the girls are already getting ready for bed with Grandma," Rebecca said, eyeing her curly haired progeny. "Everybody usually arrives closer to eight."

"Sorry, I thought things started at seven-thirty," I replied. "I was worried I might be late."

Ted offered a friendly side hug and pat to my arm. "No worries. Just make yourself at home. I'm sure Tabby and Eva will be happy to introduce themselves once they're done gorging themselves on bananas. There are days I wonder if we're raising little girls or little monkeys."

Rebecca rolled her eyes good naturedly. "Daddy's just grumpy because he forgets how messy and chaotic little children can be. The king of commercial insurance wears a very different hat at home. Girls," Rebecca said sternly, her voice carrying as much steel as Ted's mother, "put the bananas down. Time for bed."

Little Eva tossed herself onto the floor and dissolved into a fit of wails and screams worthy of any toddler tantrum.

"No fair," her older sister grumbled, but her resolve melted as Ted walked over to her. "I want to stay up," she whined. "Please, Daddy?"

I snickered quietly at the puppy dog look the mighty Margolin received from his wife's cherubic lookalike. I recognized that same internal battle of "I need to say no, but this kid is so cute" look on Ted's face, and this time, I laughed out loud.

"I'm sure this is all second nature for you," Rebecca said over Eva's petulant screams.

"It's not as cute when they're twelve," I said. "Enjoy it now, guys. Believe it or not, you'll miss this one day."

"Which is why we love having grandchildren," Rose said, scooping the squawking Eva from Rebecca's arms. Making her way toward a hallway, she added over her shoulder, "We get to play with them and then give them back when we're done."

"Gramma! Gramma!" Tabby called, releasing her hand from Ted's and jogging after her grandmother. "Wait for me!"

The strains of running water and little girls giggling quickly carried into the great room, and Rebecca exhaled her own laugh. "God bless your mother, Ted. I don't know what we would do without her."

Placing an arm around his wife, Ted kissed Rebecca's temple. "*You* are an amazing mother, you know that?"

She grinned up at him like a princess in love with her handsome prince, and I felt an ache for my own, girlhood fantasies of marriage. I had not spoken to Jared directly since the coffee shop incident, and I remained unsure how to express what God had done for me.

"Hey!" Rebecca said excitedly, her gaze turning to a handsome, blue-eyed man entering the room along with a curvy redhead. "You guys are early this week."

The man grinned, and I recognized that smile as the same one belonging to his twin sister, Jessica Goldstein.

"Hi, I'm Kyle," he said. He extended his hand out to me. "This is my fiancée, Abigail."

I nodded to the redhead and shook her hand as well. Happily noting the complete dissimilarity in appearance to either Taylor Horner or Rebecca Margolin, it seemed like Kyle Goldstein had indeed moved on with his life.

"This is Poppy," Ted finally said when he noticed my delayed response. "She works at Culver with me."

"Hope you're not stuck with Deondre's old team," Kyle said with a friendly wink.

"Poppy took over Taylor's job," Rebecca added.

"Oh." His smile faded considerably. "I guess you've heard a lot about me...or read?" he asked with a raised eyebrow.

Abigail jumped in with a soothing hand on Kyle's arm. "That's all in the past, babe. You're a new creation, and I hope that nobody would judge you based on your past when all of us have skeletons in our closets." She shot a warning look in her own blue eyes.

"Kyle, I've actually had the opportunity to get to know your sister," I said, more than up to the challenge.

"Jessica?" he asked, bewildered. "How do you know her?"

"Our parents all attend Beth Tefillah. It was one of the first things Jessica and I talked about when we met at Vincenzo's."

"How is she doing?" he asked, hungry for information. "Did she seem well? Is she still dating that guy from work?"

"Kyle, how long has it been since you've spoken to your sister? She and Patrick broke up a year and a half ago."

"Wow, she confided in you that much?" Abigail blurted out. "She barely talks to Kyle."

"Well, in the interest of allaying concerns you have about me judging Kyle's skeletons, Jessica and Patrick went on double dates with my husband and his own mistress."

Both Kyle and Abigail's eyes widened further.

"So yeah," I said with a punch of fake sunshine, "you have nothing to worry about with regards to me."

With that, I walked into the kitchen and brushed fresh tears from my cheeks.

I sensed Rebecca trailing after me before she even spoke.

"Your personal life isn't any of their business, Poppy. Abigail is just really protective of Kyle. You didn't have to do that."

"Do what? Set their minds at ease that I wouldn't mention all of Kyle's past indiscretions that you and Taylor laid out in your books?"

Rebecca winced. "We did change his name."

"Anybody who knows Kyle in real life knows that it's him. The twin sister reference is just in case anybody was really unsure that it was *Kyle* Goldstein and not Chad or Drew or Scott Goldstein instead."

"What's really going on? Obviously, you're upset about something."

"I don't know," I said bleakly. "Maybe I just got triggered hearing Abigail use the phrase, 'judging Kyle based on his past.' It was one of Jared's favorite accusations against me."

"Oh, I see. My father used that line on me all the time too. My whole family did. It was the fastest way to trivialize my feelings and their abuse toward me. Their version of forgiveness meant *carte blanche* ability to treat me like garbage and then shame me for doing anything other than roll over for more."

"Do you ever wonder if all of these people attend the same narcissistic charm school?" I asked. "The behavior is so scarily similar."

"Personally, I think it's all the same demon at work," she said without hesitation.

"Demon?" I croaked. "Look, the Jesus shtick was enough of a hurdle to overcome. Don't turn this into some supernatural, young adult novel."

"What about what happened with Jared? Do you think he just made up that demonic snake in his apartment?"

"It wouldn't be the first lie he's told me. Look, all of the spiritual hocus pocus just makes me uncomfortable. Jews don't believe in Satan."

Rebecca offered a sympathetic smile rather than the condescension I might expect from the man in question. "Even though I discovered my Jewish heritage later in life, Ted grew up with it. We've both wrestled with and prayed against all kinds of demons. You know my story," she said, "the stuff I put in the book and then everything else I've told you on top of that. We do have a real enemy out there, and he has his own fallen angels. We're in a war for eternity, Poppy, and it's our souls that are at stake."

"I...I just don't like talking about it," I said, shifting away from her.

Rebecca nodded. "I get it. It's a lot to take in. Jesus told His disciples not to rejoice over the demons they cast out, but that their names are written in the Book of Life. There are plenty of people, and even full-time ministries, who have gone off the rails with demon obsession and constantly searching out Satan."

I shuddered. "Why would you even want to do that? That stuff scares the snot out of me. I can't watch the movie trailers for half of the films they make nowadays."

"People get enamored with signs and wonders, of worshiping the miracles rather than God. Jesus talks about it in *Matthew 25*, the people who claim they've cast out demons in God's Name and performed all of these miraculous things, yet Jesus says He never knew them."

"What do you mean? How could you do those things without God?"

Rebecca's smile grew pained. "I saw a lot of phony baloney nonsense at my father's church and later at SBC. Scarier still, I do believe there are people performing false miracles or using demonic power while pretending it's Jesus."

"Why would somebody do that?"

Rebecca rubbed her fingers together in the universal sign for *money*.

"Really?" I gaped.

"How do you think my father got his millions?" Rebecca said with obvious revulsion. "Take a look at some of these preachers out there telling their gullible followers that God wants them to give money so they can buy their own private airplane 'for ministry,' let alone a second or third one."

"That's disgusting."

"I know!" she said, throwing her hands in the air. "Why do you think I couldn't stand living in the Ivy Palace? I knew what horrible people my parents were behind the scenes. At that, I had no idea about so many other things until I saw Bud Riley's written confession."

I tsked. "How did he manage to stay loyal to your father knowing all of their dirty secrets?"

"My father had plenty of leverage on him, and Bud got in so deep, he knew he'd wind up going down with my father if he ever exposed him. He believed his stomach cancer was punishment for all he helped my father cover up."

"Have you tried reaching out to Bud's ex-wife or kids?" I asked.

Rebecca shook her head. "I don't really see a need to do it. Technically, the one related to them is Ada, not me, but my sister is in complete denial about everything."

"Is she still living at your parents' home?"

"No, my mother kicked her out after she was released from jail and saw what my sister had done to the place."

"Oh, really?" I smirked. "You mean your deadbeat sister didn't keep the palace in tip top shape?"

Rebecca let loose her room-dazzling smile. "For once, the blame couldn't fall on my shoulders. My aunt tries to be sensitive about sharing too much with me, but her imitation of my mother squawking about my sister ransacking the place was worth it."

"Ransacking? Did she hock their stuff?"

"And then some. Apparently, she cleaned the place out. My sister hasn't worked a day in her life and has always mooched off of a girlfriend or my parents. Much to Ada's surprise, the bills didn't pay themselves. She sold off most of my parents' artwork and furniture, and not nearly for what they're actually worth."

"Wow."

Rebecca shrugged. "It's hard to feel bad for my mother since she and my father built that entire lifestyle on deceiving and manipulating their congregants."

"Sounds like instant karma."

"Justice," she corrected. "Divine justice."

"So, what happens now?" I asked.

"The house is already under contract to be sold. My mother has a mountain of legal fees, and all of her assets were frozen when she and my father were arrested. The government snatched up most of it on various tax evasion and fraud charges."

"Do you plan to contact her?"

"I don't think so. Aunt Eleanor surprised me when she refused to let my mother stay with her and my Uncle Barry. She said my mother needs to learn to stand on her own two feet, and she's tired of enabling her."

Before I could respond, Ted poked his head into the kitchen area. "If you ladies are done discussing all of the recent, Ivy family shenanigans, we're about to start Bible study."

"Come on," Rebecca said, putting her arm around me. "Time to get into God's Word."

CHAPTER 24

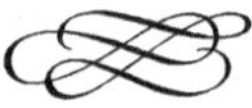

When I arrived home three hours later, I found the kitchen overhead light on and an unexpected visitor at my breakfast table. I stopped short, not sure if my eyes deceived me.

Jared looked me up and down. "Were you on a date? It's almost eleven o'clock."

"Why are you here?" I retorted, tossing my purse on the counter.

"I took the kids out to dinner, and then we came back here to watch a movie. Do you have a problem with that?"

"Why would I?"

"Do you have to answer all of my questions with your own question?" His eyes held humor rather than irritation.

I released the pent up breath I didn't realize I was holding. "What do you want? Obviously, you were waiting up for me. Was it to make sure I didn't bring home a new stepfather?"

The wounded look on Jared's face was immediate. So was

the nudge in my gut that my "joke" crossed the line from humor into a deliberate sucker punch.

"Sorry," I said.

Jared acknowledged my apology with a jerk of the chin. "I haven't seen you since you walked out of the coffee shop, and I want to explain what happened."

I held up a hand to stop the story forming on his lips. "I already know about Jessica Goldstein's past indiscretions. It's too late to drive a wedge in that friendship hoping she doesn't share your dirty secrets."

"Dirty secrets?"

"Yeah, all of the lies you spewed to her and Patrick so you could justify your relationship with Leah. Jessica made it a point to track me down and apologize for her part in everything."

"Oh."

"You painted quite a picture, Jared. It's amazing that you didn't change my name to Medusa to fit the description."

"Poppy, can we talk? Please?"

"About what?" I folded my arms across my chest.

He gestured for me to join him at the table, but I shook my head. He sighed and rubbed the back of his neck. "I want to fix our marriage."

"I've heard all of this already."

He met my eyes and held them for a long minute. "Let me rephrase. I want to fix our marriage by fixing myself, and I need your help to do that."

I felt an immediate roll of anxiety swell from my stomach up into my shoulders. "What do you mean?

"I need you to be honest with me about what I need to change. I have a few ideas, but there's probably a lot more that I can't see. I know I've blamed you for a lot of my issues, and I'm sorry."

I inhaled and exhaled, my chest tight. "I don't really know what to tell you, Jared. The root of almost all of the issues in our marriage came from your selfishness. I could list out specific things like taking care of the kids, cleaning up after yourself, or lack of appreciation, but it all just boils down to you being so self-absorbed that nobody else mattered."

"What else?" he asked in a pained voice. "What else do I need to fix?"

I raised an eyebrow. "Where are you going with all of this?"

He looked up again, surprising me with a sheen of moisture in his eyes. "God's been showing me how I've hurt the kids and how I've hurt you. He showed me my own behavior through your eyes."

"Empathy," I breathed.

"You didn't deserve what I did to you, and I don't know how to ever make it right. How do I atone for everything I stole from you and from our kids?"

"And Leah," I said, though it pained me to mention her name.

"Leah too," Jared added easily. "I just have so much sorrow and regret for what I've done to all of you. And I," his voice broke, "I'm amazed that God can forgive me."

My own throat closed as tears welled in my eyes. Thinking back to that evening's Bible study about the parable of the wicked servant, I struggled to release the words I knew I needed to speak aloud.

"I forgive you, Jared," I choked out. When his startled gaze came flying up to meet mine, I repeated more clearly, "I forgive you."

"How?" he asked. "After everything I've done?"

I swallowed back a lump of emotion and forced the words past my lips. "I forgive you because I'm tired of being eaten up with bitterness and anger. I forgive you because I'm tired of crying myself to sleep at night. I forgive you because…"

"Because you still love me?" he prodded gently.

I shook my head. "Because I know that Jesus has forgiven me of so much more."

Jared's face went white as his eyes widened. "What did you just say?"

"You heard me," I snapped, wiping tears from my eyes.

"When?"

"Two weeks ago."

His eyes widened further. "Why didn't you tell me?"

"I didn't want to. I didn't want you using it as some way to weasel back into my life."

"I understand why you would feel that way."

"Good, because it doesn't change anything between you and me." Adding steel to my tone, I said, "I've already been warned about the 'submissive wives' Bible verses you might try to throw at me. You're not the only one who's picked up a Bible and read some of it."

Surprise and delight took over his face rather than offense. "Really?"

"Yes, *really*," I said, annoyed.

Jared rose to his feet. "Will you pray with me? This could be the beginning of so many wonderful things!" He reached for my hands.

I took a step backwards. "I don't want physical contact with you, and I don't want you taking advantage of me."

"It's *prayer*, Poppy."

Reminded instantly of my brief time with Joe Trautweig, I pursed my lips. "The answer is no. I don't trust you, I have no reason to trust you, and I would be a fool to do it now." I held up a hand, anticipating his next counterpoint. "And spare me the 'I've changed,' song and dance number. I've heard it all before."

He frowned. "I thought you said you forgive me."

"I do, but forgiving you is not the same thing as welcoming you back into my life with open arms. I'm tired of spoon feeding all of the ways you've hurt and abused me over the years. We've spent hours arguing about so many issues, and it's insulting that you would need me to remind you what they are. If you still have zero insight into your own behavior, let alone remorse, there is nothing I can do for you. That's something you need to take up with God, not with me."

"I didn't say I was unaware of what I've done, Poppy. I just admitted a bunch of things. I simply asked if there was anything I missed."

"Tell you what," I said, retreating further behind the barbed wire fence around my heart, "when I hear you start owning your behavior in specifics, not just sweeping generalizations like, 'I know I've been selfish' or 'I know I've hurt you and the kids,' then we can revisit the idea of praying together. You've fed me this contrite routine too many times for me to take it seriously."

"But you said you forgive me."

"It's what I said, Jared. It doesn't mean the bill gets wiped clean, and you don't have to face what you've done. There's a verse Rebecca showed me from *1 John* tonight, that we have to confess our sins in order to be forgiven by God. If we go around pretending we've done nothing wrong, then we're just a liar," I said pointedly.

"I *have* confessed what I've done. I apologized to you that night at the gas station for how I've hurt you and the kids. I apologized for stringing you along."

"You're right, you did. But it's not enough."

"What do you want from me?" he asked, exasperated. "Blood?"

I maintained my calm and studied him. I wasn't convinced the *real* Jared Levine wouldn't make an appearance. "As far as what happened in our marriage, I want you to stop making it my responsibility to tell you what you did wrong instead of *your* responsibility to do some serious soul searching and figure that out on your own. I haven't been a Christian for a very long, but I know when God tells me how I've messed up, it's never in generalities. He shows me exactly what I did."

Jared's frown became a thin line.

"So, if you want to try to convince me that you're serious about fixing our marriage, let alone yourself, then I want to see evidence of your walk with Christ. I'm done with the super spiritual lip service."

"When did you get so comfortable with saying, 'Christ' and 'Christian?'" he asked with a note of disdain. "You do know you don't have to stop being Jewish to believe in Jesus, right?"

"Nitpicking how I express my faith doesn't erase the work you need to do, and don't try changing the subject. I'm not hung up on this *Jewish identity* mishigas like you are. I grew up Jewish, and our kids will too. I don't have anything to prove to anyone. Pointing out some non-existent flaw of mine won't take the heat off yourself. All it shows me is that nothing has really changed, no matter what you say to the contrary."

"I'm not trying to 'take the heat off' myself, Poppy. I'm genuinely concerned. How do you think you'll reach any unsaved Jewish people if you don't make an effort to use words that aren't so offensive? There's still a lot you need to learn."

"By sharing with them what God did for me and how He's changing my life for the better. Nobody is going to get saved because you say *Yeshua* instead of Jesus. It was a sixty-four-year-old black woman who led me to Christ. I needed to know God was bigger than my problems, that He loves me, and that He's in control. Anything else is just window dressing. You can wear all the *tzitzit* you want," I said, gesturing to the traditional, Jewish fringes hanging from Jared's waist, "but your hypocrisy always spoke so much louder than any of this Jewish identity stuff you're so enamored with."

He swallowed back words his eyes burned to speak. Surprised at his self control, I threw him a bone.

"Look, I'm still figuring things out, but I know what's real and what works. The Margolins are just as Jewish as they are Christian, but they're not ostentatious with it. They just are who they are, no apologies, no fuss."

Jared nodded slowly. "I see."

"Neither of us were very religious growing up. All of the Jewish trappings in the world aren't going to make us more or less holy to God. Does your Messianic synagogue teach something different?"

"We're Jewish, Poppy. God's called us to keep the Torah. We're not supposed to assimilate. I can show you Bible verses in both the Old and New Testament about it."

I raised an eyebrow. "Being Jewish, didn't keep you from acting like a selfish jerk, even after you claimed you saw the light. Yeah, you left Leah, but you still treated me horribly and used the kids as pawns. I hadn't seen any real changes in you until you said you had that snake experience in your apartment. That's when I saw a difference beyond using the Bible as a way to manipulate me."

Jared hesitated, then buried his head in his hands. "I'm so confused," he moaned.

My heart stirred with both compassion and trepidation.

Inching closer to the table and away from my fears, I said, "What are you confused about?"

He looked at me with soulful eyes. "I just don't know what's true and what isn't anymore. Some of the things Rabbi Lebow said are legitimate."

"But..." I filled in, seeing the word on Jared's lips.

A small smile appeared on his mouth, seeing how easily I'd read his thoughts. "But, every accusation he made about mainstream Christians or Jews also happens in that synagogue. He talks about Jewish people worshiping tradition, but Beth Shalom goes out of their way to mimic all of those same traditions. He talks about Christians and their manmade holidays, but then ignores how the actual story of Chanukah has nothing to do with oil burning for eight days, for example."

"What?" I said, stunned.

"I've read the entire story in *1 Maccabees*. There's no mention of oil burning at all. It talks about the defeat of Antiochus and the rededication of the temple, even an eight day feast with golden decorations, but no miraculous oil."

"So, why do we have a menorah? Why have we taught this to our own kids?"

Jared grimaced. "Because, some rabbi way back when decided that, 'Jews are against war,' and that we should focus on the 'spiritual' aspects of Chanukah instead."

"Meaning what?"

"Meaning that instead of talking about the violence of war, they made up a miracle about eight-day oil so people would focus on God in a more benevolent way, I guess."

"Wow," I breathed.

"When I told Rabbi Lebow, he gave me this condescending look and said we can't go changing traditions willy-nilly. He said it would offend Jewish people in the synagogue and any who would come to visit."

"So, your rabbi is more concerned with maintaining status quo than with the truth?"

"As I've come to learn," Jared said wearily. "It bothered me back then, especially when he brought up the importance of Jewish traditions the following week. He acts like Beth Shalom has the perfect marriage of Christianity and Judaism."

"Ah," I said, recalling Rebecca's stories of Jessica's ex-fiancé, Nathan Fein, and the same sales pitch he'd given her about the synagogue. I took another step forward and eventually sat down next to Jared at the table.

He held my gaze before sighing and slumping back in his chair.

"What?" I asked.

"I feel like I'm really seeing you for the first time."

"What do you mean?"

"You've always been beautiful, Poppy—no matter what horrible things I've said about your looks. None of that was true, by the way. You care about people, and I know I put you and the kids through hell long before I got together with Leah. You put up with more from me than any other person would, and I resented you for calling me on it. I was a selfish monster."

My jaw fell open.

"I treated all of you like pests instead of falling down in gratitude that you loved me despite myself." He grabbed my hands fervently into his own. "It's like I'm seeing this montage of all the times I took my frustration out on you or the kids or avoided all of you so I wouldn't have to deal with the reality of being a father—or any kind of a husband."

"Yes," I whispered.

Voice breaking, he said, "I have no idea how you can forgive me, how I could ever earn back your trust or be worthy of you or the kids, but when you told me you forgave me, something changed. It was like I could finally see everything. All of the ways I destroyed our family. Me. I did that. Nobody else." With his last confession, Jared began to sob. Unable to hold back my own watershed of tears, I cried with him.

CHAPTER 25

I DON'T KNOW WHEN OR HOW I WOUND UP IN JARED'S arms, only that we found comfort in an embrace of condolence rather than romance. Jared wept into my shoulder, and I stroked his back maternally. Eventually, his cries subsided, and he reached out to hold my face in his palms. His thumbs caressed my cheeks.

"I can't believe how blind I was. You're so beautiful it makes my heart hurt."

I smiled back at him. "Thanks."

"How...how do I make this right?"

"You can't," I said, my expression sobering. "You can't fix what's been broken."

"So, what do we do?"

Peeling Jared's hands from me, I placed them gently on the table. The air was growing thick with the way he looked at me and my heart's deepest longing to believe it was real. There was too much history to deny the desire that still simmered between us. Instead, I uttered words I never thought I'd say. "We start over."

"How?"

I shrugged and exhaled a deep breath. "Assuming you don't pull a 180 on me and pretend this conversation never happened, I guess we go forward."

Jared made a face, then relaxed as he acknowledged the truth of my words. "I know I've done that to you a few times."

I nearly balked at the difference between "a few" and the hundreds of instances that came to mind, but I held my tongue.

"I have to make this work," he said.

"And I've already told you that you can't. Not on your own anyway."

"With God, all things are possible," he quoted from Scripture.

"Do you even believe what you're saying, Jared?"

"Of course, I do! Why would you even ask me that?"

"You just said *I* have to make this work. God making 'all things possible' doesn't mean you just do whatever you think is best, and then God blesses it. That's no different than how you handled everything when we were married. Only now, you're hiding behind Jesus to justify the same selfish behavior."

"Selfish?" he demanded, his voice rising. "I'm trying to change!"

"In your own power, however you see fit," I argued. "You want God to bless you, but you're not willing to ask the tough questions of what you're doing wrong and what He actually wants you to do instead."

His tone hardened. "What suddenly makes you such an expert on God? You didn't believe in any of this a month ago."

"You know you're just proving my point, right? This is

exactly what you used to do, Jared. I tell you something you don't want to hear, and you pout like a child. Even Maddie does a better job of dealing with constructive criticism and correction."

He raked a hand through his hair. After a long moment and a heavy sigh, he met my eyes. "No matter what you think, I *have* missed your spunk."

I raised an eyebrow.

"You were the only person I knew who would tell me the truth."

"And you hated me for it."

"And I hated you for it," he admitted.

"I'm wondering if you still do," I said candidly. "Your knee jerk response is to shift blame back on me and shoot the messenger instead of taking responsibility. All that says is that you may want to change, but you're not ready to do it."

"I *am* ready," he insisted. "I want this for us and for our kids. I want to love all of you the way you deserve. Especially you, Poppy."

I leaned back in my chair, creating more physical distance. Joe's rejection and Jared's repentance were too much for my battered heart. The yearning to be seen and cherished along with Jared's impassioned pleas to do just that made me ripe for the plucking. As the realization struck, peace washed over me. I was no longer the naïve sixteen year-old dazzled by Jared Levine's attention. I was his much maligned, beleaguered wife who would no longer settle for empty promises and bread crumbs of effort.

"Jared, I tried to help you for twenty years, and it blew up in my face. I appreciate you asking for input, but I don't think I'm the person to help you deal with your demons. There's too much hurt on both sides. Having sexual chemistry doesn't make up for everything that's been lacking in our relationship."

"So, what do we do?" he asked. "How do we heal? How do we go forward, like you said? That's what you want, isn't it?"

"I'm not sure what I want, to be honest. As far as rebuilding trust, we start from the bottom and work on listening to each other instead of reverting into our old patterns. If for nothing else, then so that we can co-parent peacefully. We get into counseling. We pray."

"Together?" he asked hopefully.

I shook my head. "Not yet. I'm still figuring things out, and prayer is too intimate." I pushed away thoughts of Joe and the remembered feeling of my hands in his. It felt wrong to think about another man while discussing the potential for reconciliation with my ex-husband. Miss Belle's admonition rang in my ears.

Breaking through my thoughts, Jared looked at me with such warmth that my cheeks reddened and thoughts of Joe dissolved back into memory.

"When did you get to be so wise?" he murmured.

"Life. Experience. Pain."

The dreamy expression left his face. "And I'm the cause of all of it."

Surprising both of us, I laughed. "Don't give yourself too much credit. You contributed plenty, but I'm not without my faults either. We both know I have a temper, a strong tendency for sarcasm, and I wasn't always kind in how I talked to you. I was angry, and rightfully so," I added, "but that doesn't mean I didn't hurt you too."

"Wow."

I offered a half smile. "I'm not letting you off the hook, by the way. Owning my choices doesn't exonerate you from yours. It works both ways. We're both responsible for our own feelings and how we choose to deal with our pain."

He nodded. "I won't argue that, Poppy. I know I hurt you too."

"You did," I said. "You also used my anger and my reactions to justify your behavior. Out of one side of your mouth, you blamed me for whatever stupid or selfish choice you made. Out of the other side, you didn't do anything wrong, I was just over-reacting to 'no big deal,' and then overreacting yet again by being upset at you for not taking responsibility. It's called *gaslighting,* and it was probably one of your favorite tricks to use against me."

Jared's mouth flattened into a thin line. "Am I supposed to think you were right about everything, and I was just always wrong?"

I inhaled a deep breath, not sure if Jared was baiting me into an argument that proved my point or if he sincerely believed his own baloney.

Silently praying, I responded by speaking the words I heard as if directly uttered from heaven. "Why keep score over who's right and how many times? What matters is that I was hurt by something you did. Even if you think I'm being completely ridiculous—and yes, you're free to think and feel however you want—when our kids have a meltdown over something silly, our go-to response isn't arguing with them about their feelings. We don't berate them for it or act like they need our permission to have an opinion."

Jared cocked his head to the side, considering my words.

Pressing on, I said, "You used to treat my feelings and my pain like they were nothing, like you got to judge what I was allowed to feel. It was condescending and controlling and exactly why I got so angry with you. My role as the unap-peasable, dragon wife didn't happen in a vacuum."

Jared's mouth tightened.

"I'm not saying I'm completely innocent, for the record. I'm the one who is ultimately responsible for how I respond to you. Regardless, you don't get to decide how much your behavior is allowed to hurt or affect me. Do you remember how Natalie used to interpret any little thing we said to her as the worst kind of criticism?"

"I remember." Softly mimicking Natalie's whining tones of younger years, he said, "You just don't want me to have anything nice...ever!"

I chuckled. "Did we tell Natalie that she wasn't allowed to feel that way, even if we knew she was being melodramatic?"

"You never did," Jared admitted. "I argued with her."

"And what did that accomplish?"

"Nothing. It just got uglier, and she got more upset."

I watched and waited for the proverbial light bulb to go off above Jared's head. When that effort began to prove futile, I spoke up instead. "I'm just asking for the same consideration and patience you would show our kids, especially when you think I'm wrong."

"Oh," he drawled, "I see."

"Do you?"

"I think I'm beginning to, yeah."

"Jared, we've been mad at each other for a long time. We have almost two decades of stored up resentment and hurt. I may not agree with why you have offenses against me, or vice versa, but arguing over whether or not you have the right to feel them doesn't work. We can keep fighting about who was wrong, or we go forward. Somehow, we have to forgive each other, let go of the past, and work on building something new."

His dark eyes dove deep into mine. "Is that what you really want, Poppy? Do you want to make our marriage work?" Bated breath expanded his chest, and I was immediately reminded of how much I used to love curling up against it. I glanced away, frustrated and confused by the betrayal of my own emotions.

Taking my rose-colored memories captive, I forced myself to recall the pain of our marriage instead. "Outside of the bedroom, our marriage never worked. It was doomed before it got started. But," I said, as he started to interrupt, "we can try to create something *new* as long as both of us are willing to work at it. We're never going to repair a broken vase that's been shattered into powder."

"Shattered into powder," he repeated. "You always did have a way with words."

I shrugged with a mischievous grin. "Eh, maybe I'll write a book one day. Seems to be a popular hobby for the marketing department at Culver."

"Are you going to change my name?" he teased with dimpled cheeks.

"Let's see how our story ends, and I'll let you know." My own smile widened as the atmosphere in the room felt brighter.

"Mommy? Daddy?" Maddie toddled into the kitchen and covered her eyes from the overhead light. "What are you guys doing?"

"Just talking," Jared said, opening his arms so Maddie could tuck her face against his heart. She wrapped her arms around his waist.

My heart warmed and tightened, remembering a younger Natalie doing the same thing.

"Is Daddy staying here?" Maddie asked.

Jared glanced at me and then back at our daughter. "Not tonight, sweetheart. Maybe another time."

"I asked God to make you guys love each other again. Did it work?"

Tears burned my eyes as Jared's gaze seared into mine.

"From the mouths of babes," he whispered with a smile, stroking her hair.

Needing a reprieve, I stood up and escorted Madison back to bed. I took a few extra minutes to kiss her forehead and soothe her, reminding myself that no matter how horrible my marriage had been, I would always be grateful for the three, beautiful children that same marriage had also created.

When I returned to the kitchen, Jared was standing by the back door.

"Heading out?" I asked.

He nodded. "It's almost one. I have to go to work tomorrow, and so do you."

"Bring on the Vincenzo's," I deadpanned, stopping short as I realized Jared may interpret that as an invitation.

"So, do you really like that place?"

"Yeah," I said warily. "Why?"

Jared glanced over to the coffee maker with two bags of Vincenzo's grounds resting against it. "Just a question, Poppy. Don't assume the worst."

"I'm not assuming anything," I snapped but immediately regretted my harsh tone. "I'm just tired. This has been a lot to take in."

He closed his eyes and reopened them. "You have no idea how badly I want to kiss you. And not what I did to you two months ago."

"I don't think that's a good idea."

"I agree," he surprised me by saying, "but I thought you should know that I only have eyes for one woman."

"What happened to looking for love in all the wrong places?" I asked, reminding Jared of his senior yearbook quote.

He blew a raspberry. "I was young, stupid, and had no idea what *love* was."

"And you do now?"

"I'm learning," he admitted, "and we both know I have a long way to go."

Dismayed by how easily my heart shed free of its barbed wire fence, I took a step away. His gaze felt like a caress, and I was not immune to its effect on me.

"Poppy, what's wrong?"

"It's just a lot, like I said."

Taking a risk, he stepped toward me, cupped my cheeks, and kissed my forehead. Rather than pulling away from him, I leaned in and allowed myself a brief moment of weakness. I let my forehead rest against his lips and then resisted the urge to tilt up my mouth for more.

"I'm so sorry," he whispered.

"I don't know how this is possible," I murmured. "It shouldn't be possible at all. I was ready to hate you for the rest of my life." With that last confession, I pulled away from him, frustrated at how three years of celibacy, hatred, and bitterness had been so easily erased. "If you think you're going to white-wash everything that's happened by getting into my pants, you're wrong. That's exactly how we started this mess in the first place. I won't stop fighting the lust."

"I want a real marriage, Poppy. I want our kids to have better than what I had with my parents. I hated my dad for leaving my mom, and I hated my mom for marrying Gary. I hate myself for doing the same thing to our kids."

I knew how much that admission cost him. I searched his eyes for any shred of deception or mockery.

"I want this to work," he said again. "For the kids, obviously, but even more for us. I want us to grow old together and to love each other more every day."

"That was all I ever wanted," I whispered.

Jared smiled tenderly and turned toward the door to let himself out. "Good night."

His self-restraint proved the undoing of my own. Impulsively, I grabbed onto his arm and pressed a quick kiss to his cheek. "Drive safely."

With a smile more dazzling than any I had ever seen, he said, "I love you," squeezed my hand, and then exited the room.

CHAPTER 26

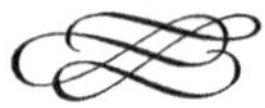

"I wasn't sure I'd see you back so soon," Jessica Goldstein said, joining me in our usual, stuffed chair corner of Vincenzo's. She gave me a brief, once over. "You look different."

I touched my face. "Do I?"

"Yeah," she said. "You look happy."

"I don't know if *happy* is the right word. Maybe hopeful, I guess."

"I assume that means things are going well with you and your friend from work," she said with a grin. "He's really handsome!"

I shook my head. "That's been over for a few weeks. Not that it ever really got started."

She seemed both shocked and disappointed. "Are you sure? I saw the way he looked at you, Poppy."

I shrugged and took a deep sip of my Italian roast. "Looking at me isn't the same thing as a relationship, no matter how much Joe or I wanted it at the time."

"Well, if it's not Joe, then who's your mystery man?"

Not sure how Jessica would receive the news, I muttered, "I think Jared and I are going to try to make things work."

She froze, took another sip of coffee, then seemed to contemplate my words. "Are you sure you know what you're doing?"

"No!" I laughed. "I'm not sure at all."

Jessica smiled on my behalf, but it didn't reach her eyes. "It's hard picturing you and Jared together after seeing him with Leah. He also said some pretty horrible things about you."

"I haven't forgotten. You've already told me the worst of it, and Jared knows his secrets aren't secret anymore."

"So, what changed?"

"I think we both did. God's been working on each of us."

"God?" she repeated in disbelief. Her honey brown eyes grew wide as realization dawned. "You became one of those Jesus weirdos, didn't you?"

"Not exactly," I said, steeling myself with more caffeine. "I got to my breaking point and had nothing left to lose. I don't know if Rebecca ever mentioned Miss Belle in our office, but she's the one who led me to Christ."

"Led you to Christ? What does that even mean?"

I smiled, perfectly understanding Jessica's confusion. "Miss Belle talked about the power of what Jesus did on the cross. Not just about Him dying for my sins, but how He took my shame and the weight of the burdens I'd been carrying."

"So, Jesus is a crutch," she said dismissively.

"He's my everything!" Tears of gratitude sprang to my eyes. "Jessica, I was so lost. When I prayed with Miss Belle, I had peace for the first time in my life. God wasn't just some abstract concept anymore. I felt hope in something bigger than me or my problems."

"My brother said something like that."

"He misses you," I said, watching her expression turn to shock. "I met him and his fiancée at the Margolins' house last night."

"How did he seem?"

"He looked happy. He cares about you."

"What did you tell him about me?"

"Not much. He was stunned that I knew you, and he asked how you were doing."

She nodded slowly. "It's hard, Poppy. After Kyle got into all of this Jesus shtick, he preached to me about adultery and fornication. This is the same guy who slept his way through half of my friend list on social media."

I winced.

"And now you're one of them. Just like Rebecca, Taylor, and all of the other loony Jews."

"So, what if I am?" I asked, unwilling to let Jessica's pain push me away. "I didn't get a lobotomy three weeks ago. I'm still the same person...only better."

"Well, what about Jared? Did you sabotage a potential relationship with that Joe guy because you suddenly got Jesus?"

I shook my head. "Calling off the relationship was Joe's idea, not mine. I had no plans for reconciliation when Joe ended things."

"You never told me what happened," she said. At my hesitation to respond, she added, "Not that it's any of my business anyway. I was just curious."

I sighed. "I didn't want to do to my kids what Jared and Leah have already done. Neither did Joe. On paper, I am still married to Jared. Joe didn't feel right starting a relationship before the divorce was finalized. Spending time together was just throwing us in the path of temptation and potential disaster. I was devastated when Joe ended our friendship, but I respect him even more now because of it."

"That took a lot of guts. For both of you." Silence stretched as Jessica seemed lost in thought. I realized she was probably thinking about Patrick and the very different decision they two of them had made.

Determined to buoy up the heavy turn of our conversation, I said, "I did encourage Joe to ask you out, by the way."

"Oh really?" Her face brightened, and she smiled prettily. "What did he say?"

I winked back at her. "You never know."

Her smile grew, turning a lovely face even lovelier. "He seems like a nice guy."

"He is," I said, "but Joe's got his own skeletons and issues just like anybody else. If you run into old green eyes one of these days, you have my blessing."

"Good to know." The corners of her mouth remained upturned as she finished the remains of her coffee.

Our conversation grew lighter and more superficial, and I eventually took my leave. Strolling leisurely to the Culver high-rise, I savored the sights, sounds, and blessing of working uptown. It was a gulp of air before submerging under waves of work emails and deadlines.

"Thank you," I breathed heavenward. "Thank you for my job, the fall weather, and an opportunity to share with Jessica about what You've done for me."

Not minding where I was going, I managed to bump right into the pair of green eyes I'd just offered up to my coffee buddy.

"Poppy!" Joe exclaimed.

I averted my gaze immediately. I felt sheepish over my

behavior during our fight, moreover, like an eternity of events had transpired since the last time we spoke.

"How are you?" he asked.

I inhaled a fortifying breath before I dared a glance above his suit lapels. Though I still found Joe's eyes beautiful, they no longer pulled me in beyond admiration of God's handiwork in designing them.

He cocked an eyebrow, noticing the change of atmosphere, or rather, the lack of mutual longing. "You got back together with him," he suddenly said, searching my face for confirmation.

My mouth opened and shut, stunned at his perceptiveness.

"When?" he choked.

Finding my own voice, I said, "Jared and I aren't officially anything right now. We're working toward the possibility of reconciliation, but we have a long way to go."

"But the divorce is off?"

I nodded. "For now anyway."

"I see."

"Joe, a lot has happened since the last time we saw each other. Feels like a lifetime."

"I don't want to flatter myself, but I hope you didn't go running back to Jared because of me." His green eyes held sincere distress on my behalf. "He didn't treat you right. Please, don't settle for less than what you deserve."

Surprised by Joe's passionate plea, I fought back against so many thoughts of "what if" with regards to our brief flirtation. Remembering instead the peace of God, the Bible verses I'd read just that morning about the Lord's faithfulness through temptation, I inhaled and exhaled slowly. I met Joe's eyes and smiled, hoping to reassure him.

"A lot has changed in the past few weeks," I began again.

He looked me over. "You seem more settled since the last time I saw you. Is that Jared's doing?" Unable to hide the edge in his voice, he added, "Everything's kosher when you're still technically married, right?"

Ignoring the insinuation that I'd fallen back into my ex-husband's arms as well as his bed, I replied, "Not Jared. Jesus."

"Jesus?" he repeated, eyes widening.

My mouth curved into a beautiful smile. "Yes. Miss Belle shared the gospel with me. She talked about the power of the cross and what Jesus did for me. She made it real, and I couldn't deny how much I needed God anymore."

"Why was this different than all the times Rebecca or Ted talked to you about it?"

"Because I saw how much I needed God to fix what I couldn't. Because I had made such a mess of things with you, with my marriage, and with my life. Because I needed to hear that Jesus loves me, and I don't have to spend the rest of my life burdened by shame and regret over all the mistakes I've made. I wanted to be free and to have peace."

"And do you have that now?" he asked, searching my face.

I smiled. "I do, Joe."

"Well, then I'm glad for you. I can't say I don't have concerns about you and Jared, but that's not any of my business anymore."

"No," I answered softly. "No, it isn't."

He held my gaze for a few moments, regret and resignation on his face.

"Joe, you made the right decision," I said, placing my hand on his arm, "and I acted like a complete brat."

"You were hurt," he said, "and I'm not holding it against you, Poppy. There's a hole in one of my condo walls courtesy of my fist. You weren't the only one dealing with disappointment and frustration over how things ended."

Feeling my heart stir again, I removed my hand from his arm. I had made my choice, and there was no going back.

Joe glanced at the now empty space and then back to my eyes. "I didn't end things because I *wanted* to. I just hope to God I didn't push you back into that monster's arms."

Recalling the tears shared at my kitchen table with Jared, I snapped in anger. "Do you think I'm so desperate for male attention that I'd throw myself at Jared just to get a quick fix?"

Joe said nothing.

Offended, I glared at him. "This isn't loneliness or self-destructive apathy motivating me. I had to forgive my husband so that I could be free of the bitterness and anger eating me alive. Jared has shown remorse for a lot of things too. He is legitimately changing, and my attitude toward him has also changed because of it."

"I just...I don't understand, Poppy. How can you go back to him after everything he's done to you? To your children?"

"What difference does it make now anyway? Nothing happened between you and me. Like you said, it's none of your business anymore."

"I think about you all the time," he blurted out. "I keep kicking myself wondering if I've made a horrible mistake, and now you're back together with the enemy."

My offense and anger melted at his confession. "Joe," I said gently, "even if all of your worst fears turn out to be true, you didn't force me to do anything. I understand why you feel the way you do, and you have no idea how touched I am by your concern. But it's misplaced."

"I didn't push you away because I don't care about you."

"I know," I said, "and I respect and admire you for it. Rest assured, the only arms you pushed me into were the arms of Jesus. I will be forever grateful for that."

"Are you happy? Truly?" he asked.

"With Jesus? Yes."

"And Jared?"

"Off limits. We can't go there anymore."

"Fair enough." he replied, his face grim. "I want you to be happy, Poppy."

"So do I!" I exclaimed, hoping to inject some levity into the conversation. "Being miserable sucks, and I'm done with it!"

His eyes brightened, though his mouth remained downturned.

"Look, I have to get to the office, but I'm glad I got to see you today, Joe. Hopefully, this puts some closure on things for both of us. You're a good guy, and you deserve your own happy ending. After everything you've been through, you deserve it."

He nodded. "Thank you."

I smiled back at him. "When we prayed on the benches, we assumed God would answer our prayers by bringing us together. And in a way, He did."

He looked intrigued. "How so?"

"Well, we both learned that there's life after our painful marriages, and we can open our hearts to someone new."

"But you went back to Jared," he objected.

"I didn't *go back* to anything. I will never settle for what our relationship looked like before, and Jared knows that. I'm not the same person I was when we got married twelve years ago, and neither is he."

"What about two months ago?" he pressed. "You were scared out of your mind and asked me to rescue you. I find it a little hard to believe he's changed that much in only a few weeks."

"*My* life changed when I opened my heart to Jesus."

"You said Jared got Jesus two years ago, but we both know that didn't stop him from abusing and manipulating you. How do you know you're not being played all over again?"

"You're just going to have to trust that I know what I'm doing. I have to trust God that He knows what He's doing too. I don't necessarily have an explanation for anything, but I also don't owe you one either."

"Yeah, you've mentioned that."

"So, take the hint," I said gently. "Believe me when I tell you that only Jesus could have worked things out between me and Jared—and that's not a done deal yet either. I'm taking it one day at a time, but God willing, my kids will get to see a happy, healthy marriage with both of their parents. After more than twenty years of waiting, I'm finally seeing the promise of what I wanted in this relationship from the beginning."

"Then, I'm glad for you," he said, smile taut. "If this is what you really want, and you're truly happy, then I can't ask for anything more."

Meeting his pale eyes one last time, I said, "I will be praying for the same for you."

CHAPTER 27

THE FIRST, OFFICIAL MARRIAGE COUNSELING SESSION for Jared and me did not go exactly as planned. I blamed myself for unmet expectations, of thinking the husband and wife team would immediately recognize Jared's culpability and my twenty years of long-suffering. I'd forgotten how naturally charming he could be, how easily words slid off his tongue to impress the listener. Despite the obvious changes I'd witnessed in Jared, our session also revealed many areas still left untouched by his recent reformation.

"That went well," he said, smiling at me over a shared basket of curly fries at Burger Palace.

I took a bite and swallowed before answering. "I guess so."

He raised an eyebrow. "What's wrong? Don't you like Tom and Anna? I thought they had some really good insights into our marriage."

I offered a noncommittal shrug and ate another fry.

"Poppy," Jared said, his expression growing concerned, "I

don't like it when you're this quiet. First, I get the silent treatment, and then you explode on me."

Bristling at the unfair characterization, I used a gulp of ice water to swallow down the harsh response I wanted to give him. After an uncomfortably long pause, one that left my glass half drained of its contents, I felt no less calm than after my first sip.

"Cat got your tongue?"

"Enough!" I growled.

Jared recoiled as if he'd been struck. "Why are you taking my head off? What did I do?"

"Why do you have to push me into saying something when it's obvious I'm not ready to answer? Back off."

"Sheesh, forget I asked!"

"Don't be a jerk," I said, rolling my eyes. "You provoked me until you got the response you wanted, and now you're playing the victim. Just like you did when we were married."

He held up his hands in innocence. "What is all this? You didn't show this much hostility with Tom and Anna."

"How could I? You were so busy talking the entire time and schmoozing them over. Do you even believe the stuff coming out of your mouth, or do you just change it for your intended audience? Dreams of full-time ministry, Jared? Are you serious? Of course, they ate all that up. They're *Christian* counselors."

His expression soured as I felt myself slipping back into familiar, combative emotions. Knowing that I needed to change my own reactions if I wanted any hope of change in our marriage, I inhaled and exhaled slowly. I raised my gaze to Jared's and felt a pang of remorse at the pain I discovered in his eyes.

"I'm sorry," I said quietly. "I didn't think things would go the way they did today, and obviously, I'm not handling it very well."

"What did you think was going to happen?"

I shrugged, feeling tears sting my eyes. Wiping them away hastily, I looked away.

"Did you think they would pounce on me for cheating on you? That they'd take your side off the bat and then point out every horrible thing about me?"

My eyes shot back up to his in shock. "How did you…?"

He cut me off with a wave of the hand. "Because I thought they would do the same thing. I didn't expect them to be so kind or understanding."

"Too understanding," I muttered.

"Look, you may not want to hear this, Poppy, but you're not totally innocent either."

"Excuse me?" I hissed, the old anger resurrecting once again. "Did I force you into bed with Leah? Did I encourage you to ignore your wife and kids because you couldn't be bothered to think about anyone other than yourself?"

"Poppy, I've already admitted to doing those things, and I truly am sorry. You didn't deserve what I did to you, and I made my own choices. None of that was your fault, and I'm not blaming you for it either. I know I used to do that, and it was wrong. I'm sorry."

The burden of bitterness lifted at his admission of guilt, but I felt even more confused. "So, what are you trying to say?"

He took a deep breath, a smile of relief on his face. "I should have chosen my words more carefully just now. I meant that you hurt me also."

"How?" I asked, bracing myself for a sucker punch.

"Your anger, Poppy. You called me worthless, helpless, stupid, and incompetent among other things."

"That's how you acted!" I said a little too loudly. Slinking down as several restaurant patrons turned around, I added more quietly, "Are you the only one allowed to have feelings, Jared? Any normal person would get upset with how you treated me and the kids."

"You had every right to be upset, but you also verbally abused me."

"Verbally *abused* you?" I repeated in disbelief. "And how would you describe your own behavior, Jared? Do you remember how you nitpicked me all the time and the horrible names you used to call me? Of course, I finally lashed out! The difference is that what you said was completely untrue. Everything I called you actually described your attitude and behavior toward me and the kids."

"Look, I'm not saying you were wrong to be angry with me or that you didn't have a right to express yourself, Poppy. The day I confessed to the affair with Leah, I know I was so ugly to you."

I fought back the urge to scream in frustration. Instead, I said through gritted teeth, "You can't compare me being upset with your chronic, selfish behavior with what you said to me that day. I had been putting up with your abuse and neglect for over almost two decades. The things you said were intentionally cruel, and it was all to cover up the fact I figured out you'd been cheating. You just needed to hurt me badly enough to shut me up."

The struggle of Jared's emotions played out on his face. "This is hard," he finally said, raking a hand through his hair. "I want to argue, but it doesn't get us anywhere."

"No, it doesn't."

"Where do I draw the line between being argumentative versus wanting to defend myself against lies?"

"Which *lies* are you referring to?" I hissed, my voice hardening again.

Noting the change in my tone, Jared met and held my gaze. Exhaling a long sigh, he said, "You know what, it's not worth it. It was wrong, no matter the reasons why I said it, and I know I hurt you more than just that one day."

"I'm not quite ready to see your side of things," I admitted. "I don't know that I could understand, let alone sympathize with any justification you made for sleeping with Leah."

"Oh really?"

"Are you kidding me right now? I never once thought about cheating on you."

"So, I didn't find you sobbing your eyes out at a gas station over that Joe guy? You sure talked him up to Tom and Anna, how he kept you from going past the friend zone until our divorce would have been finalized. Sounds like you wanted something more, if you're being honest with yourself, Poppy."

Grudgingly seeing my own hypocrisy, I offered a morsel of acknowledgement in the form of a head bob.

"Look, I'm not trying to say that what I did with Leah is the same thing as you and Joe," he began.

"Good, because it's not," I interrupted. "I didn't string Joe along for fifteen years as my get out of jail free card to our marriage."

"I'm not asking you to excuse my behavior because you toyed with the idea of a fling, Poppy. I'm just saying that nobody is infallible, not even you as the jilted wife."

Not willing to surrender, I said, "There's a huge difference between you cheating on me for a year while we were *still married* versus me contemplating a relationship with someone after you and I were well on our way to divorce court. We haven't lived in the same house for over three years. I also never acted on my feelings for Joe."

"That's not what you told Tom and Anna," he retorted. "You almost kissed Joe the night you ran away from me. You also said you threw yourself at him, and he ended the friendship. You make him sound like some kind of saint instead of a lonely coworker who's been sniffing around you for a while and then got cold feet."

I dug in my heels. "Still not the same thing."

"You're right," Jared said, "it's not. I'm not condemning you either, Poppy. Your mistakes don't wash away mine. I'm the one who put you in the position to be seduced by that guy anyway."

"Seduced?"

"It's my fault you were in a vulnerable place, and this Joe guy took advantage."

"How can you say that?" I demanded. "The feelings were mutual. Joe didn't trick me. We both wanted a relationship. He just had more self control than I did not to act on it."

As soon as the words escaped my mouth, I realized I'd fallen into Jared's trap. Here was his "gotcha" moment to prove I was no better than he was. Although the circumstances were not comparable in terms of scope, I could no longer draw and quarter my husband for succumbing to the same temptation that total desperation had created within me. While I could argue I hadn't *technically* committed adultery with Joe, I knew from both Scripture and the conviction in my own heart that I would have followed through if given the opportunity. I sighed wearily.

Jared noted my defeated posture and said, "Look, I hold myself partially to blame for what happened. I told you I wanted to reconcile, but I was also manipulating you at the same time. You were hurt and confused...and easy prey."

"I don't know what to say, Jared. You're painting Joe like some lecherous vulture and me like the innocent victim. Neither is true."

"Why are you going out of your way to defend him? You keep throwing yourself in the line of fire instead of letting Joe have any culpability for what happened—or *almost* happened—between the two of you." He watched me cautiously before asking his next question. "Do you still have feelings for him?"

"Did you ever care about Leah?" I shot back.

"No," he said sadly. "I cared about myself."

Stunned by Jared's confession, I said nothing.

"I don't mean to cause you extra pain, Poppy. What you wanted to do with Joe is not the same as what I actually did with Leah. I had reasons for the decisions I made, and most of them were selfish and petty. Blaming you for everything made it easier to justify the affair, but you're right that nobody forced me into bed with her. It's a mistake I'll have to live with for the rest of my life."

"Wow."

"And whether you agree with me or not, I hold myself responsible for what almost happened with you and Joe."

"Jared, I keep telling you that—"

Cutting me off, he continued, "If I'm being honest, I'm actually grateful to the guy for having more self control than I did. Hard to stay mad at him when he's part of the reason you and I are even sitting here right now. He helped give our marriage a second chance."

Wishing the truth were far more black and white than the shades of gray beginning to make themselves known, I shook my head and slouched in my seat.

"Can we try to start this conversation over again?" Jared asked. He gauged my reaction as he helped himself to a fry.

"No, I'm emotionally exhausted. Can we talk about work, Natalie's bat mitzvah, or just anything other than our relationship?"

He acceded with a quick nod and a sip of his beer.

"How is it?" I asked, gesturing toward his frosted mug.

"Eh," he said with a shrug. "Not the worst I've ever had. It does the trick."

After another long pause, one that saw our basket of fries emptied and water glasses refilled, Jared finally broke the silence.

"I didn't think it would be so hard to date my wife," he said.

"Is that what this is? Feels more like a battlefield."

"For lack of a better word," he replied, a smile hovering around his mouth. He followed with a flirtatious wink. "Let's take a break from all the heavy stuff and just try to enjoy each other's company."

Despite myself, a small grin appeared. Jared's dimples emerged in response.

"How are things at Culver?" he asked.

"Busy, as usual. Phil says they've finally found potential candidates to help in the office."

"That's got to be a relief." His tone was casual, but his eyes leveled me with their heady combination of intimacy and hunger. Jared's gaze traced over each plane of my face as if memorizing it.

"What?" I asked.

"What?" he answered back.

"Why are you looking at me like that?"

"Like what?"

"I don't know...you're just...you're staring at me."

"Am I?"

I cocked my head and pursed my lips. "I'm not blind, Jared."

"Neither am I."

"Meaning what?"

"Meaning that I like looking at you. Your face is so expressive, and you have this incredible way of shaping your lips when you talk. It's hypnotic."

Dumbfounded by his response, I said nothing.

"You do have beautiful lips, by the way," he said, his eyes traveling to my mouth again.

"I appreciate the compliment, but it's not going to get you an invite." I sat back in my seat and flattened my *beautiful lips* into a thin line. "Seems like the only person trying to seduce me is *you*."

"It was a sincere compliment, and I don't have any hidden agendas in saying it. You asked me why I was staring, and I'm explaining."

I inclined my head with a slight blush. "Okay, fair enough."

"I mean, I will always have an agenda to kiss you, but I didn't think that was a secret."

Swallowing another cold sip of water, this time for the raised temperature I felt creeping through me, I looked around the restaurant. I needed something to distract me from the potency of Jared's gaze and my increasing receptiveness to it.

I hated the fact I could still be so hurt and angry with his behavior, yet somehow feel desire for him at the same time. It didn't seem right...or fair.

CHAPTER 28

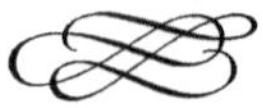

"So, tell me about the bat mitzvah," Jared said.

Unwilling to prolong eye contact beyond a brief, accidental meeting, I looked away. "What do you want to know?"

"What can you tell me?" he quipped back, also skilled in the ability to answer one question by asking another one.

Pausing, I met his dark gaze. Though he may not have fully understood the source of my tension, Jared certainly knew my avoidance tactics like the back of his hand.

"It's okay," he said. "Trust takes time to build."

"Rebuild," I corrected. "You've changed some things, but there's still a long way to go."

"What is God telling you?" he asked.

"What do you mean?"

"Exactly what I said. I assume you're praying about our marriage, reading the Bible, and looking for guidance, right?"

"Yeah," I drawled.

"So, what is God saying when you ask Him?"

"The only thing that gives me any peace is just to trust that He's got it handled. That He will protect me and the kids."

Unrelenting, Jared pressed on. "So, what about our marriage?"

"What about it?"

"Come on, Poppy. This is like pulling teeth."

"I don't know what kind of answer you're expecting here. I know you like to quote that Bible verse about God restoring what the locusts have eaten, but that's not what He's telling me about the situation."

"Oh," he said, the smile slipping from his mouth.

"Look, I don't know what the future holds for the two of us. If nothing else, I hope we can have a non-adversarial relationship for the sake of our children. I never agreed to remarry you or promise you happily ever after."

"We're *still* married," he growled.

"In name only," I shot back. "You wanted out more than I did, remember?"

"Things changed."

"So, they did. But it doesn't mean everything will work out the way you want it to."

"What about what happened in your kitchen the other day? I thought we really made some progress. Are you telling me that one marriage counseling session later, and you're just throwing in the towel?"

"Don't twist my words! We have a huge mess to untangle, and that's not going to happen overnight. As frustrated as I am with how the counseling session went today, I wouldn't be sitting here if I didn't think there was some kind of hope for a future together."

My words mollified him, and his shoulders visibly slumped in relief.

Our server arrived with matching mushroom and swiss burgers, seeming to anticipate a break in our heated conversation.

"So, you're back to eating milk and meat?" I asked, gesturing toward Jared's sandwich. "I thought you were keeping kosher."

"Bible kosher, not rabbi kosher."

"Is there a difference?"

"Yeah, a pretty big one actually. Bible kosher says don't boil a baby goat in its mother's milk. It was a pagan fertility ritual at the time. Rabbi kosher says no milk and meat, separate dishes, separate kitchens and on. I'm still trying to figure out this Jewish identity thing, and I don't want to cause offense to any Jewish people who might be open to hearing about Yeshua. At the same time, I don't want to be a slave to man-made rules or traditions."

"Can I share something that Rebecca and Ted talked about at their Bible study last week?"

He gestured for me to proceed as he quickly prayed and then chewed through a bite.

"We got on the topic of evangelism, specifically how to share Jesus with our own families. Everyone in that room has Jewish family members we want to see come to faith."

"I'm with you," he said, swallowing down the remains of his burger with a sip of beer.

"One girl there, Abigail, used to be a member of Beth Shalom."

"Abigail?" Jared repeated in surprise. "Abigail Klein?"

"Do you know her?"

"She sang on the worship team." Thinking for a moment, he said, "She left about the time she started dating some Jewish guy. I don't remember his name."

"Kyle Goldstein," I supplied for him. "Jessica's twin brother."

Jared's eyebrows raised halfway up his forehead. "Small world."

I smirked. "No kidding. Do you know anything about him?"

"Just that Jessica complained about the grief he gave her for dating Patrick. One time, she got a text in the middle of dinner and left the table crying."

"Oh," I said softly.

Jared shook his head and sighed. "I still can't believe how interconnected all of our lives seem to be."

"Do you know if Jessica and Leah still keep in contact?"

He eyed me suspiciously. "No, why?"

"Just curious."

He frowned. "So, you were saying about Abigail?"

I took his cue and continued on with my story. "Well, Abigail mentioned all of the seminars she'd attended on Jewish evangelism at Beth Shalom as well as the synagogue's crazy rules. She said people weren't allowed to wear crosses, couldn't use the words, 'Jesus' or 'Christ,' and they could only use Messianic lingo."

Jared nodded. "She's telling the truth. Rabbi Lebow was a stickler for appearances. He didn't want anyone to accuse Beth Shalom of looking like a church."

"From all accounts, that place sounds more like a cult than a church anyway. At the very least, a members-only country club with some pretty ridiculous guidelines."

Jared squirmed in his seat. "It wasn't like that, Poppy. I did find Yeshua there."

"How did you even wind up at that place? I have a hard time picturing Leah in a synagogue with the kind of life I know she's lived."

He gave a throaty chuckle. "She was furious with me for going, even more so when I came home and told her I'd been saved."

"Probably wasn't too different from my reaction when you told me."

"You looked horrified, Poppy. Leah just blew it off and asked if I was drunk."

"So, what happened when you told her it was real?"

"At first, she told me she didn't care. She said it was my life, and if religion made me happy, then go for it. A week later when I told her that I couldn't live in sin with her anymore, she threw me out and called me a hypocrite. When I told her I needed to work on my marriage with you, she called me every curse word under the sun. Then, she called Larry to smear my reputation at the bank and any other mutual friend we had."

"What happened after that?"

"She was furious when most people sided with me instead of her."

I swallowed a bitter lump of commiseration. "Well, you do live a charmed life, Jared. You up and leave your wife, then your mistress, and somehow, you're the one who walks away with a team of flying monkeys to rally behind you. My own family, included."

He scowled. "That's quite an assumption you're making."

"Enlighten me, by all means," I clapped back. "I'm just wondering if you ever feel the consequences of your selfish choices."

With the escalation of animosity between us, we both took a pause before resuming the conversation.

"Are you ready to listen?" Jared asked coolly. "Without interrupting?"

Resisting the urge to roll my eyes, I gestured for him to continue.

"You assumed," he began again, "that people sympathized with my side of things. They didn't. Nobody gave me a free pass for cheating or abandoning you and the kids. There wasn't much anybody could say to me while Leah and I were living together because I wouldn't have listened anyway."

"True," I said, remembering all too well that horrible season of litigation and court-ordered, child support payments.

"Leah didn't realize she was in an indefensible position. She was the homewrecker who ruined the life of her best friend and godchildren. Nobody was going to defend her, no matter how crazy they all thought I was for becoming a believer."

"I see."

"At first, I flaunted my relationship with Leah and basically dared anyone to say something. I ran into Patrick at a fraternity mixer while he was with Jessica, and I finally found someone who could understand how miserable it was being married. We found common ground in resenting our wives."

Stung and betrayed by his admission, I said, "You weren't the only one who was miserable being married."

His eyes looked pained. "I know, Poppy. I didn't want to see it then. I do now, and the regret and shame I feel is overwhelming."

"And all of this remorse began with some snake demon in your apartment?" I asked, daring to go to the one place that scared me more than any other of Jared's confessions.

"Did you talk to Rebecca?"

I nodded. "I also did some research online. Stumbled on an exorcism video on YouView."

Jared's eyes widened.

"Won't ever do *that* again," I deadpanned.

"Don't mess with that stuff," he warned. "It's real."

"Trust me, I know. I was married to it, remember?"

His pained expression increased. "I wish I could forget."

"I know I never will. I felt smothered by a fog when I tried to talk to you. My words were always twisted to mean something they didn't. You would rage or project your own behavior on me, and then you'd throw the most vile insults as possible. You knew exactly how to hurt me, and you seemed to do it with glee."

Jared swallowed a large mouthful of water before responding. "It's been hard finding someone to talk to about all of this. I don't trust anyone from Beth Shalom, and any other friend thinks I'm crazy for leaving for you, crazy for trying to make it work, or crazy for believing in Jesus. The army of flying monkeys, as you put it, isn't quite as big as you think."

"Why don't you come with me to the Margolins' this Sunday?" I heard myself ask.

"Won't that be weird?"

"There are other Beth Shalom survivors there," I said and listed off some names. "They'll probably understand your situation better than most. And as far as Leviathan goes," I shuddered as I uttered the word, "there's nobody I trust more than Rebecca Margolin to try to explain what that thing is. Other than her mother-in-law, maybe."

"I did get around to reading Rebecca's book," Jared said, rubbing the back of his neck. "I had some digital credit for ebooks."

"When were you planning to mention that?"

He smiled. "Now, I guess."

"What did you think?"

"She's a talented writer."

"So, you think it's pure fiction?" I asked, ready to defend my friend.

"Don't put words in my mouth. Let me finish."

"Sorry," I mumbled.

He exhaled a heavy sigh and continued. "Rebecca described everything I experienced at Beth Shalom perfectly—even though it's not easy to admit. I wish I could say I was surprised or outraged by the behavior of her father or her old pastor, but I saw myself in both of them. It wasn't a pretty picture. You mentioned talking to her about Leviathan, but I think it's Ted's mother who seems to have a lot of answers about this thing."

Thinking back to my brief interactions with the Margolin family matriarch, I knew Jared was headed down the right path.

"Rose is a pistol," I said with a grin. "She's gentle and loving, but she won't pull any punches either. After she gets the granddaughters down to bed, she joins us late for the Bible study. Most of the people there hang onto her every word."

"Did her husband ever get saved?" Jared asked.

I shook my head. "He's on the list of family members we're all praying for. Rose hoped that Steve would soften once Ted came to faith in Jesus, but it seems like he's doubled down instead. Her daughters are apathetic about all of it, but the younger sister, Amanda, is coming around some."

"You know, if you had told me twenty years ago that you and I would be sitting here talking to you about Jesus, I would have said you were crazy."

"We're a long way from Moose Grunwald's graduation party, aren't we?"

Jared met and held my gaze. "Yes, we are. Thank God."

"Thank God," I agreed.

CHAPTER 29

THE KIDS AND I ENJOYED OUR FIRST THANKSGIVING
with Jared since he'd moved out nearly three years earlier. We
continued to work through old grievances privately and in
marriage counseling, and the common ground of Jesus gave us
both an anchor in the midst of troubling topics. After my heart-
to-heart with my mother, she and my father welcomed Jared
back into the family fold, albeit hesitantly. Their former enthusiasm gave way to more reserve around Jared, and they made no
secret of their skepticism regarding his most recent change of
heart. It was humbling to realize all of the resentment I felt in
my parents pushing toward reconciliation didn't result from a
need to control me but from their misguided belief they were
helping me.

Jared began attending Bible Study with me on Sundays, and
much to my surprise, he struck an instant rapport with Kyle
Goldstein. His connection via Abigail and their shared experiences at Beth Shalom also helped solidify the burgeoning

friendship. Jared's ties to Jessica brought peace of mind to a brother missing his relationship with his sister.

Jessica and I continued to meet at Vincenzo's several mornings a week, and we avoided certain conversational pitfalls in order to maintain normalcy in the friendship. I answered questions as she asked them with regards to Jared, her brother, or Rebecca, but I finally mustered the courage one early, December morning to inquire about another mutual acquaintance of ours.

"So, do you ever talk to Leah?" A double shot of espresso bolstered my resolve in hearing the answer.

Her honey brown eyes widened in surprise. "As in Jared's ex-girlfriend?"

"The one and only."

"Not really, why?"

Not one to demur, I said, "Because there are things Jared has shared that Leah should know. Things that might help bring her closure."

Jessica nodded. "I get what you're saying, but you're probably the last person she'd want to talk to right now. Even less than Jared."

I cocked my head. "What do you mean?"

"Because you won, Poppy. As horrible as it's been for you, Leah's the one who wasted half of her life pining for Jared. She has nothing to show for all of that time other than jealousy and bitterness. I don't expect you to feel sorry for her, but I hope you can understand why she wouldn't want to speak with either one of you."

I raised an eyebrow. "This doesn't sound like you barely talk to Leah. In fact, this sounds fairly recent."

Jessica shrugged. "You can call me a hypocrite if you want. I know I gave you grief about being friends with Rebecca and

Taylor, but I know Leah would die if she found out I meet up with you for coffee."

"Why would she die, Jessica? Because you'd be someone else in her life who chose me over her—even though that's hardly the case?"

"Leah's just super insecure. Jared played on all of that too. I don't know what she would do if he called her, especially now that she's pregnant."

My gaze flew up to Jessica's in alarm, and she covered her mouth.

"I'm...I'm sorry," she stammered. "I'm so sorry, Poppy. I didn't want to tell you with things going so well Jared. I knew you'd be devastated and I—"

I cut her off with a wave of the hand. "Jared's not the father."

"He's not?" she gaped, mouth open in shock.

I shook my head. "Is she claiming the baby is his?"

"She didn't say one way or the other, but she definitely left me with that impression. I wasn't lying when I said I don't really talk to her. Leah messaged me out of the blue about a week ago in a panic. She said she didn't have anyone else to talk to who would understand."

"Is she planning to tell Jared?" I asked. "Because if she does, she won't like his answer."

"How can you be sure he's not the father?"

"Jared left Leah a year and a half ago," I said. "That, and a few other reasons."

"Leah said she's twelve weeks pregnant. She had her first ultrasound before Thanksgiving. Is it possible Jared hooked up with her behind your back?"

Thinking back to the time frame, it would have been when

Jared showed up at my front door. It might have explained his immense guilt and shame, but deep down, I knew better.

"I'm sure, Jessica."

She pursed her lips, took a sip of her coffee, and said nothing.

"I'm not turning a blind eye to Jared's cheating or lies," I said, "but I have a lot better reason than his recent changes to believe that Leah is making it all up, or at least, the part about him being the father."

Jessica's dubious expression changed to curiosity. "Why's that?"

"Jared had a vasectomy as soon as we found out we were pregnant with Madison. She was our surprise third baby, and Jared was adamant that he didn't want any more kids. I didn't find out he'd gotten the procedure until after the fact. I was furious with him."

"Oh," Jessica murmured. "Then that means Leah has been seeing someone else."

"Leah's never been short on male company. Despite some personality issues, she can be charming and vivacious too. I'm sure you saw that when you were with Patrick."

"She and Jared argued a lot, actually. I can't remember a time where things didn't seem tense between the two of them. Patrick said he didn't see it lasting very long. He said Leah was too selfish and demanding."

"What about Jared?" I asked, offended on Leah's behalf. "I'm not saying she's an angel, but knowing the two of them for as long as I have, the one who acted more spoiled and entitled was always Jared."

Jessica nodded. "I hear you, Poppy. Patrick was just as selfish as Jared. It was easier for him to blame Leah than blame Jared. He'd have to look in a mirror."

I took note of her crestfallen expression, the shame easily read on her face.

"Don't tell me I didn't know," she sniffled, wiping her nose with the back of her hand. "I was mad at the world, and I wanted revenge."

"I know," I said softly. "And there's something I need to tell you about Nathan Fein. I haven't been sure when would be the right time, but I think you should know."

"What?" she asked bitterly. "We both know my ex-fiancé is happy and healthy and moved on with his life. He found his perfect little wife to marry."

I shook my head. "No, unfortunately."

"No?" she repeated in disbelief.

"No," I said. "Nathan just got better about hiding his issues. You dodged a bullet, my friend."

"What do you mean?"

"The catalyst for all of these changes in Jared is Nathan's addiction to pornography."

Jessica faltered, her shoulders beginning to shake. I reached out a steadying hand. "Nathan downloaded underage porn onto the synagogue computers. He got busted by the police, and they raided the congregation."

"Are you serious?" she gasped. "I remember the stuff I found on his laptop. I know the girls looked young, but I had no idea they were actual minors."

"Yes, Jared told me. He said the rabbi covered up the entire scandal. He blackmailed all of the leadership to keep quiet about it, and then he preached a sermon to keep the members from asking any questions."

"What the heck! That's disgusting!"

"Jared said that's what it took to open his eyes and see his own sin. Then, he said he wrestled with some snake demon in his apartment named Leviathan."

"Don't say that word!" Jessica exclaimed, jumping to her feet.

A recent conversation with Rose Margolin had left Jared and me with faces nearly as white as Jessica Goldstein's. "This isn't just about Rebecca's book, is it?" I asked, watching her.

She shook her head.

"Did you have a nightmare, or did you wrestle with this thing like Jared did?"

"I'll sound crazy if I tell you," she whispered.

"No, you won't. In fact, every person I talk to who has encountered this monster all say the exact same thing. They feel 'crazy' for the things they're seeing and what it all means. They said it feels like they're living out a horror movie happening in real life. Believe me, it's not just you."

"Have you ever…?" she trailed off, slowly sitting back down.

"I was married to it," I said. "Jared said he wrestled with the demon that tried to destroy him, but I lived with that monster trying to destroy me through my husband."

"Oh, Poppy," Jessica said sadly. "How can you ever trust Jared again? Even if he didn't father Leah's baby, how do you know he wasn't still sleeping with her behind your back? It seemed like the only thing Jared and Leah had in common was revenge against you. You said Jared was furious when he found out you were seeing Joe. What if they hooked up again?"

"Because he's not the same person. Whether you believe in demons or not, my husband was delivered from the monster controlling him. He hasn't been the same since he found me at the gas station and said he got free of that thing."

"So, now Jared just blames this demon for how he treated you?" she asked, suspicion in her eyes.

"No, he's taking full responsibility for it. He's apologized over and over to me and to the kids."

"Well, that's good, at least."

"Jared struggles with guilt over what he's done the same way you do about your relationship with Patrick. Madison doesn't notice a difference in her father, but the older kids do. They don't fully trust him, and I can't say I blame them. Thanksgiving wasn't stress free, but it was probably the most healthy interaction the kids have ever seen between me and their father."

"Wow," she said. "I can't even imagine Patrick having a change of heart like that."

"The changes had nothing to do with Jared, and everything to do with the power of Jesus," I said.

"The power of Jesus?"

"Yes," I answered with a large smile. "Jessica, other than thinking I'm nuts for trying to make it work with Jared, haven't you seen the differences in me?"

"Yeah," she drawled. "You're definitely a lot less angry than you were. Less bitter."

Pained to remember my former state, I also thanked God for the peace that regularly guarded my heart and mind every time I dove into my Bible and prayed. "Only Jesus could have taken my nightmare of a marriage and even more nightmarish divorce and turned it into something *good*. If you want to talk about 'crazy,' try to imagine a Bible study at Ted and Rebecca's house attended by me, Jared, your brother, and his Messianic Jewish fiancée."

Jessica snickered. "If you had asked me five years ago, I would have called it impossible. I still can't believe Rebecca is married with two kids. Kyle and I sometimes joked about Rebecca and her constant tales of misery."

I frowned. "That's not very kind, especially when you know what Rebecca's family was like. How could you make fun of the abuse she endured?"

"I didn't make fun of it!" she said defensively. "It just seemed like Rebecca was always depressed about something. She would get upset with whatever stunt her parents or sister pulled, but then she'd just go right back to it all over again. Usually right after her pastor gave her some kind of pep talk."

"Ah yes, Pastor Sociopath," I said. "Another sleazeball in the pulpit."

"Ugh, I don't know how she ever trusted that creep. I mean, how do you not realize your pastor is a pedophile?"

I raised an eyebrow. "Let she who is without sin cast the first stone, my friend."

Jessica's expression turned remorseful. "Sorry, I know you're right. I just feel like Rebecca made a lot of her own messes. She could never say no."

"Why did you stay friends with her if you looked at her life with so much disdain?" I asked. "It seems like you pretended to comfort Rebecca, but then privately took delight in her misery. What's a little *schadenfreude* among friends, right?"

"No!" Jessica protested. "Look, I loved Rebecca like a sister. I hated how her family treated her, and she'll tell you that too. It's just hard being friends with someone whose life is constant drama. It's emotionally draining. I wanted Rebecca to be happy, but now that she's living her dream life, she's constantly throwing it in my face."

"Constantly?" I said, not buying it. "I thought you guys don't even talk anymore."

"She still talks to my parents and sends them pictures. My mom hates the fact that Rebecca and I aren't friends, so she shows me all this stuff thinking I'll want to reconnect."

"Sounds like you need to talk to your mother."

Jessica sniffed in offense. "Rebecca got the dream life, and I got the nightmare. She tells my mom all this stuff knowing that I'll see it. I guess she's getting back at me for all the boyfriends I had after she got dumped by Jason."

"That's quite a pity party you're having over there," I said coolly. "You can't muster an ounce of happiness or compassion for your friend who has genuinely suffered, yet you're still wallowing in the consequences of your own, stupid decisions. It's more than just hypocritical, Jessica. It's revolting."

"What?" she gasped.

"You could get another job if you want to, but you choose to keep working in a place that makes you miserable. I don't know if you're punishing yourself to atone for Patrick or if you just like playing the victim, but it's appalling how you can sit and disparage your former best friend. You have a lot more in common with Leah than I think you realize."

"Poppy! How can you say that!"

"Leah has always been jealous of me," I said, continuing on. "Yes, Jared had a large part to play, but even in high school, Leah put me down to feel better about herself. She had everything materially, but she was still miserable. Compared to her, I didn't have very much, but I knew myself and what I wanted."

"What does that have to do with me and Rebecca?"

"I'm beginning to wonder if you listened to all of my issues with Jared so you could feel better about your own, sorry choices in life. Do you make fun of me when I'm not around the same way you did to this friend you supposedly loved like a sister?"

Stunned by my outburst, Jessica said nothing, but her eyes brimmed over in tears.

"Jessica, I say this in love, but you need to grow up. For all of Rebecca's 'tales of misery,' I have never seen her give into the self-pity I've witnessed from you time and again. Yes, you made stupid mistakes. We all have. Own them, move on, and quit with the petty jealousy. The real reason you resent Rebecca is because you can't better yourself at her expense anymore." Finished with my speech, I stood up and tossed my coffee cup into the trash.

I bumped into Ted Margolin on my way out the door just as Jessica dissolved into tears. He met my eyes then glanced over to Jessica, apparently catching the last bit of my diatribe.

"Let it be," I said and exited the coffee shop.

CHAPTER 30

"Mom, are you okay?" Natalie asked following a meeting with the rabbi of Beth Tefillah. We sat at our kitchen table while my mother kept Ryan and Madison occupied with a matinee movie at the theater.

"Yeah, honey. Why do you ask?"

"Well, Rabbi Cohn had to ask you three times if you heard what he said about picking *aliyah* candidates."

"I'm sorry sweetie," I replied. "I just have a lot on my mind. Do you know who you want to come up and chant the blessings?"

"Daddy knows the Hebrew, right?"

I smirked, knowing the one good thing that resulted from Jared's attendance at Beth Shalom was his newfound ability to recite traditional service liturgy. Jared grew up in a fairly secular Jewish home, but it seemed like he'd made up for lost time while attending the messianic synagogue.

"Mom?" she prodded.

"Sorry, sweetie. Long week at the office. Who else did you

have in mind to come up and chant the blessings? You only need four people, right?"

"Minimum of four," she corrected.

I raised an eyebrow at her vehemence. "Don't you have to learn an extra three lines of Hebrew for every aliyah that comes up to the bima to chant the blessing?"

"So?" She flicked her hair as if chanting three-thousand-year-old Hebrew directly from a Torah scroll was about as arduous as tying her shoes.

"It's your bat mitzvah, honey. If you're up for all of that singing, I say go for it. Have you written the *drash* for your Torah and Haftarah portions yet?"

Natalie shook her head. "I'm still trying to figure it out. I get the basic idea of obey God or bad stuff will happen to you, but there's got to be more than that. I mean, it feels silly to just stand up there like I'm reading a book report on the Torah. This is supposed to be my own interpretation, right?"

I smiled at my smart cookie. "Well, we know Rabbi Cohn won't let you mention Jesus, but there's no reason why you can't talk about how to apply these Bible verses to modern day life. Jews still believe in God, honey."

"I wouldn't talk about Jesus anyway. You know I don't agree with you and Dad."

I smiled and met her eyes. "I know, baby, and it's okay. I guess I was just thinking about what I would say if I was in your shoes. Regardless," I said, noting that I was rapidly losing my daughter's attention, "there's plenty to use from your *parsha*." I gestured toward the yellow workbook containing her individualized, Torah portion with interlinear Hebrew and English printed inside. "Don't forget, there's other Bible translations we can use too."

"But they're not Jewish."

"It's still the Bible, Natalie. Those chapters you're reading from *Numbers* are exactly the same as any Christian Bible."

"But the Torah is Jewish, Mom. The Bible is Christian."

"No, sweetheart. The Torah is the first five books of any Bible, Jewish or Christian. The only real difference I've seen is in the order of the books in the Old Testament. The Jewish Bible has the books arranged one way, and the Christian Bible a different way. Believe me, I've checked them side by side. Sometimes, they phrase things a little differently, but the gist is generally the same."

"Oh," she said quietly.

"I was using a Bible app on my phone and found one translation I liked so much that I bought a paperback." I stood up to retrieve an *Easy to Read Version* Bible from my kitchen counter. Noting the look of condescension on my daughter's face, I said, "Just humor me, okay? Open your workbook to your parsha and then turn to *Numbers 14* in the ERV Bible. You said you were having trouble trying to explain what the portion means in your drash. See if my Bible makes it a little easier to understand."

Natalie offered another raised eyebrow before comparing her Torah workbook with my Bible. Her forehead furrowed in surprise, then a small smile began to spread across her mouth.

"Wow," she breathed.

I grinned back at her.

Reading aloud from verse 11, she said, "And the LORD said to Moses, "How long will this people spurn Me, and how long will they have no faith in Me despite all the signs that I have performed in their midst?"

Tears filled my eyes thinking of my own season of pain and bitterness with how my life had turned out. I had shaken my fist in God's face, angry that He had thwarted my attempt for an affair with Joe. I had wanted to be done with Jared Levine and forget the past. Instead, we were revisiting and healing each wound one at a time. Reminded of my own anger in the midst of suffering, I silently prayed and thanked God for the gift of Jesus and the freedom I felt.

"Knock, knock," said the man of the hour himself, entering our kitchen with a bag full of groceries.

"What's all that?" I asked.

"Dinner," Jared answered proudly. "I thought I'd cook for you guys."

"Seriously?" Natalie's voice squeaked out almost an octave higher. "Who are you, and what did you do with my real dad?"

I winced for Jared, especially since her joke did not fall that far from the truth. He grimaced before shaking off the pain and pushing through with another bright smile.

"Believe it or not, your father has learned how to cook."

"Is that so?" I teased.

He dropped the grocery bags on the counter. "Food Station University. I'm auditing classes on TV," he said with a grin.

I smiled back. "The kids love Food Station. Maddie watches all the kid baking shows, and Ryan is obsessed with anything involving Elton Braun."

"What about you?" Jared asked me. "Do you watch any of the cooking shows, or is it still R.D. Hampton once the kids go to bed?"

I blushed. "Yeah, about that..." my voice trailed off.

Jared raised an eyebrow, awaiting a response that never came.

Natalie glanced back and forth between the two of us. With a sparkle reminiscent of *Parent Plan* mischief, she said, "Why don't I leave the two of you alone for a while?"

Jared rolled his eyes with a grin as Natalie scooped up her

bat mitzvah paraphernalia along with my Bible. She offered a saucy wink over her shoulder before she left the room.

"You look great," Jared said, walking toward me at the table.

I scoffed as I glanced over my stained t-shirt and jeans. "You might want to get your eyes checked. I hear everything goes downhill after forty."

Jared chuckled, and I would have recognized that come hither look anywhere.

"Are you serious?" I laughed.

"I'm not looking at anyone else, darling."

I blushed. "You and the cornball lines."

"Not a line," he said, sitting down next to me.

"I don't think you've looked at me like that in twenty years." A rush of electricity surged down my arms to my fingertips. I balled my hands into fists to keep from yanking at his shirt and pulling Jared into the same kiss I knew he wanted to give me.

"I don't think I've looked at you like this *ever*," he said. "Every time I see you, I feel like I fall more in love with you. I can't believe you're mine."

His final statement served as an ice bucket to my kindling passion. I wanted to correct him, but felt a nudge from the Lord to hold my tongue. Scripture verses I'd just read from *Song of Solomon* immediately came to mind.

"*Ani l'dodi v'dodi li*," Jared said softly in Hebrew. "I am my beloved's, and she is mine. I didn't mean for that to sound like I see you as some kind of a possession, Poppy. It's from the Bible."

I blushed again as Jared seemed to read my thoughts. I recalled other passages from that intimate book that rivaled some of R.D. Hampton's racier scenes. I forced my mind away from a heated montage of memories with Jared.

"How is any of this even possible?" I asked.

His dark eyes glowed. "Forgiveness is a beautiful thing."

"So is repentance."

The dreamy look from Jared's face faded. "Why'd you have to say that? We were having a moment."

"You mean the truth?" I asked, stunned. "Forgiveness is what you needed from *me*. Repentance is what I needed from *you*. We never had a shot of working this out if you never faced what you did."

He sighed wearily. "Are we back to this again? Bringing up how I need to, 'own my behavior?'" he said with condescending air quotes.

"Don't you dare make light of what you did to me or the kids. It wasn't a one-time event. You deliberately hurt all of us *for years*."

"I'm not making light of anything," he argued. "I just wish you could move on already and stop bringing it up."

I shoved away from the table and away from Jared. "You know what? Maybe this was a mistake after all. Take your groceries and go."

"Are you kidding me?" His voice rose along with the rest of his body out of his chair. "Why does it have to be so all or nothing with you? This is a stupid fight, and you act like it's the end of the world. We can't move forward if you keep looking back."

"It's not a stupid fight!" I yelled. "How are you still so clueless after three months of counseling? This bizarre version you have of 'forgive and forget' doesn't exist in the Bible."

"So, you don't believe Jesus washes away our sins?" he demanded. "How can you say you forgive me when you keep throwing everything back in my face?"

"Jared, if you hit someone with your car and break their leg, they might forgive you, but they still need to wear a cast and go through rehab. Forgiveness isn't some magic eraser that pretends like nothing happened. Bad behavior has consequences, and I'm not going to play this game with you anymore. I'm the injured party, and you're the one who injured me. You don't get to tell me when I'm supposed to 'get over' something you did to hurt me. I'm allowed to have whatever feelings I want, and I don't need your approval or permission to have them."

He exhaled a ragged breath, clearly just as frustrated as I was. "I just don't see how we can go forward when you're still stuck in the past."

"I didn't bring up forgiveness, Jared. You did."

"Yes, but you had to throw repentance in my face."

I pursed my lips together, praying God would take hold of the anger steadily brewing inside of me.

"Maybe we should just table the conversation," Jared finally said. "I didn't mean for this to turn into an argument."

"Did you mean for it to turn toward my bedroom? That seemed to be where things were headed before you stuck your foot in your mouth. Probably a blessing in disguise."

Not liking my choice of words, I watched Jared catch himself from another angry outburst. I noted the self-restraint, pleased to see that we both seemed to be making progress.

"I wasn't trying to do anything other than let my wife know that she's desired by her husband. That's it. As for the rest, obviously, you and I have some unresolved issues."

"I'm just tired of going twenty rounds with you about this, Jared. We have to figure out a way for the topic of forgiveness to stop being a trigger for both of us. I do feel like you rub it in my face as if everything is supposed to be *forgotten* simply because you want it to be."

"And I don't understand how you can say you forgive me, but you act like I'm the only one who needs to change."

"When did I ever say I was perfect?" I shot back. "I've already admitted to having a bad temper. You may not want to remember what it was like living with you for eighteen years, but it's going to take me a lot longer than three and a half months to heal. Put yourself in my shoes for just a second. I'm guarding my heart. I hope you can understand why."

He inhaled a pained breath, empathy not a second-nature quality of Jared's, but a skill I knew he'd been actively cultivating. "I think I see," he said. "It's hard when you hold up the mirror. It's not a pretty picture."

The tension slowly released from my shoulders. "No, it's not. I promise I'm not trying to make you feel like even more of a jerk. You sincerely apologized for what you did to me and the kids, and I see that. I also see the changes you've made. A year ago, this would have been a knock-down, drag-out fight."

"True," he said with a half smile. "I'm proud of us, Poppy."

"Me too."

"I'm sorry I took your head off. I know we both have to unlearn a lot of bad behavior. As much as I want you to be patient with me, I realize I'm not being patient enough with *you*. I did a lot more than hit you with a metaphorical car, and you're right that I'd rather forget about it. To think about all of the stupid, selfish choices I've made is overwhelming and depressing."

"Jared, you know I'm working *with* you on healing from all of this, but we both have to face what happened. I have to deal with all of the anger I have from it, and you need to root out the selfish attitude that ever let you think it was okay to hurt your family. You're going to have to face and accept responsibility for the pain you've caused to me and the kids. I think it's the only way you'll stop yourself from doing the behavior again."

"Thank you," he said simply.

"For what?"

"For not letting me steamroll you anymore. I need your spunk more than you know."

I smiled back at him.

He slipped his arm around me for a side hug, and I didn't protest when it became an extended embrace. From beyond the doorway, I caught my twelve year-old eyeing her father and I with two thumbs up held in the air.

CHAPTER 31

AFTER MY BLOW UP WITH JESSICA GOLDSTEIN, I noticed she stopped coming to Vincenzo's. Joe Trautweig also became a ghost, perhaps finding a new location for his pre-work caffeination. My own routine shifted as I found new reading material for those precious moments sandwiched in between the crazy school rush and the start of my work day. Instead of my R.D. Hampton novels, I opened my Bible or I tried out a new Christian author recommended by Taylor. The more I grew in my faith, the less tolerance I had for Hampton's steamy love scenes. Where they used to provide pulse pounding delight, they now left me feeling empty and unclean. When I caught Natalie skimming one of my well-worn novels, I threw out my entire collection.

My mother seemed both curious and terrified of my faith in Jesus, and she asked questions here and there. My father acted mostly ambivalent, happy that I was happy, but not interested for himself. Despite my warnings against it, Jared wanted to use the Messianic apologetics he'd picked up from Beth Shalom to evangelize to my parents about Jesus. He felt like his well-rehearsed talking points presented the gospel as a simple and "logical" choice. When Jared dismissed my concerns as needless worry, I held my tongue and trusted God to handle things.

As expected, my parents weren't interested in being argued into the Kingdom of Heaven. Angrily, they told Jared to take care of his own issues before trying to "save" them. Comforting a dejected Jared, I reminded him that neither one of us came to faith because we'd lost a Biblical debate. Conceding the point, he confessed his own arrogance and actually apologized to my parents. Jared's new-found humility bolstered my hope for reconciliation, especially after our marriage counseling sessions began to stall.

Jared complained about Tom and Anna's one-size-fits-all mentality for our marriage, and I struggled with feeling constantly misunderstood. Their over-emphasis on a "spiritual covering" and incessant push to attend church glossed over Jared's traumatic experience at Beth Shalom. They also seemed bewildered that neither of us wanted to abandon our Jewish background. I broached the subject with Rebecca Margolin, looking for accountability and an outside perspective.

"Poppy, if you don't have peace about it, then take a break from counseling," she said before our Bible study.

"I feel like I'm just giving up if we stop going. How do I know the difference between being offended versus feeling legitimately unheard? Any time I argue, they act like it just proves their point."

Mrs. Margolin frowned. "That's not cool at all. Your counselors are supposed to help you, not shame you for disagreeing with them."

"I was hoping I was wrong about this. If I'm being totally transparent, I expected Tom and Anna to be able to fix our marriage. I thought they had the winning formula, and all Jared and I had to do was follow it to the letter. That's definitely how they present themselves."

Rebecca grimaced. "Those are some pretty ridiculous expectations to set, and it removes them from any kind of accountability."

"How so?"

"If Tom and Anna think their techniques are infallible, then if something doesn't work, they can just blame the couple. It gives them way too much power. As long as you go along with everything they say, they'll praise and commend you for all of your 'growth' in therapy. The second you or Jared think for yourselves and expose a potential issue in their methodology, they'll go on the offensive to get you in line."

"I think you hit the nail on the head," I said, sighing in resignation. "I can't take another week of having to explain myself or bringing up the same old stories to prove my point. The second I do, they throw out the unforgiveness accusations instead of trying to understand. They either blow off what I'm saying, or they shut me down and tell me that I'm not 'moving forward.' It's so frustrating!"

Rebecca placed a comforting hand on my shoulder. "Poppy, you're getting controlling behavior and manipulation. What Tom and Anna are doing is called *reactive abuse*."

"I've never even heard of that."

She smiled encouragingly. "This was a recent discovery for me too. Reactive abuse is when people treat the *reaction* of the victim as the problem rather than the abuser's behavior that triggered the response. It's a form of gaslighting, and abusers will also use it in their smear campaigns against their victims."

"Like Jared going around painting me as Medusa but always out of context. He had the snapshot of me saying something out of anger, but he conveniently excluded his own part to play and why I was so upset in the first place."

"Exactly," Rebecca replied. "With regards to Tom and Anna, I got plenty of that same treatment from Pastor Sociopath. When I went crying to him about my family's toxic behavior, he trivialized or excused whatever they'd done—he always made my *reaction* the problem. He shamed me as being ungodly for having a completely normal, human response to their abuse. What I didn't realize was how he was also grooming me for his own designs."

"That's just evil."

"I agree. Assuming that Tom and Anna are at least well intentioned, it's obvious they're not helping you and Jared."

"Then, why do I feel so guilty? Tom and Anna are always drilling into us how you can't just quit on your marriage. Whenever Jared or I bring up an issue with their advice, they remind us that we both committed to making our relationship work."

"Poppy, you're not giving up on your *marriage* if you stop going. The only thing you're giving up on is Tom and Anna's ability to provide the counsel you guys need. You'd fire a lousy mechanic or hairdresser if they didn't do the job right, and a counselor is no different."

I fought back the sting of their newest accusation. "At our last session, Anna told me I don't handle criticism well and only want to hear what I want to hear. In my heart, I know it's not true, but I still wonder if maybe I'm just blind to my own faults."

The look of horror on my friend's face was a balm to my wounded soul. "You're being gaslighted, and I'm absolutely furious on your behalf. I've been seeing my own counselor for almost four years, and she has never made me feel the way you're describing with Tom and Anna. The people who can't seem to take criticism are your counselors, not you, Poppy."

Released from the weight of false guilt, I felt God's comforting reassurance instead. I inhaled a deep breath of freedom. "Thank you for that, my friend. I'm glad I'm not going crazy."

She smiled. "You're not crazy."

Getting to the real crux of the matter. I said, "Jared and I keep getting stuck on this issue of forgiveness, and I'm wondering if anybody can help us get past it."

"Have you considered that maybe God wants both of you to rely on *Him* rather than some all-knowing marriage counselors? People can promise you all kinds of results, especially if their livelihood depends on it."

"Well, that's not a very comforting thought," I said dryly.

Rebecca shrugged. "The love of money is the root of all kinds of evil. I'm not saying that Tom and Anna are as greedy as my father, but they do make their living selling people on the idea they have the answers for a perfect marriage. Making you or Jared feel like dirt because you dare to disagree is not healthy or godly. It's manipulative, at best, and the exact opposite of what you guys need."

My heart constricted as tears burned in my eyes. "I needed to hear someone else say it."

"Poppy, are you okay?" Jared approached the two of us in the Margolin kitchen. "Bible study is about to start."

Turning toward him, I briefly summed up my conversation with Rebecca. She affirmed what I said and added a few other anecdotes regarding similarly bad counsel she'd received from Pastor Sociopath. My husband listened in stoic silence, glancing over at me periodically to see if I shared Rebecca's sentiments.

"Poppy, I had no idea it was bothering you so much," he said. "Why didn't you say anything sooner?"

"I didn't know how. I was afraid you might agree with Tom and Anna. You don't say much in counseling when they start spewing all of this garbage on me."

He looked remorseful. "At first, I agreed with them, and that's my own fault for being selfish and petty."

"And now?" I asked.

"And now I agree with you, Poppy. I thought Tom and Anna were helping us, but I think Rebecca's right. I'm sorry, honey."

Mrs. Margolin smiled as Jared put his arm around me and pulled me into an embrace. She excused herself so we could share a private moment.

One week later, Jared became the one in need of comfort when he showed up at my door looking dazed and shell shocked.

"Hi," I said, greeting him with a smile. "I didn't think we'd be seeing you until later." Taking note of his lack of color, I asked, "What's wrong?"

"Leah," he said. "She's—"

"Pregnant," I finished for him.

His eyes met mine. "How did you know?"

"Come sit down, and I'll fill you in." I opened the door for Jared and ushered him toward the kitchen table. He plopped down like he had the weight of the world on his shoulders.

Wordlessly fixing him a cup of coffee from the remaining Vincenzo's brew in the carafe, I set a mug in front of him.

"Drink," I commanded.

"Got anything stronger?" His hand trembled as he raked it through his hair.

My tension grew, and I sat down beside him. "This baby isn't yours, is it?"

He refused to look at me.

"Jared," I asked weakly, "you told me you had a vasectomy. Was that a lie?"

He nodded but continued to stare at the table.

Understanding dawning, my stomach dropped. Voice tight, I asked, "How long ago did you sleep with her?"

"The night you left me for Joe. I showed up at her penthouse. It was a stupid mistake, and one I may regret for the rest of my life."

I quickly pieced together the sequence of events. "So, all of those horrible text messages you sent me, the ones that our daughter accidentally saw, was actually *your* guilt?"

Jared finally looked up, his eyes bloodshot and tormented. "I'm so ashamed of myself. I...I don't even know what to say. I'm so sorry. I wish I could go back in time."

I closed my eyes and took a deep breath, steeling myself against tears ready to fall.

"Poppy?" Jared's voice quivered. "Please, say something. Anything. Yell at me. Curse at me. Tell me what a rotten, disgusting excuse of a believer I am. I deserve it. I'm the worst kind of hypocrite!"

"Did you use protection?" My voice possessed a calm I didn't think was possible.

He shook his head. "Leah was on the pill for other hormonal issues, and I didn't think I could get anyone pregnant anymore."

"So, there's a chance that this baby *is* yours," I said, "that you and I will be tied to Leah for the rest of our lives."

Jared buried his face in his palms. "I'm so sorry, Poppy. I ruined everything. One selfish decision, and I've ruined everything for you, for our kids, for Leah, and for this baby."

"When were you planning to tell me you had slept with her? If Leah hadn't wound up pregnant, would I have ever found out about this? Jessica Goldstein told me about the pregnancy back in December."

His eyes flew to mine. "What? You knew all this time?"

Fighting off regret and self pity, I said, "I *defended* you, Jared. I told Jessica there was no way you could be this baby's father because you said you hadn't been anywhere near her."

"It was true the night I said it. I hadn't seen Leah before I stopped by her place back in September."

"Why didn't it come up in counseling? Why didn't you confess?"

"Because I knew I'd ruin any chance of getting back together if I told you. You'd say nothing had changed, and you would have been right. You'd be on your way to marrying Joe Trautweig, and my kids would still despise me. It was selfishness and self-preservation."

I silently prayed, beseeching God for strength I didn't feel, wisdom I didn't have, and forgiveness I couldn't muster without His help. "What are you going to do?" I finally asked. "Have you talked to Leah yet?"

He shook his head. "She doesn't need any money from me, but she might go after child support out of spite. This baby didn't ask to come into the world, and I think it would be wrong to abandon Leah and our child. I...I can't have that on my conscience again. Not after what I did to you and the kids."

"Take a paternity test."

Jared raised his eyebrows in surprise.

"Take a paternity test," I repeated. "Leah made it a point to tell Jessica Goldstein about her baby, and I don't think that was by accident. She still hasn't contacted you directly, has she?"

"Her father did. He showed up at work and made a huge scene. He told me he felt sorry for my stupid ex-wife who was going to finally see what a worthless scumbag I am."

Puzzle pieces beginning to take shape, I felt a strengthening from the Holy Spirit. "Take the test, Jared."

"What about us?" he asked, searching my eyes. "I feel like a heel even asking for your forgiveness. Not after everything I've already done to you and the kids. Even if you can find some way to forgive me, Natalie never will."

"Slow down," I said, holding up a hand. "I'm still in shock, but no one has said this sin is unforgivable."

He looked at me wide-eyed. "Poppy, I'm lower than dirt. I wouldn't blame you for jumping ship. You deserve better than me." He jerked abruptly from the table. "I can't even stand to have you look at me right now. Everyone would be better off without me."

Hearing the dangerous turn of his voice, I leapt from my chair and grabbed his arm.

He tried to pull free. "Let me go."

"No," I said firmly. "If you take your life, you really *will* ruin everything for me and your children. Leah's included—if that baby is actually yours."

His voice broke. "How did you know?"

I reached a palm to the side of his face. "Face your demons, Jared Levine. Do you really think the monster who wrestled you in your sleep is going to give up so easily? That thing has tried to destroy both of us. Why do you suppose that is?"

"Poppy, I—"

Cutting him off, I continued, "Don't you remember what Rose Margolin told us about how relentless Leviathan is? What about Bible study last week? Kyle Goldstein shared his entire testimony knowing his fiancée would be exposed to potential gossip or embarrassment. Instead of being ashamed, though, Kyle and Abigail rejoiced because his story shows that God can save anybody—no matter how atrocious their sins are."

"Kyle did all of those things before he got saved, Poppy. I have no excuse."

"There is no sin that Jesus hasn't already overcome. The cross has the final word. Not Leah. Not her bully of a father. Take the test, Jared. If the baby is yours, we'll ask the Lord how we make this situation work. Regardless, you need to pray and thank God He exposed your sin instead of allowing it to fester and eat you alive."

He kept his head bowed but nodded in agreement.

"That being said, there better be no more lies. No more half truths. If you are truly committed to making our marriage a *real* marriage, then I want only the truth from here on out."

He sighed heavily before finally mustering the courage to meet and hold my gaze. "No more lies. I want this marriage to work for us and for our family. I'm sorry I've been covering this up and even more sorry that I ever slept with Leah in the first place."

I took his hands in mine. "Then, we start with prayer. Together."

CHAPTER 32

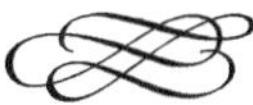

I CONFIDED THE MOST RECENT SERIES OF EVENTS TO Rebecca and Taylor, trusting both of them to pray and keep matters quiet. I also asked Rose Margolin to intercede against Leviathan without further details. She nodded dutifully, vowing to fast and seek God on our behalf. My first few prayers with Jared felt awkward, but we eventually became less guarded and fearful of one another.

Jared's requests for a paternity test went unanswered, and we both suspected there was more to the story than whatever version of events had been presented to Jessica Goldstein. Leah's silence drove Jared and I closer together and closer to Jesus. Old Jared and old Poppy would have been at each other's throats, me lambasting Jared in anger and betrayal, Jared responding with cold cruelty or blame shifting to avoid responsibility. I had a feeling Leah counted on history repeating itself, especially as my mother relayed stories of gossip hounds sniffing for details during her Jewish Federation meetings. With a sly smile, my mother said she relished the disappointment on their faces when she informed them Jared and I were planning to renew our wedding vows. The crisis that should have obliterated the Levine family instead solidified our reconciliation.

I had never seen my husband more truly broken than in those early days when he confessed what he'd done to me and our close friends. After much prayer, we agreed to keep the news from our children until we had conclusive evidence to believe they would be welcoming another sibling. Ever observant, Natalie began questioning Jared about his more recent, agitated state. Privately, she pressed me for further details, anxious that we had resumed divorce proceedings. Once I reassured her that Mommy and Daddy were still getting back together, she let the matter rest.

With no word from Leah following the twenty week mark of her pregnancy, Jared and I resolved ourselves to wait and trust the Lord. Rose Margolin encouraged us with Bible verses about God shielding us from the wicked and exposing their schemes. Rebecca and Ted gave us similar Scriptures about God being our strong tower in times of trouble. As Jared and I prayed separately and together, we began to intercede for Leah, determined that God would somehow get the glory from the mess that we'd made of our lives.

"What a night," Jared said, his arm slung around me as we finished a movie at home. "I'm on a date with my wife, the kids are all bunking over at my mom's, and you don't hate my guts. Can't get much better than that."

"Listen, I'm just as shocked as you are that your mother stepped up after all this time. The kids really warmed up to her and your step-dad."

Jared shook his head and chuckled. "Gary wasn't expecting an apology from me after twenty years of pretending he didn't exist. Neither was Mom."

"But look where it's brought us," I said, staring into his eyes. Jared's look of contentment transformed into pain and regret, and I knew depression wouldn't be far behind. "You're already forgiven. Stop."

He removed his arm from me and ran both hands through increasingly silver hair. "It's the not knowing that's killing me, Poppy. Even if it's the worst case scenario, at least we'd have an answer."

"And you don't think Leah knows that?"

Jared raised a brow. "It doesn't change what I did."

"No, it doesn't," I said, "but watching you torment yourself over something you can't control is gut wrenching. After all the times I hit you over the head about showing remorse, God used this fiasco to help both of us get free from the past. I see the changes, Jared. Even Tom and Anna would be proud."

A small smile appeared on his lips. "Well, there's certainly no shortage of forgiveness and compassion coming from you either. They thought they had you pegged as angry and holding onto offenses."

I rolled my eyes, thankful their arrow of accusation now fell helplessly to the ground. "It still blows my mind how grateful I am that God allowed this to happen."

"Grateful?" Jared croaked.

"Not for the circumstances," I amended quickly, "but for God helping us conquer our old issues and move forward." I laced my fingers through his.

"So, this is what real forgiveness feels like," Jared said, holding up our joined hands and studying them. "Knowing that you absolutely don't deserve it, but being loved anyway. I will always be grateful to you, Poppy. You have no idea how much."

I smiled. "This is salvation. Because He did this for us first."

"I love you," he said softly. "I don't think you've been more beautiful to me than you are at this moment."

I leaned over and gently kissed his lips. "I love you too."

He combed his fingers into my hair, resting his forehead against mine. "How did you do it? How did you forgive me after everything I've done?"

"That was all Jesus," I said. "I know beyond a shadow of a doubt that God was speaking through me when you first told me what happened. It's been God filling my heart with peace despite the storm going on around us. You and I were both so hurt and caught up in the past, but thank God, we're free now."

"What if we're not really free?" Jared pulled back and looked into my eyes. "What if we're tied to Leah forever, like you said?"

I sighed heavily, desperate to hold onto God's peace rather than my own worry. "We don't have all the facts yet. I'm guessing Leah is waiting for you to come crawling back or for me to wash my hands of you. She's never seen you truly walking with God, and it's unlikely she knows that I got saved last fall."

"She hates you, Poppy. Even more than she hates me, which is saying something."

"And I loved her. I still love Leah, despite what she's done and what she's doing."

"How?" he asked incredulously.

"Because I see someone who has everything the world can offer, but she's always been the most lonely and insecure person I know. Leah could have been happy with her own family by now, but she set her sights on you and refuses to let go. She wants what she can't have because she's been taught to believe she's entitled to anything her heart desires."

Jared shook his head, releasing his hands from me. "Most of

that is my fault for leading her on. It's not like I didn't know what I was doing, even back in high school."

"I know," I said quietly, "but Leah had her part to play too. You both were selfish and self-absorbed. I compounded the problem by enabling the two of you. Instead of holding either of your feet to the fire, I made excuses for bad behavior, took the blame, or kept the peace. It was a perfect storm for codependent dysfunction."

"Those were still my choices, Poppy. I can't blame you for enabling me because I didn't give you much of a choice. It was survive or be eaten alive. I was a bully, and we both know it."

I marveled at Jared's show of contrition, of the stark contrast between the haughty man I had married versus the man who had been humbled and broken into a new creation. "Yes, you were a monster, but you're not that man anymore. My parents see it too, by the way. It's made a bigger impact on them than any of that messianic stuff you tried on them back in December."

He looked stunned.

"Jared, the most disarming thing in the world is genuine remorse. You can't stay mad at someone who sees themselves through your eyes and actually feels the hurt they've caused."

"You could if you're Leah," he said bitterly.

"And that's her own choice. She's also got a lot on her plate, whether she's actually pregnant or whether this baby is actually yours. She's thirty-eight, never been married, and her one-night-stand is trying to reconcile with the person she's envied for more than twenty years. That doesn't even include hormones or potential pregnancy complications."

"You're amazing." Jared's eyes shone in admiration. "Leah's been your enemy for so long, all while pretending to be your friend. How can you show so much compassion for her even while she's trying to destroy you?"

"I remember Leah Halpern as the snotty, fourteen year-old in P.E. class who suddenly found herself humiliated because she forgot her gym shorts. There were some nasty girls in our class who couldn't wait to take Leah down a few pegs. I'll never forget the look of gratitude on Leah's face or the triumphant way she decided I was her best friend for what I'd done."

"So, it was your need to be needed?" Jared asked. "To be able to help someone else because you couldn't do anything about your brother?"

"I wouldn't go that far, but I do enjoy helping others. Probably too much. The new girl at work, Carly, treats me like a mother figure. When we're not training, she tells me about her boyfriend drama or asks my opinion on whether she should move out of the house she's renting with her roommates."

Jared laughed. "Maybe it's a practice run for Natalie."

I smirked. "Could be, but I think Nati has a better head on her shoulders, even at twelve. She's gone a little boy crazy this year, but I've also seen our daughter grow up a lot."

Jared's smile disappeared. "Did I steal her childhood, Poppy? Is that one more thing I'm going to have hanging over me the rest of my life?"

"Natalie is *still* a child," I said, taking Jared's hands in mine. "You are going to have to make peace with the mistakes you've made. No amount of regret is going to change or undo them. However, you can move forward and change your trajectory so that you're not going around in circles. All any of us can do is our best, and we have to accept it as good enough."

"And what if it's not good enough?" he asked in an anguished voice. "What if I screwed up Natalie so bad that she goes out and marries a jerk just like me?"

"Jared, do you trust God?"

"What do you mean?"

"Exactly what I said. Do you think you love Natalie more than Jesus does? That He isn't interested in her welfare or protecting her even more than you are?"

"What about free will?" he argued.

"What about it? We can't micromanage our children thinking it will protect them from making mistakes. You saw how well that worked out for my mother and me. It pushed me away, and I rebelled any chance I could. Jared, you need to trust that you are loved, our kids are loved, and that the cross has the final word."

A tiny smile touched his mouth. "You say that a lot."

"It's what Miss Belle told me the day I got saved. I don't have to carry the weight of the world on my shoulders anymore. I'm not constantly stressing that if I make one little mistake, the entire world will fall apart. It's God's job to run the world, not mine."

Eyes glowing, Jared leaned in and cupped my face. More than just physical passion, there was intimacy and a sense of belonging in his touch. This man was mine just as much as I was his. A simple kiss grew heated and intense as emotions were communicated with lips but no words. I dug my hands into his hair, and a low growl rumbled from his throat. Jared pulled me sideways onto his lap and broke the kiss. He held me tightly and pressed my head against his thundering heartbeat.

"We have to stop," he said, panting. "If we don't, we won't. I know we're legally still married, but I feel like we need to do it right."

Gently pushing his arms away, I turned so I could look him in the eyes. "Who would perform the ceremony? Rabbi Cohn?"

He shook his head. "No, and obviously not Rabbi Lebow either."

"Do you want a Jewish wedding or a Christian one? Do we even want a formal ceremony? Do we need one? I don't want to over complicate this."

"I'd like to make real vows, Poppy."

"As long as you know that vows in and of themselves aren't going to make or break our marriage. It's our responsibility to keep them after the ceremony. Otherwise, they're just empty promises that sound great for an audience."

He considered my words for a moment. "What about that other rabbi?"

"What other rabbi?"

"The one who did the *bris* for your friend, Taylor?"

"Rabbi Peretz?" I asked, raising an eyebrow. "I suppose he probably officiates weddings even though he's a professional *mohel*. Why did you bring him up?"

Jared shrugged. "I don't know. He just popped into my head."

"He's an Orthodox rabbi. I know he doesn't mind performing circumcisions for Messianic couples as long as they don't push Jesus on him, but do we want an Orthodox wedding ceremony?"

"Not the whole ceremony. We can't afford it anyway since we just got done paying off the divorce attorneys, but I was thinking we could go through the vows portion and the blessings."

"I don't know," I sighed. "It's been forever since I actually attended a Jewish wedding, and I'm not sure if he'll let us cut and paste everything. I feel like it might be a dangerous slope anyways. One second we're just doing our vows, and before you know it, we've got a full blown, Jewish ceremony because it won't feel right including one piece and not another."

"So, what do you want to do? I want to make this official, and I know you do too."

"We pray. If God gives us the go ahead, we'll call Rabbi Peretz and see if there's an abridged version he can do for a vow renewal. If not, maybe we just do our own ceremony at Danbury Park."

"Why the park?"

"I love the gazebo," I said dreamily. "The daffodils should be out in full bloom too."

"Ah, yellow," he said, matching my smile. "Should have known."

CHAPTER 33

ALTHOUGH SURPRISED BY MY PHONE CALL, RABBI Peretz was delighted to talk to me about a vow renewal ceremony, particularly when I mentioned my friendship with Taylor Horner. He said he would be happy to meet with Jared and me to discuss our vision for the event. My father seemed mystified at our choice to have a traditional Jewish wedding, but he was still supportive. Jared's mother and stepfather were elated to be included.

Jared and I met often for lunch, his midtown office only fifteen minutes away from the uptown sprawl of Parkview. Most days, we shared our packed lunches at a picnic table outside of the Culver highrise. However, as we drew near to our original, March 22 wedding anniversary, we made the fateful decision to eat at Los Bravos on a Tuesday.

Our last encounter at the restaurant ended with me storming out on Jared. As we greeted Carlos at the host stand, he smiled in surprise to see the two of us together. A glance down at our joined hands widened his grin.

"*Bienvenidos, mis amigos!* Glad to see you worked it out. *¡Feli-cidades!*"

I blushed, and Jared looked mildly embarrassed. "Thanks, Carlos," I said quietly. "How have things been going?"

"*Aye, tan loco como siempre*...crazy drama," he said with theatrical annoyance. He pointed to an arguing couple seated close to the bar. "That man comes here all the time, but always with a different woman. He used to come with *mujer muy linda*, very pretty girl, but not anymore. One time I think he comes with *la esposa*, but this time, *es—*" Carlos caught himself suddenly, grimacing as he looked at Jared. "I'll be right back, *amigos*," he said, dashing away in embarrassment.

Confused, I looked up at Jared, noting that my husband was captivated by whatever spectacle was going down with the mystery couple. Glancing over and wishing I'd brought my glasses for distance, I squinted and tried to make out their faces.

"No way," Jared murmured.

"What?"

"That's Leah...with Moose."

"What!" I said shrilly, causing a few heads to turn.

Thankfully, our allied enemies remained oblivious.

"I'm assuming you've taken Leah here before," I said, realizing how Carlos recognized my former best friend and her connection to my husband.

Jared's mouth thinned into a line. "Unfortunately."

I glanced at an empty booth behind the clandestine couple. "Jared, do you think we could...?"

"We could try," he said with a shrug. He eyed my recent haircut that had transformed my shapeless sheet of curls into a bouncy bob. "I don't think Leah will recognize you from the back."

"What about you?" I asked. "Leah would spot you anywhere. How are we going to get close enough to hear anything?"

Like an answer to prayer, Kyle Goldstein materialized from behind us, and he approached with surprised delight. "Fancy seeing you two here on Taco Tuesday! What's up, guys?"

Jared and I shared a simultaneous aha moment and worked quickly to convince Kyle to go along with it.

"So, pretend I'm on a date with Poppy?" he asked, raising an eyebrow.

"Yes," I said. "Leah and Moose won't recognize you, and even if they recognize me, they have no idea Jared will be close by."

"I'm not sure if eavesdropping is kosher," he said warily.

"Please," Jared begged. "I know this is asking a lot, but if we can find out anything today, it would give Poppy and me some peace of mind. Plus, any dirt you dig up on Patrick might help your sister move on with her life too."

Kyle glanced over at me, well aware of my last conversation with Jessica.

Picking up where Jared left off, I said, "Your sister has to get mad enough at Patrick to stop feeling sorry for herself. Jessica admits he's a jerk, but I don't think she knows how much Patrick took advantage of her. She's still blaming herself for everything. You'll be helping all of us get some much needed closure."

Before Kyle replied, Carlos arrived, ready to escort Jared and me to our table. He took one look at Kyle and then began speaking in rapid Spanish. Kyle replied with ease, glancing at me and Jared, and then apparently giving Carlos instructions on how to help us with our mission. By the end of their conversation, Carlos puffed out his chest as if playing the role of "man in the chair" helping out his superhero buddy. Jared gave my hand an encouraging squeeze as Carlos grabbed two menus from the stand.

"Every day is a *novela* here," Carlos said with an exaggerated eye roll. "You two, come with me," he said, gesturing to me and Kyle. "I'll get you a table in a minute," he said to Jared.

"I can't believe I agreed to this," Kyle whispered close to my ear. He wrapped an arm around me and blocked my face from Leah with his body. Carlos put us in a booth behind them, Kyle sitting back-to-back with Leah, and me facing forward. I could see most of Moose's face towering above the shared partition between his table and ours. I kept my gaze furtive to avoid eye contact and possible recognition.

"Thank you," I mouthed.

"I felt your husband glaring at me the second I touched you, and I don't think Abigail would like this either," he said in a hushed voice.

"Text her," I whispered back. "We can use all the extra prayer we can get. And don't worry about Jared. He's just anxious for the vow renewal and to have *his* hands all over me."

Kyle chuckled at my frankness. "Okay, well I can't fault him for that. Abigail and I are in the same boat." He whipped out his phone and sent off a series of texts to his fiancée. She responded with a .gif of a woman doing a spit take.

"Apparently, she finds this humorous," Kyle said wryly.

"Can you hear anything?" I asked.

Kyle shook his head.

Glancing at the menu and speaking softly, I said, "Hey, can you order for me in Spanish? Better that Leah doesn't hear me." I pointed at a lunch combo, and Kyle nodded.

Carlos approached with chips and salsa, temporarily halting Moose and Leah's conversation. I kept my gaze averted as Kyle placed our order. He handed over the menus, and Carlos retreated back to the kitchen. My grand plan to eavesdrop on Leah was quickly becoming an exercise in futility and unnecessary anxiety. I prayed for God to intervene and help us uncover the truth.

Looking bored and somewhat irritated, Kyle munched on a chip. "What now?"

I shrugged in apology, feeling like a fool. I glanced over at Jared, and his eyes darted to Moose and Leah, silently asking if we had uncovered anything. I shook my head. Like a moth to a flame, Leah inhaled sharply, and I knew she'd just spotted the object of her twenty-year obsession.

"Put your head down," she hissed at Moose. "He'll see us."

"Who?" Patrick said loud enough for half the restaurant to hear.

"Jared, you idiot! He can't find out!"

Feigning surprise at hearing his name, Jared sauntered over to their table. He met my eyes briefly, inclining his head as if to say, "Called an audible. Just go with it." He turned his attention quickly to Leah.

"Well, isn't this cozy?" he said grandly.

"Jared, what are you doing here?" Leah replied with feigned indifference.

"I could ask you the same thing. Patrick, why am I not surprised? Never could resist an opportunity to take advantage of a girl in crisis, huh? Feels just like your graduation party all over again with Leah."

My eyes widened at that new bit of information. Like a court reporter, Kyle took notes as fast as his fingers would allow him.

"You have some nerve," Leah spat. "You're the one who got Poppy drunk so you could take her virginity. Did you ever tell her you spiked her drink, or does she still think that night was meant to be?"

"Oh, she knows," Jared said, glaring daggers at Leah. "What she doesn't know is that her best friend told me to double the amount of alcohol. You called Poppy a sheltered baby who needed to grow up. If we're going to talk about taking advantage of Poppy's trust, you might want to look in a mirror."

With a sickening feeling, I saw how my "best friend" had ruthlessly served me up like a lamb for the slaughter. Leah had intended for me to be traumatized by my first sexual experience and forsake all designs on Jared as a result. As I mentally recounted the events, I remembered how she had hounded me for details afterward, especially since she had lost her own virginity that night too. She never told me the identity of her mystery man, only that it was painful, and he'd abandoned her when it was over.

Naïvely, I had assumed Leah was just jealous that her experience had been significantly less satisfying than mine. Twenty-three years later, I now realized that Leah's furious tirade was due to frustration that her sadistic plan had backfired. I swallowed down a lump of bile at her betrayal. Stealing my husband wasn't the worst thing Leah Halpern had ever done to me.

Jared glowered at Leah with the same disgust I felt for her. "I assume this is Patrick's baby, not mine. I mean, that's why I saw the two of you arguing, right?"

"You're the one who showed up ready for a late night house call," she said smugly. "I'm sorry your ego can't handle how easily you've been replaced, but this *is* your baby. Does it bother you to know he'll be calling Patrick, 'Daddy,' instead of you?"

I did not mistake the look of alarm on Moose's face, clearly not expecting Leah to volunteer him for co-parenting duties. Jared saw it too, unfazed by the ridiculous notion that a father who barely made time for his own children would be interested in raising one that belonged to another man.

"So, the two of you are planning to do this together, is that it?" Jared asked. "I wonder how Moose's wife will feel about that. Maybe I should give her a call. I'm sure Katie Bishoff would love to hear from her old friend at Hillcrest High."

As expected, Moose balked at the idea and Leah raged in response.

"Stay away from my wife!" Moose growled. "Not unless you want me to tell Poppy how you knocked up your ex-girlfriend while you were trying to reconcile with her."

Ignoring Moose's empty threat, Jared said, "I want a paternity test, Leah. Why else would you give me the silent treatment for the last two months unless you knew that I wasn't really the father?"

"Spare me the self righteous indignation," she scoffed. "You're just mad that I screwed things up with Poppy. This is your mess, Jared Levine, and I'm not letting you get away with it."

"I still can't believe you're getting back together with your wife," Moose sneered. "Does becoming a Jew for Jesus make you deaf, dumb, and blind too?"

Jared glared daggers at him. "Hypocrite much?"

Moose exhaled a haughty chuckle. "I just did it for the money. What's your excuse, Levine? You said Poppy got fat and ugly and ragged on you all the time. It's got to be the kids, because nobody's buying this holy man routine you're trying to sell. You wouldn't have shown up at Leah's place looking for an easy lay if any of this was real."

I winced at the same time Kyle did, and he mouthed an apology. I shook my head that I was fine, thankfully already aware of Jared's old insults.

Derisively, Leah added, "Poppy's the only person on the planet stupid enough to believe anything about you has changed. I would say that you two deserve each other, but frankly, neither one of you deserves to be happy after what you've done to me."

"And what does that make *you*?" he asked pointedly. "You're still trying to steal from your best friend what you think belongs to you."

"I want nothing to do with you, Jared."

"Is that so?" His eyes flicked to what I imagined was her distended belly. "Then, why did you tell Jessica that this baby was mine? Why did you send your father down to the bank? Why refuse to answer my request for a paternity test if this wasn't all some hare brained way to trap me into getting back together with you?"

"Because you deserve to suffer the way I have!" she roared. "I want you to know that your son will grow up hating you the same way I do. He can join his other siblings in knowing what a miserable excuse they have for a father." Her remark hit too close to home, and it took Jared longer to recover.

"Wait, why did you tell Jessica?" Moose interrupted, his gaze narrowing on Leah.

"Because she's my friend."

Moose let loose a string of profanity that said otherwise. "You really are a psycho, Leah. I don't know whose baby this is, but I feel sorry for that kid."

"Patrick!" Leah hissed. "We talked about this already. The baby is Jared's."

"Moose, did she tell you that you're the father?" Jared asked, ignoring Leah. "Is that what you guys were arguing about?"

"Yeah," Patrick said, glaring at Leah. "Princess got mad after you dumped her, and she convinced me to break up with Jessica so we could start hooking up again."

Kyle stopped typing, his hands beginning to shake. Reaching

across the table, I took a hold of his wrist, trying to keep him calm.

"Sorry, to interrupt the *novela*," Carlos said, arriving with plates balanced on his arm, "but we have other customers here." He placed our lunches in front of me and Kyle and then turned to Jared. "*Señor*, you need to sit down and order food, or you need to leave."

"I've lost my appetite anyway," Jared said with one last glance at Leah. "God help that innocent baby, because it deserves a lot better than the two of you as parents." He turned on his heel and walked away. I heard Leah burst into tears as Moose seethed.

"You ruined everything!" he growled.

"Me?" she choked. "The second he mentioned Jessica, you lost your cool. Why did you have to tell him anything?"

"Leah, you can have your sick little games with Jared, but you're not going to run a con on me too."

"What are you talking about?"

"You took a cheap shot at my ex-girlfriend, and you know it. You just had to rub it in her face that you're having my baby, right?"

"Like she even knows you're the father," she replied with irritation. "I let her think it's Jared's baby. What difference does it make anyway?"

"Everything's a competition with you. You were jealous of Katie in high school, so you hooked up with me at my graduation party. You've been holding a torch for Jared for the last twenty years, and you sabotaged his marriage. You hated that I was having a good time with Jessica instead of keeping up with the 'benefits' part of our friendship after Jared left you. Jessica never knew about us, so how do you win by throwing this baby in her face? If Halpern Industries wasn't my biggest client, I'd forget I even knew you."

Carlos kept his eyes downcast as he overheard the last bit of Moose's speech and replenished their water glasses. Muttering under his breath in Spanish, he moved on to another table quickly.

"What's so special about Jessica Goldstein anyway?" Leah demanded, her infamous jealousy the only thing she cared to discuss. "You said she was an easy mark and that you liked the convenience of you guys working together. Are you going to pretend you actually cared about her?"

"Kyle," I said quietly, seeing his hand ball into a fist on the table.

"This is wrong," he whispered back angrily. "I want to deck the guy."

"Remember what happened with Mitch and Chloe," I said, referring to Taylor Horner's ex-husband and her former sister-in-law who had carried on an affair. Kyle had discovered them together at Los Bravos and confronted them about their cheating ways. Chloe eventually repented and reconciled with her husband.

"This is my sister they're talking about," he hissed.

"You're not going to do her any good unless you lay low," I said. "Start praying, because I know I am."

Grimly, Kyle nodded and closed his eyes, inhaling a slow breath through his nose.

Trying to find my place in the midst of Moose and Leah's heated exchange, I heard Moose say, "You're the one who said she was weighing me down, Leah. I was never going to leave Katie, but Jessica and I had a good thing going. If you think I'm going to help pay for your bastard kid when I can barely afford to keep my own in private school, you're dreaming."

Leah scoffed. "I don't need your money, and you're lucky your wife enjoys her country club membership too much to divorce you. The only thing I need from you is to keep your mouth shut. Even with a negative paternity test, as soon as Poppy finds out Jared cheated again, she'll go nuclear on him. That'll be the end of their marriage. Finally."

"What exactly am I supposed to keep quiet, Leah? I thought you wanted Poppy to find out Jared cheated."

"We never slept together that night," she said. "He just thinks we did."

CHAPTER 34

"W HAT DO YOU MEAN HE *thinks* YOU DID?"

Kyle and I exchanged wide-eyed glances, feeling like we could hear a pin drop as we awaited Leah's answer.

"Jared came over to my place furious because he caught Poppy with some guy from work. I gave him two glasses of wine to calm him down because he was scaring me. I had to take a phone call, and when I got back, Jared had passed out on my couch. When he woke up, I told him we'd had sex so he'd give in and do it again. Instead, he just yelled at me and then started texting all of this garbage to Poppy. It's always about *Poppy*," she spat.

Moose whistled and shook his head. "Look, if he wants to live with his fat, ugly wife, then let him! Move on already, Princess. You're going to ruin that kid's life before it even comes out," he said, gesturing to her belly.

"My sister is going to raise the baby," Leah said primly, ignoring Moose's jab. "I don't need to be tied down with some brat, and Amy loves kids. She already has three anyway. What's one more?"

I breathed a sigh of relief, thankful that God used Leah's own vanity to spare an innocent child from being aborted or being raised by an ungrateful mother. My new co-worker, Carly, had enough horror stories to share about a childhood like that. Although I didn't know Leah's younger half-sister that well, I remembered her as a sweet girl.

"Why didn't you just get rid of it?" Patrick asked. "Even if it's my baby, I don't want another kid, and it's obvious you don't care about it either." Answering his own question, he said, "You were going to trap, Jared, weren't you? You'd get the ultimate revenge on Poppy, and nobody would be the wiser, right? Leah Halpern finally gets her fairy tale ending after twenty long years," he mocked.

"I hate you!"

Moose rolled his eyes at her outburst. "Poppy may not be the hot, young thing she used to be, but it's obvious why Jared picked her over you."

"Get out of my sight!" Leah banged her fist against the table. "I wish I'd never slept with you in high school or the night after Jared came over. I'm glad this baby will never know what a pathetic loser his father is."

"Or what a selfish whore his mother is," Patrick replied with icy disdain. "Call me after you've had the baby. I'm sure you'll be lonely. You're always lonely. Poor, little rich girl who has to pay people to love her."

Leah grunted in feral rage, and Patrick laughed in her face. Smirking, he left the booth without sparing her a backward glance. Kyle looked over at me, his expression enigmatic. I could only imagine the thoughts running through his mind about what his sister had endured being involved with someone like Moose Grunwald.

Eventually, Leah lumbered out of her seat, and I caught her side profile. Her pregnancy was legitimate even if none of the rest of her story was true. Though disgusted and enraged by her deception, my heart hurt at Patrick's cold indifference toward his unborn child and its mother. I saw a broken woman desperate for happiness but stubbornly refusing to let go of the past. Sighing heavily at my own, conflicted emotions, I sent Jared a text and invited him back inside the restaurant.

"I...I'm speechless," Kyle said once I tossed my phone back in my purse. "My poor sister! I hate that she's wasted even one second wondering what's wrong with herself. Patrick is even more of a creep than I gave him credit for. The guy's a full blown psychopath!"

"Leah didn't choose Moose by accident, but she's definitely met her match. Patrick seemed to genuinely take delight in hurting her. You didn't see his face, Kyle, but it looked demonic."

"Probably better that I didn't. I would have decked him."

"I believe you," I said, seeing the angry vein bulging in his forehead. "I just hope Leah's serious about giving her baby up for adoption. It may be the only unselfish thing she does in her entire life. That poor child deserves so much better than the two of them as parents."

"What did I miss?" Jared asked, approaching us.

Seeing the pale and pained expression on my face, he frowned. He motioned for me to scoot over so he could sit next to me.

"Well?" he prodded.

"Moose is the father," I said quietly, "and nothing happened with Leah. She made it up."

"What!" he said, doing a double take.

Kyle answered for me. "After you crashed on the sofa, Leah lied about you guys sleeping together so you'd cave for another round. She admitted everything to Patrick. She just wants you to *believe* it happened."

"To do what?" Jared rasped. "Make me torture myself with regret?"

"That too," I said, "but mostly so I would find out and divorce you for cheating again. Even if Leah had agreed to the paternity test and it was negative, nobody would have been the wiser about what didn't happen at her penthouse that night. She's still counting on it."

Instead of showing any sign of relief, Jared seemed even more tormented. "Poppy, those messages I sent you," he said, meeting my eyes in anguish. "Leah kept insisting that since you were sleeping with Joe, there was nothing wrong with her and I getting back together. She thought if she got me mad enough at you, that history would repeat itself. Instead, I just took all the guilt and frustration I felt and attacked you with it. I blamed you for what happened with Leah. Or what I *thought* happened," he amended. "I'm such an idiot!"

Before I could respond, Kyle said, "I'm going to give you guys some privacy to hash through all of this. I have to call my sister anyway. She may not want to talk to me, but she needs to know what a slime Patrick is."

I nodded, still reeling from all of the deception and needless suffering my kids and I had endured.

"Poppy?" Jared asked weakly. "Talk to me."

"There's more."

"More?" he repeated in disbelief.

"You were right when you confronted Leah. Her original plan was to trick you into thinking the baby was yours. She hoped you'd leave me to start a new family with her. It's the only thing that kept her from having an abortion. We can thank God for that at least."

Jared raked anxious fingers through his hair. "And we both know how close she came to getting her wish. Why, why, *why* did I lead her on all those years?"

"It wasn't just you, Jared. Moose called out Leah for trying to ruin our marriage. She's not the innocent victim any more than you are."

"But you were." His grieved expression left me in no doubt of his sincerity. "Poppy, I know I've apologized already, but I'm so sorry. I am the worst kind of hypocrite and I'm so ashamed of the things I said to you that night. They were ugly and cruel, and then Natalie saw everything! I'm not sure she's totally forgiven me for that…or if she should."

"I know," I said, placing my hand tentatively on his. "I've forgiven you, Jared. I'll keep saying it until you believe it."

"I don't understand how," he said bitterly. "I'm scum. I don't deserve it."

"Because I want a life together with you and our kids. I want a chance to have a real marriage with God at the center. The truth is ugly, but we're finally free."

Jared nodded, inhaling deeply and exhaling. "So, now what?"

"Well," I said, pulling my plate of food closer, "I eat my cold lunch, get back to work, and then try to process everything we found out today."

"Jared! What are you…oh!" Leah gasped, standing before us with her cell phone in hand. It took her a second to recognize me, and her eyes doubled in size.

"Hi," I said, eyeing Leah from head to toe. "Bet you didn't realize I was sitting behind you the whole time you were talking to Moose, did you?"

Apparently not, because she paled and swooned.

Earning himself an extraordinarily large tip, Carlos caught Leah before she hit the floor. He pulled her into the same booth she'd exited a scant, ten minutes earlier. Jared and I popped up immediately, standing beside Carlos as he placed Leah gently in the seat.

"She said she left her cell phone at the table," Carlos said to me and Jared. "Should we call 911?"

"Leah?" Jared called. "Are you okay?"

She groaned, her eyes fluttering.

"Leah," I said, realizing her fainting spell was no mere performance. "Do we need to call your OBGYN? Can you hear us?"

"What do you care?" she snapped, clearly feeling more like herself. "You'd be happy if this baby died, wouldn't you, Poppy?"

"Would you?" I asked gently.

Her icy blue eyes opened and met mine, taking in my appearance and sizing me up. "You're not fat and ugly," she said wearily. "Yet another lie."

"Leah," I said, "are you alright? Is the baby okay?"

Her eyes narrowed. "Are you planning to steal my baby or something? Have Jared sue for custody and raise my kid and tell him how horrible I am?"

I recognized Leah's favorite trick of projecting her own sins onto others, and I paused before answering. Although briefly tempted to throw her words back in her face, I felt the Holy Spirit urging me to hold my tongue.

"Are you better now, *señorita?*" Carlos asked Leah.

Leah waved him off. "I'm fine. I'm sure you remember all the times I came in here with him," she said pointing to Jared. "This is the horrible woman who's been ruining my life for the last twenty years. They think they're in love," she said with enough acid to make Carlos wince. He excused himself and Jared and I sat down opposite Leah.

"Is this an intervention?" she asked with a sarcastic laugh.

"This game that's been going since high school needs to stop. *Now*," I demanded. "You're not a kid anymore, and that stunt you pulled at Moose's graduation party would have gotten you arrested if it had happened today."

She sneered as she looked down her nose at me. "You could hardly call it rape, Poppy. Not with the way you wouldn't shut up about how *magical* it was."

"How could you do it?" My voice broke as I recalled the entire evening in my mind. "I thought you were my friend."

"High school was a hundred years ago."

"I'm talking about all of it. How could you betray me? Your godchildren? How could you deny my kids their own father so you could pretend Jared is the father of this baby you made with Moose Grunwald?"

She winced at the sound of Patrick's nickname, but she hid her discomfort under an armor of arrogance.

"How can you be so naïve?" she shot back. "The only person Jared Levine loves is Jared Levine."

"That's not true!" he said, countering Leah's lies before I could. "I love Jesus now, and he's teaching me how to love my wife and my kids the way they deserve. Nobody knows what a failure I was as a husband and a father better than me. I won't make that mistake again."

Leah seemed taken aback, both by Jared's confession and by his newfound humility.

"It's true," I said, searching Leah's eyes. "Jared isn't the same man I married. He hasn't just apologized for what he's done, but he also repented."

"Repented?" she repeated in disbelief. "Oh, Poppy, don't tell me he made you one of those Jesus freaks too. You're even more hopeless than I thought."

"It was *Jesus* who made me into one of those 'Jesus freaks.' It's the only way I was able to forgive Jared. Or you," I said, looking at her meaningfully. "You may not be sorry, but I do forgive you, Leah. If it wasn't for that precious baby growing inside of you, Jared and I would never have gotten over the past. We have you to thank for that, and I'm grateful."

She gaped, confused and horrified. "Don't you care that Jared cheated on you? Again?" she added, twisting the knife.

"Jessica Goldstein told me about your pregnancy back in December."

"Jessica?" she gasped. "You know her?"

I nodded. "She and I became friends last fall. We didn't discover we had you and Jared and in common until later. When she told me about your pregnancy, I told her Jared couldn't be the father."

"Why? Because he's Mr. Holier than Thou?" she mocked.

"No, because Jared had a vasectomy after I found out I was pregnant with Madison. I was furious with him at the time, and I told you all about it."

Clearly, Leah had forgotten, but she was not ready to give up the fight just yet. "That doesn't change the fact that Jared came over to my house. He wanted me, Poppy."

"I wanted *revenge,* not you," Jared said plainly, but without malice. "And if you're being honest with yourself, you never really wanted me either. You just wanted what Poppy had because you couldn't have it yourself. This has always been about your jealousy and insecurity...and my own ego."

"I don't need to put up with this abuse," she said, once again shielding herself with feigned offense.

"And I don't need to put up with yours," I retorted. "I loved you like a sister, Leah. I trusted you, and you betrayed me."

"So did Jared," she said petulantly, "yet you're taking him back. Are you some kind of glutton for punishment, Poppy? Did he blame me for everything just to get back into your good graces? And how gullible are you anyway? If you don't know that all of this Jesus shtick is just an act, then I feel sorry for you."

"Not as sorry as I feel for you."

CHAPTER 35

LEAH LEFT THE RESTAURANT SHORTLY THEREAFTER, and my heart was heavy. She assumed I pitied her for losing the battle over Jared Levine rather than the untold misery she'd caused herself. She stubbornly clung to lies she knew we no longer believed. Jared cried in bitterness and relief, aggrieved by the part he played and once again demonstrating the remorse I'd longed to see during our marriage. I saw how God had changed my own heart too. Rather than crowing in self-righteous victory, I wanted to offer Jared comfort and reassurance that God had forgiven him, and so had I.

I walked back into work in a daze, greeted by Miss Belle as I unlocked my office door.

"Ooh child," she said, looking me over. "You look like you've just been through a war. What happened?"

"Sounds about right," I deadpanned. I dumped my purse in a drawer as she followed me into my office.

She sat in one of the conference chairs facing my desk. "Can you talk, or is Carly coming back soon?"

"She took a late lunch. I didn't expect to be gone for so long either."

"What happened, baby?"

"Oh, you know...Los Bravos on a Tuesday."

"So, you saw Joe Trautweig and his new girlfriend?" she asked. "I don't know why, but all the soap opera shenanigans in this office always seem to happen at that restaurant."

I paled. "What?"

Miss Belle's hand flew to her mouth. "Oh, mercy! I should have listened to the Holy Ghost telling me to keep my big mouth shut! Poppy, I'm so sorry."

"I'm okay, Miss Belle. I'm happy for Joe. I *am,*" I insisted when she raised a penciled eyebrow at me. "Jared and I are planning a wedding vow renewal next month. You're invited, and so is Phil."

"Poppy, are you one hundred percent sure this is what Jesus wants? That you won't be thinking about Joe and his new lady friend and wishing for something else? You don't seem very 'okay' about it."

"I'm sure," I said. "I have something totally different on my mind right now. Whoever is with Joe is a very lucky woman, but I'm with the man I'm supposed to be with. Jared is not the same person I married, and I'm not the same person either."

Miss Belle finally relaxed, the tension leaving her shoulders. "Well, then I'm glad to hear it, child. I'm sorry for my loose lips."

"You're forgiven," I said, scanning through my afternoon workload. "The big news is that Jared and I ran into Leah and her boyfriend today. Do you remember when I told you Jared couldn't be her baby's father?"

Miss Belle rolled her eyes. "You're a better woman than I am to forgive Jared for being at her house in the first place, Poppy

Levine. If Mr. Vickers ever set eyes on another woman, he'd be walking around blind by the time I got done with him."

I laughed out loud knowing Miss Belle sincerely meant every word.

"So, the boyfriend is the baby daddy, I reckon?"

I nodded. "Leah also confessed that she and Jared never slept together that night. She just let him believe they did to ruin any chance of our reconciliation. I also found out she helped Jared get me drunk at a high school party the first time he and I were together."

"Ooh child!" Miss Belle gasped, pearls appropriately clutched in hand yet again.

"Jared never told me Leah's part to play in all of that. He confessed what he'd done after we had been dating for a while, but I was so in love with him that I didn't care. Now, I'm horrified to look back and see how much they both took advantage of me."

"There are a lot of people who would call you crazy for taking him back," Miss Belle said. "Me too, if I didn't know how our mighty God has been working in both of y'all's lives. It's hard to believe that a man like Jared Levine could actually change, but the cross has the final word," she declared, using her oft quoted phrase.

"I've been thinking about writing my story like Rebecca and Taylor did," I said, eyeing her for a reaction. "I want to share how God can take a situation as hopeless as me and Jared and use it for good. That there's hope for other women suffering out there in bad marriages."

Miss Belle pressed her lips together, looking like she wanted to share something but wasn't sure. Finally, she said, "Just be careful with that."

"What do you mean?"

"I'm all for giving hope, but it needs to be the right kind of hope."

"Is there a wrong kind of hope?" I asked with a nervous chuckle.

Miss Belle leveled her potent gaze at me. "There's false hope, baby. The kind that lets an abused woman keep justifying why she won't leave her man. Share your story, but make sure you remember that it was Jesus who saved your marriage."

"Of course!" I said, mildly offended. "I would never try to take credit for what happened. I just thought I could help other people in difficult marriages. You know, like if God did this for me, He can do it for you too. Why would that be wrong?"

"Wishful thinking is a dangerous drug."

"Wishful thinking?" I repeated angrily. "How is it wishful thinking to believe that God can save someone from their sins? Isn't the definition of faith believing in something you can't see yet?"

Miss Belle looked at me patiently. "You can't have salvation without repentance, baby. Even the thief on the cross had to repent first. Just because you have faith for someone else to get saved doesn't mean they'll choose to do it. They have to surrender to God."

"So, how do I offer hope to anyone, Miss Belle? Are you saying it's wrong to believe that salvation is even possible? My friend, Rose, has been praying for her husband for more than forty years. Should I tell her to just give up?"

"No!" she said emphatically, "but you can't make guarantees about anybody's salvation without asking God first. The Word says that He chose His followers before the foundation of the world. We have a responsibility to share the gospel, but only God decides where that seed will take root and grow. As much as we pray for anything in this life, it will always be the sovereign will of God that prevails. We can't make God do anything. To preach otherwise is the height of arrogance and foolishness."

"Why is giving hope to women who are suffering such a bad thing?" I asked, desperate for one more attempt to plead my case. "I get what you're saying, Miss Belle, but don't you think our story could encourage someone else?"

She shifted in the chair, looking increasingly agitated with my stubbornness. "What happens if one of these women you want to help decides to play martyr and thinks she's 'suffering for the Kingdom?' What happens if the husband never repents, and she winds up wasting her life living with a monster? You can't tell me you'd want anyone to suffer like that, Poppy. There's plenty of fools out there shaming women about how they're not praying hard enough for their marriage or they don't have enough faith."

"God forbid!" I said, outraged.

"You just have to be careful, that's all I'm saying. You were flirting with an affair when God started working on your heart. Your husband claimed faith in Jesus but was still walking in his own pride and self-righteousness. The only part either of y'all had in putting your marriage back together was humbling yourselves and crying out to Jesus for help. He did everything else. If you want to give hope to women suffering like you were, that's what you should tell them."

Considering her words, I finally said, "I just don't understand why God would save our marriage but not every marriage."

"Baby, I don't know why God does what He does," she said softly. "I don't understand why he'd give your husband a second, third, and fourth chance and not somebody else. What I do know, though, is that His plans are bigger than ours. I do believe your story will help people, Poppy, but maybe not the way you were expecting."

Pride wounded, even with good intentions, I was thankful Miss Belle threw me a bone. Continuing, she said, "The story of you and Jared isn't so much about your marriage, but about how God can take even the most ugly situation and use it for our good. He can take what was broken and make it beautiful."

"*Tikkun olam*," I murmured.

"What?" she said. "You're speaking another language, child."

"I am," I said with a grin. "*Tikkun olam* is Hebrew for 'repairing the world.' For my mother and her Jewish federation, it means social justice and charity work, but I think there's something more."

"Go on," she said, intrigued.

"I was thinking the other day about my marriage, just praising God for what He's done. I remember hearing about *tikkun olam* in Hebrew school, but I felt a nudge to do some research online the other day."

"And what did you find, child?" she asked, eyes sparkling.

"The whole concept means to take something that's broken and not just repair it, but improve it. We make it even better than what it was before."

"Like your marriage," she said in understanding. "That's beautiful, Poppy."

I beamed at her, thankful not only for the restoration of my marriage, but for the changes I'd seen in my children as well. Ryan, especially, blossomed under the new and improved Jared. I never realized how much my son desperately needed his father's love and approval until Jared began to pour it out lavishly. Maddie was her usual, effervescent self, even more so seeing her parents together and happy. Natalie's surly disposition also improved tremendously. She began asking questions about Jesus when she saw the changes in me and Jared.

Four weeks later on April 16, Jared and I renewed our wedding vows in my parents' backyard. We stood underneath the *chuppah*, the wedding canopy, and each grandparent held a metal pole that lifted the canopy above our heads. We chose to use Jared's *tallit* for the chuppah cover, and Rabbi Peretz said the outstretched, Jewish prayer shawl represented the creation of a new family before God. Jared and I also viewed the tallit above our heads as God's protective wing covering our marriage and our family.

We had several small rows of folding chairs set up just beyond the chuppah, and our children sat in the front row, dressed in white and smiling brightly. Rebecca and Ted Margolin sat just behind them with Steve and Rose Margolin holding their granddaughters. Taylor and Ian couldn't make it for the ceremony, but Culver Incorporated was proudly represented by Phil and Miss Belle. Kyle and Abigail also attended as well as several other members of our small Bible study.

Jared and I chose to omit some of the standard, Jewish traditions, one of them being the *hakafot*, or the bride encircling her husband seven times. We prayed about which traditions to keep and which to leave out, and Jared and I both felt that the traditional explanation of a wife "protecting" her husband or building some sort of invisible wall seemed more mystical in origin than Biblical. We also wanted to avoid tradition for the sake of appearance or ascribing supernatural power to any of the religious customs in and of themselves. When my mother balked at the idea that it wouldn't be a *real* Jewish wedding without the hakafot, I asked if it was the tradition that made it Jewish or the two people standing beneath the chuppah. That had effectively ended the argument.

"We are here today to celebrate the renewal of marriage vows between Jared Michael Levine, *Ya'akov Moshe ben Yosef*," Rabbi Peretz said, using Jared's full Hebrew name, "and Poppy Esther Berman, *P'nina Eliora bat Chanah*. Jared and Poppy are here to rededicate themselves to one another, to their marriage, and to *Hashem*, our almighty God. As Poppy told me last week, they are bringing tikkun olam to the Levine and Berman families."

Jared caught my eye and gave me such a beautiful smile, I forgot to breathe.

"We will begin with the blessing over the wine, and this cup will only be shared by Jared and Poppy. It represents the unity of their marriage, that they are reserved for one another and no one else."

I met Jared's gaze again, wary of finding any pain or lingering guilt. Instead, his dark eyes glowed at me.

Rabbi Peretz chanted, *"Baruch atah Adonai, Eloheinu melech ha'olam. Borei p'ri hagafen. Amen."*

Our small audience also responded with an, "Amen."

"Blessed are you, Hashem, King of the Universe, who creates the fruit of the vine," Rabbi Peretz said in English. He handed the wine glass to Jared. After he sipped, Jared lifted the glass to my lips so I could also partake.

"Now for the exchanging of rings," Rabbi Peretz said. "Who has the ring for Jared?"

Jared looked over to Gary, and he produced my old wedding band from his pocket.

"I have a surprise for you," Jared whispered. Angling the gold band, I saw he'd had my ring engraved with *Proverbs 31:29*.

I grinned at him.

"Jared, please repeat after me," Rabbi Peretz said. He recited the vows in Hebrew and then in English.

Jared dutifully repeated the prayer in both languages, sliding the ring on my finger and saying, "Behold, by this ring you are consecrated to me as my wife according to the laws of Moses and Israel."

"Now for Poppy," Rabbi Peretz said.

I glanced over at my mother who was miraculously holding herself together. She handed me Jared's ring. Smiling beautifully at my husband, I said, "I have a surprise for you too," and showed him where I'd also had his ring engraved.

"*Ani l'dodi,*" he whispered, reading the tiny Hebrew script now etched on the band.

"Poppy, please repeat after me," Rabbi Peretz said, and I recited the feminine version of Jared's vows.

Next, Rabbi Peretz read the *ketubah,* our Hebrew wedding contract. We had signed the beautifully decorated parchment the night before during a small, rehearsal dinner Jared's mother hosted for us. Barbara had then mounted the certificate inside of a gilded frame. Jared and I planned to hang the ketubah over our bed once we moved into our new house together.

Rabbi Peretz then chanted the *Sheva Brachot,* the "Seven Blessings," signifying the shift in the service order from the "betrothal" to the "marriage." He began with a prayer of thanksgiving to God for creating all things for His glory. The next blessings were for the creation of man and woman, of children, and then, the blessing of our wedding. It resounded with a joyful note, the lilting Hebrew chants of, *"kol sasson v'kol simcha, kol chatan v'kol kalah,"* as Rabbi Perez proclaimed the joy of both bride and groom celebrating their marriage.

The searing look Jared gave me would have melted iron, and I swallowed hard, thankful for another wine blessing and an opportunity to wet my mouth that had suddenly gone dry. Rabbi Peretz completed the Sheva Brachot with the same prayer said earlier over the fruit of the vine, and Jared and I took another sip from the wine glass.

As the final stage of our wedding, Rabbi Peretz took the wine glass Jared and I had shared throughout the ceremony and placed it inside of a velvet drawstring bag. He explained that we break the glass to remember the destruction of the Jewish temple in Jerusalem and to symbolize the first act that Jared and I would perform as a married couple. Likewise, the glass was also shattered so that no one else could partake of the cup Jared and I had shared.

Jared stomped on the glass, and a chorus of *"Mazel tov!"* erupted from the parents holding the chuppah as well as our small gathering of guests.

Rabbi Peretz announced, "May I present to you, Mr. and Mrs. Jared Levine."

Our small contingent burst into applause and cheers.

"Not that you need my permission, but go on and kiss her already," Rabbi Peretz said to Jared. "We've all seen the way you've been looking at your wife."

As our audience laughed, Jared cupped my face and kissed me like a man dying of thirst. Ignoring the raucous cheers of our friends and the shrieking embarrassment of our children, I staked my claim on the man who had captured my heart at sixteen years-old.

"Enough, enough!" I heard my father say through our passionate haze. "You're embarrassing my grandchildren."

Smiling and laughing, Jared hugged me, and we spent the rest of the afternoon and evening celebrating all that God had done.

CHAPTER 36

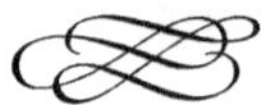

It was a bittersweet moment when I finished packing the last of our boxes, staring at the bare, basement apartment my children and I had shared for nearly three years. Jared and I were able to purchase a small house not far from my parents. Although not nearly as large as our previous home together, it felt like a mansion compared to our basement set up.

"I'm going to miss having you here," my mother said, coming up beside me.

"What are you going to do with all of the space?" I eyed the empty walls, amazed that we'd managed to all fit four of us inside of 1,000 square feet.

"Your father and I haven't decided yet. We've actually been thinking about selling the house."

"Oh, really?" I said with a sly smile. "You know, I hear they're building an active seniors community across the street from us. Jared and I could just drop the kids off, and it'd be just like old times."

My mother stuck her tongue out at me. "I'm serious, Poppy. We don't have a need for all this house, and your father isn't comfortable renting the basement out to strangers."

Sobering, I turned and looked at my mother. "You guys have been here forever. Are you sure this is what you want to do? I grew up in this house."

"I know," she said, "and maybe it's time for us to move on like you and Jared did."

I smiled at the mention of my husband's name. The bitterness of eighteen years felt like nothing compared to the sweetness of the past four weeks. My mother took notice.

"You have no idea how happy it makes me to see you so happy," she said, tears forming in her eyes. "You look radiant, Poppy. The way a new bride should look."

I felt moisture quickly blur my own vision. "Jared and I have made so many mistakes along the way. This really is nothing short of a miracle."

Hoping to preempt another conversation where I gushed about what God was doing in my life, my mother switched topics. "Oh, did I tell you what happened to Leah Halpern? Apparently, she's not doing very well."

"What do you mean?"

"Well, Mindy Friedman's been dating Bruce Halpern, you know. She acts like she's hit the jackpot dating Leah's father. Mindy's had her eye on Bruce for a while, and she made her move once the divorce was finalized with the last trophy wife."

"Mom," I said, straining for patience, "what does this have to do with Leah?"

"Well, Mindy says Leah's been very depressed since she lost the baby."

"Lost the baby?" I asked, my voice coming out higher than usual. "Are you sure about that?"

"How else do you explain going into the hospital nine months pregnant and then coming out empty-handed?"

"Oh," I said softly.

My mother raised an eyebrow. "Do you know something I don't?"

"Yes," I answered honestly, "but it's nothing that needs to be repeated and shared for the Jewish Federation gossip chain. Thanks for letting me know about Leah. I'll make sure to pray for her."

My mother tsked and shook her head. "You and all of this Jesus mishigas. Sometimes, I wonder if it's made you go soft in the head. How can you forgive that girl for all of the suffering she's caused you? To your children?" she said with a meaningful look.

"I don't know what to tell you, Mom. I've had a soft place in my heart for Leah Halpern since the day I met her. I'm not excusing anything she's done because it's truly horrific. Sometimes, even Jared thinks I'm nuts, but I just see someone doing everything possible to sabotage herself. You can call me crazy, but I think it's just compassion for someone who's been lost her entire life."

"I'm calling it crazy," my mother said dryly. "If your father and I had known what kind of a horrible influence Leah would be for you, we never would have allowed you to be friends."

"You also never would have had your three, beautiful grandchildren without Leah, so let's not gripe about the past. We can't change it anyway."

My mother pressed her lips together, and I knew her thoughts had gone back to River.

"It's okay to miss him, Mom," I said, putting my arm around her. "It's okay to have regrets, to wish you could have done things differently. But you're going to have to forgive yourself if you ever want to heal."

"Forgive myself?" she repeated, shirking off my comfort. "Don't you start with that Jesus mishigas, Poppy."

"Who said anything about Jesus? I've been watching you beat yourself up for more than thirty years. I want to see you finally be at peace with what happened."

"Don't you dare tell me to 'let it go,'" she said with watery eyes. "You have no idea what it's like to lose a child!"

Seeing the pain beyond the rage, I calmly met her gaze. My mother shuddered and sighed wearily. "I'm sorry, Poppy. I'm not mad at you."

"Are you mad at God?"

Her eyes flashed angrily. "Don't I have a right to be? He took my son!"

"And He gave His own," I said gently. "He gave His only Son to die for the entire world. He gave His Son so that we could be set free from the weight of pain and grief."

"I knew you would do this!" my mother fumed. "Why does everything have to be about Jesus?"

"Because everything *is* about Jesus for me! You saw what a mess I'd made of my life. You saw what Jared did to me and the kids. Yet, here we are, three years later. You can't tell me that anyone else is responsible for these changes. I know you don't want to hear about Jesus saving you from your sins. What about Jesus saving Jared's life from suicide and depression? Or mine? What about Jesus saving my marriage? You don't have to believe, Mom, but give credit where it's due!"

My mother pursed her lips again and held her tongue.

Sighing heavily, I let the matter rest. My mother helped me empty the cupboards, and our conversation slipped into less contentious topics. Halfway through, Jared called to let me know he had finished dropping everything off at the house and was returning with the rental truck.

I heard him pull up several minutes later, the screeching brakes announcing the truck's arrival. I greeted my sweaty husband who had been lugging boxes and furniture along with Ted Margolin and Kyle Goldstein.

"Wow," I said grinning up at Jared as he switched off the engine. "You guys look as bad as you smell."

As Ted and Kyle exited the passenger side, Jared hopped down to stand in front of me. "I think," he said wryly, "the words you meant to say were, 'thank you for being such big, strong men and loading and unloading all of my worldly belongings into my new home.'" He leaned down and planted a firm kiss on my lips.

"I just got a text from Rebecca," Ted said. He wiped the sweat from his brow and then replaced the baseball cap on his head. "The kids are having a great time playing together. My mom stopped over as back up."

"Thank you," I said, keeping an arm around Jared and looking over at the mighty Margolin. "I really appreciate both of you helping us out. I know it's not the most fun way to spend a Sunday in this heat and humidity."

Jared used the back of his arm to unstick hair that had been plastered down on his forehead. "At least we'll have a few weeks to get settled in before Natalie's bat mitzvah."

"What's left?" Kyle asked, apparently having some energy left.

"A few boxes in the family room, and some bags of food in the kitchen," I said. "My parents are still inside. My mom mentioned she wanted to pass along some heirlooms, so you can ask her what she had in mind."

Kyle nodded and took Ted with him back to the house,

joking that fatherhood had transformed the mighty Margolin into a tired, old man. Ted gave a return jab as they entered the basement kitchen.

"Heirlooms?" Jared asked, meeting my eyes. "What's going on?"

"Mom said she and Dad are thinking about moving. I don't know how serious she is, but I think she might be ready to stop living in old memories and embrace some new ones."

"Is she ready to take down the shrine for River? They haven't touched that bedroom in thirty years."

"More like her shrine of guilt about it," I said sadly. "The Lord gave me an opportunity to share about what He's done for you and me, and I took it."

Jared studied my face. "I'm assuming it went about as well as expected. You'd be a lot more excited otherwise."

"Pretty much," I said with a resigned sigh. "I planted seeds at least. God willing, they'll grow." Feeling Jared's perspiration seep into my own clothes, I pulled away and fanned myself with my t-shirt.

"Sorry for making you so hot," he said with a grin and dimples. "I'm pretty irresistible."

I laughed and rolled my eyes. "Don't flatter yourself. You're covered in sweat, and now I'm covered in it too."

"We could always try out our new shower," he said suggestively.

I swatted him in the arm. "Sounds like you need a cold shower."

His grin widened. "I'd still ask you to join me."

"Is that so?" I trailed my finger on his upper arm, adding a cartoonish squeal when I felt his bicep. With a growl, Jared pulled me into his arms and kissed me soundly.

After an indeterminate amount of time, we heard an awkward cough and stifled laughter from behind us.

"If the two of you are finished," Ted began, his tone all business, "we can wrap up the move, and then you can pick up where you left off once we're gone."

Chuckling, Kyle said, "I'd tell you guys to get a room, but that's exactly what we're helping you do anyway."

"Says the happily married newlywed," I retorted, smirking at Kyle. "Didn't I catch you and your wife mauling each other before Bible study last week? How soon can we expect a baby announcement?"

Ted gaped, Kyle gulped, and Jared laughed uproariously. Apparently, my husband did enjoy my spunk after all.

We settled into our new home fairly easily, and I thanked God for such a smooth transition. Natalie and Madison still shared a bedroom, but this one was much larger and boasted a walk-in closet. Ted helped Jared build loft beds for the girls so we could fit desks and bookshelves underneath. Ryan had a smaller bedroom to himself, and Jared and I shared a master suite with an adjoining bathroom.

We hung the ketubah over a new, queen sized bed, a surprise wedding gift from my parents. Gary and Barbara bought us bedding to go along with it, saying we deserved a fresh start. Jared and I vacillated on whether to include old photos in our bedroom to decorate, but we ultimately decided to put the pictures into an album and use framed shots from our vow renewal instead.

A week before Natalie's bat mitzvah, I heard a rap at my office door and welcomed my visitor without looking up to see who it was.

"Hi, stranger," Joe Trautweig said.

My head whipped up in disbelief and mild alarm. Meeting

the familiar pair of green eyes, I saw something different in them. I raised an eyebrow in silent question, and Joe answered with a smile and a nod.

"When?" I asked breathlessly.

"About a month ago. One of these days, you might even see me at Bible study if that wouldn't be weird for you...or Jared."

"Of course not!" I exclaimed. "Oh, Joe, I'm so happy for you!"

He smiled, taking delight in my enthusiasm. "Mazel tov, by the way," he said, clearing the air of any tension. "Marriage definitely suits you. I'm happy for you, Poppy."

I beamed at him. "Have a seat," I said, gesturing to the office chairs in front of my desk. "Did Ted or Kyle lead you to the Lord? What about this mystery girlfriend Miss Belle told me about? She mentioned she saw you with someone at Los Bravos."

Joe laughed as he sat down. "One question at a time! Mystery girlfriend isn't a mystery at all. Miss Belle made an assumption. She's actually a friend of yours."

"My friend?" I asked, confused.

"Jessica Goldstein. I interrupted a conversation she was having with some jerk, and I played a knight in shining armor."

"Oh no," I murmured, having a strong hunch I knew which "jerk" Joe meant.

"So you've met this Patrick character?" he asked, reading my expression.

"Unfortunately, yes. He's one of the most vile human beings I have ever had the misfortune of knowing."

Joe nodded. "That was the impression I got. He belittled Jessica in one breath and then tried to seduce her in the next. I've never seen anything like it. She just sat there like she deserved to be treated that way. I was horrified."

"It's how Patrick maintains control over his harem," I said in disgust. "He acts like they should be grateful for his attention while keeping their self esteem in the toilet."

Joe studied my face but kept his thoughts to himself. Pressing forward, he said, "I recognized Jessica from that time we met at Vincenzo's, and I put two and two together from everything I've heard Goldstein share about his sister. He was surprised when I told him I'd already met Jessica."

"So, what happened?"

"I slid into the seat next to Jessica, told her how much I had missed her, and begged her to take me back."

CHAPTER 37

"Take you back?" I said, confused.

"We've never dated," Joe said quickly, "but it was the first thing that came to mind."

"Jessica must have been pretty surprised."

"Poppy, I've never seen such a grateful look on anybody's face before! Honestly, I was shocked she remembered my name, but Jessica played along like we'd planned the whole thing."

"The plot thickens," I said, totally intrigued by Joe's story.

He grinned. "As I'm sure you can imagine, Patrick wasn't having any of it. He started yelling and cursing at both of us. The entire restaurant went silent."

"Did you give Patrick a black eye? It's the least he deserves."

"Even better, there were some cops eating lunch a few tables away. They threatened Patrick with arrest for disorderly conduct and ran him out of the restaurant. Jessica hugged me and just kept saying thank you. That's probably the part Miss Belle saw, but Jessica Goldstein and I definitely aren't dating."

"I'm glad you were there to help her."

"She told me I was an answer to prayer." He watched my face for a reaction. "She's not the first person to call me that."

"You do have a knack for rescuing damsels in distress."

"I suppose I do," he said.

"Did you guys stare into each other's eyes, realize it was all beshert, and then the rest is an R.D. Hampton novel waiting to happen?" I asked with a grin.

Joe held up his hands and laughed. "Slow down! Nothing like that."

"Tell me you got her number at least."

"Ease off, Poppy, I'm not interested. I was happy to help, but that's as far as it goes."

"Oh," I said. "I'm sorry, I didn't mean to push. I just remember when I introduced you two, and you guys seemed to hit it off."

"I think Jessica's a very nice person, but she's got some things she needs to sort out. I made the mistake of pursuing a woman still dealing with a bad break up. It didn't end so well for me."

"Oh, Joe," I said softly.

"Don't feel sorry for me. I know this was the best possible outcome for you and your kids, and I can't begrudge you that. All I can do is hope for my own happy ending."

"You deserve no less," I said, meaning every word. "Men like you are a rare breed, Joe Trautweig. I don't doubt that God has someone wonderful for you. When we prayed together last year, I know God heard us. I have to believe that if He answered my prayers that day, He's going to answer yours too."

"Speaking of," Joe said, "you asked how I came to faith in Jesus. That's the reason I'm here."

Joe began to share his story, joined by the mighty Margolin who had initially stopped by to deliver updates for an RFP. The three of us talked for almost thirty minutes. I sat with my jaw on the floor as Joe's miraculous salvation story unfolded. Before I could ask any questions, Joe's cell phone buzzed, and he looked down at the number and frowned. Taking the call, I quickly realized he had an unhappy client on the other line. Joe waved an apologetic goodbye as he spoke in alternating strident and soothing tones to the caller.

"Looks like I showed up not a moment too soon," Ted said, his eyes following Joe as he exited the main office through a side door.

"Did you really think I was in danger?" I glanced at a recent photo of me and Jared on my desk.

"Poppy, I don't think you realize the effect you had on Joe," Ted said. "The effect you *still* have on him."

I snapped back defensively, "What are you talking about? Every word I said to him was sincere. It wasn't a come on or a tease."

"I'm not accusing you of acting inappropriately. I just remember the way Joe looked at you before you reconciled with Jared, and it's clear he still admires you."

"*Admires* isn't the same thing as *loves*, and Joe knows I'm crazy about my husband. One of the first things Joe did when he came here was congratulate me."

Ted sighed and closed the door to my office. "Joe omitted a few details when he shared his testimony."

"Are you planning to share what they are?" I asked. "There were times I felt like both of you were being evasive."

"For good reason. Can you please trust me that I'm trying to protect you and be a good friend?"

"Ted, you're scaring me, and I hate all of this cryptic garbage. Just come right out and say something. Don't waste my time or yours hinting around and leaving me to guess what it is. I still don't understand why you and Kyle didn't say something a month ago when all of this happened."

"Poppy," he said, using the same tone that probably cowed countless competitors in the commercial insurance world, "you may not think you're in any danger of temptation talking to Joe alone, but that doesn't mean Joe isn't."

"I didn't invite him here," I said, offended.

The mighty Margolin exhaled a weary sigh and sat down. Leaning forward and clasping his hands between his knees, he said, "Do you remember how Joe said Jesus appeared to him in a dream?"

"Of course," I said. "It's an incredible story."

Ted grimaced. "It wasn't exactly a dream. I just didn't want you to feel responsible for what happened or to consider rekindling a romance if things get tough with Jared."

I sat back in my chair, mortified and insulted.

"That's what I thought."

I grit my teeth. "You thought *what*, exactly?"

"That I screwed up," Ted said, effectively loosening the lid on my emotional pressure cooker. "Rebecca told me you could handle it, and I should have listened to my wife. This was my own fear, Poppy, not a reflection of you."

Frustrated, I said, "Ted, what are you talking about?"

"Kyle was working with another producer at Cooper & Jaye for a joint, CID/Benefits deal with Joe. The producer said he couldn't get a hold of Joe, and Kyle felt the Holy Spirit gave him a nudge to check on him. Kyle and I have been meeting Joe for lunch every other week, and he remembered Joe saying there

was a park he liked. Kyle found him passed out on a bench over-
looking a small duck pond. He called 911, and then he called
me. Kyle and I were both there when Joe had his stomach
pumped. He tried to overdose on sleeping pills."

"Oh," I breathed, feeling ashamed of my earlier resentment.

"When Joe came to, he said he'd had a vision of someone
named Yeshua, and he asked us if it was Jesus."

I smiled through my tears. "Wow."

"That's what we said. Our friend didn't mention that we led
him to Christ in a hospital room because he didn't want you to
feel responsible for what he chose to do. He said something
about his first wife and that he'd gotten so low, he wanted to
see her again."

"Poor Joe," I said. "Ted, I feel so stupid."

"Don't," he said brusquely. "None of this is your fault. Joe
doesn't blame you for anything that happened."

"I know," I said, aggrieved. "He blames himself."

Ted sighed. "I'm sorry, Poppy."

"No matter what any of you say, I know I have to own my
part in this too. I didn't lead Joe on, but I did throw temptation
in his face. It was Joe's integrity that kept me from making a
complete disaster of my life. I hate that he's suffered so much
because of my own selfishness. I shouldn't have tried to pry
that door open, no matter what I thought of Jared at the time."

The mighty Margolin shifted uncomfortably, then glanced
through the glass wall of my office to the curious onlookers just
beyond.

Reading his thoughts, I said, "I'll text your wife later. This is
probably a better conversation to be having with her anyway. I
appreciate you telling me what happened. I will pass it along to
Jared so we can pray."

Ted nodded, standing from the chair, and opening the door. My new coworker, Carly, entered the room and noted my red-rimmed eyes with a look of concern. She raised an eyebrow but said nothing as she circled around the mighty Margolin to her desk. Usually, it was Carly crying on my shoulder about her "toad" ex-boyfriends or her mistake two years she couldn't forgive herself for. Her angelic face hid many secrets, and she was about to learn one of mine. Ted excused himself, and I texted my husband before confiding in my golden haired officemate.

My husband responded immediately.

Are you okay, Poppy? I don't know how I feel about Joe just showing up at the office.

I'm fine. I just feel bad for Joe. This is partly my fault for playing with fire.

You didn't force any pills down his throat.

No, but I shouldn't have put either of us in the path of temptation either. I'm not taking blame for everything. I'm just saying that I had a part to play.

Do you still have feelings for him?

I paused, angry that my husband could even ask after all we'd been through together. I typed and deleted a scathing response involving Leah Halpern. Instead, I stopped to pray, exhaling out shades of the old Poppy and my legendary temper.

Poppy? Jared asked via text. *Are you still there?*

I'm here. Just hurt you asked me that. I needed to pray because I was about to rip your head off.

You're right. I'm sorry. I trust you.

I sighed deeply, my heart overwhelmed with too much information to process all at once.

After another long pause, Jared wrote, *Listen, I'm in the middle of a crisis at work, but I want to talk about it when I get home.*

Fine with me. I'll see you later.

I threw my phone into my purse with an uneasy feeling in the pit of my stomach. I stared at the picture of me and Jared again, wondering what would have happened if things had worked out differently. Shaking my head, I took those poisonous thoughts captive, instead lifting the entire situation to heaven and asking God to intervene.

Two days later, I literally bumped into Jessica Goldstein at Vincenzo's, and she seemed both surprised and delighted to see me.

"Poppy!" she exclaimed. "It's been way too long!" She pulled me into a hug.

"Hi," I said, wondering at the overly friendly greeting. I noted that Jessica had cropped her long locks to just below her shoulders, the ends dyed lighter than her roots. Her face looked the same, but the sadness lingering around her eyes and mouth had disappeared.

"I have to thank you," she said, taking me by the arm and leading me to the overstuffed leather chairs.

"For what?" I was curious to hear her version of events and wondered how the Los Bravos incident factored into everything.

"Well, you told me to grow up and stop feeling sorry for myself. I took your advice."

"Oh?" I asked above the rim of my cinnamon latte.

She nodded eagerly. "Patrick called me up about a month ago. He said he'd made a huge mistake breaking up with me. Stupidly, I agreed to meet up with him at Los Bravos. He created this huge scene, but thank God, some cops showed up to get him out of there."

When she didn't supply further details or rapturous praise of Joe, I raised an eyebrow. "Is that all of it?"

"Oh," she laughed, "there's so much more! I always knew

Patrick was a bully, but I never felt like I had the power to do anything about it. Seeing him grovel to those police officers showed me a completely different side of him. For all of his arrogance, Patrick's a spineless weasel, and I realized I deserve so much better than him. Or Nathan," she added with newfound confidence.

"That's wonderful," I said sincerely. "Is that what's put a sparkle in your eye, or is it something...or maybe *someone* else?"

Jessica gave a breathtaking smile in response. "Oh, Poppy, I've met the most wonderful man! My brother introduced us two weeks ago. It's a crazy story how all of it happened, but I never thought I could ever feel like this again. He's so amazing!"

I relaxed, grateful I wouldn't have to dash any hopes about Joe. "I'm so happy for you, Jessica. What's his name?"

"Micah," she said. "Micah Ballinger. He's the brother of Lexie Arterton in your office."

Suddenly realizing the extended connection, I almost laughed at God's sense of humor. Micah Ballinger was the step-brother of Jessica's sworn enemy and Kyle's ex-girlfriend, Taylor Horner. Although Jessica and Kyle had reconciled, the subject of Jesus had been relegated to "agree to disagree." Throwing Micah in the mix would suddenly upend all of that. I anticipated a text from Taylor sooner rather than later asking for more information. My grin widened as Jessica provided every little detail about their first date. She swooned over everything Micah had said or done as if it was the most perfect, wonderful thing in the history of mankind. She asked a fleeting question here or there about Jared, but then she'd remember an attribute of Micah's and launch into another series of exaltations.

Smiling into my coffee cup, I felt someone looking at me. I glanced over to see pale green eyes studying me and Jessica with sadness and relief. I looked at Joe questioningly, but he shook his head and then exited the coffee shop.

As Jessica happily prattled on, I closed my eyes and prayed. I prayed God would send Joe Trautweig someone so wonderful that he'd forget all about me. When I mentioned it to Jared, he had no problem agreeing with me in that prayer.

Over the next few days, I noticed an increased possessiveness in Jared, as if he had something to prove to an invisible force beyond the walls of our home.

"Ow, you're hurting me!" I said, pushing him away from me in our bedroom.

"What? I can't hug my wife?"

"Jared, what is the matter with you? You've been in a bad mood all week, and Natalie's bat mitzvah is tomorrow. It's supposed to be a happy occasion for our family, but you've been snapping at the kids too. I haven't seen you act this way since before we separated."

The second those words escaped my lips, I knew tension would escalate. I felt the presence of something evil in our bedroom, an old foe I didn't think I would ever face again. My stomach dropped.

"Maybe you wish it was Joe here instead of me," Jared said, giving voice to his insecurities.

"How can you possibly say that?"

"Go ahead," he taunted. "Throw Leah back in my face and call me a hypocrite. I know you want to!"

"Jared," I said slowly. "I'm married to *you*. I love you. If I wanted to be with Joe Trautweig, that's where I would be."

"Right," he said contemptuously. "The honorable Joe Trautweig willing to die for your unrequited love."

I sucked in a breath at Jared's cruelty and silently cried out to Jesus to intervene. Like wings to a prayer, the word *jealousy* came to mind, and I began to see Jared's irritability through a different lens. When we were married before, Jared's outbursts resulted from narcissistic entitlement. He thought it was the job of me and the kids to reorder our lives around his ever-shifting moods. Thinking back to the past few days, Jared had been on edge, but not with the same, selfish disregard. I knew my impromptu meeting with Joe was the trigger, and I begged God to show me how to reach my husband.

"What's the matter?" Jared demanded. "Are you still feeling sorry for your beloved Joe and coming up with ways to rescue him from himself?"

Shuddering, I recognized the presence of our old foe, Leviathan. It had plopped itself right on top of our home, trying to crush us under its oppressive weight. I could not shake the sensation of that same, suffocated feeling I had known for the first eighteen years of my relationship with Jared. Although not as comfortable as Rebecca or Rose Margolin when it came to the idea of "spiritual warfare," I knew our argument was a plan from the pit of hell to ruin Natalie's bat mitzvah celebration.

"Jesus, help me!" I cried.

My outburst gave Jared pause, and he silently studied me rather than working himself into an even greater frenzy. Already, I knew the Holy Spirit was at work, and I felt some reassurance in that. At another time and place and time in our marriage, Jared would have launched one barb after another, pelting me with machine gun blasts of insults and accusations. Likewise, I would have held up my armor of anger and cut Jared off at the knees. We had been together long enough to know exactly how to rip one another to shreds.

Jared's nostrils flared in simmering anger, but his expression held pain and uncertainty.

Calmly, I said, "I'm not going anywhere. What happened with Leah and with Joe is in the past. We rededicated our marriage to the Lord and our lives to one another. That hasn't changed. You don't have to be afraid."

He searched my eyes for any hint of a lie, and I squared my shoulders, daring him to find any. As if mummified inside of his own helplessness and fear, Jared stood stiff as a board. Slowly, his bunched shoulders relaxed, and I imagined wraps of mummy gauze unraveling around him. The dark and heavy presence was losing its foothold, and I silently rejoiced in God's victory.

"I'm sorry," he said bleakly. "I don't know what came over me."

I took a tentative step toward my husband and reached a hand to his cheek. He jerked away from my touch. Using my other hand, I turned his face back toward me and rubbed my thumbs against his temples.

"Jared," I said softly. "You're afraid I'm going to do to you what you did to me and the kids. I promised to forsake all others two months ago. I meant those words then, and they're still true now. Nothing has changed."

"I don't deserve you, Poppy. I know I don't, but I don't like hearing you talk about Joe Trautweig. You get this dreamy look on your face. You may not think you still have feelings for the guy, but it's obvious to pretty much everyone else."

"Jared, how many times do I have to tell you that nothing happened?"

"You've got him up on a pedestal, and you know it. You treat him like some brave knight from one of your novels. Joe Trautweig can do no wrong because you can reinvent him into some kind of fantasy. It wasn't so long ago you asked him to rescue you, remember?"

"I threw out all of those R.D. Hampton books," I said. "I don't want or need a fantasy love life. I have the real thing. You asked me if those novels were enough for me. They're not."

"Then how do I get you to stop thinking about him? You've mentioned Joe at least ten times in the last two days. I feel like I'm losing you, Poppy, and there's nothing I can do other than watch you slip away from me."

I dropped my hands. "I'm just praying for him. That's it."

"You need to let somebody else pray for Joe Trautweig and his love life. I think you're crossing a huge line here. I can't compete with a fantasy, and honestly, I shouldn't have to, no matter my past sins."

I sighed wearily. "Jared, for the nine millionth time, Joe is just a friend. This jealousy is out of place to the point of being insulting."

"He's more to you than *just a friend*. You may not think you're playing with fire again, but you are. Joe's living in your heart and in your mind. Maybe you're not in love with him, but I think you're in love with helping him."

I frowned, not liking the implication of Jared's words. "Do you think that one automatically leads to the other?"

"All of this stuff you've been saying about Joe having a special place in your heart is dangerous. You might be keeping appropriate physical boundaries, but emotionally, you're still tied up with the guy. You need to let him go. Completely."

I felt resentment creep up my spine at Jared's hypocrisy. Biting my tongue instead, I wrestled for a calm I didn't feel.

Reading my thoughts, Jared said, "Poppy, do you think I'm still beating myself up about what happened with Leah and her baby?"

"Well, aren't you?" I demanded. "Isn't that what all of this jealousy about Joe is really about anyway? Misplaced anger at yourself?"

"No," he said firmly. "I made peace with what I did. I repented, and I had to accept that Leah was responsible for her own choices. I feel bad for the situation that she's in, but I don't feel personally at fault for putting her there anymore."

"So, what are you saying?"

"You act like the happiness of Joe Trautweig depends on your intervention. You're convinced that all of your intentions are holy and above board because you're praying for him, but it's the same, codependent garbage all over again."

"Excuse me?" I hissed.

"Poppy, you've taken on this burden for Joe's love life like it's your personal mission to fix. You think it's okay because you're not meddling with him and Jessica Goldstein anymore, but now, you're using God to play matchmaker. You've been going around like you and Jesus are in cahoots to get him married off."

"*Cahoots*? Really???"

"What I'm saying," Jared said through obviously strained patience, "is that you're hiding behind God to justify your attachment to a guy you almost fell into bed with."

"That's rich," I said, glaring at him.

"I'm not a hypocrite for pointing out what's going on here, so get off your high horse. If anything, I'm an expert on the subject. I know firsthand how dangerous it is to keep the door open for an old flame. I nearly destroyed the lives of everyone I love because of it."

I grit my teeth, grudgingly admitting to myself that Jared was owning his sins, not projecting them. I felt both offended and exposed by his assessment of the situation, and I wanted to argue. As I opened my mouth, I instead saw my own sin held before me as if looking into a mirror. While I was not responsible for Jared's emotions or jealousy, I also saw that I was not as innocent as I presumed to be. I was not innocent at all, in fact.

"Poppy?" Jared prodded.

I bit my lip, wanting to cry. God lovingly but painstakingly showed me the self-righteous hypocrisy and bad behavior I justified with good intentions. As God shined the light even further into my heart, I realized that even those "good intentions" were being fueled by sin. I was flattered by Joe's devotion, misplaced as it was. Feeling responsible for his happiness also gave me an excuse to hold a candle for him. I saw my own vanity, and I was ashamed that I had tried to make God my accomplice.

"You're right," I said, my voice breaking. "I'm so sorry, Jared. You had every reason to be jealous. I didn't want to see it or admit it, but I did like knowing I had that power over someone else. Here I was, guns blazing, ready to nail you to the wall, and I was so blind to my own pride."

My husband looked at me tenderly. "Thank you."

I nodded, disgusted with myself.

"I know I hurt you too, Poppy, and it was wrong. I'm sorry."

With tears trickling down my cheeks, I looked into Jared's eyes. "We're quite a pair, aren't we?"

He took a step toward me and enfolded me in his arms.

Pressing me into his chest, he kissed the top of my head. "If not for the grace of God, we would both be such a mess."

I sniffled and chuckled, burying my head against his heart. "We still are a mess."

Jared pulled back and looked down into my face. "This is both of us growing together despite ourselves. This is the power of Jesus keeping us from spinning our wheels for the next thirty years making the same mistakes over and over."

I smiled, thinking of Miss Belle's oft-quoted phrase. "The cross has the final word," I whispered.

Jared planted a kiss on my forehead. I stood on my tiptoes and lifted my face to give him my mouth instead. Sometime later, bodies and hands entwined with one another, I marveled at the grace of God. Jared pulled me closer to him as he drifted off to sleep. Tempted to pray for Joe and his own share of companionship, I instead prayed for God to forgive me of my arrogance. Jesus could easily handle Joe's love life without my self-appointed assistance.

"Mom? Dad?" Natalie called the following morning. She opened the door to our bedroom. "Ew!" she shrieked. "Oh my gosh! Please, tell me you guys aren't *naked* under there! Oh, my eyes! My eyes!"

She slammed the door, loudly lamenting the need for bleach as she stalked down the hallway and toward the kitchen.

I heard Jared's laughter rumbling in his chest behind me. "Little brat," he murmured into my hair. "That'll teach her to knock first."

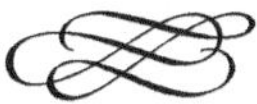

CHAPTER 39

Jared and I dodged the inevitable birds and the bees discussion as the bat mitzvah pre-party madness began. I took Natalie to my mother's salon to get her hair, makeup, and nails done. I also enjoyed some pampering myself while Maddie sat next to me in a pink princess chair. Halfway through my foot massage, Jared sent a few frantic texts from the synagogue with questions from the caterer and deejay. I told him to direct everything to my mother since she had insisted on—and paid for—all of the party extras. Beyond that, I knew giving my mother something to worry about made her less likely to go in search of some imagined, potential catastrophe.

I glanced over at Natalie, and she soaked up every minute of the hair styling and beauty tips. Her little sister chattered on about a multitude of things, much to the amusement of the salon techs. Maddie had questions about why they needed so much nail polish, had anyone ever slipped and fallen, and what happened if they accidentally dyed someone's hair the wrong color. Gina, one of the newest hires, looked up at me with amusement in her eyes as she finished with ruby red toe polish that matched my lipstick.

Forgoing any hairstyling, I left my hair natural with abounding curls. Maddie, however, insisted on a "princess" updo like her sister. While my mother's stylist, Emma, pulled and pinned Maddie's loose curls on top of her head, Natalie changed into her bat mitzvah outfit. When my thirteen year-old emerged from the bathroom, I simply stared. I could hardly reconcile the baby I had nursed in a garage sale recliner with the beautiful creature standing before me. I fanned my eyes with my hands, trying to keep the tears from ruining my newly applied eye makeup.

"Oh, baby girl," I breathed.

"Do you like it?" Nati asked. She held out the navy, peplum overskirt of her dress, daring to believe she looked as beautiful as she felt. The sleeveless dress was elegant and age appropriate, and I smiled at my mother's tasteful selection. She and Natalie had snuck off to the mall and told me I wasn't allowed to see anything until the big day. The sparkling, jeweled belt and knee-length, sheath skirt lent an extra dose of sophistication.

"Nati, you look so pretty!" Madison squealed, running up to hug her sister.

"Do you have something to cover your shoulders?" I asked. "You can take it off for the after party, but you won't be able to go bare shouldered during the service."

She nodded, the curls of her updo bobbing along with her. She reached into a shopping bag and pulled on a silver cardigan. Placing it over her shoulders, she looked even more beautiful than she had a moment earlier. I took a deep breath to hold back the bittersweet tears of just how fast my baby was growing up. Emma had used a light touch on Natalie's make up, enhancing her features without making her look like a Diva Doll.

"Emma, you're a genius!" I said.

"Text me pictures," she said with a grin. "I know your mother will be showing them off next week, but I could use a few more for my brag board."

"Do you really like it?" Natalie asked again, searching my eyes. "Do you think Caden will like it?" she said more shyly.

"He'd be a fool if he didn't." I pressed my cheek to Natalie's, giving her an air kiss rather than a red lipstick stain on her face.

"You look pretty too, Mom," Natalie said, eyeing my purple wrap dress. "Daddy's going to give you that crazy look again."

"What crazy look?"

"The same one he does when he sees a piece of strawberry cheesecake."

"Ah," I said, chuckling softly. Jared held his favorite, childhood desert in high esteem. There were times I'd even asked if he and his cake needed a moment alone together.

"Mommy!" Maddie said, tugging on my dress. "Do I look pretty too?"

I smiled down at my little cherub in her pleated, sailor dress. "You look beautiful, Maddie."

She beamed at me, her wide smile overtaking her face. She twirled around in red, ballet flats, her dress ballooning in the air and making her giggle. At that moment, I wondered if it was possible for one's heart to literally explode from so much joy.

After a sizable tip for Emma and her team, I loaded the girls into the minivan and headed toward Temple Beth Tefillah. The synagogue seemed deceptively small from the outside, but it boasted three floors of classrooms plus a sanctuary, reception hall, gift shop, and clerical offices. Amidst the hoopla of family photos, fawning grandparents, last minute instructions from

Rabbi Cohn, and Natalie's nerves, Jared locked eyes with me from across the rabbi's office.

Smiling, he walked toward me and wrapped his arm around my waist. He whispered close to my ear, "I can't believe we made it."

"The day's not over yet. You still have to chant from the bima."

"Slacker," he said with a grin. "You took the English prayers instead of the Hebrew."

"I already sang for these people twenty-five years ago at my own bat mitzvah. Natalie will do a much better job than I did."

Jared looked over at our precocious thirteen year-old seated in front of the rabbi's desk. She seemed so grown up as she listened to Rabbi Cohn's final instructions.

"I still can't believe this is possible," he said. "That I'm standing here with my wife and children about to celebrate Nati's bat mitzvah. Our lives could have gone a hundred other ways."

I glanced up at Jared, marveling at how dapper he looked with his salt and pepper hair and black suit. There was an old school, Hollywood charm about him, and I couldn't remember him ever looking so handsome. Jared stared back at me just as intently, his eyes lowering to my ruby red lips. I suddenly felt like a piece of strawberry cheesecake.

"If the parents are done canoodling in the back," Rabbi Cohn said from behind his desk, "I have a few things the two of you need to be aware of."

The rabbi locked eyes with Jared, his gaze narrowing. "We are a synagogue, not a church," he said. "I want no talk of Jesus or any other messianic chazarai from my bima. Mr. Levine, I've approved the speech you prepared to say to Natalie, and I expect no deviation from it. You can talk about your Christian beliefs on your own time, but they have no place in a Jewish synagogue."

Jared tried to reassure Rabbi Cohn he meant no disrespect, but the rabbi wasn't finished scolding my husband for offenses not even committed.

"You and your wife may have chosen to turn your backs on Judaism, but I will not allow my pulpit to be turned into some kind of Baptist revival. I will cut the bat mitzvah short or have you forcibly removed from my synagogue if that becomes a problem." He gave us a haughty look down his nose as if this was no idle threat.

Jared and I stared at one another in horror, stunned by Rabbi Cohn's snide remarks and assumptions. I felt rage at the injustice done to Natalie and her four years of hard work, but the Mama Bear instinct roared even louder in my mother. She answered the rabbi before I had a chance to respond.

"You have some nerve!" she growled, visibly shaking in anger. "How dare you threaten my granddaughter and her parents right before they're about to go on the bima! You ought to be ashamed of yourself, Rabbi Cohn! Today is about Natalie's bat mitzvah, not your personal vendetta with Jews for Jesus."

"Harriet!" my father said, stunned by her outburst.

Still glaring daggers at Rabbi Cohn, she continued, "I'm not saying I buy into all of this Jesus stuff my daughter does, but I did my own research after your last teaching on Messianic Judaism. I picked up one of Poppy's Bibles and even read from the New Testament. I thought, surely, I would find this anti-Semitic Jesus you mention in all of your lectures."

Jared looked sharply at me, silently asking if I knew about any of this. I shook my head.

"Do you know what I found, Rabbi?" my mother asked. "Jesus, the anti-Semite, doesn't exist. Instead, I saw a man fed up with religious hypocrites who enjoy lording their position of authority over others. Maybe you hate Jesus so much because his words hit too close to home."

"Harriet, I mean this with all due respect," Rabbi Cohn said coolly, "but you don't know what you're talking about."

"*Nu?* I don't have two eyes? I can't read for myself, you pompous little *macher?*"

That response finally wiped the arrogant smirk from the rabbi's face. It took a lot to get Harriet Berman truly angry, and Rabbi Cohn had no idea what kind of wrath he'd just called down upon himself.

Taking a step closer to his desk, my mother towered over Rabbi Cohn as she wagged her finger in his face. "I've seen the way you've condescended to members of this synagogue, Arthur. You've talked down to friends of mine who *built* this synagogue fifty years ago. You prance around like some elitist, acting like you have insight into the Torah the rest of us *schmendricks* in the seats couldn't possibly understand. For all of Rabbi Epstein's flaws—and there were many—he never would have treated any member of this synagogue that way. I don't doubt that if Jesus was standing here right now, he'd talk to you the same way he did to those Pharisees. It would be no less than you deserve."

After an uncomfortable silence, my mother added, "Frankly, I don't care if my son-in-law wants to lead a Hallelujah choir up there. We paid for this bat mitzvah, we paid for the party, and our membership dues help pay for your salary," she said pointedly. "My granddaughter has worked her *tuchus* off to prepare for this day, and I won't sit by and listen to smug, self-righteous threats from a man who only has his job because the last rabbi couldn't keep it in his pants."

After my mother finished her rant, everyone in that room

wore the same, stunned expression. Rabbi Cohn had never been taken to the proverbial woodshed, too accustomed to being lauded as an all-knowing Torah scholar that no one dared to question. My father and in-laws could not believe my mother had actually read the New Testament. Meanwhile, Jared and I were shocked by the champion God raised up to speak up on our behalf. Only Natalie smiled, beaming at her grandmother like she wore tights and a cape.

"Are you finished, Harriet?" Rabbi Cohn asked. Shock had given way to defensive arrogance, and I could see my mother's diatribe had little effect on him.

"No," my mother replied, "I'm not finished at all, but I'll take that up with the synagogue board after my granddaughter's bat mitzvah. In the meantime, get on that bima and do your job."

Rabbi Cohn tried to save face with puffed shoulders and nonchalance, but the panic in his eyes was real. He and my mother both knew how much clout she carried in the synagogue and the Jewish Federation. One word into the right ear, and my mother could have him replaced. I had a feeling that was likely to happen.

As we headed backstage behind the bima, Jared pulled my mother aside to hug her and whisper his appreciation. She waved him off and told him she'd grown tired of Rabbi Cohn and the demeaning way he'd talked to Jared during Natalie's bat mitzvah rehearsals. She said it was Jared's refusal to argue or retaliate that opened her eyes to the rabbi's arrogance. She admitted that she used to respect Rabbi Cohn and had thought he was a brilliant scholar. Now, she saw him as a puffed up toad, too self important to be of much use to anyone. She aptly noted that all of the Torah study in the world had not helped him in the areas of respect or humility.

I saw a fire in my mother I'd never seen before, and I wondered if God was slowly removing the blinders and objections she had to Jesus. For my entire life, I'd watched my mother bend over backward to appease the opinions of others. Her synagogue friends, especially, seemed to enjoy dissecting the lives of whoever wasn't in the room. My mother cowered in fear of their judgment and condemnation, desperate for their approval. That day, I witnessed Harriet Berman in an entirely new light.

"Thank you, Mom," I said, joining Jared and leaning down for a cheek-to-cheek kiss.

"I thought of you, Poppy," she said, looking into my eyes.

"What do you mean?"

"I remembered the defiant look you'd get when I tried to control your life. Most of the time, you'd put me in my place, and I hated it."

"I'm sure you did," I said with a smile. "It doesn't mean how I handled myself was appropriate either. I'm sorry for hurting you with my anger."

"You're forgiven," she said affectionately. "I've been seeing a lot of myself lately too. Maybe it's old age and taking inventory of my life, but I feel like I finally saw myself through your eyes. All the times I thought I was helping you, I was really just trying to fit you into what I thought was best. I'm seeing now that it wasn't even a mold that I wanted for you. I just didn't want to be shunned by my friends."

"Yes," I whispered.

"I'm sorry, Poppeleh. It was wrong."

I nodded, too emotional to speak without crying.

"You were my inspiration," my mother said. "I thought about what you would say to a little worm like that."

I laughed through my tears. "Oh really?"

My mother nodded, proud of herself. "I have to say, it felt good. Very liberating," she said, standing up straighter and adjusting the jacket of her gown.

"It's time to start," Cantor Allen said from just beyond us. The three-hundred pound man who chanted all of Beth Tefillah's liturgy presented an intimidating exterior, but everyone knew him as a giant teddy bear. Piano music filled the sanctuary, and we filed onto the bima platform. Natalie took the seat furthest downstage and closest to the podium. Jared, my parents, and I walked in behind her. Ryan and Madison sat with Gary and Barbara down in the audience, joined by the Margolins, the Goldsteins, all of Natalie's classmates, and too many cousins to list from my side and Jared's. In the back of the room, Ian Horner bounced a fussy Ethan in his arms, while Taylor maneuvered herself and her baby bump into a seat.

I smiled out into the crowd, nervous and excited for Natalie to take her step into spiritual and literal womanhood. It wasn't until we had concluded the service that I noticed Bruce Halpern sitting with Mindy Friedman in the back.

CHAPTER 40

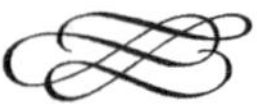

THE SERVICE BEGAN WITH A RECOVERED RABBI COHN greeting the larger than usual congregation as if nothing had gone awry in his office. He glibly talked about Natalie and her "wonderful Jewish family," and my mother shot me a side-eyed glance and a smirk. Cantor Allen sang the blessing for Natalie to come to the podium, calling her by her Hebrew name, *Netanyah Rivka bat Penina.* Jared and I smiled encouragingly as Natalie stepped forth to begin the service.

"Good morning," she said, her eyes looking over the crowd. "Please rise and turn in your *siddurim* to page 135 for the *Bar'chu.*"

From there, Natalie led the liturgical service as if she'd done it her whole life. Countless hours of practice showed in her perfect Hebrew pronunciation and singing. Rabbi Cohn even seemed impressed by her poise, though I suspected he would have schooled his expression regardless.

Following twenty minutes of responsive Hebrew and English liturgy, the pinnacle of the bat mitzvah service arrived. The doors to the ark were opened, and Rabbi Cohn retrieved a Torah scroll for Natalie to march around the congregation. The massive scroll was adorned with a burgundy, velvet cover featuring an embroidered golden crown in the center. Surrounding the crown were vines with budding flowers also embroidered onto the fabric. Covering the top scroll handles were two, silver Torah crowns featuring intricate, filigree design. The *yad*, or pointer, dangled from around both scroll handles, hanging like a pendant necklace halfway down the Torah cover.

As Cantor Allen continued to chant in Hebrew, Rabbi Cohn passed the Torah from my mother, to me, and then ultimately, to Natalie. She braced herself with two legs to carry the heavy scroll. Rabbi Cohn then led the processional through the congregation, and we followed her off the stage throughout the room. From the front row, Gary and Barbara joined us along with Maddie and Ryan. The synagogue regulars as well as our friends knew what to do, and they reached out their *siddurim*, touched it to the Torah scroll, and then kissed the prayer books. Though the origins of the kiss had been conflicting, Jared and I found the simplest explanation was that the kiss showed deference to God and delight in His Law.

As we passed by the Margolins, Rebecca squeezed my hand, whispering words of encouragement. Ted's parents grinned at us, warmly shaking hands with my parents. Shyly, Natalie approached her classmates, not sure how many of them would understand, let alone follow, the traditional Jewish custom.

Noting her flustered response to one particular brunette, I surmised this was the infamous Caden Jones. Dressed in a navy blazer and khaki pants, the boy was definitely a heartbreaker. So long as he didn't break my daughter's heart, he would have no problems with me. He glanced nervously at me and Jared, sizing us up. Jared took notice, acknowledging Caden with a slight lift of the chin before meeting my eyes in amusement.

As Cantor Allen finished his last, booming strains of *Hinei Ma Tov*, we returned to the bima, and Rabbi Cohn began the process of removing the Torah ornamentation and unrolling the scroll for Natalie to read.

Cantor Allen started the liturgical process of individually calling the *aliyot*, or Torah readers, to the bima. He started with Natalie's cousin, Brett who got up from the audience to join her at the podium. Reciting the opening blessing for the reading of the Torah, Brett squeaked through the Hebrew with a voice one would expect of a thirteen-year-old boy who'd recently undergone a bar mitzvah himself.

Cantor Allen held the silver yad onto the Torah scroll, careful not to touch the parchment with his fingers. Natalie began chanting the first three Bible verses of her parsha in ancient Hebrew. Cantor Allen moved the pointer as Natalie read, singing quietly along with her. Once she was finished, Brett recited a closing blessing for the Torah, and then went back to his seat. The same process began again when my mother and father came to the bima for their aliyah. My mother chanted the Hebrew while my father recited the English translation.

Flawlessly, Natalie chanted the next three lines of the Hebrew. My heart swelled as I felt the weight and enormity of what we entered into as a family. Though I ascribed no supernatural power to the rites in and of themselves, I felt the presence of God so strongly upon us. Once Natalie finished, my parents recited the closing blessings in Hebrew and English, and then rejoined Jared and me in the stuffed chairs situated to the side of the bima.

Cantor Allen then summoned Jared and me to the podium, and I saw a glimpse of nervousness flicker across Rabbi Cohn's face. Jared and I flanked Natalie on either side. With a grimace, Rabbi Cohn announced that Jared and I had a few words to share about Natalie before we proceeded further.

Clearing his throat, Jared unfolded his printed speech from his coat pocket and began to read.

"Baby girl, I can say without a doubt that your mother and I would not be standing here today if it wasn't for you. You surprised us when you announced your arrival into this world, and I knew my life would never be the same."

Jared paused to wipe tears from his eyes while Natalie looked adoringly at her father. He held her heart in his hands. I swallowed back the lump in my own throat, silently praising God for the healing and restoration of the Levine family.

"Natalie, you bring so much fire and warmth into this world. Your passion for life, for truth, for right and wrong, are gifts from God. Never lose sight of the truth, Nati. It will always set you free."

I caught Rebecca's eye and the knowing gleam there. Rose beamed at us from just beyond her.

Jared continued, "There are so many things a father wants to say to his daughter, especially on a day like today." He turned from his sheet and met her eyes, not needing to look down at his paper for this part. "Nati, you are loved. You are special. You are beautiful. I'm so glad you're my daughter."

Jared reached out to cup the side of Natalie's cheek and wipe the lone tear that had fallen. An audible gasp and cooing came up from the pews.

"I want to do more than just praise you for a job well done on the bima, although trust me, you're killing it!" Jared said with a grin. That elicited some light chuckles from the crowd. "Your perseverance, your work ethic, and your commitment to excellence has been put on full display in front of our family, our friends, and the members of Beth Tefillah today. Nobody who has watched you up here could ever question your commitment to God, your Jewish heritage," he shot a glance at Rabbi Cohn, "or your commitment to your family. Your mother and I love you very much, and we are so proud of you."

Jared and I leaned in to hug Natalie simultaneously while the crowd clapped approvingly. Rabbi Cohn seemed relieved Jared hadn't invoked the name of Jesus, and he seemed almost smug as Jared and I recited the Torah blessings and Natalie flawlessly read another three verses in Hebrew.

As the fourth—and final—aliyah, Cantor Allen once again called on Natalie by her Hebrew name. She recited the same Torah blessings that had now been chanted three times already.

"*Bar'chu et Adonai ham'vorach.* Praise the One, to whom our praise is due!"

In response the congregation once again said, "*Baruch Adonai ham'vorach l'olam va'ed.* Praised be the One, to whom our praise is due, now and forever!"

Natalie repeated the same blessing uttered by the congregation and then continued, "*Baruch atah Adonai Eloheinu melech ha'olam. Asher bachar banu m'col ha'amim. V'natan lanu et Torahto. Baruch atah Adonai, notein haTorah. Amein.*"

"Amen," the congregation chanted.

Reciting the blessing in English, Natalie said, "Praised be the Eternal God, Ruler of the Universe. You have chosen us from all peoples by giving us Your Torah. Blessed is the Eternal One, giver of the Torah. Amen."

Turning her attention over to Cantor Allen, Natalie read the final in her quartet of stanzas, a beatific smile radiating from her face as she concluded her Torah reading. Following the closing blessings, Rabbi Cohn then picked up the Torah scroll and stood in front of the ark. With arms outstretched to display the Torah unfurled, he chanted in Hebrew and then said in English, "This is the Torah that Moses placed before the Israelites—the mouth of Adonai at the hand of Moses."

Bringing the Torah back to the podium, he rolled the scroll back together and used a velvet clamp to keep the sides from coming apart. He then lifted the naked Torah scroll and placed it in a stand just behind Natalie. Once complete, he closed the doors of the ark and motioned for the audience to be seated.

Rabbi Cohn came beside Natalie and offered praise for a job well done. She smiled tightly, not sure of his sincerity.

"Natalie will now be sharing her Torah drash," he announced. "This is her interpretation of the passage she chanted so beautifully for us in Hebrew." He made a sweeping gesture with his hand as if giving Natalie the floor. My mother was not able to keep her eye roll to herself, and I saw Ted snicker next to Rebecca. As told, the mighty Margolin did not miss much.

After a deep sigh, Natalie began, "A few months ago, I wasn't sure how much I would have to say during my drash. I asked my mom about it, and she had me read a different Bible translation to see if it would help."

Unable to resist, I looked over at Rabbi Cohn. He shifted in his chair on the opposite side of the stage. Whatever write up Natalie had provided to the rabbi beforehand, it was clear she was going off script. I chuckled silently, thinking that Rabbi Cohn would have been better off scolding Natalie instead of Jared in his office.

"It's an honor to read from the Torah in Hebrew," she said, "but if you don't know what you're reading, then what's the point, right?"

I heard an awkward cough from the audience, wondering just how many toes my daughter was about to step on.

I could not have been more proud of her.

"I know that praying means so much to my mom and my dad. I've seen it change their lives and their marriage." She paused as emotion welled up. Jared reached over to hold my hand, eyes shining. Sniffling down her tears, Natalie forged on. "So that's what I did. I prayed. In my parsha, Moses talked to God, and God had plenty to say too. I don't think I'm as good as Moses, but I also don't believe that God would only speak to one person, like *ever*. So, I prayed too."

A pin drop could be heard in the room.

"I didn't hear anything like Moses did," Natalie gave a self-deprecating laugh, "but all of these ideas started coming to my head. I knew I didn't want to come up here and just give everybody a book report from the Torah. My mom said I should find a way for my parsha to apply to our lives today, and that's what I wanted to share with everyone."

Rabbi Cohn rose stiffly from his seat, ready to cut off Natalie's speech. Shocking everyone, Cantor Allen blocked him and said, "Sit down, Arthur."

Shocking us even more, Rabbi Cohn sat.

Natalie shot a grateful look over to Cantor Allen, who nodded for her to proceed.

Inhaling and exhaling her nerves, Natalie said, "One of the things I learned from this whole experience is that praying to God isn't just the *Sh'ma* or the liturgy we say every week in synagogue. Moses talked with God, and God talked back to him. So, that's what I did too. My parents talk to God, and they tell me all the ways they think God answers them. To be honest, it made me a little jealous. So, that's what I decided to do."

Shuffling through her prepared speech, Natalie located something she wanted to share. She looked back out into the crowd. So did I, seeing Rose's lips move silently and knowing she was interceding on behalf of my daughter.

"One of the things that didn't make sense to me was why the people who saw God deliver them out of Egypt during Passover would want to go back to being slaves again. Didn't they see God part the Red Sea? But there they were, actually complaining about it. It says they were ready to kill Caleb and Joshua because they had good things to say about going to Israel. I just couldn't understand how they could do that. And then it hit me: they were afraid."

"Yes," I murmured, seeing courage pull my baby's shoulders back as she continued on with her drash.

"God got so mad at the children of Israel that he wanted to destroy them and start over with Moses. It made me wonder why God would get mad at people because they were scared. That's when I started praying. I had no idea if I'd get an answer, but I figured I had nothing to lose."

Natalie pushed a curled tendril away from her face, never looking more beautiful. "I can't tell you that I heard a voice out loud like Moses did. But I realized something after I asked my question. God wasn't mad just because the people were afraid. I went back to re-read *Numbers 14:11* in my Mom's Bible." She glanced shyly over at me and then back to her speech. "God was upset that they didn't trust Him. Even after all the miracles, they didn't believe He was real." She turned her gaze briefly to Rabbi Cohn, well aware of his disdain for anyone who believed the Torah was more than an inspirational, suggestion guide. "I want to tell you that God is real. My baby sister Maddie told me that Jesus lives in her heart and makes her happy. I said I want that too. We prayed together, and something changed. I wasn't angry anymore. I didn't hate my parents or my life. I knew I had something worth living for."

"Oh baby," I whispered, tears running down my cheeks.

"So, whatever you think of my Hebrew chanting is great," she said, daring to look out at the crowd, "but I want everyone in this room to know that Jesus Christ is God's Son, and if he can take away the pain I had in my heart, He can do it for you too."

CHAPTER 41

It was Cantor Allen who officiated the rest of Natalie's bat mitzvah. As soon as Natalie uttered the name Jesus, Rabbi Cohn turned apoplectic and stormed off the stage. Cantor Allen seemed troubled, but more by the rabbi than by our daughter. He finished the Torah proceedings, re-dressed the scroll with all of its ornamentation, and placed it back inside the ark. Cantor Allen then joined Natalie back at the podium, not bothering with a pithy joke but moving full steam ahead with the service. Natalie navigated easily through more liturgy and then recited her *Haftarah* blessings and coinciding Hebrew verses from *Joshua 2*. Her drash for the second portion was far more conventional than her first. Even Rabbi Cohn would have approved had he not decided to remove himself from the building.

The rest of the bat mitzvah went on smoothly, my mother beaming at Natalie the entire time. We posed for photos afterward, Cantor Allen's smile definitely forced. To his credit, the man did his duty by our family, specifically Natalie and my mother.

"Never thought I'd see the day," he said low, talking to my mother just behind me.

"Harvey, I've seen a lot in my time," my mother said with a laugh, "but even this one takes the cake. That's certainly one way to run off a rotten rabbi."

That brought a baritone chuckle from the portly man. "I don't know if I will recover from the shock of that, Harriet. Your granddaughter has some *chutzpah*, that's for sure. I guess the apple didn't fall far from the tree. Tell me what exactly you said to Arthur in his office, because he gave me an earful before we went on stage."

Peeling away from my mother, I went in search of my oldest daughter. I walked past a poster sized photo of Natalie on an easel, framed in white cardboard and ready to be signed by the attendees. I replaced the caps on several markers dangling from the top of the frame, feeling like I had performed my due diligence to keep the markers fresh. I noted several well wishes by Natalie's friends, most accompanied by hashtags and drawn emojis. Snickering at how much times had changed since my own bat mitzvah, I continued my search for Natalie within the reception hall.

A few of the older guests had already found their way to their assigned tables, no doubt eager for the extravagant buffet my mother had ordered. The deejay booth played instrumental, big band music while the caterer and her team set out platters of traditional Jewish fare. After a quick scan of the room yielded no sign of my daughter, I went back into the lobby area. I finally spotted my oldest daughter surrounded by a gaggle of her friends.

"Natalie, that was totes amazeballs! Slay, queen!" one classmate squealed, donning a pastel, floral dress. "Like, I can't believe they let you say 'Jesus' here."

"Oh. Em. Gee," another girl said before laughing at herself. "Like, it's *literally* OMG. Look!" she said, holding out her forearm. "I have actual goosebumps right now. That doesn't even happen to me in youth group! Natalie, are you like, extra special or something because you're Jewish too?"

One of the Mendel cousins on my mother's side piped up, pushing round glasses up the bridge of her nose. "Sorry, but you can't be Jewish and believe in Jesus. That's just crazy, Natalie. I can't believe you actually said that in the middle of your bat mitzvah."

"I told the truth," my daughter said, turning to face her cousin, Avery. "And you don't get to tell me if I'm Jewish or not. We're at my grandparents' synagogue celebrating my bat mitzvah. I think that's Jewish enough for most people."

"You can't just talk about Jesus in a synagogue," Avery insisted. "I mean, you just don't do that! My grandmother said what you did up there was a *shanda*."

Natalie ignored the jab courtesy of my Aunt Susan, refusing to accept the Yiddish accusation of 'disgrace' leveled at her. "Avery, my parsha was about having faith in God. You may not believe that Jesus is God's Son, but I do. What happened with my little sister was real. You don't have to believe it, but it did happen."

Her cousin scoffed while the rest of Natalie's friends watched the exchange like a ping pong match. Avery dug in her heels. "Maybe it was real, or whatever, to you, but that makes you a *Christian*, not a Jew." She spat the word with the same contempt I had done so many times myself. "Your *goyishe* friends just don't know any better. That's the only reason why they think it's cool."

Most of Natalie's entourage seemed confused, but a few knew enough to be offended. Recognizing my cue to jump in, I eased past a couple of open mouthed middle schoolers and put my arm around my daughter.

"Didn't Natalie do an incredible job chanting all of that Hebrew?" I asked the group at large. Some of the girls nodded, unsure of what else to do. I turned my full attention to my niece. "Hey, Avery, maybe you can ask Nati for some pointers for your own bat mitzvah next year. I'm sure she'd be more than happy to help. That's what family is for, isn't it? You know, to encourage and build each other up. Your cousin could probably teach you a few things about how to do that."

Natalie looked up at me gratefully while Avery's mother, Samantha, approached. She looked at me and my daughter as if Avery might catch *Jesus* the same way one contracted the flu. She pulled her daughter away with a less than gentle tug. Suppressing the urge to roll my eyes, I instead smiled brightly at the rest of the girls and complemented their dresses. That spurred the conversation to lighter topics, and I left my daughter to navigate the wilds of adolescence.

Moving back toward the reception hall, I spotted Jared. He had apparently witnessed the entire scene and walked purposefully toward Samantha. He stopped her midtrack, and she smiled for him. Being second cousins had never stopped Samantha from flirting with Jared as my boyfriend back in high school nor with my husband at my daughter's bat mitzvah.

I found my way to Jared's side, easing an arm around his waist. I smiled sweetly at my cousin. "Hey Sam, long time no see."

"That was quite a show your daughter put on," she said, voice dripping with sarcasm. "I've never actually seen a rabbi storm off in the middle of a bat mitzvah before. You two must be so proud."

"Of course we are," Jared said, holding me tighter and forcing me to sheathe my claws. "Did you hear how beautifully Natalie chanted her Hebrew? It was absolutely flawless. I'm sure Avery can't wait to do just as good a job as her cousin did today."

Samantha pursed her lips, unwilling to acknowledge any of Natalie's hard work.

Jared's smile dimmed as his expression grew thunderous. "It's rude to insult the guest of honor at their own party. Considering the snotty way your daughter just talked down to mine, I think Natalie handled herself with class. A lot more than you're demonstrating right now, Aunt Samantha."

Samantha cleared her throat, recognizing the challenge. In her eyes I saw retaliation, but she also caught my mother's curious gaze from just inside the reception hall. Whatever insult my cousin wanted to land remained behind seamed lips.

"Nobody is asking you to agree with what we believe," I said, "but when my mother asks you about Natalie, I expect you to give my daughter the praise she deserves. You were invited here to celebrate your niece. I suggest you do it."

"Or what?" she demanded, unable to hold back the taunt.

"Or you'll be asked to leave," I said simply.

Samantha scoffed. "Yeah right, Poppy. You don't have the power to do anything other than make empty threats. We both know your mother paid for the party anyway. Aunt Harriet won't do anything because she's too scared of what my mother would say."

A small, brittle smile appeared on Jared's lips. "By all means, Sam, go and repeat that trash to Harriet and ruin her granddaughter's big day. I don't think your mother would approve, no matter what she says about Harriet or Natalie behind their backs. And by the way, you're setting a horrible example for your own daughter." He glanced down at Avery, who had been all but forgotten by her mother.

"Speaking of horrible examples, I'll be sure to send your regards to Leah Halpern." She gauged Jared's face for a "gotcha" reaction. I knew Leah considered my cousin to be one of her acquaintances, and she had obviously shared some version of the truth with Samantha. I frowned at the thought.

Conversely, Jared's smile became more genuine. "I hope you do send my regards to her. Please, tell Leah that Poppy and I pray for her daily. Jesus loves her, and He loves you too."

Aided by Avery's impatient tugging on her purse, Samantha gave an acrid smile and excused herself.

I looked up at Jared and smirked. "I don't think you're supposed to use Jesus to scare off annoying relatives, but thank you anyway. Sam was being awful."

He grinned back. "I meant everything I said."

"I know, but now she'll go report you to Aunt Susan. My mother doesn't need any stress from her sister after all the mishigas with Rabbi Cohn. Plus, I think she'd verbally vaporize anybody at this point. We've unleashed a beast!"

Jared's irresistible dimples appeared. "The talking down she gave Rabbi Cohn will probably be added into the annals of Mendel family scandals."

"Speaking of scandals," Bruce Halpern said, approaching us with Mindy Friedman on his arm, "I don't know what's more appalling. The fact that your daughter is up on the bima spouting off about Jesus like some Jesuit priest, or the fact you abandoned *my* daughter in her hour of need."

From the frying pan into the fire, I prayed silently for God to start the party so Jared and I could disappear inside the reception hall.

"Hour of need?" Jared repeated. "Bruce, the baby wasn't mine. I haven't touched your daughter in over two years."

Taking a step closer to Jared, Bruce's voice lowered. "My daughter is in a mental hospital because of what you've done to her. Twenty years of jerking her chain, and for what? Empty promises and a dead baby."

"Now, Bruce," Mindy cooed, stroking his arm. "That's not quite fair to Jared." She looked up at both of us pleadingly. "I'm sure you can understand a father's love for his daughter on today, of all days. Amy was able to adopt a baby just when Leah lost her little boy, so it's been hard for everyone. Postpartum depression can be so ghastly too. Leah hasn't handled things very well."

Bruce's eyes narrowed onto Mindy, clearly unhappy with her loose lips. She shrugged as if to say she was just trying to help.

"What I did to your daughter was wrong," Jared said, squaring his shoulders and talking to Bruce man-to-man. "It was wrong in high school and every year after that. I've apologized to Leah, and I've also forgiven her for the harm she caused to my wife and children."

"Harm?" Bruce choked, nearly as apoplectic as Rabbi Cohn. He turned his attention over to me. "Leah said you ran off your husband with your temper and you've called him a lousy father since day one. If you ask me, it sounds like my daughter did you and your kids a favor by taking Jared off your hands. Only a fool would take him back after that."

"Leah was my best friend," I said, voice tight. "You can spin the narrative however you want, Mr. Halpern, but she was an aunt to my children until she ran off with their father. I trusted Leah, and she betrayed me."

"So did Jared!" Bruce fired back.

"You're right," I said, "but Jared has taken responsibility for his mistakes. I've watched him struggle to forgive himself even though the children and I already have." As Bruce began to huff, I said, "You don't have to believe me, Mr. Halpern, but Jared and I don't need your permission to be happy. I'm sorry to hear that Leah is struggling with the loss of her baby. I can't even imagine that kind of pain."

Surprised by my response, he said nothing.

Going for broke, I said, "No matter what you think about Jesus, your daughter needs to know that God loves her. That he sees her. That the years she spent wanting something she couldn't have don't need to be a total waste." Stepping closer and looking into the same, icy blue eyes as Leah, I whispered, "Even if it's just as, 'Aunt Leah,' your daughter can still have a relationship with her son. Amy didn't adopt that baby boy by accident."

Bruce's eyes widened, and he swallowed convulsively.

"Yes," I said, briefly squeezing his hand.

Tears filled Bruce's eyes. "Leah denied and denied it, but I just *knew*. It was too coincidental. Too easy."

"What was?" Mindy asked from just beyond him.

Bruce waved her off, looking at me with new eyes. "I shouldn't be thanking you at all, but I'm grateful. I know my daughter can be a handful." Cutting himself off, he shook his head. "Nevermind, we both know how Leah is. You're a real friend, Poppy. Better than I think my daughter deserves. I'm sorry you're stuck with *him* though." The momentary softening in his eyes turned back into daggers for my husband.

"Don't be," I said, meeting that familiar, icy stare. "When Natalie said that only Jesus could have made this day happen, she wasn't lying. It's by the grace of God that any of us are standing here today. This is tikkun olam."

"Tikkun olam?" he said skeptically.

"Yes," I said, feeling the Holy Spirit well up within me. "Nothing is so broken that God can't fix it. My daughter said the same thing from the bima today. When we remember the things God has already done for us, we can find peace and hope that He'll be faithful to answer the prayers we have today. God loves you, your daughters, all of your grandchildren," I said meaningfully, "and as long as we're still breathing, our lives have a purpose."

"Poppy!" my mother called from just beyond the door, "they're about to start the party. Get in here already!" Noticing Leah's father and his girlfriend, her joyous expression fell immediately. "Hello, Bruce. Mindy. I didn't realize you came to *shul* today."

"Beautiful bat mitzvah," Bruce said, walking over to kiss my mother's cheek. "You should be very proud of your grand-daughter."

Mindy wore the same shocked expression as my mother. Grinning ear-to-ear in amazement, Jared said, "*Anything* is possible with God."

EPILOGUE

To no one's shock, Rabbi Cohn tendered his resignation before my mother could get him fired by the synagogue board. Rumor traveled far and wide over the verbal smackdown she gave before his sudden departure. I had no doubt Cantor Allen helped spur those stories along, always a longtime fan of my mother's. The old guard yentas suddenly looked to Harriet Berman for approval rather than the other way around, and I'd never seen my mother so happy or vibrant. She wholeheartedly clung to her Judaism, but she no longer acted squeamish regarding our family's faith in Jesus. Sometimes, I wondered if she might secretly believe herself, but Jared told me to trust God and not force the issue.

Taylor and Ian Horner welcomed a second little boy into their family, and as Taylor put it, "survived another bris." In the midst of our friend's joyous, new arrival, Rebecca suffered a miscarriage following a surprise pregnancy. Ted blamed the stress of wrangling two toddlers plus the burden of weekly Bible studies for the loss. Though Rebecca didn't agree, she was grateful when Kyle and Abigail Goldstein offered to switch off hosting duties to ease the load from the Margolins. The group continued to grow, many members suggesting the Margolins and Goldsteins start up their own congregation. Knowing Rebecca's history well enough, she politely declined, instead asking Ted, Jared, and Kyle to look for other people in the group to disciple and create more home group leaders.

Jessica and I continued to meet periodically at Vincenzo's, but our visits grew more sporadic as her relationship with Micah became serious. One frigid, December morning, she stopped by with a gold band on her finger and informed me that they'd eloped over the weekend. Wondering at the speedy nuptials, I got my answer when early signs of a pregnancy appeared a month later. Jessica never mentioned Taylor or her relationship as Micah's step-sister, but her new husband was close with Taylor's brother, Gabe. I caught bits and pieces of Gabe's gradual acceptance of Jessica into the family, more so when she and Micah announced their pregnancy. Micah's sister, Lexie, did not take the news so well because of her own fertility issues, and I continued to lift the entire family in my prayers.

Jared and I ran into Bruce and Mindy at various Beth Tefillah functions, and tensions had thawed considerably since Natalie's bat mitzvah. Bruce always had new pictures to show of his "beautiful grandson," and Mindy rolled her eyes good naturedly. What became readily apparent was baby Noah's marked resemblance to Halpern Industries' long-time, corporate attorney. Patrick continued to lie about the baby's paternity, but his potent DNA did not. Bruce eventually fired him at Leah's behest.

Cuddling with Jared in bed one early, Sunday morning, I dared to broach a formerly taboo subject. "So, I got an email from Joe Trautweig yesterday."

Jared paused from playing with my hair before answering. "What did he say?"

"He's been attending First Baptist of Parkview," I said, referring to the mega church close to the Culver highrise. "He said he likes the anonymity and being able to sneak in and out."

I heard the frown in Jared's voice. "So, how does Joe connect with anybody there? The guy needs some kind of fellowship. It's one of the things I love about our home groups. Everybody knows everyone else."

"That's just it," I said, lifting my head from Jared's chest so I could meet his eyes in the dim light. "God had plans for Joe Trautweig, even though *he* had plans to remain invisible."

Jared grinned playfully. "Does that mean Jesus found him a girlfriend without the help of the all-knowing Poppy? I'm shocked!"

"Why, yes it does," I said with a swat to Jared's arm. "The crazy part is that her name is Leah."

Jared's face paled immediately.

Laughing, I said, "I knew that would get your attention! You can relax because it's not Leah Halpern. Her name is Leah Smith and she's a commercial realtor in midtown. Joe said they hit it off, but they're taking things slowly."

"Wow," Jared said, processing all of the information. "Sounds like all of our friends and family are either married, pregnant, or accounted for. What's left to do?"

"Sit back and enjoy it," I said, smiling at my husband.

Pulling me closer, Jared did exactly that.

ACKNOWLEDGMENTS

MK Stein for your support, friendship, and awesome editing suggestions. God bless you for helping a sister out!

Lydia, my original beta reader, who asked if I could include a Jewish wedding in one of my books. I had already planned on the bat mitzvah, and you gave me a fun, extra challenge.

Barbara Kellyn, your beta feedback completely changed this novel for the better. Thank you for your honest critique and suggestions.

Hannah Linder and Catherine Posey for the gorgeous cover and interior design work. Your patience is always and forever appreciated.

Derek and Todd for aiding a mom in need and answering my distress signal. May I never have to put together another set of bunk beds.

Mike and Kasea for blessing me and my kids beyond what I could ask or imagine. No words, y'all. Can't wait to visit and see your new house!

To my three babies, the litigator, the leader, and the entertainer, I love you guys for everything you are, everything you're not, and everything you will become. Thank you for the privilege of being your mom.

To Jesus, my King and my first love, thank you for delivering me from evil, protecting me and my children, and for providing beyond my wildest dreams. Time for Phase II!

COMING FALL 2023

BOOK 4 IN THE BEAUTY FOR ASHES SERIES:
LEV TAHOR: A HEART REDEEMED

CARLY MILLER LOVES READING THE TRIUMPHANT memoirs of her friend and co-worker, Poppy Levine. Having survived a tumultuous upbringing with her hyper-religious mother, Carly is happy for Poppy's story of healing and faith, but she believes her own sin is unforgivable. Equally inaccessible to Carly is Poppy's former suitor, Joe Trautweig, whose story from Poppy's book captivates Carly. When she encounters those jade green eyes in real life, the lines between the printed page and the man himself begin to blur. Joe has his own, painful secrets, but Carly fears her past will be too much for their mutual attraction to overcome. Can Carly accept the idea her own heart could be made clean (*lev tahor*) and that both she and Joe can embrace what forgiveness truly means?

EXCERPT FROM LEV TAHOR: A HEART REDEEMED

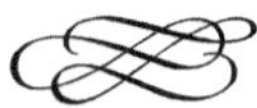

AFTER A QUICK BOWL OF MICROWAVE SOUP IN THE office break room, I made my way to the covered walkway separating the Culver Incorporated highrise from its parking deck. Referred to as "tornado alley" when the wind picked up, the bolted down benches kept the furniture from flying. On a whim, I'd decided to grab some frozen yogurt from Let it Fro-yo, my favorite little shop situated outside the parking garage.

I spooned the comfort food into my mouth as I studied Parkview's finest trek between the two buildings. I often found myself inventing backstories about the locals just for fun.

"So you're a fan of the taro flavor too?"

I glanced up to see Joe Trautweig standing over me. A mound of purple frozen yogurt sat on top of a waffle cone in his hand.

I managed a smile, still stinging from my Poppy's remark about having a book crush on Joe. "Looks like," I said impassively.

"I've seen you around with some friends of mine at Culver,

so I figured I'd stop by and introduce myself since I already know your name. I used to work there too, once upon a time. Mind if I join you?" he asked.

I shrugged.

Joe sat down and met my eyes. With a bit of a grin, he said, "Japanese sweet potato is a very popular choice with Culver employees past and present. I applaud your good taste, Carly."

I temporarily forgot about Dylan, Zach, or the three toads in between. Joe's innocent remark landed like high praise, and my stomach flip flopped. I blushed and looked away.

"I don't bite, I promise," he said. "My name's Joe."

"I know who you are," I said quietly.

"Ah," he said with a grimace, "you've read the books." Joe rubbed the back of his neck with his free hand. "Kyle Goldstein says to embrace it as an opportunity to share about Jesus, but I'll admit I'm not quite as open with my past as he is."

"They did change your name," I said, glancing back at Joe. "I mean, for anybody that knows you guys personally, it could be a little awkward, I guess." My eyes drifted to the oblivious Parkview workforce as they walked past us on the bench. "Most people around here just see a businessman with an ice cream cone. I think your secret identity is safe."

Joe exhaled a soft chuckle. "I can't remember if it was Rebecca or Taylor who gave me that ridiculous last name."

I genuinely laughed this time, and Joe's expression altered. His gaze shifted from humor to curiosity, and my stomach flopped again. He studied me for a moment.

"Carly, how much of what Poppy wrote about you is true?" he asked.

Taking the opportunity to hide from his scrutiny, I scooped another bite of yogurt into my mouth. "None of it," I answered honestly, "but that's my own fault."

Joe raised an eyebrow over pale, wide set eyes. Nothing in Poppy's memoirs had been fictional about the intelligence and intensity of that jade green gaze. The brief thought flickered that there might be life outside of Dylan and my perpetual mantle of shame. Shaking off that wishful line of thinking, I stared down into my yogurt cup. "I had a bad breakup. I didn't handle things so well after. That's what Poppy saw."

"Ah," he said. "How long ago did things end?"

"Too long," I said. "Everyone keeps telling me to get over it, but it's not that easy."

Joe nodded. "Don't let anybody ever tell you how long you need to recover from trauma. If you rush the process, you'll wind up hurting yourself even more. Nobody has the right to judge the pain you've been through, especially if they've never experienced anything like it."

Touched by his words, I smiled at him appreciatively. "Thank you. I have a couple friends who probably need to hear that."

He smiled back. "There's a lot you learn when you get to be my age. Getting old has its advantages."

"Old?" I said, figuring that Joe was still a few years younger than the mighty Margolin. "I'm sure they invented the wheel before you were born, right?"

Joe's eyes sparkled in amusement. "Please, tell me you know better than to eat laundry detergent pods."

"That's Gen Z, not me."

"Ah, a millennial. Society's new favorite scapegoat."

"Okay, boomer," I retorted, sticking my tongue out at him.

Joe gave a hearty chuckle. "My parents are actually baby boomers. I fall under the Gen X category."

"Got it. Grunge music, teen angst, and a lot of flannel."

"Mountains of flannel," he said. "Enough to keep any lumberjack or hipster millennial happy."

I smirked. "Poppy says she doesn't understand why girls my age want to dress like the *before* in a '90s teen makeover movie."

I expected Joe to laugh again, but a strange look crossed his face. Ruefully, he said, "For a minute there, I forgot the connection between the two of you."

"I don't mean to pry," I drawled, "but I think you probably know the next question I'm going to ask."

Joe laughed mirthlessly. "Jared Levine has nothing to worry about. I've made peace with everything other than my own regrets."

"Funny you should say that," I said, feeling my defenses lower at Joe's admission.

"Why's that?"

"I struggle with regret too."

He offered me a sympathetic smile. "I guess it's not relegated to any one age bracket, is it?"

"Definitely not. I may not be as old as you, but I feel like I've made enough mistakes to last a lifetime."

"That's surprising," he said, studying me. "You have the face of an angel."

"Hardly," I muttered.